W9-BCL-932

For Lt. Col. Joe Kulmayer —

Warm thanks for your contribution to the great Galen caper of 1978, and for not lacing his copy with Anthrax powder.

With warm personal and high professional regard —

Ben Schemmer

THE RAID

By the same author

Almanac of Liberty

THE RAID

Benjamin F. Schemmer

Harper & Row, Publishers

NEW YORK, HAGERSTOWN, SAN FRANCISCO, LONDON

1817

Cartoon on page 285 printed by permission of Washington *Star*.

THE RAID. Copyright © 1976 by Benjamin F. Schemmer. All rights reserved. Printed in the United States of America. No part of this book may be used or reproduced in any manner whatsoever without written permission except in the case of brief quotations embodied in critical articles and reviews. For information address Harper & Row, Publishers, Inc., 10 East 53rd Street, New York, N.Y. 10022. Published simultaneously in Canada by Fitzhenry & Whiteside Limited, Toronto.

Designed by Sidney Feinberg

Library of Congress Cataloging in Publication Data

Schemmer, Benjamin F
   The raid.
   Bibliography: p.
   Includes index.
   1. Vietnamese Conflict, 1961–1975—Campaigns—
Sontay Raid, 1970. 2. Vietnamese Conflict, 1961–1975
—Prisoners and prisons, North Vietnamese. I. Title.
DS557.8.S6S34   959.704'34   75–30345
ISBN 0–06–013802–5

   78 79 10 9 8 7 6 5 4 3 2

To the men who tried to bring them home
and the men they tried to rescue

In memory of my wife,
CYNTHIA BLYTHE SCHEMMER,
*who understood little about war but all about life,
and who asked me in a note I found only after she died
to tell "the other half that hasn't been printed"*

Contents

Illustrations

MAPS

Prologue

Eight days before Thanksgiving of 1970, President Richard M. Nixon met in the White House Oval Office with four of his closest advisers to hear one of the most dramatic briefings of his presidency. It was Wednesday morning, November 18, a cold and cloudy day so bleak in Washington that the National Weather Service would record only four-tenths of an hour of sunshine all day long.

Nixon was deep in conversation with national security adviser Henry A. Kissinger, Central Intelligence Agency Director Richard M. Helms, Defense Secretary Melvin R. Laird, and Secretary of State William P. Rogers when Admiral Thomas H. Moorer, Chairman of the Joint Chiefs of Staff, was ushered in precisely at 11:00 A.M. The tall, soft-spoken Moorer greeted the President, nodded to the other men with a warm yet business-like smile, and opened a large map case full of 20- by 30-inch briefing charts. As he set them up on an easel between the President's desk and the overstuffed chairs and sofas which flanked the Oval Office fireplace, Rogers noticed the Top Secret designation on the charts' cover-sheet. Of all those present, he was the only one for whom the subject of Moorer's briefing would be a total surprise. The United States' Secretary of State was about to learn for the first time that an 'invasion" of North

1

Vietnam had been planned for months.

Nixon laid his ever-present yellow legal pad on an end table beside his chair, a sign for Moorer to proceed. Moorer opened his briefing book, a carefully tabbed, three-ring black binder with the words "Top Secret—Chairman's Eyes Only" stamped in gold on the cover. "Mr. President," he began, "the code name for this operation is 'Kingpin.' It provides for a raid on North Vietnam to be conducted by Army Special Forces personnel assaulting the Son Tay prisoner-of-war camp, 23 miles west of Hanoi, in Air Force helicopters assisted by a Navy air diversion near Haiphong. The most advantageous period for this undertaking is between November 21 and 25."

Standing beside the easel, Moorer uncovered a large map of North Vietnam to pinpoint the location of the Son Tay compound. He then unveiled charts and detailed diagrams of the compound itself and the surrounding area. He calmly described the compound's layout and said, "This is the only confirmed active POW camp outside Hanoi, Mr. President. The Son Tay camp has a prisoner population of 70 Americans. Of these, 61 have been tentatively identified by name and service: 43 Air Force, 14 Navy, 4 Marines . . . We propose," Moorer said, "to rescue them all."

As Moorer began to describe how the rescue mission would be timed and executed, Kissinger quietly picked up a phone; within minutes, his deputy, Major General Alexander M. Haig, entered the Oval Office and took the chair farthest from Moorer's briefing charts. Flipping through the charts one by one, Moorer took 18 minutes to relate the details of the raid. Despite the "Pentagonese" in which the briefing was written, his proposal was full of drama, rich in detail. He knew the subject well, and referred only sporadically to his briefing book.

Finally Moorer paused; he had a flair for dramatic effect. Then he spoke very slowly: "The ground commander is positive that the operation will succeed, Mr. President."

The President, one participant at the briefing would recall, was lapping it up "like an eight-year-old at his first cowboy movie." He told Moorer, "Sounds great, Tom. What else?"

Moorer gave a short intelligence summary which focused on the "threats" that would present the operation with its greatest risks. Then he paused again: "A final word, Mr. President. If resources in support of this operation reveal that the enemy may have determined our objective, the operation will be canceled." He let the word "canceled" sink in.

"Damn, Tom, let's not let *that* happen," Nixon said. "I want this to *go.* "

During the briefing, Moorer realized, the President had scribbled only a few notes on the yellow legal pad at his side. That was good, Moorer thought; he'd kept the President's attention and there wouldn't be many questions. Nixon had only two. He asked when Moorer had to have a final decision. Then he asked what cover stories had been devised in case the raid failed.

The raid on Son Tay had been postponed once before, for political reasons. But now Nixon said, "How could anyone *not* approve this?" Then he told Moorer, "Tom, I know you guys have worked months on this. I want those POWs home too . . . Hell, if this works, we could even have them here for Thanksgiving dinner, right here at the White House."

Five days later, it was Moorer's turn to listen to a briefing, this time by an uncomfortable secretary of defense standing in front of 55 newsmen at the Pentagon. It was Monday, November 23, a dark, cold and not very friendly day in Washington.

The Pentagon press corps knew that a big story was about to break. That morning, the daily news briefing known as the "eleven o'clock follies" had been postponed until 3:30. By then, so many rumors had spread around the pressroom that there was a "full house" waiting when Melvin R. Laird strode into "the studio," the newsroom just off the Pentagon's Mall Entrance. He was accompanied by Moorer and two officers unfamiliar to the "regulars" who covered the Department of Defense for the nation's newspaper and radio/TV networks. One was Leroy J. Manor, a slim, suave Air Force brigadier general; the other was Army Colonel Arthur D. Simons, a gruff, barrel-chested, mean-looking rock of a soldier whose blouse bore an array of parachutist and combat infantryman badges, six rows of decorations and campaign ribbons, three distinguished unit citations and the shoulder tab of the famous World War II 6th Ranger Battalion.

Laird stepped to the microphone and told the reporters that he wanted to give them details of an "operation that took place north of the 19th Parallel this past weekend." A raid, he announced, had been made on a prisoner-of-war compound "approximately 20 miles west of Hanoi." Its purpose was to rescue "as many of our prisoners as possible." Laird then introduced Manor and Simons to the Pentagon press corps. Three minutes and two seconds into his carefully worded briefing, he delivered the punch line: "Regrettably," he said, "the rescue team discovered that the camp had recently been vacated. No prisoners were found."

Laird talked for two more minutes, describing some general details of the raid. Finally he opened the press conference to questions. He turned most of them over to the two officers flanking him. General Manor had been the overall commander of the raid, Colonel Simons had led the assault on Son Tay; but because of "security," they weren't allowed to add much detail, even though the reporters had a flock of questions. Apparently the raid itself was a success: no American lives had been lost. But the question uppermost in the reporters' minds went unanswered. Why were there no prisoners at Son Tay? Twelve minutes and five seconds into the press conference, a reporter summed up a conclusion every journalist in the studio had reached by then. "On whom do you blame the intelligence failure?" he asked.

At 4:12, Laird cut off any further questions with, "Thank you very much, gentlemen." That was the end of the Son Tay press conference—and the opening page of a news story that was to dominate the papers for weeks.

The next morning, an eight-column banner headline across the front page of the *Washington Post* read:

U. S. Raid to Rescue POWs Fails

About one-third of the paper's front page was devoted to the raid on Son Tay. Three of the other nine articles on that same page fleshed out the story:

Incursions by U. S. Raise
New Peril for Nixon Policy

Paris Session Canceled
As Reds Protest Raids

Senators
Appalled
At Forays

Many of the news stories that followed were off the mark. There were several details of the raid that the Pentagon did not want made public, and some which it did reveal would prove to be untrue. As a result, a host of questions remained unanswered. Was the raid on Son Tay a daring and courageous mission—worth the risk, even though it failed to rescue a single American prisoner of war? Or was it, as many editorials suggested, a foolhardy and provocative act which needlessly endangered the lives of the raiding force and invited retaliation on the POWs who still remained in North Vietnamese prisons? How and why was the raid planned? What actually happened during the 27 minutes that the raiding force spent on the ground in a remote—and empty—POW camp deep in the heart of enemy territory? How had the Pentagon been able to obtain such detailed intelligence about the names and number of POWs held captive at Son Tay? Why was the camp empty? Why didn't the Pentagon learn that the camp had been vacated before the raid was launched? Or did it? And if so, why wasn't the raid canceled? Was the raid an act of desperation by a government and military machine that had been frustrated at almost every turn in the war in Vietnam? Or was it a useful card in the Byzantine game of power politics? Was the raid on Son Tay a failure? Or did it, in the end, achieve an ironic success?

The raid on Son Tay was an archetypical event of the Vietnam war, a complex political and military operation that encompassed the ponderous bureaucracy of the Pentagon and the White House, the rigidly compartmentalized work of and sometimes counterproductive rivalry between America's various intelligence agencies, meticulous planning and training, and, finally, the incredible bravery of the men who carried out the mission. But in a very real sense, the raid on Son Tay was the highlight of the last three years of that traumatic decade called Vietnam. From early 1969, when America began withdrawing its forces from Vietnam, until early 1973, when 566 American POWs were finally released by North Vietnam, the Viet Cong, and Communist China, there was only one purpose left in the war. America spent 20,683 lives and over $62 *billion* in those five years to achieve what a small party of brave men tried to do at Son Tay—bring those prisoners home.

ONE

Son Tay Prison

In North Vietnam early in 1970, Air Force Captain Wes Schierman was fighting for his life in a cold, dingy, cramped prison just west of a small town called Son Tay Citadel. For weeks he had been gasping for every breath of air. His fellow prisoners watched him "almost die" several times, unable to help him, outraged when the guards ignored their cries to get him a medic.

The men at Son Tay had learned that flying over North Vietnam was not an easy way to earn a living. So had hundreds of other POWs held captive elsewhere in North Vietnam.

Navy Lieutenant Everett Alvarez, Jr., was the first American to find out what a North Vietnamese prison was like. His fighter-bomber was one of two planes shot down in 1964 during the August 5 retaliatory strikes over Haiphong Harbor ordered by President Johnson after the Tonkin Gulf incidents. As Southeast Asia exploded into a full-scale but undeclared war in 1965, air strikes over the north mounted rapidly, averaging about 70 planes a day. So did the number of planes shot down and Americans taken prisoner. By the end of that year, 61 American pilots were held captive. They were the "lucky" ones. Most of the air crews in planes that were shot down, almost one plane every other day in the north, never lived to see the inside of a North

7

Vietnamese prison. In 1966, 223 planes a day were hitting the north—but the North Vietnamese had built up the heaviest air defenses ever seen in the world and their gunners shot down an American airplane about eight out of every ten days. That year, 86 more Americans found themselves in "Heartbreak Hotel," that part of Hoa Lo Prison, the huge old French jail in downtown Hanoi, where North Vietnam took new captives for their first weeks of interrogation—and torture. Hoa Lo was aptly named—in Vietnamese, it meant "the place of the cooking fires."

By the end of 1967, air strikes over North Vietnam were averaging close to 300 planes a day. And almost daily, one of them fell mortally crippled from the skies over Hanoi, Haiphong, or the Vietnamese panhandle above the Demilitarized Zone. Despite heroic efforts, search and rescue (SAR) helicopter crews were able to recover less than 13 percent of the airmen shot down during this entire period. Pilots who bailed out over the sea, between Yankee Station in the Gulf of Tonkin and Dixie Station off the northern part of South Vietnam, stood a much better chance of being rescued. So did airmen shot down over land in South Vietnam, Laos, or Cambodia. But the odds were not very good over North Vietnam. Chances were almost nine to one that pilots who got "smoked" there would die—or end up a prisoner.

Every other day that year of 1967, the most intensive and costly of the air war in the north, another American airman was taken prisoner. By the time President Johnson ordered a total bombing halt over the north on October 31, 1968, 143 more planes had been shot down and 56 more Americans had been thrown into North Vietnamese prisons. Somewhere outside those prisons, and possibly in them, another 917 Americans were missing in action. In all, North Vietnam had bagged 927 planes and 356 prisoners by late 1968 when flights over the north were limited to reconnaissance sorties.

Many of the men shot down over North Vietnam were in grave trouble before they even hit the ground. Under normal circumstances, over 90 percent of crewmen who have to bail out of an airplane land uninjured. Over North Vietnam, it was a different story. Seven of every ten men who lived to tell what happened suffered injuries so severe when they ejected that they were incapable of even *trying* to escape or evade capture after they hit the ground.

Flying under great stress in skies full of exploding flak, missiles and small arms fire, already drained of reserve energy after a flight to the target that had lasted over an hour, sometimes two hours, these men were pushing their planes, and themselves, to the outer boundary of safe "design limits." Many of the planes were flying at 400 knots or faster when their crews had to eject. In some cases, the planes were in a dangerous nose-down attitude, screaming toward impact with the ground. In other cases, they were also rolling, tumbling out of control —or just plain disintegrating. Sometimes traveling at supersonic speeds, the men had to strain against four to eight times the force of gravity, their bodies pressed against their seats or the sides of the cockpit as they struggled to eject.

Ejection seats ("life support systems," as airplane designers call them) were not designed very well for those extreme conditions. Once a crew member pulled or pushed the eject handle, he was supposed to be shot out of the airplane (usually by a 37 mm. cannon shell beneath the seat) into a "smooth ballistic trajectory" until his parachute opened automatically and the seat fell comfortably away while he prepared for a parachute landing. It didn't happen that way in North Vietnam. Ten percent of the men reported extreme difficulty in even locating or activating their ejection controls. Others found it impossible to get "squared away" in their seats when the time came to "punch out." Improperly positioned to eject, 40 percent of the men experienced "flailing"—spinning through the air out of control, a tumbling mass of arms and legs torn by near-supersonic forces.

Fighter-bomber pilots were supposed to fly with their shoulder straps "locked," to restrain them in their seats even under heavy gravity forces. But most of the air crews over North Vietnam loosened those shoulder straps—so they could relax a bit on the long flight, bend over their back seat radar scopes, read the bomb sights better as they rolled into the target, or look over their shoulders to check for enemy MIGs. Once their planes were hit, there was too little time to actuate the locking mechanism that tightened their shoulder straps and positioned their bodies to eject. Twenty percent of the men broke their elbows and arms or knees on the sides of their cockpits, or suffered other "major injuries," because American technology had not devised a way for those shoulder straps to be pulled taut automatically a split second or two before the ejection charge went off.

The men who had been injured during ejection had no hope of evading their captors. Even those who ejected and landed safely were usually captured very quickly. They were robust, tall, very white or very black Americans and they were very conspicuous in a land of 21 million short, thin Orientals. It took North Vietnam only three weeks to pick up the longest evadee. A Navy pilot, he decided to head inland instead of toward the coast, hoping to reach a friendly CIA outpost on the Laotian border. But the North Vietnamese found his flight helmet and tracked him down with dogs. It took them only 12 days to nail the second-longest evadee, Colonel George E. Day. He was a forty-year-old "half blind" F-100 pilot who lost his eyeglasses when he ejected on August 26, 1967. But he escaped soon after being captured, even though his right arm was broken in three places, his left knee badly sprained and his body numb with pain from his initial torture. He almost made it across the Demilitarized Zone. How he thrashed about the rice paddies and stumbled through the hills and jungle of North Vietnam that long before being caught again was something even he can't explain, except that he wanted to get home "very badly."

Captured quickly, their bodies broken and bleeding before they hit the ground, pummeled by irate, over-exuberant villagers worked into a frenzy of hate by local political cadres, spat upon and beaten on their way into Hanoi's Heartbreak Hotel, the Americans were ill-prepared for what followed.

Torture.

Torture of the most inhuman, crudest kind. It wasn't sophisticated. It just hurt—beyond comprehension, beyond the limit of human endurance. The most common form was going "on the ropes." After their initial interrogation periods, when most prisoners were beaten savagely but gave only the "name, rank and serial number" required by the Geneva Convention, these debilitated men found their captors impatient—but effective. Their arms were bound behind them until wrists, then elbows, touched. A rope was looped through the bonds, pulled up behind their necks, strung over a hook or bolt in the ceiling, and pulled taut until their arms were raised behind their backs to the point where their shoulders were often literally pulled out of their sockets.

The men were left to hang there. Until they talked. Some held out for a week or ten days.

Once a prisoner talked, he was finally fed. A typical meal was a bowl of insipid pumpkin or cabbage soup. Often, it was infested with vermin. For one four-month period, the prisoners' diet consisted of two bowls daily of unspiced, boiled cabbage soup—240 consecutive bowls of it, nothing else. Diarrhea, dysentery, scurvy, beriberi, and hepatitis were forever present in the bare, unventilated cellblocks.

Hoa Lo Prison was the "Devil's Island of Southeast Asia." Built by the French 40 years earlier, it was known intimately by many of North Vietnam's highest officials. Some of them had been imprisoned there as long as 10 to 12 years, by the French and then the Japanese.

The prison stank. Years of urine, blood, vomit, and feces permeated every crevice. Rats and long flying cockroaches were Hoa Lo's real landlords; the North Vietnamese guards were just the caretakers. Mice, spiders and ants were all over, mosquitoes so profuse that one prisoner said of his first night there, "The insects nearly carried me off." American POWs dubbed Hoa Lo the "Hanoi Hilton."

Other parts of Hoa Lo were filled with North Vietnamese civilian convicts. Some were children only fourteen years old. When they were brought into the courtyards for "exercise," the Americans could see through their cell windows that many of the children were chained together.

Rules for the POWs were strict: no whistling, singing, or talking. Just silence. As the prisoners tried to communicate, they

learned quickly that their captors spent much of the time looking for excuses to punish them. Catching the men communicating was a favorite excuse.

The 356 Americans held prisoner by 1970 had bailed out in
the prime of their lives. The "average" POW—if the word "average" can be used for men who were to endure what they did
—was only about thirty-two years old, a captain in the Air Force
or a Navy lieutenant, married and the father of two young
children. About 85 percent of them had flown more than 15
missions over the north when their "number came up."

One of the unluckiest prisoners of all was Lieutenant Colonel
Richard P. "Pop" Kiern, shot down on July 24, 1965, the seventh Air Force crewman bagged in the Vietnam war. A B-17
copilot in World War II, Kiern had been shot down on his first
mission over Germany and spent nine months as a POW. An
F-105 pilot in Vietnam, he was shot down on his third *day* in
Southeast Asia. Kiern experienced only a few hours in combat
but spent almost ten years as a prisoner of war. After his release
in 1973, he would joke that the Air Force had become much
smarter; it was impossible, he said, to find a pilot dumb enough
to fly with him. Asked to compare captivity in Southeast Asia
with his experience in World War II, Kiern said, "Captivity in
Germany was rough, but at least I was treated like a human
being. Captivity in North Vietnam was unreal, unbelievable,
not of this world."

Air Force Lieutenant Colonel Robinson Risner became a prisoner on September 16, 1965, while flying an F-105 over the
north. A Korean war ace with 109 combat missions and eight
MIGs, he had been shot down over North Vietnam six months
earlier but managed to make it to the coast and bail out over
the water. An SA-16 flying boat plucked him out of the water
while the other planes in Risner's flight strafed the North Vietnamese boats rushing from shore to capture him. The crew
which saved him was on its first combat rescue mission and
could barely get its plane airborne.

Time magazine wrote up the mission; Risner's picture was on
the cover. When he was shot down again, he came "to regret
that *Time* had ever heard of me." The more senior a prisoner

was, the more "famous" or the more important, the more impatient the North Vietnamese were to break him, to have him confess his "crimes against the North Vietnamese people" in front of visiting peace groups or foreign newsmen, to hammer him into submission as an example to other prisoners that there was no use resisting because their senior officers had already talked.

Risner was to spend seven and a half years in captivity. The "distinctive character of imprisonment in North Vietnam," he would report, "was the suffocating monotony. . . . Bodies built for movement were confined to closet-like boxes. Active minds were forced to be idle with the numbing nothingness of four walls in a dingy little cell. Men trained to fly sophisticated machines at incredible speeds and breath-taking heights were caged like animals. . . . But worse than that, no people to be close to."*

Navy Lieutenant John M. McGrath had a rough bailout when his A4-C was shot down on his 178th mission in Southeast Asia. By the time he hit the ground, his left arm was broken and badly dislocated; he also had two fractured vertebrae and a broken left knee. In their haste to rip off his boots, the North Vietnamese militiamen who captured him hyperextended his broken knee six times; en route to Hanoi, frenzied villagers twisted his injured leg and dislocated the same knee. McGrath was "sure" he would not reach Hanoi alive. He did—but soon wished he *had* died. During his initial interrogation, the North Vietnamese dislocated both his right shoulder and right elbow. They denied him medical treatment, but when he begged them to shoot him, he was told, "No, you are a criminal! You haven't suffered enough."**

The men suffered.

Their families suffered almost as much. It's hard for a woman not to know whether she's a wife or a widow, for a son or daughter not to know if their father is dead or alive. It hap-

The Passing of the Night: My Seven Years As a Prisoner of the North Vietnamese by Colonel Robinson Risner. New York: Ballantine Books, 1973.

**Prisoner of War: Six Years in Hanoi* by Lieutenant Commander John M. McGrath. Annapolis, Md.: Naval Institute Press, 1975.

pened not to just a few hundred, but to *thousands* of families. For every 12 men who were killed in Southeast Asia, there was another man listed as a POW or MIA. At one time or another, 4,705 American families had a husband, father, or son who was either "missing in action" or held as a "prisoner of war." Three years after the Paris peace agreements that terminated American involvement in Vietnam, less than one in five of these men has been accounted for.

Carroll Flora's wife was typical of those kept in limbo so long, not knowing if a husband was alive or dead. Sergeant First Class Carroll Flora became missing in action on July 21, 1967, during an Army Special Forces night action. For six years, his wife didn't know if he had been killed, captured, or was still trying to evade capture in the jungles and hills of Laos. She never received one letter from him, or he from her. On Saturday, January 29, 1973, 2,017 days after he was listed as MIA, the North Vietnamese released his name in Paris as one of the prisoners who would be returned home. Flora was only one of 53 men released about whom North Vietnam had given out no information whatsoever during the entire time they were held prisoner.

Some families knew that a husband or father had been captured or seen in prison, but never got a letter from him or knew if he was getting theirs. Even though North Vietnam eased many restrictions on POW mail from 1970 to 1973, 95 of the 566 prisoners released in 1973 had never received a letter from home; 80 families had never received a letter from the prisoner.

For still other POW/MIA families, there was the agony of knowing that a husband or son had been taken captive but was seriously wounded, and that North Vietnamese medical treatment was primitive and torture frequent. Of every 100 men taken prisoner, 11 were to die in captivity. The Commander-in-Chief, Pacific, Admiral John S. McCain, Jr., lived with this kind of agony for five and a half years. His son, John S. McCain III, a Navy attack pilot, was shot down over Hanoi on October 26, 1967, just three months before his father was named to command all of the Army, Navy, Marine, and Air forces prosecuting the Vietnam war. Young McCain was known to have been seriously wounded when his plane was hit. His wing man saw the North Vietnamese fish him out of a lake in downtown Hanoi, apparently unconscious. In August of 1969, two prisoners who were released early by North Vietnam reported that McCain was near death, tortured beyond the believable limit of human endurance. He had been given only enough medical care to stay alive, sometimes in a semi-comatose state, and had been held in solitary for the past 15 months.

His captors knew who McCain's father was, and the North Vietnamese had offered him an "early return" in July of 1968. Jack McCain, however, declined—and was tortured repeatedly because he refused the chance to go home. His fellow prisoners begged him to accept the offer; they were afraid he would die if not given better medical care. But McCain didn't want the North Vietnamese to propagandize his "groveling" for an early release, as he felt sure they would, while fellow POWs languished in Hanoi's cells.

The prisoners suffered all the more knowing the anguish and uncertainty their families were going through. Bent by brutality, dispirited because they had "talked," weak from malnutrition, suffering from primitive or nonexistent medical attention, confined in solitary—some men for as long as four years, one Navy captain for 58 months—tortured when caught trying to talk with their fellow prisoners, it was a miracle that the POWs retained their sanity. Some didn't.

The night he was moved to Son Tay, December 10, 1969, Air Force Major Elmo C. "Mo" Baker thought he might have lost his. He had been a prisoner for two and a quarter years, shot down on his 61st mission over the north on a strike against the Bac Giang bridge 28 miles northeast of Hanoi. Bac Giang was not a target pilots liked to visit very often; photo interpreters had counted 138 guns around it. Baker had flown against it the month before and won the Distinguished Flying Cross for knocking the bridge out. But the bridge served one of the only two railroads coming down from China, and because it was vital to North Vietnam's supply system, it was quickly repaired. Colonel Bob White led a new F-105 attack against the bridge; Baker led the roll in to the target. The "golden beebee" caught up with Mo Baker that day, August 23, 1967.

Baker was thirty-five years old, a tall, soft-spoken native of Kennett, Missouri, who got his Bachelor of Arts degree from Syracuse and a master's degree in electrical engineering just before going to Vietnam. When he ejected, his F-105 was porpoising and Baker broke his left thigh bone in a painful fracture. As his parachute neared the ground, he could see and hear North Vietnamese all around him. He had no chance for escape or rescue. The North Vietnamese took him to Hanoi by helicopter, straight into Heartbreak Hotel. His introduction to North Vietnamese "culture" was excruciating: instead of the usual torture, the guards twisted his left foot, first one way, then another, rotating it almost three-fourths of a circle each time.

Three weeks after his initial interrogation, Baker's leg was finally set in Bac Mai Hospital. He stayed there 30 days, then was sent to the "Plantation," the "show" prison in Hanoi where visiting peace delegations were often taken. The prisoners hated those visits: they got "tromped up" before a delegation came, and again after it left. Baker was used as a prize exhibit to show that the POWs were getting "hospital care." He met his first delegation, headed by peace activist Tom Hayden, on October 11, 1967. The North Vietnamese, of course, didn't tell the visitors that the thigh bone Mo Baker had snapped while ejecting was used for torture for three weeks before they finally "repaired it," and that it now had a radial fracture as well.

The North Vietnamese had a list of 17 questions they knew visiting delegations would always ask, and the prisoners were "instructed" beforehand on how to answer. If a prisoner "got on a preaching stump" or was too recalcitrant, the North Vietnamese had a stock answer: "You shall know pain."

Baker's cellmate at the Plantation was Air Force Captain Larry E. Carrigan, shot down the same day he was. Carrigan was picked to meet some visitors from the Women's Strike for Peace. Instead of admitting contrition for his "criminal acts" against the North Vietnamese people, he told the group he was proud to be an American pilot. After the delegation left, his captors hung him "on the wall" and Carrigan knew pain. Ropes bound tightly around his wrists were hoisted through two eyebolts on the wall until he hung there like a crucifix. One of his arms came out of its socket. The pain Carrigan knew from that one session would last for five years.

Twenty-seven months after their shootdown, on December 9, 1969, a guard came into their cell late one night and told Baker and Carrigan to "roll up"—gather their few belongings and roll them up in their rice pad blankets. It was a "scary thing" for the POWs, being moved to another camp, usually at night, always on short notice. There was never enough time to collect the carefully hidden homemade pencils, paper, nails, or pieces of string and wire that they hoarded like treasure and used to communicate from cell to cell or in some other ingenious way.

The guards blindfolded Carrigan and Baker, tied their wrists to each other, and threw them into a mini-bus along with several more prisoners. Guards were put between groups of the POWs to make sure no one lifted a blindfold or talked. The North Vietnamese didn't want them to see who the other prisoners were or where they were headed. But Carrigan and Baker managed periodic peeks through their blindfolds. They could see they were headed west. As the bus rumbled on, Carrigan told Baker, "I think we're going to Laos." That bothered them; they were sure that prison in Laos would be even worse than Hanoi. Baker dispelled the idea with a curt, "You're crazy, Carrigan." Another 30 minutes went by, but the bus still headed west. Carrigan lifted his blindfold again and told Baker once more, "I think we're headed for Laos." Baker told him to "quit smoking opium." Thirty minutes later, Baker managed to lift his own blindfold. The bus was in open country and still rumbling west. He blurted out involuntarily: "Sweet Jesus, I think we're going to Laos."

Late into the night, the bus turned off a road and stopped in front of a steel gate. Carrigan and Baker were led through it. All they knew was that they were a long, long way west of Hanoi. They found themselves in a small compound courtyard roughly 140 × 125 feet. In it were three small buildings: one of them was to their left, in the southeast corner; the other two buildings adjoined each other just inside the compound's north wall. They were taken to a cell in one of them, the building on the right, and locked up with Air Force Major Irby D. Terrell, Jr., a January 1968 shootdown who had been on the bus with them. It was the first time they'd had another roommate in 837 days of captivity.

The building they were housed in was called the Opium Den; it contained three other three-man cells. The building beside it was known as the Beer House and the one farther away, in the compound's southeast corner, as the Cat House. Baker noticed that the walls of his building were made of brick and mortar; they would carry sound real well. Each of the three new inmates put an ear to one wall. Baker was "astonished" to hear that "it was alive, humming with tapping conversations." They decoded the loudest tapping: "Two guys just came into the Opium Den. One is bald-headed."

Baker hit the wall solidly with his elbow; the "Ka Thump" was a standard warning signal, an order to be obeyed instantly —"guards coming" or "stop communicating." The walls fell silent.

Baker then "initiated comm"—"Shave and a haircut, two bits," he tapped, meaning "I want to communicate." He tapped out the code: "I am Major Elmo Baker," and then added, "the bald guy." He tapped again: "Just arrived from the Plantation with eleven others. Where are we?" He got an immediate response from the camp's senior ranking officer (SRO), Navy Commander Render Crayton, a February 1966 shootdown. "You're at Camp Hope, near Son Tay Citadel. It's isolated as hell out here. Eleven men have just been moved out."

Suddenly, communication was interrupted by another sharp "Ka Thump" from somewhere. The "V"—North Vietnamese— had "heard the walls vibrating"; guards began patrolling, and they looked agitated. Son Tay fell silent. Baker and the new arrivals wondered what lay ahead for them in this God-forsaken prison outpost.

That Thursday morning, December 11, 1969, Baker and his cellmates awoke early. The day was bright. A stern guard told them, "This is a *working* camp." He took them outside. Baker was given a steel pipe about a foot long and told to break up a pile of old bricks. They would be used, Baker learned later, for the foundation of a new interrogation building. Baker was elated: "They couldn't have given me a better telegraph key!" And he was outside, in fresh air, basking in the cool sunshine. The compound was even smaller than he had pictured it in the dark and everyone would be able to hear him.

He started pounding on the bricks, "sending out the news." He described and named the new prisoners, then told that Neil Armstrong had walked on the moon. The guard was so pleased over his industrious prisoner that he brought Baker a new pile of bricks. Baker pounded out a new message, "This guy don't read code," and announced that a turbine-powered car had led the Indianapolis 500 for 197 laps. Signals from the Beer House told him it was great: none of Son Tay's holdover prisoners had heard that. Almost half of them were 1965 and 1966 shoot-downs, the rest 1967; none of the prisoners were 1968 or 1969 captives. The camp, Baker learned in turn, had become active on May 24, 1968, when 20 POWs were moved there from Hoa Lo Prison; on July 18, 1968, another 20 men were moved in. The last group of 15 had moved in on November 28, 1968.

Wes Schierman was one of that last group. He had been a prisoner of war for over three years. Shot down on August 28, 1965, he was the eleventh Air Force pilot to be taken captive in North Vietnam (of 321 finally released in 1973). Like the other POWs, Schierman had been moved from one camp to another—first from Heartbreak Hotel to another part of Hoa Lo, then to a camp near Ap Lo in the country far to the west of Hanoi which the prisoners quickly dubbed the "Briarpatch." Late in 1968, Schierman was moved to still another camp, this time to the shabby little compound called Son Tay. It was not a bright or cheery place, but the sun broke out that Thanksgiving Day of 1968 and the prisoners decided to nickname their new home Camp Hope.

Compared with Hoa Lo and Briarpatch, Son Tay was "great" in one respect. There were as many as ten prisoners in some of the cells. Most of the POWs had spent their captivity in solitary or with only one or two cellmates, listening to the cries of a fellow American being tortured in a nearby interrogation room, wondering how soon their turn would come again for the same agony. At Son Tay, they were able to see and talk to each other. It was "a new world."

"The new companionship was unbelievable," Navy Lieutenant Ralph Gaither would say of the changed circumstances. "We were able to share knowledge and help each other over the rough spots. We could have fellowship in church services, in games, in shooting the bull."* Like Wes Schierman, Gaither had been a prisoner for five years; a 1965 shootdown, he was the forty-second American to be taken prisoner in North Vietnam (of those eventually released in 1973).

Gaither's F-4 Phantom had been hit on October 17, 1965; he spent his first 15 months of captivity in solitary, initially in Heartbreak Hotel, then in a prison on the southeast edge of Hanoi called the Zoo. His cell there was lit 24 hours a day by a glaring, bare light bulb, and he was kept in handcuffs after getting caught cutting a peephole at the bottom of his cell door. On December 1, 1965, he was moved to the Briarpatch. There, still in solitary, Gaither became deeply depressed. Through the tap code, he asked his fellow prisoners for help. From a cell next door, an Air Force officer and POW he had never met, Wes Schierman, established contact and kept talking to Gaither. Schierman helped him get through "a deep spiritual crisis."

Gaither got his first roommate on January 20, 1967, after 460 days of captivity. But three weeks later he was moved back to the Hanoi Hilton, and from there he was moved again for three months to the Hanoi power plant; Ho Chi Minh had made good his threat to "chain" POWs to the power plants if they were ever attacked by U.S. air strikes, and they were now being targeted regularly. It was a flagrant violation of the Geneva Convention agreements, which specified that prisoners of war would not be held near a target area and that POW camps would be clearly marked. On October 25, 1967, after two prisoners nearly escaped from a little camp called Dirty Bird on the other side of the power plant, Gaither and most of the prisoners were moved back to the Hanoi Hilton.

* *With God in a POW Camp,* by Lt. Cdr. Ralph Gaither, as told to Steve Henry. Nashville, Tenn.: Broadman Press, 1973.

A year later, on Thanksgiving eve, 1968, Gaither was moved without explanation again—to Son Tay. There he found that one of his roommates was a former neighbor from an adjoining cell in Briarpatch, that unseen, friendly "voice" who had helped him through his crisis almost three years before—Wes Schierman. Another cellmate was John Frederick, a forty-six-year-old Marine Corps chief warrant officer. Shot down on December 7, 1965, while flying as radar intercept officer, he was one of the last Marine Corps warrant officers still on flying duty. An avid fisherman like Gaither, the two became fast friends. Raised on an Illinois farm, proud of having "carved life out of earth" with his own hands, Frederick dreamed of retiring from the service and buying a small farm. He never got to buy that farm. He would die in a North Vietnamese prison.

Life at Son Tay was "pretty quiet" compared to other prisons. But the torture continued. Wes Schierman was one of three cellmates who "caught it" time and again. So did Marine Corps Captain Orson Swindle, a 1966 shootdown, and Air Force Captain Julius S. Jayroe, a 1967 shootdown who was the senior man in their cell. They had what the North Vietnamese called "bad attitudes." Their refusal to stand at attention or to bow to their captors sent them repeatedly to the interrogation room. There, they were made to sit on stools for days on end, legs clamped tightly in irons, never allowed to sleep. After one grim session, Jayroe was taken back to his cell exhausted, his ankles and feet cruelly swollen from the leg irons. A day later, the camp commander had the gall to invite him to join some North Vietnamese officers for tea. It was September 2, 1969. They were going to celebrate North Vietnam's National Day. Jayroe curtly refused the luxury and the North Vietnamese cut their party short. Once again, he had "won" and made his captors lose face. It was a small victory but an important factor in maintaining the POWs' morale and self-respect. Word of the incident quickly passed from one cell to another and each of the prisoners "stood a little taller." They knew they were "beaten but not broken."

Periodically, the North Vietnamese would move the senior ranking prisoner out of Son Tay. It usually happened whenever the "V" were displeased because prisoners were being obsti-

nate in their interrogation sessions or caught in a lot of infrac-
tions like not bowing to the guards, or communicating between
cells. Julius Jayroe was SRO when Ralph Gaither moved into
Son Tay late in 1968. By the time Mo Baker arrived in December of 1969, Render Crayton was SRO. But the North Vietnamese moved him late that month or early in January. Marine
Corps Major John H. "Howie" Dunn, a December 1965 shootdown, took over from him, but Dunn was shipped out in May
of 1970. Lieutenant Commander Claude D. "Doug" Clower, a
prisoner since mid-November 1967, then took over as the senior American in Son Tay Prison.

Like all SROs, Clower had the prisoners tabulate and keep
current a mental "data bank" of every American any prisoner
had seen alive on North Vietnamese soil. By May of 1970, there
were about 370 names on the "corporate" list. Mo Baker had
357 of them in his data bank. And Clower kept encouraging the
men to pass on every shred of information they could garner on
the lay of the land outside those compound walls.

The prisoners at Son Tay got to spend more time outside
than in other camps because the North Vietnamese were en-
larging the compound, building a new interrogation room and
a small kitchen-dining hall for the guards. Before Mo Baker
arrived and began his enthusiastic assault on the brick pile,
Ralph Gaither and the other POWs had been put to work
building a new compound wall, about 60 feet beyond the
north wall that lay just outside the Opium Den and Beer
House. The interrogation room Mo Baker was breaking up
bricks for and another small cellblock were being built just
inside the new wall.

The North Vietnamese were improving Son Tay in other
ways. They had the prisoners plant two steel pipes to hold poles
for a volleyball net—so the guards could play, not the prisoners.
One day, Air Force Captain Richard C. Brenneman, a November 1967 shootdown, brashly shimmied up the volleyball pole,
right in the middle of the compound, and took a look outside
the walls. It was "pretty obvious," a big "no no." A guard in the
tower by the front gate spotted him. The North Vietnamese

were "irritated." They threw Brenneman "under the tower"—
a favorite form of torture at Son Tay. Brenneman was locked up
in a small shack for 30 days, baking by day, freezing at night,
choking in the stench of his own excrement. The guards hauled
him out only long enough to beat him when he refused to admit
that he had climbed the pole on anything but a whim. Brenneman took it well, but finally got an order from the camp's SRO
to write an apology to the North Vietnamese before they broke
him and extracted something critical, like the real purpose of
his trip up the pole, or communication methods and codes.
Brenneman wrote the note. It said something harmless like
"I'm sorry I was a bad boy," and the camp commander ordered
him to be released.

Brenneman wasn't the only climber. Whenever they saw the
guards in the towers dozing off, the POWs would climb the
compound wall for a quick look at the area outside. They got
away with it often enough to piece together a mental mosaic of
the countryside around them. They were in the middle of a
farming area, surrounded by rice paddies and irrigation ditches.
A few hundred yards to the south, there was some kind of a
canal. It flowed from a river which ran to the north just outside
the compound's west wall. There was a pumphouse where they
intersected. One POW swore that it had a skull and crossbones
on it, but others passed it off as an odd mud smear, the kind of
image clouds seem to form. It didn't make any sense; it was
incongruous for the North Vietnamese to be painting a skull
and crossbones on anything.

The winters in Son Tay were the hardest. The camp was
primitive, cold, and damp. Very damp. The Song Con River
flowed by just outside the compound wall, often so high that the
compound came near to flooding. Medical care was cruelly
lacking and the prisoners were weak from years of malnutrition
and torture.

Wes Schierman developed asthma problems. They became so
severe in the winter of 1969 that he almost died. He would gasp
for breath, sitting up night after night for weeks at a time to
keep from smothering in his own phlegm. In April of 1970,

even though life in prison had "eased" considerably for most of the prisoners in the preceding six months, Schierman was again fighting for his life. The sound of his gasping for breath filled his fellow prisoners with terror because they were so helpless to aid him. When they asked the guards to get medical help for him, their pleas were ignored. Sometimes Schierman could not even get up enough strength to take the occasional bath the prisoners were allowed and always looked forward to as a luxury. Yet his fellow POWs never heard him complain.

During their long months of captivity, the prisoners at Son Tay thought mainly of going home. Escape, they knew, would be impossible. But the camp's location in an isolated farming area gave them another idea. Rescue. Yet who the hell knew they were there? American reconnaissance aircraft flew over the north almost every week, photographing installations with walls around them. But from the air Son Tay might pass for a barracks, a farm compound, or a schoolyard. The prisoners devised a plan.

On work details in the prison yard, the POWs dug ditches and moved rocks under the watchful eyes of the guards. The guards did not notice that the rocks and dirt from the excavations were piled up in odd ways. The prisoners were put to work digging a new well, since the old one in the compound had dried up. The POWs dug and dug; they never reached water level, but the dirt was piled up very carefully. Allowed to dry their laundry in the prison yard when the sun came out, the prisoners hung up their clothes in an unusual way.

One day the camp's auxiliary generator, which was located just outside the compound and powered the lights around the compound wall, failed. The North Vietnamese couldn't get it to run. They asked if any of the prisoners knew anything about machinery. It was an excellent opportunity to pick up more intelligence about the area outside the compound. Two men were taken to inspect the generator. They examined it knowingly, debated about what was wrong, argued over how to fix it—and took hours to explain to their captors how they could get it running again. But they were careful to leave out an essential step or two. The North Vietnamese still couldn't get it running. A few days later, they pressed the prisoners to take another look at it. Two POWs made their second reconnaissance of the world outside Son Tay, this time with new instructions . . .

"Polar Circle"

Fort Belvoir, Virginia

Fifteen miles from the White House, on the Potomac River just south of Mount Vernon, Air Force Technical Sergeant Norval Clinebell and his bosses were sure he had made a "breakthrough." They were working their usual Saturday morning stint in the heavily secured, isolated compound that housed the Air Force's 1127th Field Activities Group at Fort Belvoir, Virginia. Not many people knew what went on inside the high chain-link fences that sealed the 1127th off from the Army Engineer Center in the northern part of the sprawling, 9,237-acre post. A big 5- by 8-foot sign inside the gate said only, "1127th USAF FAG." One of the unit's men used to complain about it: "My Army friends keep asking why we need such a big cage to hold the 1,127th queer caught in the Air Force."

The 1127th was, in fact, an "oddball" unit, a composite of special intelligence groups who "conducted worldwide operations to collect intelligence from human sources." The men of the 1127th were "con artists." Their job was to get people to talk—Russian defectors, North Vietnamese soldiers taken prisoner in South Vietnam, anyone who might have information and was willing to "sing." In addition, the 1127th processed intelligence on American prisoners of war and designed programs to help downed airmen evade capture or escape from prison. The latter work went on in a small section called the Evasion and Escape Branch. Two of its members had been prisoners themselves. Personnel assigned to the branch were dedicated to their work, good at it—and frustrated by it. They knew there were more than 462 American POWs in Southeast Asia, 80 percent of them held captive in North Vietnam. Over half of the POWs were fellow airmen. Another 970 American servicemen were missing in action; many of them were probably prisoners as well. Some of the POWs had been imprisoned over 2,000 days, longer than any serviceman had ever spent in captivity in any war in America's history. Some, they knew, had died; others were near death, and all the POWs were being held in conditions so primitive and brutal that they sometimes wondered if any of them would return home sane.

The date was Saturday, May 9, 1970. Twelve days before, President Nixon had launched the invasion of Cambodia. It was not going well; about all the White House could announce was that 65 tons of rice had been discovered in the Fish Hook area. Earlier that week, four students at Kent State University had been shot to death by National Guardsmen called out to control a campus protest against the war; 11 others had been wounded. The day before, 75,000 protesters had demonstrated at the White House, which the Secret Service decided to seal off by a bumper-to-bumper ring of buses borrowed from the D.C. Transit Company. Early that Saturday morning, a sleepless President drove to the Lincoln Memorial to mingle with the protesters, mostly college students, in a gloomy, drizzling rain. He talked with them about football, then the war. Their "dialogue" lasted almost an hour. Later that day, two of Henry Kissinger's deputies mounted their own protest by resigning from the National Security Council staff.

The invasion of Cambodia had torn America apart. About the only issue the country wasn't divided on was the POWs and MIAs. Everyone wanted them home. But there wasn't much prospect of that happening soon. In Paris, the North Vietnamese had made it clear that the prisoners were hostages.

They would be released only when the United States pulled all of its forces out of Vietnam. President Nixon's withdrawal program was under way, but there were still 428,000 American servicemen in Southeast Asia. Nine hundred and twenty of them would be dead before the month of May was out, 4,291 others wounded in action, about 20 taken prisoner; 25 more would be missing in action.

Information on where those prisoners were held, and where the missing might show up, had the Pentagon's highest intelligence priority and became one of the nation's top ten Key Intelligence Questions. The intelligence community had gathered reams of "input" from a variety of sources, but useful, "hard" information was difficult to come by. One of the steps taken early in the war was to photograph regularly every installation in North Vietnam with a wall around it. That made a sizeable target list, however, in a country where almost every family raised pigs and chickens and didn't want them running loose in the middle of a nation short on food, and where almost every school had its own closed-in compound.

There were, of course, many sources of intelligence besides reconnaissance photographs: enemy propaganda films, news releases and broadcasts; and the interrogation of defectors and enemy prisoners of war, which had proved especially valuable when a captured North Vietnamese turned out to have a brother or cousin or brother-in-law who was a guard in one of the POW camps. In one case, a previously unknown prisoner, Air Force Lieutenant Colonel Willis E. Forby, had been positively identified when a North Vietnamese soldier taken captive in the south revealed that he had captured Forby when he was shot down early in the war, September 20, 1965. Sometimes information came from foreign visitors to North Vietnam or members of American protest movements allowed to visit there. Other tidbits were passed along, often purposefully gathered for the United States, by military attachés and diplomats stationed in Hanoi from friendly and neutral nations—and occasionally, even from an unfriendly one. Another source was mail from the POWs themselves, when they were allowed to write those cruelly short and uninformative letters home. Only about half the prisoners were being given that privilege, however. Finally, there were the nine Air Force and Navy prisoners who had been released by North Vietnam after several months to several years of captivity. But that was a rare occurrence; and in mid-1970, almost a year had passed since the last one, Air Force Captain Wesley L. Rumble, had been released.

Late in 1966, efforts had begun in earnest to exploit every such source of intelligence on a systematic basis. At that time, the Air Force alone had 264 men down in North Vietnam, but only 29 of them were known to be POWs, including one man shot down over the South China Sea who was being held prisoner in China. The other 235 were "missing in action." North Vietnam announced very few captures. It had become evident that Vietnam was going to be a repeat of Korea, with the enemy refusing to make systematic reports on the identity, location, and treatment of its American prisoners as required by accords of the Geneva Convention, which, contrary to many impressions, North Vietnam had signed in 1959.

In October of 1966, at the urging of the Air Force Casualty Branch, a small, informal meeting of intelligence specialists and casualty representatives from all of the services took place, its purpose to find new ways to collect POW and MIA data, and better ways to analyze it. There were two immediate goals: one was to identify those held prisoner so that the concern and anguish of their families could be somewhat alleviated. The other was to locate the POW camps and place them "off limits" to Air Force and Navy planners who were targeting the "Rolling Thunder" bombing campaign in the north. Yet while every effort was made to avoid hitting known camps, the campaign itself made a grim contribution to the POW problem. In November of 1966, for instance, 7,257 planes had bombed North Vietnam with 11,142 tons of explosives. Over 20 of the planes never made it back.

The meetings quickly grew both in size and frequency, from "as needed" to at least weekly. The group normally met every Friday morning, at first in the Air Force's Pentagon personnel center, then in more formal sessions chaired by the Central Intelligence Agency (CIA). By August of 1967, it was formally chartered as the "Interagency Prisoner of War Intelligence Committee,"—IPWIC—and headed by the Defense Intelligence Agency (DIA). At times the meetings included as many as 20 or 25 people, representatives from each of the military services (Belvoir's odd Air Force unit, the 1127th, for instance, had two full-time members, sometimes more), the CIA and the DIA. The State Department, the FBI, the Secret Service—and even the Treasury Department and the United States Post Office participated when required. Treasury, for example, was called in when a few POW wives began getting letters asking, "Please send me $20 so I can buy some fruit" or "$50 for vegetables." When they tried to send the money, they were told it was illegal. Neither North Vietnam nor the United States had formally declared war, but North Vietnam was an "enemy" and the Foreign Assets Control Regulations administered by the Treasury Department prohibited "all unlicensed transactions by Americans with North Vietnam," including payment of any kind for "accommodations or for services." Treasury and the Post Office finally found a way for the wives to get international postal money orders to some of the prisoners, but it took special approval from Congress. A Marine Corps officer who was a member of IPWIC was nevertheless against having the money sent. At one meeting, he protested, "I'm damned if we'll let anyone send money to help North Vietnam's war effort." He calmed down when an Air Force member suggested that if $50 would help North Vietnam win, the war had already been lost.

The Post Office also worked with international postal authorities on ways to expedite POW mail to and from Hanoi. But as of mid-1970, almost three-quarters of the mail reaching the POWs got to them not through postal channels, but was hand-carried by peace activist Cora Weiss, co-chairman of the Committee of Liaison with Families of Servicemen Detained in North Vietnam. The last mail received *from* the POWs by post had arrived from Hanoi on May 13; from then on, Hanoi saw to it that Cora Weiss was the *only* conduit through which the families could communicate.

Gradually, as IPWIC spelled out new "collection requirements" and priorities and took a closer look at the data it already had, its work began to pay off. Late in 1968, for instance, information from enemy prisoners, visitors to Hanoi, and the first three American POWs to be released by North Vietnam indicated that Americans were being held in a "walled installation" located "approximately 30 miles west of Hanoi." At that time, four POW camps in the north had been located and identified. Three were in Hanoi proper; the fourth was 25 miles to the west. The physical characteristics of the fourth camp, however, did not match the rough description of the camp supposedly five miles further west. Nor did the presence of "walls" offer much help. Practically every walled installation in the north deemed capable of holding POWs had been photographed; many of them were located in an area that could be loosely described as "approximately 30 miles west of Hanoi."

Members of IPWIC worked hard to pin that camp down. But the DIA had an impossible load of other intelligence requirements, from new Russian intercontinental ballistic missile sites to new Soviet ballistic missile submarines, from new tank parks in East Germany to Chinese atomic bomb tests in Sinkiang Province, from increased construction of Egyptian air defenses opposite the Suez Canal to Viet Cong rice caches in Cambodia. For the DIA's senior member of IPWIC, it was only one of two dozen other top-priority assignments.

Nor did he always have the best help in the world. Both the DIA and the CIA were almost suffocated by intelligence data, but it was the men who collected it, not the men who analyzed it, who were getting promoted. Blocked from promotion in jobs analyzing data, many of the bright, senior civilians in the intelligence community spent a lot of time working their way into transfers to posts where they could collect it—and, they hoped, a promotion as well. The net result, as a senior staff member of the National Security Council would sum it up, was that "95 percent of the U.S. intelligence effort has been on collection, and only 5 percent on analysis and production."

New civilian talent shied away from the intelligence agencies, which simply could not compete with the rest of the federal government in enticing aboard the "big brains" who might bust open the intelligence logjam. The DIA, for example, had

3,088 civil service employees, but only 15 "supergrades." The 776-man National Highway Traffic Safety Administration, in contrast, had 36 supergrade billets. A job as an intelligence analyst—or "spook"—was a dead end.

On the military side, the situation was equally bad. Not until 1973 would a single Army colonel or Navy captain assigned to the DIA be selected for promotion to general or admiral. The DIA was a graveyard. It was an environment that was hardly conducive to producing brilliant analysis. Notwithstanding the dedication of some very hardworking people, pinpointing the location of North Vietnam's POW camps suffered accordingly.

At Fort Belvoir, a few men in the 1127th Field Activities Group devoted almost full time to unraveling the reams of raw data from the DIA and the CIA. Finally, on May 9, 1970, Norv Clinebell was pretty sure he had discovered something "hot" on that POW camp west of Hanoi. He was an intelligence technical specialist, an old hand at the game who had worked in Laos long before overt American operations began there. Just under 6 feet tall, slightly overweight with receding blond hair, close to retirement, Clinebell was known for his patience even when things didn't fit together right away. His work was like trying to cook a three-star French dinner out of garbage, but he stuck to it. Late in April, he had started to assemble various tidbits of information, both old and new. There were *two* camps west of Hanoi. He was sure of it. And within a short time he had identified one of them; it was at Ap Lo, 31 miles west of North Vietnam's capital. But a close comparison of old and new reconnaissance photos of the area revealed much more, Clinebell thought. He went to his boss, Colonel George J. Iles, and asked if he could "bounce some ideas" off him.

Iles headed the 1127th's Programs Division, of which the Evasion and Escape Branch was part. He had more than an average interest in his work: he had been a POW himself in World War II, shot down over Italy in a P-51 Mustang. Together Iles and Clinebell laid out the bits and pieces, everything they knew, the "total take" from the intelligence community—and their own latest, if small, collection of raw data. They came up with an almost simultaneous discovery.

The jigsaw puzzle seemed to fit. If their analysis was correct, there were *two* POW camps west of Hanoi: the one at Ap Lo, and another nearby in a walled compound just west of the provincial capital called Son Tay. Until Clinebell compared old and new reconnaissance photos of the area, no one had noticed that the Son Tay compound was being enlarged; there was a new wall and a new guard tower in the northwest corner. Through an ingenious code spelled out in hieroglyphics on the ground, someone in that camp had revealed that there were 55 prisoners at Son Tay. Six of them were calling for an urgent rescue mission; they had devised a desperate plan that, Iles and Clinebell felt, might just work—if it was acted upon quickly.

Iles and Clinebell asked two men for their assessment. One was Colonel Rudolph C. Koller, the 1127th's commander; the other was Claude Watkins, a retired Air Force master sergeant back in service as a civilian intelligence specialist in Iles's Evasion and Escape Branch. Both Watkins and Iles were members of IPWIC. Like Iles, Watkins was inordinately interested in his work. He had been a prisoner of war in World War II for 15 months, a B-17 waist gunner shot down in a raid over Germany. He had spent from 1950 until that May 9, 1970, meeting, with the exception of one year, totally immersed in POW affairs. Koller, a tall, jovial, crew-cut officer, also cared deeply about the POWs. Many were fellow airmen, not just statistics in an intelligence report. Thus, Koller and his men were much more personally involved with the POWs than higher echelon intelligence analysts from the CIA and the DIA. It was not surprising that when the White House had asked for a full POW "update," the 1127th was picked to give it, not the DIA or the CIA. By December of 1972, Watkins was to give one briefing, "Captivity in Southeast Asia," 364 times in all parts of the world. It was updated every week. American peace negotiators in Paris thought it was "gangbusters."

Koller had given men like Iles and Clinebell the license they needed to do a near-impossible job with imagination. And when they came to him with information about Son Tay—and the request for an urgent rescue mission—he went to the telephone, called the Pentagon, and asked Major General Rockly

"Rocky" Triantafellu, Air Force Assistant Chief of Staff for Intelligence, if they could meet with him early the next morning. He had something "hot."

Claude Watkins worked late that night putting together a briefing and making the necessary "flip-charts" to spell out what Clinebell and Iles had unraveled. He was excited.

Son Tay—located on the Song Con River where it flows into the Red River as it bends east toward Hanoi—had been identified a year and a half earlier as the possible location of a prison compound. A North Vietnamese soldier captured near the Demilitarized Zone had revealed that his battalion had bivouacked near the site on its way south. Sent to draw water for his platoon from a well outside the compound, he had seen several prisoners working in the open courtyard. He was "pretty sure," but not positive, that they were Americans. Now Iles and Clinebell had come up with reconnaissance photos of new construction at Son Tay—and photos that showed POWs outside the compound. Watkins had seen many photos of prisoners inside a compound that had already been identified, but this was the first time he had seen POWs working outside a camp. It was also the first time that he had seen POW uniforms hung up to dry inside a compound the way those in Son Tay were arranged. Some were spread on the ground and seemed to spell out the code words for "SAR"—a search and rescue mission. It also seemed as if some POWs had tromped out the letter "K" in the dirt in one corner of the compound. "K" was a code letter for "Come get us."

There was more. Clinebell had unraveled a message the prisoners had worked at for months to get back to the States through a new version of their "tap code." It called for the rescue of six POWs—fast. The prisoners had managed to communicate where the pickup should be made, a spot just far enough from the compound to be workable. They had even made known who the six men were; one of them was in "pretty bad shape."

"Jesus," Watkins thought as he worked on his briefing charts that night at his home in Reston, Virginia, "someone really worked to spell it all out." Then the thought struck him, "God, what if they've been caught?" He drank a beer with his wife, Millie, and asked her to wake him up no later than six the next morning. And would she explain to their son, Kelley, that they would have to postpone working on that go-Kart? It might be a long day.

It was.

Rocky Triantafellu was convinced the 1127th Field Activities Group had something. As soon as he saw how positively the reconnaissance photos and the hieroglyphics designed around the tap code seemed to confirm the request for a pickup, he called in other specialists. "Christ knows, we've waited long enough for something like this," he told Koller. Triantafellu could hardly believe how clearly the prisoners had drawn the Pentagon a veritable road map for a daring and desperate escape. Son Tay was located approximately eight miles northeast of Mount Ba Vi in the foothills approaching Laos. Objects arranged by the POWs in the compound suggested an arrow pointing to the west and the number "8." The prisoners were calling for a pickup at Ba Vi. Clinebell had speculated that work parties from the camp were sent there on certain days of the week, perhaps to chop hardwood for the camp's kitchen fires, perhaps for timber for whatever was being built inside the compound. Triantafellu was convinced the rescue would work. He asked Koller to call Arlington Hall Station, the DIA's annex three miles from the Pentagon. He wanted Navy Captain John S. "Spots" Harris and some of his POW specialists to hear the briefing. Harris headed IPWIC. Meanwhile, Koller was told to begin work on a rescue plan.

Harris brought his team to Triantafellu's Pentagon office early on Monday, May 11. Some of them weren't impressed, a few of the participants recall. One told the Air Force team it was "all a bunch of shit." He conceded that there was a camp near Son Tay and that Clinebell had a "hard lock" on 55 prisoners in it. But he thought that the Air Force interpretation of a bunch of photographs and that odd message calling for a rescue was a "pile of crap."

Nevertheless, the Air Force team was "positive" it was right.

Triantafellu and Koller were convinced that a rescue should be attempted. They were concerned about the POWs at Son Tay. Why had the North Vietnamese put them in such a remote, isolated camp? Why weren't they locked up in downtown Hanoi, where most of the prisoners were known to be held? Triantafellu wondered if these were the "basket cases"—the prisoners who were most seriously injured, the most tortured, or ones who had gone insane. That would explain why the North Vietnamese wanted them out of Hanoi, far out. That way, there would be no risk of a visiting peace delegation seeing them. Triantafellu felt that if peace activists like Ramsey Clark or Jane Fonda or Cora Weiss ever saw how badly some POWs had been treated, they might "turn around 180 degrees." All they saw were the "showcase" prisoners, men who had been beaten into submission before their visits, or the few POWs who were cooperating to save their own hides—and sanity. North Vietnam would go to any length, Triantafellu knew, to keep those peace delegations from realizing how few prisoners were getting such "humane" treatment and what torture the others were still enduring.

But finding prisoners was Triantafellu's job; *rescuing* them was someone else's. He decided to take Koller, Iles and Watkins to Room 4D1062 to see Brigadier General James R. Allen, Deputy Director for Plans and Policy under the Air Force Deputy Chief of Staff for Plans and Operations. Allen was impressed by their evidence; some of the participants recall that he got "real excited." For the next few days, Koller, Iles and Watkins went back and forth from Fort Belvoir to Allen's and Triantafellu's offices in the Pentagon. They ended up in Allen's office "with a big crowd," outlining a "cursory conceptual study" of rescue possibilities and a proposal for an unusual mission.

Allen agreed with their proposal. Tall, lean, serious—a non-bureaucrat with a long face and sense of humor that didn't often show—Allen was a "doer, not a ration-drawer." Asked to describe him, one of his subordinates at the time said later, "Well, when he came up with something, he'd run like hell with it." Allen wasn't the kind of general who needed a big staff study to prod him into gear. But the proposal for a rescue mission at

Son Tay was "way out" of his authority. Allen had little patience with the rituals and delays of bureaucracy; in this case, however, he had no choice. He called an office in the Joint Chiefs of Staff and took Koller, Iles and Watkins—charts, photos, maps, and all—down to a little-known office in the Pentagon basement, Room 1E962. It was now Monday, the 25th of May.

SACSA

Not many of the 27,840 people who worked at the Pentagon in 1970 knew what the acronym "SACSA" meant. Fewer still had any inkling of what the group really did. It was headquartered in the prestigious "E" ring just beneath the office of the Chairman, Joint Chiefs of Staff. Five United States Capitol Buildings could rest comfortably within the Pentagon's walls and two and a half Washington Monuments could be stretched end to end across the same space, so proximity to the "E" ring executives was an important indication of where an individual or office stood in the military hierarchy's "pecking order." SACSA stood pretty close to the top.

SACSA was Donald D. Blackburn, a sandy-haired, 6-foot, 180-pound Army brigadier general, the "Special Assistant for Counterinsurgency and Special Activities" to the Chairman, Joint Chiefs of Staff. He looked far younger than his fifty-three years, and after greeting Allen, Koller, Iles, and Watkins that Monday morning, he picked up the telephone to ask a fifth man to join them from down the hall. This was Army Colonel E. E. "Ed" Mayer, a tall, stocky North Dakota-born clandestine operator who looked like an affable, mild-mannered Midwestern farmer, but one whose patience should not be tested unnecessarily. There was something in his bearing that hinted he could break the average man in two with a sudden whack of his forearm. Mayer headed a small group in SACSA called the Special Operations Division. His work never made the newspapers; for one thing, it took far more than a Top Secret or "Q" clearance to find out what Special Operations did.

The five men sat down around a conference table. Then Allen asked Watkins and Iles to go through the briefing they had prepared for General Triantafellu, showing how the 1127th had positively identified prison compounds at both Ap Lo and Son Tay, and how they had pieced together the urgent request to rescue six prisoners held captive at Son Tay.

The briefing over, Allen told the group that he thought the men could be rescued. He wanted to know if Blackburn could arrange for a clandestine agent to be put into the area. Contrary to many impressions, agents in most of North Vietnam were a military responsibility, not the CIA's, and their missions were "laid on" and controlled by SACSA. Early in the sixties, President Lyndon Johnson had limited the CIA's coverage to the western part of North Vietnam within 15 miles of the Laotian border. The CIA had a number of operating sites there and some coverage into North Vietnam was a natural fallout. But organizing the rescue would be largely the responsibility of SACSA.

Allen's plan was simple. Rescue helicopters with a small Army Special Forces team would stand by only 105 miles away from Son Tay at one of the CIA's border stations in northern Laos. Meanwhile, the SACSA agent would infiltrate the area around Mount Ba Vi, find out when and how often the work party from Son Tay was there (if that's how the prisoners were getting to Mount Ba Vi), and when the situation "looked propitious," call in a rescue team. He could signal for a rescue on a small radio that Allen was pretty sure the North Vietnamese couldn't monitor. Two beeps would mean: "Come get us. They're here." One beep: "Come get me. They ain't here. I've been watching a week and they're not around." If he signaled for helicopters to come in and bring some prisoners out, Allen said, the whole operation would come off very quickly: less than half an hour from "Beep beep" to when six American prisoners of war would be in friendly hands and on their way to an American base in Thailand.

Several factors seemed to favor the operation. North Vietnamese radar might pick up the helicopters coming in from Laos, but the enemy air defense system would have little time to react. Mount Ba Vi was in a remote area of the country, outside the heavy flak coverage, and the main threat to either the prisoners or the rescue force would be small arms fire from guards accompanying the work party. The agent could help mark a landing zone for the helicopters, alert the prisoners that a pickup was imminent, and perhaps even help overcome the guards if necessary.

Allen and Blackburn discussed the idea in more detail. If the operation succeeded, six POWs could be brought back to the United States within a week, two at the most. And besides recovering six Americans who obviously needed help fast, they felt the rescue would pay off in several other ways at this juncture in the war. The Paris peace talks were stalemated; the POWs were North Vietnam's strongest bargaining chip. Rescuing some of them would focus even stronger world attention on the POW/MIA tragedy—and pressure North Vietnam to negotiate more seriously toward release of the others. Unlike the nine POWs released earlier by North Vietnam, the rescued POWs might be permitted to talk publicly about conditions of their captivity. Few of the POWs whom the North Vietnamese had so far released had been badly treated, although they reported knowing that others were undergoing brutal torture, some to the point of death. Coming from a rescued prisoner instead of a released one, news of North Vietnamese brutality would have a tremendous impact. World opinion might then persuade North Vietnam to treat the prisoners more humanely.

Blackburn and Mayer shared Allen's enthusiasm for the rescue, but they had another idea. Why go for just six prisoners? Why not bust into Son Tay and bring out all the prisoners? Blackburn asked to look at the aerial reconnaissance photos again. The two camps Koller's men had identified were in isolated parts of North Vietnam and looked like the most vulnerable of any POW camps located so far. Perhaps they could hit both Son Tay and Ap Lo in the same raid.

Allen had not considered a larger rescue operation. And even if Blackburn thought one was feasible, he pointed out, it was out of his purview. It was something the Joint Chiefs of Staff would have to decide. During World War II, 29 years earlier, a regimental or division commander could have okayed such a mission on the spot. But this was the Vietnam war: the decision to attempt to rescue American prisoners in North Vietnam would probably have to be made in the Oval Office of the White House, 9,500 miles from the battle zone.

Blackburn told Allen he would talk to the Chairman of the Joint Chiefs of Staff personally. He would get back to Allen just as soon as possible, the next morning at the latest.

Claude Watkins left the room disappointed. He too wanted to get more than six prisoners back—but he had a vague sinking feeling that a larger rescue operation would "slow things up."

Watkins was right. There were several problems connected with the rescue plan that Blackburn and Mayer couldn't talk about. Chief among them were the effects of the bombing halt over all of North Vietnam ordered by President Johnson in 1968. The military no longer had the authority to mount special operations or agent "insertions." Its authority was now limited to mounting immediate rescue attempts if a reconnaissance plane or one of its armed escorts was shot down. President Johnson had also forbidden any missions to resupply the CAS teams ("Controlled American Sources," as the agents were known) that were operating in North Vietnam at the time. Nine teams, 45 carefully trained Vietnamese, had been simply abandoned. For months, about all they were told in guarded radio messages was to "hang in there"; there were "problems with resupply," but they were being "worked out." It was one of the biggest, most secret tragedies of the Vietnam war. Reconnaissance flights and propaganda leaflet drops were still being flown over the north regularly—but not one CAS resupply mission. In time, some of the men had been picked up by the North Vietnamese; a few had defected; others had simply died, more than a few of outright starvation. Ironically, one of the last CAS teams to remain in contact had set up a "safe site" on Mount Ba Vi. It was one of several hill tops in Laos and North Vietnam whose location was given to aircrews so they could try to make their way there if shot down and get "exfiltrated." Just a few months before Allen's visit, SACSA finally lost contact with the CAS team there.

Blackburn and Mayer had pointed out, before the meeting

with Allen and his men broke up, that even if SACSA could get an agent request approved now, insertion would be difficult and the timing uncertain. Often CAS agents were parachuted into the north in conjunction with search and rescue missions; that way, the planes flying them in wouldn't attract undue attention. But no air strikes were being flown over North Vietnam in May of 1970, planes weren't being shot down, and there were no SAR missions to use for a cover. They couldn't point out, of course, that recruiting new CAS teams had become very difficult since President Johnson left the last nine of them "twisting in the wind."

Moreover, Blackburn and Mayer weren't sure if the six POWs expected to reach Mount Ba Vi on a work detail or after escaping from Son Tay. They were very leery of attempted POW escapes. They knew of six such attempts. All had failed. Some of the POWs had been killed trying to escape; all of the others had been recaptured, and some of them later tortured. One had apparently been tortured to death. In some cases, Mayer had worked hard to foil escapes which, he had learned, the prisoners were planning. Several POWs got word out of one camp, for instance, that they would "bust out" in two months, steal a boat or make a raft, and float down the Red River at night toward Haiphong Harbor. They had devised signals so they could be picked up en route. Ed Mayer agonized over that one, but finally got a message into the camp telling the POWs not to try: the Red River had just been mined.

Without detailing all of these problems, Blackburn and Mayer had agreed with Allen that something should be done. And Blackburn was the man who could do it. Brigadier generals didn't normally pick up the telephone and ask to see General Earle G. Wheeler, the Chairman of the Joint Chiefs of Staff. But as SACSA, Blackburn had special access when he needed it; if he had something "hot," he could get in to see Wheeler without going "through channels." It was a ticket he didn't punch unless necessary. On May 25, however, he and Mayer left his office soon after Allen had departed and walked upstairs to Room 2E873. There, 30 yards off the Pentagon's imposing River Entrance, Blackburn asked the colonel who guarded the chairman's "inner sanctum" to see General Wheeler on a priority matter. They were admitted immediately.

In Wheeler's office, Blackburn and Mayer told the chairman in three or four minutes of the new prisoner intelligence that the group at Fort Belvoir had put together. Then they described the Air Force request to insert an agent and launch a rescue mission to pick up six POWs on Mount Ba Vi. But, they pointed out, if the rescue was hastily mounted and botched, it would compromise chances of a follow-up mission. Even if the raid was successful, that in itself might preclude a later attempt to rescue their fellow prisoners. Blackburn and Mayer proposed their alternative: a larger, more carefully planned raid to rescue all of the prisoners at Son Tay, possibly even those at Ap Lo.

"Jesus Christ, Don," Wheeler said, "how many battalions is this going to take?" His reaction was a natural one. The last thing "Bus" Wheeler needed on May 25, 1970, hard on the heels of President Nixon's controversial Cambodian "incursion," was an invasion of North Vietnam. Moreover, at this juncture in the war, American combat deaths in Vietnam were still averaging over 500 a month. May 1970 would be a particularly bad month: 754 Americans were to die in hostile action, and another 166 would be dead from other causes. The Army's strategic reserve was down to its lowest number of deployable battalions since World War II.

Wheeler's question didn't bother Blackburn. He knew that the chairman was one of SACSA's strongest supporters. A summary compiled soon after Wheeler left office would show that close to a third of all the actions he had recommended to the Secretary of Defense for approval involved "special operations" handled through SACSA channels. During the McNamara era, however, the Secretary of Defense had not even responded to about 25 percent of the proposals.

Blackburn told the chairman he wasn't thinking in terms of battalions, but of a small group of Special Forces volunteers. With that reassurance, Wheeler asked Blackburn to think about it for a while, and get back to him as soon as possible with a recommendation. But there was another problem. Wheeler had been Chairman of the Joint Chiefs since mid-1964, just before the Tonkin Gulf incident. Worn by the war and his own ill health, he was just weeks away from retirement. He wanted Blackburn to brief his successor, Admiral Thomas H. Moorer, before the planning went too far.

With a green light from Wheeler, Blackburn and Mayer swung into action. They passed the word to only a few people that the chairman had asked for a high-priority feasibility study of a sensitive special operation. But first, they needed more intelligence about North Vietnam's POW camps. They went to see two senior general officers at the DIA, who "got the picture" quickly. The next day, Tuesday, May 26, Blackburn and Mayer were told that "DIA will handle the intelligence briefings." The operation was too important and sensitive to be based solely upon intelligence input from any one service or agency, and the DIA had some unique intelligence sources not available to the 1127th or Allen.

The second "Jesus Christ, Don," came the next day. On Wednesday, May 27, Blackburn went to his superior, Air Force Lieutenant General John Vogt, the Joint Chiefs' Director of Operations, or J-3, and told him that he had a "requirement" to put together a quick, prisoner-rescue feasibility study for the chairman. "Jesus Christ, Don," Vogt exploded. "Don't you ever tell your own boss what's going on?"

Blackburn wasn't the type of officer who tried to cultivate "Brownie points" by running in to his superiors with tidbits of information they didn't need at the time; he preferred to fill them in after the groundwork had been laid. But some of his superiors felt that he just didn't like bosses and operated "solo" a bit too often. It was a natural fallout of Blackburn's determination to keep his "access lists" small. The more people who knew about his kind of work, the greater the danger of inadvertent leaks or compromises. Just as important, the more people who were privy to his special operations, the more officers he had to "coordinate" with, any one of whom might try to second-guess or object to his proposals. Few senior officers on the Joint Staff understood his brand of warfare; fewer still were enthusiastic about it.

After his initial explosion, Vogt, a burly officer who looked like a Russian Cossack, asked Blackburn how soon he could have a recommendation for Wheeler. Blackburn said he and Mayer would get back to Vogt by Monday, June 1. "There goes Memorial Day weekend," Mayer thought to himself when told of the deadline. Home from Vietnam only since April, he was looking forward to some time with his family, and Memorial Day weekend would be their first real holiday together. As events transpired, he would also spend the July Fourth weekend and Labor Day working on the Son Tay raid.

Blackburn and Mayer were under a whirlwind deadline. For the normal "action officer," working a proposal through the Joint Staff was like swimming through tapioca. But SACSA had a unique license to work free of bureaucratic restraints. And Blackburn was in his element; a POW raid deep into enemy territory was right up his alley.

Donald D. Blackburn was a rare breed of soldier. Florida-born and educated, he had been sent to the Philippines soon after being commissioned in 1940. When the Japanese attacked Pearl Harbor, he was serving as an adviser to a Filipino infantry battalion in northern Luzon. When Corregidor fell in May of 1942 and the Japanese overran Luzon, he and a handful of other officers refused orders to surrender. Instead, they evaded capture and took to the bush. Blackburn spent the rest of the war helping to organize 20,000 Filipino guerrillas, eventually commanding one of their five regiments. The unit was made up of his favorite warriors, Igorot headhunters.

When American forces landed on northern Luzon on January 9, 1945, 235,000 well-equipped Japanese troops were defending the island. Blackburn's headhunters fought hard behind the lines. By the time the Philippines were declared reconquered, on July 5, 1945, 24 Japanese had died for every American lost. It was a remarkable kill-to-kill ratio since the attacker seldom loses fewer troops than the defender. Nevertheless, Blackburn left the Philippines with nagging questions about the Army's sledgehammer way of winning wars. One incident illustrated why.

There was an important road junction and Japanese airstrip at the town of Aparri. Ordered to seize them, Blackburn and his guerrillas crossed the Cagayan River at night, met only light opposition, and by dawn held both objectives. Blackburn rushed back to his headquarters to radio the good news to his superiors. A message was waiting when he arrived: a battalion combat team of the 11th Airborne Division was going to capture Aparri. "But we have already captured Aparri," Blackburn radioed back.

It was going to be a "public relations attack," he learned with astonishment, complete with photographers. Blackburn and his men were asked to act as "extras" in the farce. According to a later account of the incident:

> The guerrillas were bewildered but good-natured about it. They cleaned up the airstrip they had captured, and ruffled up the cogon grass they had trampled to make it look nice and fresh for the photographers. Then they took up positions from which they could defend the airstrip just in case any Japs returned. These positions were carefully concealed so that the paratroops, who had not been informed that they were capturing a town that had already been taken, would not mistake the guerrillas for Japs.*

The next morning, while Blackburn and his men watched from their hiding places, gliders of the 11th Airborne descended on Aparri, hitting the ground in "crunching collisions that left many of the men hurt and scared." Blackburn's guerrillas left their hiding places to give them first aid. Sixty-one paratroopers were seriously injured in the "capture" of Aparri— none of them from bullets.

Blackburn returned to the United States a twenty-nine-year-old full colonel. The Army didn't know what to do with a colonel that young—and, presumably, "inexperienced." It sent him on a six-months' tour of Army schools with former POWs to learn something about the Army. After he had served for a year as provost marshal of the Military District of Washington, the Army decided to turn him into a "normal" soldier and sent him

Blackburn's Headhunters by Philip Harkins. New York: Norton, 1956.

to infantry school. A two-year stint in the Pentagon followed by parachute training finally made him more respectable in Army circles.

In 1950, Blackburn was picked to teach military psychology and leadership at West Point. His department head, Colonel Samuel E. "Ned" Gee, had a unique philosophy: "It takes all kinds of clowns to make an Army work." Blackburn shared that philosophy and peppered his courses with grains of his own theories of combat, challenging his cadets to come up with ways of holding their casualties down, urging them to think unconventionally. More than once in the Philippines, he had found the unorthodox approach very effective.

Late in 1957, Blackburn was sent to Vietnam as senior adviser to the Vietnamese general commanding the Mekong Delta. During his tour there, Hollywood made a movie of his exploits in the Philippines. But the writers took so many liberties with the story that when Allied Artists released the film, *Surrender, Hell!*, Blackburn called it the worst movie he'd ever seen. Following his tour in Vietnam, he was given command of the prestigious 77th Special Forces Group at Fort Bragg, North Carolina. When President Kennedy decided early in 1960 to send a covert military advisory group into Laos, Blackburn was told to organize it. The man he picked to head the so-called "White Star" teams was a young lieutenant colonel and World War II Ranger named Arthur D. "Bull" Simons. Blackburn already had Simons in the back of his mind as the man he wanted to lead the prisoner raid into North Vietnam—if he could get it approved.

When Vietnam erupted into a full-blown war in 1965, Blackburn was back in the covert operations business at the Pentagon. He soon returned to Vietnam to command one of the most secret and little-known units in all of Southeast Asia, "SOG." The acronym, the public was told, stood for "Studies and Observations Group." In reality, Blackburn headed the Special Operations Group. It was the OSS of Southeast Asia, a hand-picked force of CIA operatives and volunteers from Army Special Forces and Air Force Special Warfare Units as well as Navy SEAL teams. Its crest sported a skull wearing a green beret in front of a burst of black and gold fire, emblematic of SOG's explosive operations. It hardly symbolized a Studies and Observations Group. Blackburn's men were never able to wear the crest on their uniforms, but inside the security of their own compounds, they sported it on beer mugs, drinking cups, ash trays—and, Blackburn suspected, probably a few jock straps.

SOG's headquarters in Saigon had about 90 people planning operations for its detachments outside South Vietnam. At Nhatrang, SOG had its own wing-size air detachment. A Navy element at Danang ran SOG's private fleet of PT boats. At a place called "Bearcat" near the village of Long Than, airborne and ground units were billeted and prepared for insertion into North Vietnam. There were 350 to 500 people in SOG's operational units, but that was just the American contingent. Another group of 400 to 500 Vietnamese "technical services" troops had been running secret "cross border" operations in Laos and Cambodia before they were combined with SOG to operate in North Vietnam. One of the few SOG missions ever made public involved the "34 Alpha" PT boat raids on North Vietnamese coastal installations by American-trained South Vietnamese crews. Some historians suggest these raids may have triggered the Gulf of Tonkin incidents in August of 1964.

Blackburn had the ideal job for a colonel, running his private international army, navy, and air force, doing "black" work only a handful of people were cleared to know about, reporting directly to General William C. Westmoreland, the commander of United States forces in Vietnam. He was very much his own boss, and he wanted Bull Simons as one of his deputies and chief troubleshooter. But getting Simons assigned to Vietnam was not easy. Westmoreland had laid down a firm policy: colonels would not be assigned to his headquarters unless they had graduated from one of the war colleges. Simons had not been selected to attend one. His efficiency reports as a leader and combat commander were among the best in the Army, but he was a reserve officer and not rated as "general officer potential." Even with Simons' Ranger combat experience, Special Forces background, and the invaluable knowledge of Southeast Asia and of the North Vietnamese which he had gained while commanding

"White Star" teams on two tours in Laos, the Pentagon had to process a special, written exception to Westmoreland's policy before he could join SOG.

Blackburn was also supposed to have, but never got, a CIA deputy. The man who objected to the idea was a covert operations specialist named William Colby. The CIA was going to run its own war, not wage one subordinate to an Army colonel. Later, Colby would head the CIA's controversial "Phoenix" operations in Vietnam and go on to become Director of the CIA.

Blackburn assumed command of SOG in May of 1965. At that juncture in the war, American advisory and combat operations were supposedly limited to South Vietnam. But Blackburn's units ranged over Laos and North Vietnam. Blackburn remembered his own guerrilla days and exhorted his teams not to risk lives needlessly. He never lost an American on the first 45 "cross border" operations that SOG mounted. He always inserted the teams by helicopter late at dusk or first light. The North Vietnamese or Viet Cong could hear them, of course, and usually knew about where the team had been landed, but the helicopters would touch down quickly in two or three places near the objective to mask the actual insertion. To foil the ambushes that the Viet Cong often set up, Blackburn told his men, "After you land, just get lost in the jungle and wait; make *them* hunt for you. When you hear them, *you* can do the ambushing."

He stopped his men from wearing the camouflaged jungle uniforms which the Army Quartermaster Corps had specially designed for such work. It was one of Simons' ideas; the suits blended beautifully with the foliage, but Simons reasoned they were a death sentence if movement was detected. "How many North Vietnamese or Viet Cong do you see dressed in jungle suits?" he reminded his team leaders when they were drawing equipment for a raid or an intelligence-gathering foray.

Experienced as they were, Blackburn's Special Forces teams were understandably nervous about going into "denied areas." Time and again, he had to convince them that it wasn't as dangerous as going on the "main line of resistance" in World War II or Korea. Still, Blackburn was worried about his men being captured; the Communists, he knew, would capitalize in propaganda forums around the world if they could prove that American combat troops were operating outside South Vietnam. So SOG made sure that Blackburn's teams mounted their more sensitive operations with a special set of maps which distorted South Vietnam's borders by as much as ten kilometers. Blackburn reasoned that even with Russia's mapping help, the North Vietnamese could never be that sure it wasn't their maps that were wrong.

One of Blackburn's best "operators" was a young Special Forces master sergeant, Richard J. "Dick" Meadows. "A real life Jack Armstrong," Meadows captured an entire battery of Russian artillery from a North Vietnamese storage point on one mission he led into Laos. It was being moved to South Vietnam, and was so new that the barrels and breechblocks were still packed with cosmoline preservative to prevent rust during shipment. He brought back the Russian-made fire-control equipment. Westmoreland was ecstatic; it was a first, just the evidence President Johnson needed to convince his critics that the Vietnam conflict was no longer a quiet little internal revolution, but a full-blown war being fought by North Vietnamese troops equipped with Russian supplies. Westmoreland asked to meet Meadows personally and was surprised to find a seasoned soldier who looked in his early twenties. He subsequently awarded Meadows a battlefield commission, the first one of the Vietnam war and one of only two which "Westy" was to award in four years as commander of American forces in Vietnam.

During the time that Blackburn commanded SOG, from May of 1965 to May of 1966, American troop strength in Southeast Asia soared from 22,000 "advisers" to more than eight divisions and a quarter of a million men. Thus, Westmoreland's attention, and the Pentagon's as well, was focused on the massive build-up of conventional forces, with the sprawling logistical base needed to support them. The military operations which everyone watched most carefully involved equally conventional land combat.

SOG's unorthodox operations never made the headlines, of course, because of their secrecy, but seldom did its work figure in the overall strategic planning for the Vietnamese conflict. Covert operations were too far down on everyone's checklist. Besides, they were closely controlled out of the Pentagon, and Secretary of Defense Robert McNamara seemed content to direct the conflict from Washington; while Westmoreland, critics said, was bent on winning the war with a few good old-fashioned cavalry charges.

Yet some of SOG's operations had a profound impact on the North Vietnamese. In one ingenious operation, SOG's covert specialists shut down North Vietnam's fishing industry for six months. To do it, SOG's PT boats picked up every fisherman they could find in the waters off North Vietnam from Vinh to the DMZ. The roundup went on for weeks. Close to 1,000 fishermen were kidnapped and brought to Phoenix Island near Danang, one of SOG's most secret installations. There, they were treated royally, but their captors explained that next time it might be different. Because North Vietnamese political leaders often used fishing boats to send contraband weapons and supplies to the south, it might be necessary to sink the boats, and some innocent fishermen might be killed. Perhaps, they were told, it would be best not to fish for a while, or not to fish too zealously—just enough to provide for each fisherman's immediate family. Then, by way of apology for the inconvenience, all the captured fishermen were given baskets of presents that contained sewing kits, cloth, fresh meat, vegetables, cigarettes, spices, garden seeds, sandals, small garden tools, pocket knives —and transistor radios tuned to a single, pre-selected frequency.

After a final sumptuous meal, each fisherman was taken back north and put to sea near his home, floating ashore in the huge wicker baskets which the North Vietnamese used as combination dinghies and life preservers. Sometimes the baskets were so laden with presents they would barely float.

SOG operatives realized that the trick was working when they began picking up "double dippers"—fishermen who had been captured before and were willing to risk being captured again for another boatload of presents. Others, however, took the hint, for in South Vietnam, newly captured North Viet-

namese soldiers were heard to complain that their diet had
fallen off before the long march south. For one thing, there had
been very little fish. They didn't understand it. The South Vietnamese units that had captured them were eating fish; sometimes it was even served to the prisoners. If there were fish in
the south, there had to be fish in the north. Why weren't the
North Vietnamese people getting any?

Blackburn believed strongly in the efficacy of such unorthodox operations. They cost few casualties, wore on the enemy
psychologically, discouraged his soldiers, distracted his attention, diverted his resources, kept him off balance, sapped his
energy—and were deniable. Back in Washington after his tour
of duty in Vietnam, he urged his Pentagon superiors to try more
of them. By May of 1970, the war was past its peak of American involvement. Since April of 1969, 115,482 Americans had
left Southeast Asia; "Vietnamization" was well under way. Yet
11,527 Americans had died in Southeast Asia that year, and
3,279 so far in 1970. Hundreds of POWs still languished in
prison. On May 20, 1970, Navy Lieutenant Everett Alvarez, Jr.,
had spent his 2,120th day of captivity in the north; in the south,
Major Floyd J. Thompson, an Army Special Forces officer from
Ed Mayer's old unit, had been a prisoner for 2,250 days. Blackburn felt something dramatic could be done to get North Vietnam to negotiate seriously toward the return of American prisoners and, just possibly, its own disengagement in the south.
Nixon's Cambodian invasion was a conventional military operation which seemed designed to fail; Blackburn wanted to try
something on the North Vietnamese that would really "rattle
their cage."

What he had in mind was a series of unannounced, unpubli-
cized, unorthodox operations by small forces, like taking out the
Lang Chi hydroelectric dam on the Red River, 65 nautical miles
northwest of Hanoi. Built with Soviet equipment and technical
assistance, it was the showpiece of Soviet-North Vietnamese
solidarity, the Aswan Dam of Southeast Asia. The dam was
nearing completion. Its three turbogenerators would turn out
108,000 kilowatts of electricity, more power than North Vietnam had ever generated. A platoon of Special Forces men,

Blackburn felt, could knock out the generators easily—and get back safely. The operation, moreover, would be "deniable." Hanoi wouldn't dare admit that American forces were operating with impunity in North Vietnam's heartland, able to destroy overnight a key installation that had taken years and close to a billion dollars to build.

Blackburn wanted to raise hell in Hanoi's back yard—just as the Viet Cong had done in the south. He knew that he could knock out that dam. Every soldier who wore a Ranger tab on his shoulder had participated in just such a practice mission as his graduation exercise. Special Forces troops often practiced similar raids, just as they trained from time to time disabling the locks of the Panama Canal. A raid on the Lang Chi Dam, and other operations like it, could become an important bargaining lever, Blackburn felt, and far more effective than the recent "cavalry charge" into Cambodia. But he needed a hunting license.

The Son Tay raid might give him one. If he could show the Joint Chiefs how vulnerable North Vietnam was to the kind of foray he had in mind; if he could get the President's attention; if people would quit asking questions like, "Jesus Christ, how many battalions?" If they would let him go north, in style, just once . . .

The "Tank"

Blackburn and Mayer made their June 1 deadline. At three o'clock that afternoon, they reviewed several rescue alternatives with Vogt and Lieutenant General Donald V. Bennett, Director of the DIA. Their briefing—vugraphs, maps, and all—lasted about 45 minutes. It spelled out several principles for an operation they called "Polar Circle." The code name had been picked at random by a Pentagon computer loaded with thousands of similar phrases. It was the first of three code names the operation would have by the time the raid was launched.

By now, Bennett's analysts had expanded significantly on the breakthrough made by the Air Force's 1127th Field Activities Group. Throughout the preceding week, working with Koller,

Iles, Clinebell, and Watkins, DIA's POW and photo-interpretation specialists had been running back and forth to a little-known building in downtown Washington only a few blocks from the Capitol called "Building 213." Even that guarded designation appeared unobtrusively only two or three times in the Department of Defense's entire 437-page-thick telephone directory. It was the National Photographic Interpretation Center, part of the National Reconnaissance Office, an agency so secret at the time that merely mentioning its name to anyone without a precise "need to know" could mean years in the federal military prison at Fort Leavenworth, Kansas. There, as well as in a suite at the Pentagon that housed DIA's "Directorate for Collection and Surveillance," and in the specially secured offices of the DIA complex at Arlington Hall Station near the Pentagon, Bennett's analysts had been scrutinizing new high-altitude SR-71 photographs of the countryside west of Hanoi. They weighed their assessment of those photos against other new "input" and confirmed beyond doubt the existence of POW camps at both Son Tay and Ap Lo. Some of their confirmatory information may have come from two unlikely sources. One was South Vietnam's vice premier, Air Marshal Nguyen Cao Ky. He was from the town of Son Tay and still had relatives there. Another was a Saigon entrepreneur known as "Mr. Trinh." A dissident North Vietnamese who had fled to the south, he had once "served time" in Son Tay Prison, and based in Saigon, he occasionally came up with an interesting tidbit on what was going on in the north. It all added up to "pretty certain proof" that 50 or so Americans were being held at Son Tay, perhaps as many as 100, given the way the compound had been enlarged in the past year.

Reviewing rescue possibilities with Vogt and Bennett at the Pentagon that Monday morning, Blackburn and Mayer advised against the original plan to insert an agent in the area who would call for a pickup east of Mount Ba Vi. If the operation was botched, or even if it was successful, it would blow chances of rescuing all of the prisoners held at Son Tay and Ap Lo. Blackburn and Mayer thought that both camps looked isolated enough to be promising targets for a major POW rescue.

One option they suggested involved launching a small, fairly simple raid into Son Tay from CIA sites on the Laotian border, 105 miles away. The sites were close enough so that helicopters would not have to refuel in flight to or from the objective. The monsoon season had set in up north and weather would make in-flight refueling a tricky proposition. Two or three extra helicopters would be standing by in Laos while the raid was under way. They could be called in to take out the extra prisoners, or to mount a search and rescue effort if any assault helicopters were shot down or forced to land inside North Vietnam. The compound at Son Tay looked just big enough to land a small assault helicopter inside the walls; that might permit a rescue party to break into the prisoners' cells before the North Vietnamese could react and hold the prisoners hostage or possibly even shoot them.

Another option would be to launch from Thailand, Blackburn and Mayer said; but that would entail a larger, more complex operation. In-flight refueling would be needed and the timing of the operation would be even more dependent upon precise weather predictions. Meteorologists had told them the first good weather "window" would not come before October. In either case, the raid should probably be made at night, Blackburn said. But weather would be the key factor, and much more meterorological data had to be analyzed to recommend the best combination of weather and moonlight. Weather uncertainties during the present monsoons ruled heavily in his mind against an immediate effort.

There was too much risk of a compromise, Blackburn felt, to launch the raid on a "standby basis" from Laos. He respected the enemy's intelligence system too much. He knew that the North Vietnamese and Viet Cong often had gained advance warning of B-52 raids launched from Guam, 2,400 miles away. It was possible that the North Vietnamese would learn that helicopters had been positioned on the border in northern Laos. They would sense that "something was up" as the helicopters waited for the weather to break, and might alert their warning systems and tighten defenses accordingly. "When you operate against a sophisticated intelligence system," Blackburn said, "don't hedge: be sure."

Blackburn also suggested the possibility of drawing North Vietnam's attention away from Son Tay with a Navy diversionary strike launched over Haiphong from the Tonkin Gulf. In the back of his mind, he wanted an operation that would have a 95 to 97 percent chance of getting in and out without a loss, not a 20 percent chance of jeopardizing the prisoners.

Vogt and Bennett agreed with Blackburn's assessment. The next step was to present their proposal to the Joint Chiefs. Blackburn recommended a two-phase approach. First, he would pull together a "feasibility study group" of about 25 people and be ready to report to the Joint Chiefs on about July 15. Phase two, the raid's detailed planning, training, and execution, would follow. Vogt thought 25 people was too large a group to be "cut in" at this early stage and reduced the study group's size by half. But he wanted the planning to move faster; he changed Blackburn's deadline to June 30.

The following afternoon, Tuesday, June 2, Blackburn and Mayer briefed General Wheeler. He was enthusiastic. "I don't see how *anyone* could say 'No' to this operation," he said. He wanted to know whether his successor, Admiral Moorer, had been "clued in." Blackburn told him that they had briefed Moorer last Friday, the 29th, though in much less detail. Wheeler said he felt it was time to let all of the Joint Chiefs and the Secretary of Defense know that a major POW rescue was being considered. He asked that a JCS briefing be scheduled before the week was out, when he would be leaving for Europe on his last visit to NATO as chairman of the Joint Chiefs of Staff.

On Friday, June 5, at one o'clock in the afternoon, Blackburn and Mayer were in "the Tank," the gold conference room where the Joint Chiefs of Staff meet almost daily. It was the first time in nine months as SACSA that Blackburn had been called into the Tank to brief all of the Joint Chiefs. Mayer made the presentation; Blackburn spent most of the time "just watching the faces" of the five senior officers present; together, they wore 19 stars. None of them had much to say, although as the briefing

unfolded, Blackburn thought some of the members were looking at him "like I was smoking marijuana." But the "Chiefs"
agreed that SACSA should proceed with an in-depth feasibility
study of how to bring home all of the prisoners from Son Tay
and Ap Lo.

Given the way things were done in the Pentagon, however,
Blackburn and Mayer would have to run through their briefing
several more times before they could even start the study the
Joint Chiefs had just approved. Right after lunch the following
Monday, June 8, they briefed the service Deputy Chiefs of Staff
for Operations in a session that lasted about an hour. Each
DCSOPS (pronounced DESSOPS) had his own special warfare
division from which SACSA could draw whatever personnel,
equipment, and funds were needed to mount the raid.

The next day Blackburn and Mayer met at CIA headquarters
in Langley, Virginia, with the director's Special Assistant for
Southeast Asia Matters, George Carver, and his deputy for prisoner-of-war affairs, Richard Elliott. SACSA and Carver's office
worked together on an almost daily basis; Elliott had served
with Blackburn in SOG and with Mayer on IPWIC. Blackburn
asked Carver for someone from the CIA to meet regularly with
his feasibility study group. He told Carver that one option still
to be considered was launching the raid from "Site 32," a key
CIA border post west of the targets. Carver agreed to support
the study.

Blackburn had his hunting license. He and Mayer now had
the approval, cooperation, and resources they needed to plan
a major POW rescue mission. But over two weeks had passed
since that mission was first proposed, and it seemed to Blackburn and Mayer that they had spent most of their time
"briefing" and "coordinating." In the way that JCS proposals
normally proceed, they knew that was pretty fast work. But was
it fast enough?

Arlington Hall Station

The first thing Blackburn needed to plan the raid on Son Tay
was more intelligence than IPWIC or the 1127th had in their

files about prison camps in North Vietnam. It would have to come from the Defense Intelligence Agency, and getting it wouldn't be easy.

The DIA was housed in an 87-acre, fenced-in, well-guarded complex at Arlington Hall Station, Virginia, a residential area that some real estate agents called the "Pentagon's bedroom." DIA's critics suggested it was so named because whenever a crisis broke, the agency was caught napping. When Lieutenant General Donald V. Bennett got word late in 1969 that he would become director of the DIA, the first question he asked himself was, "Am I being brought in to preside over a funeral?"

For half a year, the DIA had functioned without leadership. Its director, an Air Force lieutenant general, had not been in the office for six months; he was a very sick man. DIA's deputy director, a Navy vice admiral, had been in the office only one week between May and October of 1969. The rest of the time, he too, was on sick leave. The number three man, an Army major general who served as DIA's chief of staff, had retired on May 1, 1969, but had not been replaced. DIA's fourth ranking officer was an Air Force major general who refused to take over and continued running his own directorate as if the front office was still open for business.

The leadership vacuum wasn't the only problem Bennett inherited. The DIA's reputation stank.

On every new assignment in his twenty-nine-year Army career, Bennett, a 6-foot, 3-inch West Pointer, always seemed to find himself in a cage with a new tiger. As he flew to Washington to be sworn in as the agency's new director, he knew that Vietnam would be in the forefront of his problems. His wavy, short-cropped hair was salt-and-pepper gray when Defense Secretary Melvin R. Laird administered his oath of office as the nation's top military intelligence officer. Within a year, the raid on Son Tay would turn his hair white.

Bennett's first task had been to take inventory of DIA's problems. It proved to be a very long list. Heading it was the agency's lousy reputation. On New Year's Eve of 1968, DIA's copy of an urgent message from the NSA had been misplaced on a clipboard. It warned of intercepting North Korean communications suggesting the spy ship *Pueblo* might be seized. The message was found over three weeks later, after *Pueblo* had been captured and its men imprisoned.

Later that same year, the Soviet invasion of Czechoslovakia caught the intelligence community completely by surprise, despite an obvious seven-week build-up of Soviet troops on the Czech border. The CIA, the NSA, and the National Reconnaissance Office were equally at fault, but the DIA took the brunt of the blame. In fact, the DIA continually found itself in the middle of some dispute within the intelligence community; it usually wound up on the losing end.

The DIA's estimates weren't always the best, but they weren't the worst. They were just the best publicized—probably by the CIA. It was a clever way of deflecting potential criticism of, or too many questions about, CIA's own work. And the CIA was in the driver's seat. It enjoyed a much closer dialogue with the White House and controlled the ultimate fabric of U.S. intelligence. By law, the CIA director was also the director of Central Intelligence for the President. Theoretically, every member of the intelligence community—the DIA, the CIA, the State Department, the NSA, sometimes the FBI—had an equal say with the CIA in the production of national intelligence. But the CIA jealously guarded its prerogative to "polish" the intelligence sent to the President. What ultimately reached the President's desk was the daily Central Intelligence Bulletin, a document edited by CIA. Only rarely were dissenting views ever mentioned in it, and then only by footnote.

When disagreements surfaced between the DIA and the CIA, they weren't easily resolved. The CIA had too much clout. CIA Director Richard Helms had the President's ear whenever he needed it. By contrast, until Don Bennett came aboard no director of the DIA had ever sat in on the chairman of the Joint Chiefs of Staff's daily briefing, the early morning session where "no holds were barred."

The DIA had other problems. One was a complicated charter which saddled it with so many conflicts of interest and fractionalized responsibilities that Solomon couldn't have managed the organization. Formed in 1961 at the direction of Robert

McNamara, the DIA served two masters. On the civilian side, its director was the secretary of defense's chief intelligence adviser; on the military side, the DIA served in place of a J-2, or intelligence branch, for the Joint Chiefs of Staff. On many occasions the secretary of defense and the Joint Chiefs had diametrically opposed views of what they needed to hear from the head of military intelligence, and the DIA had to come up with an analysis to support both sides of the argument. It was an impossible assignment.

Most of its assignments were. For one thing, except for the military attachés the DIA handled at embassies around the world, the agency was totally dependent upon "input" from other sources: intelligence reports from the Army, Navy, Air Force, or Marine Corps units in the field, or raw data from the CIA, the NSA, and the National Reconnaissance Office. The DIA didn't have *one* man of its own in South Vietnam.

The agency was not lacking in raw data. Far from it. At times there were 1,700 cables a day coming into its "indications center." But the agency had trouble recruiting the talent necessary to sift through that mass of information; other civilian and military departments of the federal government could offer better pay and promotion opportunities. Many of the attaches, for instance, were on their last assignments before retirement. Soon after he took over, Bennett fired 38 of them "outright" for "incompetence."

Yet with all these problems, Bennett knew that there were a host of questions his analysts would have to answer if a raid on Son Tay stood any chance of success. The odds were against the raid. Except in the Civil War, despite scores of tries, there had never been a successful rescue of American prisoners from a POW camp during all the years of America's military history. The closest to success was an armored thrust by General George Patton's Third Army into Germany to liberate a camp in which Patton's son-in-law was held captive. The "raid" succeeded, but on their way back to friendly lines the rescuers ran into a German ambush and suffered frightful casualties.

Despite the odds, Bennett was determined to give Blackburn and his planners the sharpest intelligence mosaic the DIA had ever produced; they would need it to bring the Son Tay POWs home. The men he put in charge were DIA's best. One was the agency's Deputy Director for Intelligence, Air Force Major General Richard R. "Dick" Stewart. Aggressive, demanding, a hard worker and tough boss, Stewart was DIA's top intelligence officer. One of his subordinates at the time was Army Colonel Thomas C. Steinhauser who headed DIA's Operational Intelligence Division. Steinhauser would describe Stewart as a "24-hour-a-day general," a "really hard-nosed sonovabitch" who was determined to put professionalism back into the DIA's product.

Navy Captain Spots Harris, head of DIA's Production Support and Resources Office in Building B at Arlington Hall Station, also joined the DIA team supporting Blackburn's planning syndicate. Harris was more of a bureaucrat or manager than an intelligence expert. But as head of IPWIC, he was a logical focal point to coordinate DIA's work on a prisoner-of-war rescue. He wasn't as flexible or quick to react as some of the Son Tay planners might have liked. But he was a good "front man" and cared very much about the raid. At one time, when he thought the CIA was holding some key intelligence too close to its chest, Harris was said to have told a CIA deputy director: "If I find out you've held back on one dot of information that will help free those prisoners, I'll personally commandeer a cruiser, sail it up the Potomac and blast this fucking building off the map."

Harris arranged for some of DIA's brightest people to work on the Son Tay raid. One of them was a GS-17 named John T. Hughes, a civilian supergrade who was DIA's Deputy Director for Collection and Surveillance. Hughes worked out of Room 2D921 in the Pentagon, overseeing the agency's work with the National Photographic Interpretation Center in "Building 213." A former Army enlisted man, Hughes was "hip" on photo interpretation. He cultivated contacts with firms like Kodak, Hycon, Fairchild Instruments, Perkin-Elmer, and Itek, pushing them to produce better lenses, better cameras, higher resolution film. He was not just an expert on photo interpretation, but on briefing what the photos meant. He became famous in the intelligence community in 1962 when he uncorked Russia's installation of medium-range ballistic missiles in Cuba.

For the Son Tay raid, Hughes would have even better collection tools at his disposal: Lockheed's "Big Bird" multi-sensor reconnaissance satellite; Lockheed's SR-71 reconnaissance plane, a black monster that flew three times faster than the speed of sound and higher than 80,000 feet above the earth, a system so complex and sophisticated that over 400 maintenance man-hours were needed to ready it for every hour in the air; Teledyne Ryan's "Buffalo Hunter" low-altitude reconnaissance drones; and lastly McDonnell Douglas's RF-4 reconnaissance planes that flew either at low or high altitude.

Finally, there were weather and communications intelligence experts whom the DIA could call on from within the services or the National Security Agency to support the Son Tay planners. Altogether the DIA team was an impressive one. It had to be. Without intelligence—accurate intelligence—the raid had no chance for success.

Don Blackburn convened his 15-man feasibility study group at Arlington Hall Station on Wednesday morning, June 10. It met in one of DIA's more secure facilities; nevertheless the room had been "swept" by a counterintelligence team just before the meeting to make sure that it wasn't bugged. Seven of the group's 12 officers were Air Force, three were from the Army, and one each from the Navy and the Marine Corps. Air Force Captain James A. Jacobs and Marine Corps First Lieutenant James A. Brinson represented the DIA. Army Sergeant Major Donald M. Davis was the only noncommissioned officer in the group; and there were two civilian secretaries, Frances L. Earley, a GS-8 from SACSA, and Barbara L. Strosnider, a GS-6 from Air Force intelligence.

Chairing the group's first meeting was Army Colonel William C. "Clint" Norman, a Special Forces veteran from SACSA who, in one officer's words, had been "the best team commander Fort Bragg has ever seen." Soon after the group began meeting, however, Norman went on an ordinary leave for almost a

month. He had planned it for some time. But Blackburn and
Mayer were miffed; when Norman returned, he was no longer
on the study group.

Air Force Colonel Norman H. Frisbie took over as the senior
member at the group's later meetings. Assigned by the Air
Force Plans and Policy Directorate, Frisbie was quick, gregari-
ous, and "a strong runner" when it came to "getting things
done." But in the interests of getting the job done, Frisbee took
into his confidence a few officers who had no "need to know,"
and that became a point of irritation for Blackburn and Mayer.

After Clint Norman went on his leave, the Army's senior
member of the study group became Lieutenant Colonel
Thomas F. Minor, assigned from the DCSOPS Directorate of
International and Civic Affairs. As planning for the raid unfolded, Minor was to prove himself invaluable. Slight of build,
soft-spoken, prematurely gray, he was a "detail" man more than
a broad-gauged planner. Asked to describe him, one officer said
unkindly, "He was the messenger to Garcia, the guy who could
always get us what we needed from the Army, always charging
around the Pentagon. But there were times you had to know
which stairwell he was headed for to make sure he didn't get
sidetracked en route." The same officer added, "Minor really
knew how to make the Army move."

Keith Grimes was stationed at the Air University, Maxwell
Air Force Base, Alabama, when he received orders early in June
to report to Washington for "extended temporary duty." He
was one of the officers whom Blackburn and Mayer had asked
the Air Force to detail by name. Grimes was a lieutenant colonel and meteorologist, and they had worked with him often in
Southeast Asia. His weather predictions had always been "un-
canny." Throughout the months ahead, he was to play an increasingly key role in the raid.

The noncommissioned officer in the group, Army Sergeant
Major Donald M. Davis, was detailed from the 6th Special
Forces Group at Fort Bragg. Six feet tall, he was the movie
image of a "Green Beret" type, lean, mean, hair cropped so
short he looked almost bald. Another member detailed from
Fort Bragg was Major Boyd F. Morris, assigned from Headquar-

ters of the John F. Kennedy Special Warfare Center. He was to prove himself one of the raid's sharpest planners.

Only one man in the group would actually end up going on the raid, Air Force Lieutenant Colonel Warner A. Britton. A soft-spoken, Alabama-born veteran helicopter pilot with receding gray hair and gold-rimmed glasses, he looked more like a college math professor than someone who had flown into North Vietnam on a host of hairy rescue missions. Detailed from Headquarters, Aerospace Rescue and Recovery Training Center at Eglin Air Force Base in Florida, Britton later was to recruit most of the helicopter crews who would fly into Son Tay.

There were three Air Force intelligence and operations experts in the study group: Lieutenant Colonel Lawrence Ropka, Jr., Major Arthur A. Andraitis, and Captain John H. Knops. They were all pro's. Ropka, the group's senior operations officer, was quiet, enthusiastic but subdued, poised and confident. He enjoyed everyone's respect. His cohorts called him an "inspiring guy." If there was "one real brain" in the Son Tay planning group, they said, it was Larry Ropka. Many of the changes that evolved in the original concept and some of the most important operational details of the raid were his ideas. Blackburn later said of him: "He generated complete confidence in whatever he told you"; because "he had gone through the staff procedures mentally, he commanded respect by the composition of his thoughts and their presentation, and you didn't have to look over his shoulder." He was something of a contrast to other planners who were equally imaginative, but more impetuous and whose "wild-ass ideas" gave Blackburn and Mayer occasional heartburn. They felt they could "give Ropka his leash and let him go." Ropka was sincerely convinced that the Son Tay operation *could* go, *should* go, and *would* go.

Andraitis was one of the top planners in Air Force intelligence, assigned from the "Multi-sensor Branch" of the Imagery and Data Management Division in the Air Force's Directorate of Intelligence Systems. Scholarly, slim, he was described as probably *"the* top photo interpreter in the Washington area."

Knops was young, very junior to the people he was working with daily. An intelligence specialist, he was not shaken by rank.

He was "confident and ready to stand up and be counted any time." A "nitty gritty guy who understood the big picture," he also knew every detail of the North Vietnamese warning system just as if, one member of the group later remarked, he had been sitting in a North Vietnamese radar room and "knew exactly when everyone there took a leak." If you had to get forces into the north undetected, Knops knew how to "thread the needle." Blackburn later described him this way: "A problem solver, he had a knack of foreseeing the problems and difficulties that could 'blow safe entry,' and he came up with logical ways to counter them. He knew that operational perfection on the part of the guys going in there wouldn't do any good if the intelligence behind them wasn't just as good." Blackburn called him "the shining star of the entire intelligence group."

SACSA's feasibility study group met days, nights, and weekends, and throughout its work, Colonel Rudolph Koller and Claude Watkins were called in regularly from Fort Belvoir's 1127th Field Activities Group. One outside civilian also worked closely with the group, but on an ad hoc basis—Dick Elliott from the CIA. Nevertheless, Blackburn and Mayer were concerned by the extent to which the CIA would be involved. First, there was the need for all the intelligence they could get; second, it still looked as if the raid might have to be mounted from one of the agency's border sites in Laos. When Blackburn and Mayer advised General Wheeler of this, he suggested that he sign a letter to Director Richard Helms, asking the CIA's all-out support for the rescue mission. Mayer drafted a short letter, one paragraph long; Wheeler signed it on Friday, June 19. Helms wrote back on June 25. He pledged the agency's full cooperation but said that his people were already working with the feasibility study group. Wheeler, unaware that Blackburn and Mayer had visited the CIA the day before the study group first met, seemed surprised that the agency was so deeply involved in planning such a closely held JCS operation.

The deadline for the preliminary feasibility study—June 30—came and went. Ten more days would go by before the Son Tay mission was again taken up with the Joint Chiefs of Staff. Early July of 1970 was a time of musical chairs for the military hierarchy, full of such distractions as retirement ceremonies, speeches, and welcoming parties. On Wednesday, July 1, Admiral Thomas H. Moorer was succeeded as Chief of Naval Operations by Admiral Elmo R. Zumwalt, Jr., the youngest CNO in naval history, who had been selected over 60 admirals much more senior to him. On that same day, President Nixon signaled Hanoi that America was ready to resume serious peace negotiations by appointing David Bruce, one of the country's most experienced and respected diplomats, to head the United States negotiating team in Paris. On Thursday, July 2, "Bus" Wheeler retired from military service and a grueling six years as Chairman of the Joint Chiefs of Staff during the longest, most divisive and third bloodiest foreign war in American history.

The Plan

On Friday afternoon, July 10, Admiral Moorer presided over one of his first meetings of the Joint Chiefs of Staff. A major item on the agenda was Don Blackburn's recommendation for a mission to rescue the American POWs at Son Tay. Briefed about the raid almost a month and a half earlier, Moorer was in favor of it, like his predecessor. He wanted some "focal point, something dramatic," to give the country a different, more positive perspective on the war. Rescuing some of those prisoners—or at least trying to—might do the trick. "If we could get 50 or 60 of those boys back in the United States," he thought, "and let them tell in their own words what had happened to them, it would throw a new light on the character of the North Vietnamese." And he wanted to let the POW families and wives know that the people in the Pentagon were doing more than just wringing their hands.

Moorer, moreover, felt a personal identification with the POWs and MIAs. A few days after Pearl Harbor, 29 years earlier, he too almost became a prisoner of war. He was piloting a two-engine Catalina PBY amphibian patrol plane near a Japanese-held base in the Netherlands East Indies when it was attacked by Japanese fighters. Wounded during the engagement, Moorer managed to ditch his badly damaged and burning aircraft safely downwind. He helped evacuate the crew into life rafts and they were soon spotted by a Philippine freighter. But two hours after the freighter picked them up, it too was sunk by Japanese planes. For the second time in one day, Tom Moorer found himself in a life raft. Determined not to be taken prisoner or let his men die, he improvised a small sail and alternately sailed or rowed the raft to Melville Island off Australia. There, an Australian submarine chaser finally rescued him and his men.

Twenty-six years later, on June 28, 1967, Tom Moorer was listening on the radio to an air strike over North Vietnam when he heard one of his best friends get shot down. The man was Captain William P. Lawrence, commander of the F-4 attack wing of the nuclear-powered carrier *Enterprise.* For five years, Bill Lawrence had been Moorer's executive officer and senior aide. Moorer looked upon the tall, quiet, young Texan almost like a son; Lawrence was the one person Tom Moorer could confide in. It had been six months since Lawrence had left the Pentagon to take command of his attack wing, and Moorer, flying from Saigon aboard a small Navy passenger-cargo plane to the *Enterprise* off Yankee Station in the Gulf of Tonkin, was looking forward to a good, long visit.

His plane was about one hour away from Yankee Station when Moorer's pilot asked if he wanted to listen in on some radio traffic; a large "Alpha Strike" was approaching its target just south of Haiphong. Moorer moved up to the cabin, took over from the copilot and put on the headphones.

Then he heard Bill Lawrence get shot down. For the next 45 minutes, he listened in silence as a massive rescue effort got under way. It failed. As his plane turned to land on the *Enterprise,* Moorer heard a downcast rescue helicopter pilot report that a North Vietnamese gunboat had fished Bill Lawrence out of Haiphong Harbor.

Now, more than three years later, Lawrence was still in a North Vietnamese prison camp, and Moorer heard Blackburn's proposals with more than passing interest. He could listen to a briefer with an intensity that some found unnerving. His dark eyes seemed to focus like two laser beams to dig way inside someone's mind. Yet he could be so calm and impassive that critics would describe him as a military robot—but one who wore his four-star uniform well. In his relaxed moments, Moorer was disarming, a good companion. He took his golf game seriously. He hated to lose, but he was a good loser—at golf; he didn't want to lose those prisoners at Son Tay.

By this time, DIA's "make" on Son Tay was so detailed that 61 prisoners had been identified in the camp, by name and service. There might be more, but Bill Lawrence was definitely not one of them. The DIA had also learned that the camp at Ap Lo was now empty, and Blackburn's original idea of busting both camps was scrapped. But Moorer was concerned; raids could backfire, even if they succeeded. What would success or failure at Son Tay mean to the prisoners like Bill Lawrence who were left behind, he asked? In his own mind, he knew "their treatment was pretty goddam severe" and reasoned "it would be hard to get much worse."

Bennett agreed; the question had worried him, too, and he had asked the CIA for its assessment. The job was given to Ken Brock, Dick Elliott, and William Miller, CIA's top POW specialists. One of the people whose views Brock had sought out was a young Vietnam specialist on the National Security Council staff, Dolf Droge. A towering, craggy-faced giant, Droge had served three tours in Vietnam and Laos with the Agency for International Development. He spoke Vietnamese fluently and probably understood the culture and people better than some of South Vietnam's own leaders. Brock couldn't tell Droge that a raid on Son Tay was being planned, but he asked a hypothetical question: "What would North Vietnam do to the other prisoners *if* one of the camps were raided and a bunch of POWs rescued?" Droge didn't hesitate a second before answering that, succeed or fail, it would be "the greatest thing America could do" for *all* the prisoners. Their treatment, he predicted, would improve dramatically and instantly. Brock sometimes wondered if Dolf Droge was nuts. He didn't buy that optimistic assessment. Instead, he turned in a three- or four-paragraph analysis concluding that there would be a "general tightening of security" for four or five months following a raid, but no reprisals on the prisoners left behind. The North Vietnamese, Brock and his cohorts reasoned, would look for much more specific targets for their hostility than POWs who hadn't concocted the operation.

Another problem which Moorer, Bennett, and Blackburn discussed was whether to keep the raid a secret, even if it succeeded. One of the reasons for the raid was to increase American clout at the Paris peace talks. Why not alert Ambassador David Bruce, the American negotiator in Paris, before the rescue was launched? Then the instant aircraft were on their way back with prisoners, Bruce would be notified and would ask to meet with his North Vietnamese counterparts immediately. "Let's make a deal," he would propose. "You don't want to admit that we got into North Vietnam and rescued 61 prisoners. We could really make headlines telling the world about their bad treatment. But we won't. We won't make any fanfare. We won't even tell about the rescue—*if* you agree right now to immediate and regular International Red Cross inspections of *all* the POW camps." The Joint Chiefs even considered letting North Vietnam claim credit for *releasing* the prisoners, since it would be impossible to keep their return under wraps for very long.

As the Joint Chiefs listened to SACSA's briefing, the rescue of those 61 men sounded more and more feasible. Blackburn seemed confident as he outlined the overall concept. He then turned the briefing over to Norm Frisbie, who covered the feasibility study group's plan in detail. It was obvious from the data Frisbie presented that Don Bennett's spooks were bringing together the kind of intelligence needed for the raid to be plausible.

Low-altitude photos taken by an unmanned Buffalo Hunter reconnaissance drone and high-altitude photos taken from an SR-71 confirmed that the camp was isolated and active. It was located in an area surrounded by rice paddies, at least a mile from the closest civilian habitations at Son Tay city to the southeast.

Although the prison was isolated, there were several North Vietnamese military installations within a few miles. In all, the

DIA and the CIA estimated that as many as 12,000 North Vietnamese troops were located within ten to 15 minutes' driving time, but that was under normal daytime conditions. The primary threat would be from three installations within ten kilometers of the target, to the south of Son Tay, and from troops billeted in Son Tay city. The DIA had identified them as elements of the 12th Infantry Regiment. The Son Tay artillery school was the closest military installation housing enemy personnel. Frisbie showed the Joint Chiefs the approach routes from the school to the target. In addition, there was the Son Tay Army Supply Depot with about 1,000 supply personnel, but it was about 20 minutes away under normal daytime driving conditions. Finally, there were about 500 troops and 50 trucks at an air defense installation to the southwest; in daytime, they could react within 20 or 25 minutes.

There was only one other facility near Son Tay Prison. About 500 yards south of it, across a small canal, was another compound of about the same size. On Frisbie's maps of the area, intelligence specialists had it labeled "Secondary School."

The camp at Son Tay, Frisbie explained, consisted of two separate portions, a recently enlarged, walled compound and an administrative support area, including guard quarters, outside the east wall. Bennett's analysts estimated that only 45 North Vietnamese were housed there, including a few dependents. There was only one power and telephone line in the area and it terminated at a communications headquarters building just outside the main gate.

The prisoners were thought to be housed in four large buildings inside the compound. There were three guard towers along a seven-foot-high wall enclosing the prison. Two of them were on the corners of the west wall, where the camp adjoined a river. The third tower was at the main gate on the east wall. Photo interpreters had spotted a small hut beneath it and by comparing photos taken at different intervals, even verified that POWs were occasionally shoved into it. Apparently it was where the prisoners were punished in a form of outdoor solitary confinement reminiscent of the Japanese tin oven in *The Bridge on the River Kwai.*

Photo reconnaissance had also spotted prisoners in the compound's open courtyard. It was small, the unobstructed portion
hardly as big as a volleyball court. There were trees almost 40
feet high, just inside the wall, but there appeared to be enough
of a clear area for a small UH-1 "Huey" helicopter to land inside
the compound with a six- or eight-man assault team. If that
could be done, some of the rescuers could get into the cellblocks
before the guards could react. Outside the south wall, there was
a clear area large enough for several larger helicopters to land
with the rest of the raiding force. They would blow a hole in the
wall so that more men could rush through the opening to release the prisoners and guide, or carry, them out. Some of the
POWs, the DIA knew, were very sick men. While the main
assault was under way, another part of the raiding force would
take care of the guards in the prison's support area and set up
blocking positions on a road east of the compound to prevent
reinforcements or reaction forces from reaching the area. The
ground force would total only about 50 men. Other helicopters
would fly in with the raiding force but land farther away in
some rice paddies, on call to touch down at Son Tay and help
evacuate the prisoners.

The raid would be launched at night for maximum surprise
and to lessen the chance of the helicopters being detected as
they flew into North Vietnam. Parachute flares would be
dropped over the camp seconds before the first helicopters set
down to blind the guards (the raiders would wear protective
goggles) and let the helicopters land safely.

All of this would have to happen very fast. Blackburn had
calculated that North Vietnamese troops from the Son Tay artillery school could get there in as little as 30 minutes. This assumed 12 minutes for them to be alerted, grab their weapons,
and board trucks before racing up that road. On this basis, the
plan called for the whole raid to be over in 26 minutes. The
helicopters would be airborne and headed for Laos by the time
the first truck driver spotted that breach in the wall of Son Tay
Prison.

When Blackburn and Frisbie finished their briefing, there
were quite a few questions. Most of them came from the new

Chief of Naval Operations, Admiral Zumwalt. None of his questions focused on the raid, but on whether it was necessary. Was Blackburn sure that every possible avenue had been explored in the Paris peace talks to get the prisoners released? Was there anything else the United States could do to negotiate with Hanoi on the treatment of the POWs, or to get better information on the MIAs? One of those present at the meeting (not Blackburn) later remarked, "You can describe Zumwalt's questions this way: they would have been great at the White House or over dinner with Henry Kissinger, but at that meeting, they were just plain irrelevant. He acted like a drone."

The questions from Army Vice Chief of Staff General Bruce Palmer were probing and to the point. He wanted to know how sure Blackburn was that he could get the raid in, and out, without putting more soldiers or airmen in some North Vietnamese prison. Palmer later recalled just one impression he got from Blackburn's answers: "You know, that sonovagun really convinced me; he was going to pull it off."

Blackburn explained the raid's timing. It was all weather-dependent. Monsoon rains and the risk of compromise, going in from CIA border stations in Laos, argued against an early launch; weather experts agreed that late October or November would offer the safest launch windows. Moreover, the moon would then be just high enough above the eastern horizon to give the helicopters good visibility on the 100-plus-mile flight from the Laotian border to Son Tay, yet low enough to reduce the possibility of their being detected.

The Joint Chiefs of Staff approved Blackburn's final recommendations. More detailed planning would be needed; then a joint task force would be trained to execute the raid on Son Tay.

Blackburn wanted to lead that raid, with Ed Mayer as his deputy. But his boss, John Vogt, told him that his job was to plan the raid. He'd have to pick someone else to command it. Blackburn was let down but not surprised. For one thing, he knew his name was on a special list which proscribed him even from traveling to certain "high risk" areas; he had too many clearances on too many operations and he knew too much about too many intelligence sources. So did Mayer.

Vogt nevertheless called Mayer a few days later. "I owe you an explanation," he said. "I know how intense you guys are about this. I know how much you and Blackburn would like to lead it. But it's going to take months to get this raid ready. If I could let you do it, we wouldn't need you on the Joint Staff." He did not have to explain that their sudden absence would also raise too many questions he didn't want people to ask.

Fort Bragg, North Carolina

At Fort Bragg, North Carolina, on Saturday, July 11, 1970, Army Colonel Arthur D. "Bull" Simons was busy cataloguing his collection of ancient Vietnamese brassware—spittoons, chamber pots, snuffboxes, dragon heads—a veritable horde of antiques. A big man, he was the spitting image of Telly Savalas, except that Simons had a thin wisp of hair. There was one difference. Bull Simons didn't *act* mean; he *was* mean. An officer who served under him twice in Laos described him as "the only man I know who genuinely hates people." Underneath that gruff surface, however, Simons was a very sensitive man.

The phone rang. It was Don Blackburn. He and Ed Mayer were flying to Fort Bragg on Monday. Could they all get together? Bull Simons didn't know it, but he was about to make his fourth trip to Vietnam.

After he hung up, Bull's wife, Lucile, remarked quietly, "Don Blackburn? Every time he gets in touch with you, there's bad news. Don't tell me you're going to get mixed up with *him* again!"

Simons went back to his Vietnamese brassware. He knew the history of every piece, some of them centuries old. But brassware wasn't all that he collected. He had his own arsenal, an armory of pistols, rifles, and submachine guns that would be the envy of any gun buff. In Panama years before, his officers used to kid that "the Bull" had enough arms in his attic to mount his own invasion of Cuba. For relaxation, he loaded his own ammunition. At Fort Bragg, Bull kept five or six cases of black gunpowder on the second floor of his quarters. He often took his guests up there and went about loading shells as they talked—puffing away on a cigar, oblivious of the long ash that always needed flicking.

Blackburn and Mayer landed at Fort Bragg around 10:30 Monday morning, July 13. They had two objectives. One was to find out if Simons was available to command the raid on Son Tay, without revealing to him that it entailed a prisoner rescue or a mission into North Vietnam. Second, they had to select a training site, either Fort Bragg or Eglin Air Force Base in Florida. The overall mission commander would come from whichever service provided the training site; that would ease a lot of administrative problems and minimize the kind of inter-service "coordination" that might compromise the raid. If Fort Bragg was selected, an Army officer would be the mission commander with an Air Force deputy. If Eglin was picked, there would be an Air Force commander with an Army deputy. SACSA would make the decision.

Simons met Blackburn and Mayer for lunch at the Fort Bragg Officer's Open Mess. Bull Simons, they knew, had suffered a slight stroke before the tour in Korea from which he had recently returned to serve as supply officer, or G-4, of the XVIIIth Airborne Corps. Both were relieved to see how well he looked. When Blackburn asked him how he was really doing, what kind of shape he was in, Simons told them casually he was back up to 250 push-ups a day. Blackburn looked at him and suspected it might be more like 800.

Over lunch, Blackburn asked Simons if he would be interested in leading a "very sensitive mission." It might be "kind of rough," he suggested. Simons knew enough not to ask what it was; if Blackburn was involved, it had to be interesting. "Hell, yes," he answered, "let's go. I don't need to know any more about it." There was no discussion of a raid, no mention of North Vietnam. Instead, the three began to talk about personalities, what kind of men Simons might want to have with him. A few officers came to mind immediately, men they had all worked with before. Some of them, they realized, wouldn't "fit" because they were on orders to Vietnam or Germany or had just been assigned to new posts in the United States. Recalling them or canceling their orders would raise too many questions. Several names were agreed upon, however: Sydnor, Meadows, Petrie . . .

After lunch, Blackburn and Mayer told Simons they'd be back in touch; but it might be a while, they cautioned. As they said goodbye, it was clear to them that Bull Simons would lead the raid. Whether he or someone else would be the overall commander would hinge on other factors.

Before they had left the Pentagon, Blackburn and Mayer were convinced that Fort Bragg would be the ideal training site. The sprawling 130,698-acre reservation was the home of the Strategic Army Corps; joint Army and Air Force training exercises were regular events and one more wouldn't raise undue attention. Pope Air Force Base was located nearby. All over the reservation, and in outlying areas where the Army leased additional land, people were used to the oddball training programs that Fort Bragg's Special Forces teams and the 82nd Airborne Division conducted regularly. There was a secure compound built for just such purposes. Moreover, Bragg was where most of the ground force volunteers would come from. The Air Force Special Warfare Center at Eglin Air Force Base —a vast 464,980-acre complex in the panhandle of northern Florida—offered some advantages. It had access to 44,000 square *miles* of Gulf waters for test ranges undisturbed by commercial air traffic. And it was the home of the Aerospace Rescue and Recovery Training Center as well as USAF's Special Operations Wing. Most of the helicopter crews and C-130 refueling tankers would come from those two units. But on the whole, Blackburn and Mayer favored Bragg.

After leaving Simons, they called on the commander of the Special Warfare Center. They explained that they had to pick a site for training a special force, many of whose members would come from Fort Bragg. They needed a secure area to house special intelligence assets and some very sensitive planning. Could they use the area which had been built at Smoke Bomb Hill some years earlier for just such a contingency?

"No way," the commander, a major general, told them. His Personnel Records Section and Judge Advocate General's

Office had just moved into that compound. It would "disrupt everything." But he suggested an alternative: how about the communications shack on Chicken Road near Camp Mackall? There were some empty World War II wooden barracks available there. Blackburn and Mayer explained again—without really explaining—that this was for an operation of the highest national priority. The major general wouldn't budge.

In disgust, without even visiting Eglin Air Force Base, Blackburn and Mayer flew directly back to the Pentagon. Mayer drafted a brief message for Admiral Moorer to sign: Eglin Air Force Base would be the training site for what was now to be called the "Joint Contingency Task Group" (JCTG). The message directed the Air Force to designate a mission commander. Henceforth, the operation would have a new code name, "Ivory Coast." The point of contact for JCS coordination would be Colonel E. E. Mayer in SACSA.

Meanwhile, Blackburn went to see General Palmer, Army Vice Chief of Staff. He told Palmer that he wanted to name Bull Simons as JCTG's deputy commander and to lead the raid. Palmer knew of Simons' reputation as a combat leader, and as a special operations expert since World War II. But he told Blackburn, "Jesus, I don't know if I can go along with that. Didn't Simons have a massive heart attack about two years back?" It was a slight stroke, Blackburn said, but he and Mayer had just visited Fort Bragg and Simons was back on parachute status and doing 250 push-ups a day. Even with the stroke, Blackburn told Palmer, "Simons is ten times better than anyone else."

Palmer had confidence in both Blackburn and Mayer. Blackburn's guerrillas had once bailed Palmer's soldiers out of a hot spot in the Philippines when he was a division chief of staff; Mayer won one of the two Silver Stars Palmer had awarded during American intervention in the 1965 Dominican Republic crisis. Palmer looked at the list of about ten men Blackburn and Mayer had drawn up. He put a check mark and his signature by Simons' name.

Blackburn was relieved. That choice, he felt, would increase the operation's chance of success by a wide margin. His path and Bull Simons' had crossed time and again for almost 28 years. Blackburn believed that Simons could do almost anything—and the two had a bond of mutual trust and respect so strong that, Blackburn felt, Simons would do the impossible if Blackburn told him it was important enough.

Simons' nickname was appropriate. At fifty-two, he looked like a bull—huge shoulders on a 5-foot 11-inch, 190-pound frame that seemed carved from granite. He had a lot of distinguishing features: a thick neck, receding hairline, bushy eyebrows, a wide, hawklike nose, big ears. Deep creases curved from either nostril around his mouth and down to his chin.

Those who knew him called Simons fearless. "Death is not that far away from me by other causes," he used to say. But there was a big difference between being fearless and being careless; as he put it, "I didn't want my people to get their ass shot off for nothing." That's what leaders were for, to not let that happen. The object of any operation, Bull believed, was "to kill the other sonovabitch, not your own people." He was not interested, however, in "body counts" and once told his men, "If I find one of you counting any bodies, I will break your neck right where you are standing." "Take only those losses that are unavoidable," was his philosophy, "if you can't smart your way out of it." And soldiers, he felt strongly, were "entitled" to leadership from men who could "smart their way out of it."

Leadership, Simons believed, wasn't as complicated as service schools made it sound. "Small unit combat is a pretty simple business," he later said of his work. "The guy who carries the gun wants to know what the hell kind of a man you are and he wants to know you're there with him—not up front, necessarily, but that you know your business, you've got control of the sonovabitch and if the thing really goes sour that you are going to be there with him when it's time to have it out."

He had been in enough fire fights to accept the blood of battle as "an occupational hazard"; war, after all, was "a miserable business to begin with." But Simons believed in soldiering: "If history is any teacher," he once said, "it teaches you that when you get indifferent and you lose the will to fight, some other sonovabitch who has the will to fight will take you over."

Simons became a soldier in 1941, commissioned as an artillery second lieutenant out of ROTC from the University of Missouri. He liked artillery and he liked animals, so he asked to join a "pack artillery" outfit. He was in the 98th Field Artillery when it was sent to New Guinea. The "grizzly old sergeants" in it knew their business, he thought, so he kept his mouth shut. "For the first 60 days out there," he later said, "all I saw in front of me was a long line of mules' asses." Then one day he noticed that the mules' loads weren't riding right and the animals were getting chafed by shifting ammunition cases and bouncing 75 mm. gun barrels, breechblocks, and mounts. Simons barked at one of the sergeants to "pull that mule out of the column and fix his load. It's not riding right." The sergeant "damn near fainted"; he thought Simons was a deaf-mute. Simons would later joke that his first order in combat was telling a sergeant how to make a jackass more comfortable.

The pack artillery was not effective in New Guinea and the battalion was disbanded. By then, Simons was in command of one of its firing batteries, and when he learned that the Sixth Ranger Battalion was being formed and needed some very mobile artillery, he took his battery into the Sixth Rangers.

Simons commanded "B" Company of the Sixth Rangers in the invasion of the Philippines. He landed on an island in Leyte Gulf three days before the invasion began, taking in a team of Navy men and "5,000 pounds of God damn electronic gear" to help blow the electronic mines with which the Japanese had sown the channel. The next night he had to get his company to another island to knock out a radar station. All they could find for the assault was "a bunch of God damn canoes" and a Philippine guide, who "was smart enough to jump out" as soon as they left shore. All the canoes sank, "the whole God damn outfit." But Simons stole more canoes, landed on the wrong island, carried his canoes to the other side, and paddled on to the objective. By that time, another force from the Sixth Ranger Battalion had landed to take out the radar site, "but they had some strange orders, got a couple of guys killed and decided to pull back."

Simons decided to knock off the radar site. He had only 15 men left of an 80-man company. But at two o'clock in the morning, he led them up a cliff on the backside of their objective. "It took an hour and a half to climb that cliff," Simons later recalled, "by our fingernails, you know. I mean straight up." As they reached the top, Simons saw "a young Japanese gentleman about to take down his drawers and take a crap." He was about ten feet away. "It was too bad." Simons shot him, and then he and his men proceeded to blow up the radar station.

About a month later, Simons' Rangers were emplaced on a hill near Aparri, ready to provide covering fire for Don Blackburn's guerrillas as they seized the Japanese airstrip that would later be "captured" by the 11th Airborne. But the two officers didn't meet until years later.

In 1957, Simons was stationed at Fort Bragg. The senior officer of the post, a lieutenant general commanding the Strategic Army Corps, noticed that he had earned a degree in journalism at Missouri and made him the public information officer. Simons hated the job and hated the press. They could be "conned." "The press hasn't done very well for the American soldier," he would explain later. As Fort Bragg's go-between with the fourth estate, he found the press lazy: "They never asked the crucial questions." After a year in "purgatory," he asked his boss for mercy and was posted to the Special Warfare School. By then, Don Blackburn was commanding 77th Special Forces stationed at Bragg and had just returned from his first tour in Vietnam. He put Bull Simons in charge of a battalion-level "C" team. The two men, both advocates of unorthodox warfare, became fast friends.

Early in 1960, Blackburn got word to organize a clandestine group to go to Laos for six months to train a Laotian army. The CIA had originally been assigned the mission, but it wasn't working. Blackburn picked Simons to recruit a new force. They were code-named "White Star" teams. Simons took 107 men to Laos. Before they left, he told them all, "You are going to lose your manhood. Some dumb sonovabitch from the jungle is going to tick you off. But you're going to keep your mouth shut and take it."

Simons and his men left Fort Bragg in July; when they arrived in Laos, no one could tell him whom he was supposed to train or what to train them for. But there was so much ferment in the country, so much military activity from North Vietnamese cross border operations, and so little muscle in Laos's military force (it was mainly a palace guard) that some kind of army was obviously needed. Simons decided to build one. When the government wouldn't recruit any volunteers, Simons kidnapped them. His men roamed all over the country, impressing thousands of Meo tribesmen uprooted by the turmoil in their land. He put them in compounds behind barbed wire, fed them, clothed them—and gradually taught them to soldier. They were eager to learn; life had a purpose and they were even being paid. Bull Simons kidnapped 12 battalions of "volunteers," and they proved to be such tough opposition that North Vietnam soon lost much of its appetite for the cross border raids that had torn Laos apart and almost toppled its government. When Simons' six-month tour of duty was up, he brought every member of his White Star teams back to the States alive. One of his deputies on that mission later recalled: "I would follow Bull Simons to hell and back for the sheer joy of being with him on the visit."

After Laos, Simons headed a large Special Forces contingent in Panama, then joined Don Blackburn's Special Operations Group in Vietnam. In executing SOG missions, Simons refused, in his own words, to "live with some of the restraints put on me." But, he would add, "I got away with it only because I didn't make any mistakes." He knew that if he got caught, "they'd get some other conductor for the trolley car and throw my dead body off the back." When Bull Simons undertook an operation, Blackburn later recalled, the research and planning behind it were "meticulous." He didn't believe in "foolhardy frolics." But he also came to believe that "the more improbable something is, the surer you can pull it off." This was the man that Blackburn picked to lead one of the most improbable missions of the war in Vietnam—the raid on Son Tay. The research and planning would be superb, and he was sure that Bull Simons could "pull it off."

By one of the great ironies of the Son Tay raid, on the day after Bull Simons was picked to lead it, the prisoners there were moved to another camp. A few weeks earlier the well inside Son Tay had dried up. Then the worst monsoon rains in years hit North Vietnam. The prisoners didn't know that just outside the compound, the Son Cong River was flooding water to within a foot or two of the west wall. Their move was orderly, almost casual, not the kind of "panic move" they would experience later. The guards had ordered them a few days before to take down the clothesline, then the volleyball net and posts. The next day, they loaded hogs and chickens aboard some trucks. Then they were told to inventory the dishes and blankets. Finally, they were ordered aboard buses. That night, July 14, 1970, they were all driven to a converted Army barracks at Dong Hoi, 15 miles to the east. The prisoners immediately named the place Camp Faith.

THREE

"Ivory Coast"

Volunteers

At Eglin Air Force Base, Florida, Brigadier General Leroy J. Manor received a rather vague phone call from the Pentagon. He had been designated to command a special mission for the Joint Chiefs of Staff. He was to fly to Washington by special courier plane the next day. Midway on the flight north, however, he was to land at Pope Air Force Base, North Carolina, just long enough to pick up an Army colonel named Arthur D. Simons from nearby Fort Bragg. They would be met at Andrews Air Force Base and driven right to the Pentagon. There, they would be briefed by Brigadier General Donald D. Blackburn, the JCS SACSA.

Manor and Blackburn had never met, but they knew of each other, and Manor had a good idea of what SACSA was all about. As commander of the Air Force's Special Operations Force at Eglin, the forty-nine-year-old New York-born officer trained the unconventional warfare teams which supported SOG operations in Southeast Asia. His students included American and Vietnamese airmen, Cambodians, Thais, and occasionally a few Laotians. Their subjects covered everything from jungle defoliation and leaflet drops over North Vietnam to the clandes-

81

tine insertion of special infiltration teams. Moreover, for three years Manor had been at the Pentagon as the Air Force's top briefing officer on Southeast Asia. He knew there was a lot more to the war in Vietnam than the "search and destroy" sweeps, body counts, and fighter-bomber missions which made up most newspaper accounts of the fighting there.

Like Bull Simons, Manor had seen a lot of combat—345 missions in World War II and Vietnam, 275 of them in Southeast Asia, where he commanded the 37th Tactical Fighter Wing at Phu Cat. Their reputations differed, however. In the Army, Bull Simons was respected as a combat leader, but he was a renegade whose work often made his superiors somewhat uneasy. In the Air Force, Roy Manor was a precise organizer who quickly won the full confidence of his superiors. Simons was outspoken, Manor quiet. Both were competent, dedicated, serious men, but they were different breeds of cat.

The flight to Washington went off as scheduled, and at the Pentagon, Manor and Simons first heard about the raid on Son Tay. Blackburn and Mayer told Manor that he would be in overall command, the "manager"; Simons would be the deputy commander and lead the raid itself. Blackburn and Mayer would handle the coordination in Washington, where one of their main jobs would be to keep people "off their backs" so Manor and Simons could concentrate on recruiting, equipping and training the force, and executing the mission. Whatever they needed, they would have the highest priorities the Joint Chiefs of Staff could provide. In fact, Manor would later be handed a letter by the Air Force Chief of Staff, General John D. Ryan. It was addressed to the Air Force's major commanders and directed them to give Manor their "full support" on a "no questions asked" basis.

After Manor and Simons reviewed the operational concept which Blackburn's feasibility study group had presented to the Joint Chiefs of Staff, both men felt confident the raid could be pulled off. But there was a lot of work to be done, much more detailed planning was needed, and success or failure would depend largely on the quality of intelligence behind them. At a meeting with Bennett, Stewart, and Harris of the DIA, they were relieved to hear that whatever they needed, whenever they wanted it, the DIA would "lay it on." Manor and Simons would get the best intelligence the DIA, the CIA, the NSA, and the National Reconnaissance Office could offer.

NSA's specialty was electronic surveillance; Manor knew how vital its work would be in selecting penetration and escape routes for his aircraft. North Vietnam juggled its air defenses regularly. Firing batteries were moved, communications frequencies changed, and the effective radar coverage varied from week to week. But there was one problem: not once during the Vietnam war had NSA's electronic intercepts picked up one word about the location of prisoners of war. There were thousands of reels of tape in NSA's vaults: the "Encyclopaedia Britannica" on North Vietnamese radio and telephone signals— and specious power line transmissions as well. But in all those intercepts, there wasn't a microsecond of data on the POWs that hadn't already been publicly broadcast in some propaganda forum. Thus, Manor and Simons were told, they would be almost totally dependent on photographic reconnaissance for the intelligence so vital to the success of the raid.

Some last-minute, new information might be developed through other sources, but it was not likely. Occasionally, there was a useful tidbit in mail from POWs, but the letters were weeks and sometimes months out of date. Manor's and Simons' best intelligence would come from photographs taken by the high-flying SR-71s and the low-altitude drones. The SR-71s' long focal length "technical objective cameras" produced fantastic photos. Taken from higher than 80,000 feet, they were sharp enough to let a skilled interpreter count the exact number of people moving around in a cramped compound. But sometimes SR-71 missions produced nothing but photos of cloud puffs directly over a target. The drones could fly under those clouds but had to be used sparingly; too many low-altitude Buffalo Hunter flights near an isolated target like Son Tay might tip off the North Vietnamese that something unusual was up. And Buffalo Hunter assets were scarce, so there was no way to saturate North Vietnam with decoy flights to mask the real objective. Moreover, weather would be bad over the north in the weeks ahead, and that would also limit the effectiveness of photo reconnaissance flights.

Manor and Simons had another problem. If the raid was to be launched in the first favorable weather window in October, they would have to work fast. They agreed with Blackburn on a rough timetable. They would immediately fly back to Eglin and Fort Bragg to recruit their nucleus of volunteers and specialists. Then on Saturday, August 8, they would reconvene in Washington with their hand-picked deputies for five days of detailed planning. A special security section would be organized by that time to develop cover stories and handle the counterintelligence measures necessary to prevent a leak. While the planning group was meeting, Manor and Simons would send a small team to Eglin to pick a training site and prepare it for their men to begin training early in September. The planners would have a training plan ready by August 20, and the actual operations plan laid out by August 28. Training would begin by September 9 and had to be finished by October 6. Most of the photo reconnaissance missions would be programmed in that interval. If everything went as planned, the raiding force should be ready to deploy by October 10, in time to launch the raid during the first good weather window, anticipated between October 20 and 25. It was a tight schedule, but as Roy Manor and Bull Simons left Washington to return to their home bases, they were confident they could make it.

Back at Eglin, Manor began to pick his key subordinates. He called in one of the Air Force's top helicopter pilots, Lieutenant Colonel Warner A. Britton, the operations and training officer at Eglin Air Force Base for the Aerospace Rescue and Recovery Service. Britton had been on Blackburn's feasibility study group, so he was well clued in on the mission which lay ahead. Manor asked Britton if he would volunteer for the raid. Britton told him "Yes" without hesitating. Manor believed in delegating authority; he trusted the instincts and judgments of his "operators," the men who would be in the cockpits instead of the command post. He asked Britton to select the helicopter crews that would land Bull Simons and his men in Son Tay.

Britton told Manor that he personally would fly one of the ships.

One of the first men Britton recruited was Lieutenant Colonel John Allison, a forty-four-year-old Jolly Green Giant veteran who commanded one of the HH-53 flights at Eglin's training center for the Aerospace Rescue and Recovery Service. Allison signed on immediately. But Britton had a difficult time with another "volunteer"—Lieutenant Colonel Herbert E. Zehnder. He couldn't give Zehnder any details about the mission, just that it would involve a lot of training and night flying. Zehnder had been an enlisted man for ten years; he had heard the advice too often, "Never volunteer for anything." He told Britton "No." But Zehnder had the experience and guts Britton needed. The forty-six-year-old pilot had set a long-distance record in 1967, flying an HH-3 helicopter nonstop from New York to the Paris Air Show. He had also flown counterinsurgency missions in Vietnam for a year; in sometimes hairy jungle pickups, he had saved the lives of 84 people. Britton finally "talked" him into volunteering.

Allison and Britton would fly two of the helicopters that landed Simons' assault force at Son Tay; Zehnder would co-pilot the third one. A fourth pilot, Major Frederic M. "Marty" Donohue, would also play a key role, but he was recruited later. Donohue would fly the first helicopter over Son Tay, a gunship that would knock out the guard towers. At the moment, however, he was on another special mission, preparing to fly the world's first trans-Pacific helicopter flight. Britton decided that Donohue had enough on his mind getting ready for that. The historic mission took place on August 15–24, when Donohue flew 8,739 miles on a great-circle route from Eglin Air Force Base, over Alaska, Japan, and the Philippines to Saigon, with 13 HH-53 refuelings along the way by four-engine HC-130 tankers. When he returned to Eglin, he deserved a long rest. Instead, Britton met him as soon as he stepped off the plane, asked him into the base operations office, and, as Donohue put it, "closed the door—which was highly unusual."

Donohue had flown 131 missions in Southeast Asia, four of them rescues in North Vietnam. At thirty-nine, this lanky Californian had logged almost 6,000 hours as a helicopter pilot, as much as and possibly more than any pilot in the world. He had been the project officer at Cape Kennedy on the Apollo space launches. Behind that closed door, Britton could tell Donohue only that he was needed for a "challenging mission" that would involve a lot of night flying. Donohue replied that he wanted to be "in on it."

As Manor and Britton were rounding up their volunteers at Eglin, Bull Simons corralled his at Fort Bragg. The first two men he wanted were Lieutenant Colonel Elliott P. "Bud" Sydnor, to serve as his overall deputy, and Captain Richard J. "Dick" Meadows, to head the compound assault team. Both were stationed at the Infantry School, Fort Benning, Georgia. Simons, Meadows, and Sydnor knew each other well. At the time Simons and Blackburn were in SOG in Vietnam, Meadows was the Special Forces sergeant who had captured the first North Vietnamese artillery pieces in Laos; and when Westmoreland awarded him the first battlefield commission of the Vietnam war, it was Simons who pinned on Meadows' bars. Simons and Meadows had served on many missions together, none of which Simons would discuss in detail. "If we had asked permission for some of them," he later explained, "Westmoreland would have fainted." One of them, Simons claimed, was "the most beautiful operation of the Vietnam war." It involved an "almost impossible" situation. But Meadows was "a steady boy" and he pulled off a "beautiful show—it was slick, I mean really *slick!*" Another time, Meadows, Sydnor, and Simons had taken a small Special Forces team, only about 18 men, and recaptured a major CIA outpost in Laos that the North Vietnamese had overrun and operated from with impunity for almost two months. They "cleaned it off."

Meadows had also served under Simons in Panama. There, but after Simons had left, Meadows helped pull off an operation called "Black Palm." It was a training exercise, to hone Special Forces teams in covert operations and train Panamanian National Guardsmen defending the locks. One of Blackburn's officers flew down and personally briefed the governor of the Canal Zone; he said that small teams would be operating within a ten-day period and gave him a list of seven potential targets, most of them locks along the canal. The governor briefed his troops on the period of the "threat" and the target areas; and the Panamanians quickly picked up one of the Special Forces teams and locked them up in jail. By the next morning, the men had escaped. Twenty-four hours later, the governor was told that if he had divers inspect one of the locks, they would find dummy explosives wired to the flotation chambers that gave bouyancy to the huge lock doors. Meadows' team, which had just escaped from jail, had planted them.

Simons knew that Son Tay would not be Dick Meadows' first visit to North Vietnam. In 1968, after Blackburn had left SOG, Meadows was serving his third tour in Southeast Asia. A team of CAS agents got into "a real pickle" deep in North Vietnam, at a site known as "Eagle" between Hanoi and Haiphong. Meadows was sent in from an aircraft carrier to rescue them. He arrived too late. But he got himself and his men out safely. "I can't say too much about that man," Ed Mayer would later remark. "He's truly a *great* soldier: he's not just heroic, he *performs!*"

Elliott Sydnor was "lean, mean, and tall." Mayer described him as "Gung-ho, brilliant, competent, sensible, fearless, a great team player." Blackburn called him a "mummy. You ask him to do something and he doesn't react. He just *does* it." In combat, he was "fantastic: the tougher things get, the cooler he becomes. *Nothing* flusters him. I've never seen another soldier like him in my life." Like Meadows and Simons, Bud Sydnor believed in Blackburn's line of work. "People in the rear area should never feel comfortable," Simons later said. "The idea is to discomfort the sonovabitch as much as you can."

Simons needed one other senior officer, a doctor. Blackburn's feasibility study group had listed one as essential to the mission. Many Special Forces troops were well-trained medics, but the raid needed a full-fledged doctor, not only to help in the final planning but to be on the raid and care for the prisoners—or Simons' men, if something went wrong. Simons asked the Army Surgeon General to recommend a "combat-type" doctor, but he couldn't tell the Surgeon General what for.

One day early in August, a lieutenant colonel named Joseph R. Cataldo walked into Simons' office. He told Simons, "I'm Doc Cataldo. I hear you need a doctor." Simons asked him if he knew why. Cataldo said no, but that he was available. He had been chief surgeon for the Green Berets at Fort Bragg, graduated from the Command and Staff College at Fort Leavenworth, and had just been reassigned to Washington. He and his wife, Lee, were getting settled with four young children in a home in Alexandria, but the Surgeon General had sent him to Fort Bragg to see Simons about some kind of "special assignment."

The two had never met, but Cataldo was just what Simons needed. He was new to Washington and his absence wouldn't raise too many questions. He knew what special operations were like; he was parachute-qualified, had worked with Green Berets in the field, and he "spoke my language pretty well," Simons later recalled. The only question in his mind was, "Would Cataldo volunteer?" He told Cataldo bluntly that a prisoner-of-war rescue was being planned that would involve a raid deep into North Vietnam. The "risk would be great," Simons said, and he needed a doctor to go along. That was about it. Would Cataldo volunteer? Cataldo told him, "I'm your surgeon."

Simons was surprised. "There was the word 'Surgeon' on my damn personnel check list," he would recall, "so I put a check mark next to it, asked Cataldo how to spell his name, and said to myself, 'No shit: well, now we've got one of those.' "

People described Doc Cataldo differently. One of the Son Tay planners would call him "intense, earnest, dedicated but a self-centered publicity seeker." Simons bridled at that description. "Cataldo *is* a funny guy," he said, "but I want to tell you something: you couldn't get a *captain* to volunteer for that mission. Sure, they'd be happy to come down and help with the training or give the shots and that bullshit—but go into North Vietnam? *Forget* it!" Simons almost bit through the plastic tip of a cigarillo as he continued: "So here a *lieutenant colonel* walks in and volunteers. The man's got a career worth a hundred thousand dollars a year ahead of him. He really had it made, close to retirement if he wanted, ready to make a bundle in private

practice. So I have reservations about anyone who'd run
Cataldo down. The guy *is* hyper-aggressive. Some people don't
care for him. But some people don't care for me either and I
really don't give a shit, to tell you the truth. He had the guts to
do the job and furthermore he was intensely interested in doing
it well. I really don't give a damn about motives, to tell you the
truth. I don't know why Doc Cataldo volunteered. From *his*
view, the risk was great. But he volunteered. Just remember
that."

Simons had to be discreet in choosing the rest of his force.
Through company first sergeants and unobtrusive notices in
Fort Bragg's daily bulletins, word went out that Colonel Arthur
D. Simons was looking for volunteers. Those interested were to
report to the post theater. Simons' reputation on the post was
almost a legend; shortly before lunch one day, close to 500 men
showed up to hear what he had to say. It wasn't much.

Without disclosing any details, Simons told them that he
needed men for a "moderately hazardous" mission. There
would be no extra money involved, meaning no "TDY allowance" for temporary duty away from home station. That was it.
Anyone who was interested should report back to the theater
after lunch with his company "201 jacket"—personnel folder.
Simons would personally interview every man who volunteered. Those who weren't interested needn't worry; Simons
would make damned sure that no one took roll of who came
back and who didn't.

During lunch, a lot of soldiers speculated about Bull Simons'
idea of a "moderately hazardous" mission. That afternoon, only
half of them were back. Simons spent the next three days inter-
viewing every one of them. He had Cataldo and two sergeant
majors with him; they screened every man's service background and medical records. Cataldo gave each a quick physical. Nine men were turned down because they were overweight, even though they were Green Berets. Eleven men had
psychiatrists' notations in their medical jackets of enough concern to disqualify them. Some had pregnant wives; Simons
ruled them out because he couldn't risk men with "extraneous
worries" on their minds.

While Simons probed their combat qualifications and assessed their physical condition—he was looking for soldiers strong enough to *carry* the prisoners out of Son Tay if they had to—Doc Cataldo taunted them to see how quickly they could be provoked under stress: "I see here that your liver is enlarged. What's the matter, soldier, got a drinking problem?" Many of their questions were designed to cloud the real nature and location of the mission, questions like: "Can you ski?"—"Have you ever had scuba training?"—"Do you get seasick easily?"— "How long can you walk in the desert without water?"—"Do you sunburn easily?"—"Are you anti-Semitic?"—"Any problem living in crowded confines with a lot of garlic-loving Lebanese allergic to showers?" Simons and Cataldo selected 15 officers and 82 enlisted men. About one-third of them had served under Simons before and he "knew" at least half of them. Six had never been in combat before, but Simons liked their "mettle." Ten of the men would be back-ups or alternates for roughly a 50-man assault force; the others would make up the support detachment.

On Saturday, August 8, the JCS message which Ed Mayer had drafted for Moorer's signature in mid-July was sent to unified and specified commands around the world. It told of a "Joint Contingency Task Group" under Manor and Simons' command and dubbed the operation "Ivory Coast." There was no hint of what Ivory Coast was all about. By that time, Blackburn had also moved his staff from Arlington Hall Station to a secure DIA complex in the Pentagon's basement.

Two days later, on August 10, Manor and Simons met in Washington with the people Don Blackburn had convened as the Ivory Coast Planning Group. There were 27 people present at the meeting, along with 13 others who made up "SACSA's Administrative Support/Augmentation Group." Two of that group would not appear on any Pentagon records of the meeting: Dick Elliott and Robert Donohue from the CIA. The planning group, Blackburn explained, would meet from Monday through Friday to review and modify plans for the raid. Thenceforward, the final, detailed planning would be up to

Manor and Simons at Eglin Air Force Base. Blackburn and Mayer would "run interference" for them and coordinate at the JCS level from the Pentagon.

Of the 38 planners, 11 were from the 15-man feasibility study group Blackburn had convened on June 10. Among the new faces present, besides Manor and Simons, were Cataldo, Meadows, Navy Captain William M. Campbell from the Chief of Naval Operations' office, and a "wad of intelligence types." One of them was the "Blue Max," a counterintelligence expert and Army major named Max E. Newman. Another was Air Force Lieutenant Colonel John E. Kennedy from the Pacific Air Defense Analysis Facility. He was NSA's expert on the North Vietnamese air defense network. Navy Captain Spots Harris headed DIA's four-man contingent. Of those present at the meeting, four would end up flying into Son Tay.

One of the first decisions Manor and Simons agreed on at the meeting was to send representatives to Eglin to select a training site for Simons' force and begin arranging the needed logistical support. On Wednesday and Thursday, while planning group meetings were still under way in Washington, their representatives chose Eglin's Auxiliary Field Number 3. History was repeating itself: the Doolittle Raiders had trained nearby 28 years earlier. It was an isolated, vacant cantonment used by Air Force ROTC students. There were enough parking aprons at the field to handle the helicopters, six barracks for troop billets, a theater and other classroom space, a small post exchange and snack bar, a mess hall and motor pool, and a headquarters building with barred windows that could be used for a classified operations center. Nearby was plenty of unused range area in the flat, wet Florida scrubland. Blackburn's feasibility group had proposed— and Simons agreed it would be essential—that a mock-up of the Son Tay compound be built so that the assault could be rehearsed under terrain conditions as close to those in North Vietnam as could be found in the United States. Florida's thin pine and cottonwood trees were about the same height as those inside Son Tay Prison, although the foliage wasn't as thick.

As the planning group discussed details of that nature, however, counterintelligence personnel cautioned against building the complete, realistic replica that Blackburn and Simons had in mind. Too much detail would prematurely reveal the nature of the target to the raiders and the new construction would be difficult to explain to casual observers. More important, the "spooks" pointed out, Russian photographic satellites passed over Eglin Air Force Base regularly. Like their American counterparts, Soviet photo interpreters presumably were trained to take a close look at any new construction on a military base. Cosmos 355 was passing over Eglin twice every 24 hours at that time, at an altitude of about 70 nautical miles. From that distance, U.S. Big Bird satellites could take photographs that would let a skilled interpreter spot a new outhouse in the middle of Siberia. Its heat-seeking infra red sensors could even tell how often it was being used. Every 13 days or less, the intelligence analysts knew, Cosmos' film payload was "deorbited" and examined for just such evidence. Often, Russia had two such satellites in orbit at any one time, thus shortening still further the interval before a Son Tay mock-up might be detected. Moreover, a Soviet trawler was operating in the Gulf of Mexico, clearly on an electronic intelligence-gathering mission. There was no way to mask from radar the extra flights that would be going in and out of Field Number 3; and the training couldn't be conducted in complete radio silence, although codes and frequencies could be changed. The flights and radio traffic might give the trawler enough of an "indicator" to warrant having Cosmos 355, or a specially launched satellite, take a closer look at Eglin Auxiliary Field Number 3.

But Simons wasn't about to train his men for a raid into North Vietnam with a Fort Leavenworth "map exercise." So the planners decided to build a mock-up that could be dismantled during the daylight hours. They could use 2 × 4 lumber and target cloth for the compound walls and buildings. Gates, doors and windows could be painted on or cut into the cloth. Thus, the Son Tay compound could be "rolled up" and stored out of sight; the 2 × 4s could be lifted out of their holes and the post-holes covered by lids to conceal the camp's outline. Daylight training would be limited to those four-hour-a-day periods when the satellite was not in position to photograph the area.

For cover purposes, Simons would tell his men the mock-up was a "village" they might have to fight in. But he wanted that mock-up ready fast. He had most of the information he needed to do the job. Blackburn had asked the DIA to arrange a comprehensive photo reconnaissance study of the entire target area. It was handled by the CIA and completed in August. Blackburn had also contacted Milt Zaslov of the NSA, who coordinated the Pentagon's more important requests for special electronic intelligence. Thus, DIA's "target folder" on Son Tay now filled several file drawers. In them were a special set of large-scale maps of the objective area, printed in only a few copies (1 inch on the map would equal 50,000 inches on the ground); large- and small-scale photo mosaics from Son Tay to the Black River, 65 miles to the west; special photographs showing each turning point on the route from Laos into the target; and mosaics of the objective itself in two scales, 100 and 200 meters to each grid square. The planning group knew the location of every building, every wall, every ditch, and every tree in the Son Tay compound; and within days of its first meeting in Washington, 710 6-foot-long 2 × 4s and 1,500 yards of target cloth would arrive at Auxiliary Field 3. Elsewhere at Eglin, huge trees would be dug up and transplanted to conform exactly, with respect to the mock-up, to the positions of the trees the helicopters would have to fly over to land Simons' assault team within the walls of the compound.

Equal attention had been paid to the intelligence details necessary for the long flight from Laos to and from the target area. Recent SR-71 and drone coverage, the planning group was told, showed "no major changes" near the objective, although a new early warning/ground control intercept training site was identified 3.3 nautical miles southeast of the prison, and there were more trucks and vehicles than usual south and west of the objective.

The planners were told one other thing: photos taken since June 6 showed Son Tay Prison to be "less active" than usual.

Some very odd American "air strikes" were under way over northern Laos to the west of Son Tay as Blackburn's planning group discussed the "decreased activity" which had been noted at the prison. Manor would note later in the JCS After Action Report that "Other intelligence satisfactorily explained these changes." But he did not elaborate, even in the Top Secret document, on what that "other intelligence" was—or if he was even told. For Manor and the other Son Tay planners were apparently unaware that the "changes" meant Son Tay Prison was not just "less active;" it was empty. Nor were they told that the "changes" may have been triggered by those odd air strikes over Laos that were part of an ultra-secret program called "Operation Popeye."

Operation Popeye was only one of several code names for "weather modification activities" conducted by the Department of Defense and the CIA during the war in Vietnam. Information on those operations was held in a "special channel," access to which was so limited that five years after the raid, the head of one intelligence agency would explain that he wasn't "scared" discussing the subject, he was "just shivering over it." For the suggestion would be made that the prisoners some Americans were trying to rescue from Son Tay were moved out of the target in July of 1970 because of a flood caused by covert rainmaking missions which other Americans were flying nearby. But because Operation Popeye—and its related activities—ranked among the most closely held secrets of the Vietnam war, the Son Tay planners, and the men who would go on the raid, were not told of that possibility.

The rainmaking program had been conducted under different code names: "Operation Compatriot," then "Intermediary," and when those were "uncovered," Operation Popeye. The program lasted from March of 1967 to July of 1972, and it was not a small deal. It involved 2,602 sorties, almost as many fighter-bomber missions as were flown over North Vietnam in all of 1970 and 1971. The purpose of the program was "to increase normal monsoon season rainfall," using air-dropped silver and lead iodide cloud-seeding units. This, it was hoped, would slow the infiltration of supplies down the Ho Chi Minh Trail by "softening road surfaces, causing landslides along roadways," and "washing out river crossings." Because the North

Vietnamese were using the Laotian streams that fed the Mekong to float supplies to the south—usually in barrels, which just
"bobbed" when bombed—another purpose of the program was
to turn the streams into "raging torrents." An even more highly
classified part of the weather modification program was handled by CIA teams in northern Laos who dumped tons of
"emulsifier" on trails and river banks wetted by the extra rain.
The emulsifier turned the trails into impassable, slippery pools
of quicksand, while river banks collapsed and compounded the
flooding.

At the time of the bombing halt ordered by President Johnson, on November 1, 1968, all "seeding operations within the
boundaries of North Vietnam were terminated and never rein-
stituted." But operations over Laos, and in Laos, intensified.

All of the 1969 seeding operations were flown over northern
Laos, in a small target area contiguous to the border of North
Vietnam. Most of the area was due west or southwest of Hanoi
—and Son Tay. In 1970, the seeding area was enlarged to include the eastern part of southern Laos; but the target area west
of Hanoi—and Son Tay—was also doubled. That year, 277 such
sorties were flown; the planes dropped 8,312 "seeding units,"
the third highest number in any of the six years that Operation
Popeye was under way. And most of the missions were flown
between March and November.

Did those missions cause a flood at Son Tay, or so worsen the
floods that normally occur that time of year in western North
Vietnam that the prisoners had to be moved? For reasons unknown, the vital figures for 1970 are no longer available. But
they do still exist for 1971, and in June of that year 16 inches
of rainfall were recorded in the hills of Laos west by southwest
of Son Tay; 7 of them, Pentagon analysts would calculate, were
"induced" by Operation Popeye. Yet most of the 1971 missions
were flown far to the south in the Laotian panhandle, whereas
more of the 1970 missions were concentrated to the north, in
the area west and southwest of Son Tay prison. It rained like
hell in northern Laos and North Vietnam in 1970.

The world's best weathermen would be hard-pressed to explain why it rains hard somewhere one year and not the next.

But if Operation Popeye had anything to do with the heavy summer rains over Laos and the July flood at Son Tay Prison in 1970, not many people would have been aware of it. The Defense Department would estimate that in the six years the cloud-seeding missions were flown, only 1,400 people were ever cleared to know of them. That included all of the air crews and "supporting personnel" who flew or launched the 2,602 sorties involved, and loaded 47,409 "seeding units" aboard Popeye's airplanes. Any way the numbers are divided, they averaged out to only about 230 people who were cleared to plan, load, and fly about 435 missions every year. Popeye was a *very* "close hold" operation.

A list supplied by the Pentagon would later reveal that the "Director, CIA and limited supporting staff" were made privy to the operations. The list also revealed that 14 other agencies or offices "were informed in varying degrees as to operation and scope." They ranged from the "Joint Chiefs of Staff" and "limited members of the staff of the Office of the Secretary of Defense" to the "Director of Defense Research and Engineering." There was no mention that the DIA was informed, although it must have been; and while it was the DIA that would have informed the Son Tay planners, it would become evident that some of the key DIA analysts supporting the operation were not cleared to know of Operation Popeye. Nor did the CIA always inform the Joint Chiefs of all it was doing in its "private fiefdom" in Laos.

The situation was so complex—and so intentionally vague—that it would raise a host of questions about the Son Tay raid. Did some senior members of the intelligence community know in July or early August that the prisoners at Son Tay had been moved? Were they moved because of a flood caused by American rainmaking operations; and if so, were the Son Tay planners not told of the move because they were not cleared to know about Operation Popeye? Those questions would not even be asked until long after the Vietnam war was over. In August of 1970, the Son Tay planners knew only of "decreased activity" at the prison compound. And in the weeks ahead, the men who would actually mount the operation would be confronted with

very unusual weather conditions. Roughly "five years of ty-
phoons," Manor would write in the JCS After Action Report,
"moved into the area of North Vietnam, South Vietnam and
Laos" in the two months preceding the raid. The area was
experiencing its "worst weather" in years. It meant that obtaining last-minute intelligence from photo reconnaissance flights
would be extremely difficult. It meant that timing the raid
would be difficult. Did it also mean that a Top Secret American
operation was inadvertently endangering both the lives of the
POWs in North Vietnam and the lives of the soldiers and airmen who were about to attempt their rescue?

Assets

No one at Strategic Air Command Headquarters, Omaha,
Nebraska—or anywhere else in SAC—was cleared to know anything about the Son Tay raid. Yet SAC would have to provide
the bulk of the intelligence on which Manor and Simons would
depend. SAC refueling crews, as well as its communications
relay aircraft, would also support the raid.

As Blackburn's planning group continued its August 10–14
meetings, a "package" of seven Buffalo Hunter reconnaissance
drone launches was put at Manor's disposal to give his task
group last-minute "prisoner verification" and "positive identification of the enemy order of battle." At least as many high-
altitude SR-71 missions would be available, but photo interpreters would depend on the drone photos to verify the small-scale
coverage from the SR-71s' ultra-long focal length "technical
objective" cameras, which covered a swath ten nautical miles
wide on the ground.

SAC crews would fly both sets of missions, but no one in
Omaha knew why. Nor would SAC's photo interpreters be told
what to look for. After the raid, Roy Manor was to recommend
"that in the future, if SAC reconnaissance assets are used, one
officer in the SAC Reconnaissance Center Intelligence Requirements Office be briefed on the operation." He went on to explain that "Some difficulty was experienced in coordinating the
JCTG reconnaissance requirements with the SAC Reconnais-

sance Center at Offutt Air Force Base as none of the SAC personnel were cleared for this operation." A "more intimate
knowledge of the requirements," he suggested, "would aid considerably in obtaining the desired coverage."

There was another difficulty. Due to a quirk of the military
bureaucracy, SAC was responsible for all high-altitude reconnaissance (satellites, U-2s, and SR-71s), but only *part* of the Air
Force's low-altitude reconnaissance program. SAC was responsible for "remotely piloted vehicles (RPVs)" or drones—the
Buffalo Hunters—and flew these unmanned low-altitude reconnaissance missions over North Vietnam; but the Tactical Air
Command (specifically, 7th Air Force in Saigon) planned and
flew all of the *manned* low-altitude recce missions there, usually
with RF-4s or RF-101s. The mixed bag of responsibilities drove
Pentagon planners up the wall on missions as complex and
sensitive as the Son Tay raid—especially when the JCS Reconnaissance Office couldn't tell either SAC, TAC, or 7th Air Force
what the Pentagon was looking for or when the target being
reconnoitered might be hit.

Part of the confusion was planned to prevent leaks; part of it
was accidental. But at SAC headquarters, a young lieutenant
colonel named John Dale was perplexed; as head of drone
reconnaissance for SAC, he was "laying on" a "slug" of Buffalo
Hunter missions over a part of North Vietnam no one had paid
much attention to for years. And his hunters weren't bagging
anything. Seven "shots" would be flown between early September and late October; at least two were downed by North Vietnamese gunners and four had "mechanical failures" caused by
weather, operational, or maintenance problems.

One of these, ironically, was flown on July 12, two days before
the prisoners were moved. Two of the American POWs, Mo
Baker and Larry Carrigan, were in the prison courtyard, saw
the drone approaching and waved frantically to tell the outside
world, "We're here, we're here." But something went wrong,
and of the 127 million Buffalo Hunter photos of North Vietnam
which fill the DIA's files today, none came from that mission.

The last Buffalo Hunter shot was a perfect launch. It was
supposed to bring back photos taken from treetop level, just

above the walls of Son Tay Prison, to show "the height, color, eyes and facial expressions" of every man in Son Tay Prison. The photographs were superb. But the carefully programmed drone banked an instant too soon and the perfect pictures it produced were of the horizon beyond Son Tay. When he saw them, DIA Director Don Bennett would recall, "I cried for two days." For all he could tell from the imagery, Son Tay could have been empty—or full of a visiting delegation of rice farmers.

The intelligence community agreed that flying more missions near the camp at low level could tip off the raid; it was decided to "depend upon our high-level penetration" for the remaining photos. The SR-71s would fly out of Kadena Air Force Base, Okinawa, but the film would be rushed to DIA's photo interpreters in SAC's 67th Reconnaissance Technical Squadron at Yokota Air Force Base, Japan, then back to Washington for a closer look. Since the DIA men assigned to SAC were not cleared to know of the raid, the interpreters in Yokota would look for changes in North Vietnam's air defense system and new military deployments over the ten-mile-wide swath covered by the SR-71's photo track. They did a good job. As one user of their product said later, "They located every gun barrel within 50 miles of that place." Only the DIA photo interpreters assigned directly to Manor's Joint Contingency Task Group would "read" what was going on at Son Tay itself, but it was not all that easy. Because of the unusual weather in that part of Southeast Asia in mid-1970, the objective was often covered by clouds or cast in heavy shadows.

At the DIA, Bennett and his deputy Dick Stewart decided it was time to call on other "assets." The possibility of "inserting" a CAS agent near the objective was revived, someone who could "bicycle down the road" outside Son Tay, arrange to have a flat tire or break his drive chain, take a quick glimpse or two inside that front gate, listen for an American voice.

The 1968 ban on agent insertion and resupply had been partially lifted by President Nixon. Bennett went to see Admiral Moorer. The insertion, he suggested, should be timed so that the agent would be in, and hopefully out, long before the raid was scheduled. Moorer agreed. He ordered Bennett to check with CIA and "investigate the desirability of injecting a CAS team," but on a *very* "close hold" basis.

Asked, "What came back?" Moorer would later recall: "Objections." In a country and closed society like North Vietnam, he would explain, "a white person stands out like a box. But you could never be sure whether you can trust the Vietnamese, if you had to go in there with a non-American agent. And it could reveal the fact that you were zeroing in on that point. The concern revolved around the chance that the North Vietnamese might find out about the raid and lay an ambush." Asked if he was "aware before the raid that a CAS team or agent had gone in," Moorer would pause: "No. I don't think there was one there." He would add, however, "There may have been one close to it [Son Tay] out of Laos, but the team didn't provide any information. Operations of that nature were going on up and down the North Vietnamese border, but they didn't contribute anything, as I recall, to the Son Tay raid."

Bennett's recollection would be more specific: "We did put an agent in." It was done "about two months" before the raid, but according to Bennett, he found out "nothing." Asked if the agent was recovered, Bennett would reply, "I don't know. That wasn't my end of the business. You know, we never could find out much when they were threshing around up there."

Perhaps because the operation was "close hold," or perhaps because the agent discovered nothing, Blackburn was not informed of what the CIA and the DIA had done. Apparently, even Admiral Moorer was not informed of the particulars of the operation. An "asset" that had originally been discarded because it might jeopardize the security of the raid was being used —without the knowledge of the man in charge of planning the mission. Blackburn would not learn that a CAS agent might be "threshing around" Son Tay until shortly before the raid was launched.

There was another "asset" known to only a handful of officials in the entire U.S. government. He was North Vietnamese, a "middle-level" but "well-informed" bureaucrat in Hanoi. His name was Nguyen Van Hoang, a senior official in the research office of the North Vietnamese Enemy Proselyting Office, the group concerned with administration and supervision of the POWs and their detention areas. Its "research" office, and Hoang in particular, dealt with POW interrogations. Cheerful, eloquent, and well liked—by his associates—Hoang was close to fifty years old and tall for a Vietnamese, 5 feet 10 inches. His most distinguishing features were his light skin, short dark hair, and thick eyebrows; he looked like North Vietnam's version of John L. Lewis.

For more than a year since Ho Chi Minh's death, the United States had been cultivating Nguyen Van Hoang through a contact in Hanoi called "Alfred." When the Buffalo Hunter shots "crapped out," the DIA arranged for requests to be made of Nguyen for information about Son Tay and, to mask too specific an interest in that target, other POW camps as well. It was a request that would bring much more positive results than the CAS agent insertion. But Blackburn and Mayer knew nothing about that "asset" either.

With hindsight, five years after the raid, military intelligence officials would admit there was one "ace card" they had failed to play: acoustic and seismic sensors to "spike" the camp at Son Tay. These were being used widely to "seed" the trails in southern Laos at the time, with results the Air Force claimed to be "spectacular" in directing air strikes to choke off North Vietnam's resupply of the south.

Don Blackburn had been intimately involved in the early development of the sensors. Soon after he returned from SOG in 1966, he was abruptly taken off the NATO Military Committee and assigned to a newly formed agency called the "Defense Communications Planning Group." Its job was to design and build the "electronic fence" or "infiltration barrier" with which Defense Secretary McNamara hoped, with grandiose optimism, to isolate South Vietnam. Blackburn's job at DCPG was Assistant Deputy Director, Intelligence and Evaluation, and as the sensors were developed and tested, he gained some appreciation for their potential. Later, as SACSA, he was briefed regularly on the intelligence they produced and the operations they triggered. By that time, McNamara had left the Pentagon and his "electronic fence" had been scrapped; but the sensors developed by DCPG were replacing clandestine "trail watchers" in Laos to the point where "every fourth bush on the Ho Chi Minh Trail had an antenna in it." As one Air Force officer put it later, "We wired the Ho Chi Minh Trail like a drugstore pinball machine and we plugged it in every night."

The operation was called "Igloo White," and by mid-1970, it was beginning to pay off. In January of 1971, for instance, airmen flew 25 percent fewer strikes over Laos than they had in January of 1970, but destroyed four times more cargo. The sensors were so good that an air attack against a convoy moving at night or a truck park camouflaged in the daytime destroyed about half of the trucks and cargo. Some 320 tons of North Vietnamese supplies a day were coming into Laos; only ten tons survived to reach South Vietnam.

All kinds of sensors were used. Two of them were acoustic. "Spikebuoy" was a free-fall acoustic device which buried itself in the ground after it had been dropped by helicopter, transport aircraft, or jet fighter-bombers. "Acoubuoy" was another acoustic sensor, but it was dropped by parachute and hung up in the jungle canopy. A third was a seismic sensor, "Adsid," a small free-fall device that looked like a thin mortar shell. This, too, buried itself in the ground, but a small antenna resembling a tropical plant remained above ground. A fourth sensor, "Acousid," combined acoustic and seismic features. It was free-fall, similar to Adsid, but it transmitted audio pickups of command from electronic "triggers" relayed by a high-flying EC-121R. The converted Lockheed Constellation relayed the sensors' signals to an "Infiltration Surveillance Center" at Nakhon Phanom in eastern Thailand. There, it took two IBM-360-65 computers to analyze all the signals coming in from the sensor fields. Over Laos itself, a "Lightning Bolt" C-130 command ship could monitor the signals in "real time" and direct strike aircraft or AC-123 "Black Spot" and C-130E "Surprise Package" side-firing gunships against the most lucrative targets.

There was one drawback. As even more sophisticated sensors were added to the electronic arsenal, an increasing number of the "targets" turned out to be water buffaloes, not North Vietnamese trucks—until the "bedbug breakthrough."

The Army's Limited Warfare Laboratory at Aberdeen Proving Ground, Maryland—a group Blackburn helped get started —had a "people sniffer" program. The object was to develop a sensor that could pinpoint people, not just truck engines or trembling ground. A gamut of technological devices was tested, but again, mechanical systems could not distinguish human beings from tigers or water buffalo. Bedbugs could. The Limited Warfare Lab tested all kinds, but Mexican bedbugs worked best: they had 20 percent more range. They could sense a human being at about 150 yards' distance, wet season or dry, and "got agitated as hell." The bedbugs were literally glued to phonograph needles hooked to a vibrating crystal wired to a tiny transmitter. The Pentagon soon had Mexican bedbugs glued to phonograph needles all over Southeast Asia.

What the CIA needed in Son Tay was a bedbug; but in mid-1970 the device had not yet been perfected. The acoustic sensors had, but Blackburn would later admit that he never thought of using them; he was leaving intelligence up to the spooks. And, he remarked candidly, "I didn't want to know *too* much. Doubts I didn't need. I needed a license to 'go.'" But in retrospect, he said he would have "spiked" the camp, and to mask the real objective, the Air Force could have seeded every other rice paddy in North Vietnam.

Asked about the feasibility of using sensors, DIA's Dick Stewart would say, "That's a hell of a good question." He recalled that "The idea was discussed," but North Vietnam had never been spiked and "I guess we didn't push it hard enough. We have to hold ourselves to blame because we didn't. You can say, 'Well Christ, we should have done it.'"

When Manor and Simons flew back to Florida after their August 10–14 planning meetings with the spooks, they talked about a model that Mayer had introduced them to. Her name was Barbara. Mayer had described her as "quite handsome, amply endowed, impeccably put together." When Simons saw her, he had to agree. "Barbara" was a $60,000 table-size replica of the Son Tay compound, built by the CIA in June at Mayer's request, precise in detail and rigged with special viewing devices. Through them, Simons' men would be able to see the compound exactly as the ground before them would look the night of the raid. By varying the light in the optical viewers, the camp would appear to be lit by a quarter- or half-moon, by flares, or in near-total darkness. Simons had seen similar models on other operations, but none quite this elaborate. He wanted his men to know the target in such detail that, between studies of the model and practice assaults on the Son Tay mock-up at Eglin, every member of the assault force would be able to fight his way into the POW cells even if he was blind, deaf, drunk, and wounded.

Cuba?

Cuba weighed heavily on Marty Donohue's mind. Air Force training for the Son Tay assault began on Thursday, August 20, and by the time Donohue had returned from his trans-Pacific HH-53 record-setting flight and joined the other helicopter and C-130 crews recruited by Warner Britton, they were well into the program. Much of their flying was done over water in the Gulf of Mexico, just south of Eglin Air Force Base. The rest was done at very low level, in terrain-hugging flights which twisted and turned over the mountains of northern Georgia and Tennessee, then back through the flat scrub pines of the Florida panhandle at treetop level. Often they were accompanied by a flight of aging A-1 propeller-driven attack planes, lumbering but maneuverable, tight-turning monsters left over from the Korean war, which usually escorted the Jolly Green Giant helicopters on their Southeast Asia rescue missions.

Donohue had no idea what they were training for. Few of the men did. There was a lot of night flying, refueling practice, and close formation work with the lumbering Sikorsky HH-53 rescue helicopter and its smaller HH-3—sometimes the even smaller Army UH-1 Huey. The latter two usually flew tucked into "draft" formation behind the four-engine, turbine-powered, propeller-driven Lockheed C-130s. Everyone wondered what kind of mission Britton and Manor had dreamed up; but from the duration of the training flights—and reports that the Soviets might be building a submarine resupply base at Cienfuegos in Cuba—Donohue became convinced that Ivory Coast involved a helicopter assault in Cuba.

It all seemed to fit. As HH-53 training progressed, Donohue noted, the flights lasted longer and longer, from just under two hours at first until finally just over four hours in duration. From Eglin, it was roughly 1,000 nautical miles to the southern coast of Cuba, about nine and a half hours' flying time in an HH-53 at its best air speed. But a raid from Eglin to Cuba was impractical; the actual mission would probably be launched from the huge Tactical Air Command complex at MacDill Air Force Base, south of St. Petersburg. That was the base from which strikes against Soviet missile installations would have been flown in the 1962 Cuban missile crisis. MacDill was about 520 nautical miles from Cuba, roughly five hours' flying time one way in an HH-53; but if the planes landed to refuel on the ground at Homestead Air Force Base south of Miami, the trip to Cuba would run three to three and a half hours. The "profiles fitted"—three and a half hours, lots of over-water flying, a hill-hugging, low-altitude penetration across Cuba's Santa Clara mountain range, then "Bang!" to knock out those sub pens in Cienfuegos.

Other crews in the training program shared Donohue's conviction. Cuba would be the target. They were only about 9,500 miles off.

Donohue's calculations were accurate in one sense, however. During the raid on Son Tay, the HH-53s would be airborne exactly 3.4 hours en route to the target. But there wouldn't be much flying over water, only a few rivers and lakes in Laos and North Vietnam. The three and a half hours would be spent bending around hills and mountains on winding routes the DIA and the NSA had mapped out to hide the penetration into Son Tay through precisely located blind spots in Chinese and North Vietnamese radar coverage. Every turn was carefully timed to offset the scanning intervals of enemy radar antennae.

The training flights at Eglin were long—but not monotonous.

Some of them were just plain "hairy." The C-130s, for instance, were operating at the extremes of their capabilities—at what aeronautical engineers call close to the "dead man's curve." Three C-130s would take part in the raid. One, a rescue HC-130, would assist in the early phases of navigation and refuel the heliocopters over Laos. The other two would be specially equipped "Combat Talon" C-130s, with precise, new navigation equipment and forward-looking infra red systems (never used before) which had been matched against intelligence "tracks" giving the IR signature of every turning point along the routes into the target. One of these Combat Talons would lead the assault force of five HH-53s and either one HH-3 or UH-1 into Son Tay Prison and drop flares over the camp. The second would guide the supporting A-1 strike force through and under the enemy radar net. The crews of the two Combat Talons had to practice switching roles and formations, however, in case one of them was shot down or had to "abort" en route because of mechanical failure. That was not an unlikely possibility, but it was also not the least of the problems.

Major Irl L. Franklin of the Air Force's 7th Special Operations Squadron and Lieutenant Colonel Albert P. Blosch of Detachment 2, 1st Special Operations Wing, had flown a lot of C-130 missions—but none like these. The normal cruise speed of a C-130 at low level is about 250 knots; Blosch and Franklin were now trying to keep theirs airborne at 105 knots—roughly ten knots above the airplane's "stall" speed. They had to fly that slow because the HH-3 and UH-1, one of which would land the compound assault team inside the walls of the prison, couldn't fly any faster. Nor did they have enough power to carry their own precise navigational gear plus the assault team and a more powerful, bigger helicopter couldn't be used because the clearing inside Son Tay was so small. The C-130 Combat Talon "mother ships" would have to be like Seeing-Eye dogs for the long flight into Son Tay; and both helicopters were so underpowered for the mission that they would have to fly "in draft," tucked in close enough behind the C-130s' wings to be "sucked along" in the planes' vacuum, just the way some formula race-car drivers race behind front-runners on early laps to conserve fuel and gain speed. At 105 knots, a fully loaded HH-3 or UH-1 was at the "upper boundary" of its performance envelope; at 105 knots, a C-130 was at the rock bottom of its performance curve.

It was crazy. To fly a C-130 that slow, Blosch and Franklin had to use 70 percent flaps, something they would normally call for only on landing. To stay airborne at that speed, they needed power on and all four engines in perfect tune. If an outboard engine were to fail in that "configuration," the C-130's flying characteristics were "marginal." They would be too low, of course, to parachute to safety. Blosch and Franklin might avoid a crash landing—"impact"—only if they could push the throttles "straight into the fire wall" fast enough to accelerate to 140 knots safe forward air speed. And their reaction time would be tested every second of the three and a half hour flight into the target; with 70 percent flaps, the C-130 was "unstable" and could not be flown by autopilot.

Moreover, Blosch and Franklin soon learned, "Caution must be used in making power changes or during roll in and out of turns." Leveling off from a descent in that condition was a "critical maneuver." Too much power applied too quickly would either stall the airplane or accelerate it into the ground. And at 105 knots, the C-130s could not respond fast enough from a "nose-high altitude" for their terrain avoidance radars to provide much of a safety margin. Yet the route to the target over northern Thailand, Laos, and western North Vietnam would involve scores of twisting, turning descents. The navigation tasks alone proved to be so complex that, midway through the training program, Manor decided to add a third navigator to the Combat Talon crews.

The pilot of the assault force C-130 Combat Talon, Major Irl L. Franklin, had a slug of separate problems to deal with. Once over the target, he would drop flares to light up the compound, and then release "fire-fight simulators" to distract, discombobulate, and demoralize North Vietnamese ground troops. But in early practice runs, some of the flares Franklin dropped were duds. Someone had shipped the Ivory Coast task force a "bad lot" of ammunition—only the first of many to arrive at Eglin Air

Force Base. And in addition to their pioneering test work to find out how slow pilots could fly a C-130 and still keep it in the air, Franklin and Blosch were also "cross-training" to deliver the flares, fire-fight simulators, and ground markers in case either had to abort en route.

The flying became more complex as the helicopters, C-130s, and A-1s began training together. Fully loaded with bombs, rockets, and fuel, the A-1s had to fly at about 145 knots to keep from stalling; and they, too, needed a C-130 "mother ship" to guide them into the target. Circling and S-turn tactics were devised so the planes flying at 105 knots could keep in contact with the planes flying at 145 knots. Thus, if either Combat Talon was shot down or had to abort, the motherless helicopters or A-1s could guide on the remaining C-130E.

The air crews practiced their weaving and twisting, ascending and descending ballet at night at treetop level, over the rugged terrain of northern Georgia and the Great Smoky Mountains, in only partial moonlight. So they wouldn't be spotted from the ground, the pilots had to hold these tight formations with cockpit instrument lights dimmed and without the usual external night navigation lights to help them keep station. The pilots tried electronic and night low-light-level binoculars, but the dimmed cockpit lights made them of little use. In the aft cabins, however, flight mechanics and gunners used them to keep track of the planes behind them. All of this flying had to be done in radio silence; and because weather was so uncertain over Laos and North Vietnam, they had to practice reestablishing contact after flying through clouds or heavy ground fog. In all, Manor's crews logged 1,017 hours in the air getting ready for the raid on Son Tay, without a single accident in the 368 sorties flown under these strenuous conditions. The men earned their flight pay. By mid-September, they were ready to marry up with Simons' men and move into the joint training phase, practicing night assaults on that "village" near Auxiliary Field Number 3.

Range C-2

While Manor's pilots were alternately sweating and freezing in the air, Simons' volunteers were merely sweating on Eglin's Range C-2. Every one of the 103 men was a well-honed Special Forces type, picked among other attributes for his physical strength and stamina. But as soon as they arrived at Eglin, Simons and Sydnor began "getting them in shape." For an hour before breakfast on the first day training began, Wednesday, September 9, Simons led them through calisthenics—six repetitions of Army Drill One, the "daily dozen" that every veteran will remember—and then a two-mile run. That day they ran for three minutes, walked for one, and then resumed running; but the exercise period advanced to a new stage every day, and the men were soon doing the daily dozen eight times and running the two miles nonstop. The first week, the training schedule was "relaxed"—seven hours a day of weapons firing, radio procedures and practice, helicopter orientation, demolition drill, patrolling, plus evasion, escape, and survival. And any day that training was completed ahead of schedule, organized athletics were programmed.

By September 17, night training began, starting with night firing and target recognition, both on the ground and from helicopters, with Sydnor and Meadows juggling right- and left-handed shooters to get the maximum number of rounds into the "high threat targets"—the northwest guard tower and the gate. The other training ranged from cross-country movement, village surveillance, house search, demolition placement, and house "clearing" to lessons from Doc Cataldo on how to treat battle wounds, shock, and fractures, and to inject morphine. Hours were spent on "raid and immediate action drills"; Meadows took the men through them step by step, beginning with arm and hand signals:

Thumb down: DANGER—enemy or no good—prepare weapons for firing.

Thumb down, followed by two fingers moving and pointing: EN-
EMY in that direction.

*Hand forming a fist, pumping from belly to full extension of an
arm:* AMBUSH—move away from the fist and prepare to open fire.

Hand rotating over the head with finger pointing up: FORM THE
CLOCK DEFENSE.

Thumb up: YES—all clear—okay—prepare to move out.

Meadows' training plan had eight pages of such signals and
drills. Another training annex covered drills for firing different
types, colors, and numbers of star clusters to recall the helicopters in an emergency, the use of strobe lights to mark landing
areas, and special radio procedures for the assault teams, once
they were on the ground, to communicate with each other and
call in the strike aircraft if needed.

Simons then formed the men into three groups. The first was
the compound assault team of 14 men in all, who would land
with Meadows from a small helicopter inside the walls of the
prison. Because space was so cramped in their helicopter, they
would be armed with CAR-15s, a smaller and lighter version of
the 5.56 mm. M-16 which everyone else would carry. Among
the CAR-15's other features, it had a folding stock and could be
fired with the stock folded forward like a Schmeisser submachine pistol. Sydnor would lead a 20-man "command and security group"; Simons would take in the 22-man "support group."
Both would land from larger helicopters immediately outside
the walls of the Son Tay compound. These teams would each
have two belt-fed 7.62 mm. M-60 machine guns to seal off key
approaches with a steady stream of tracer ammunition. On the
raid, the three teams would be code-named "Blueboy," "Redwine," and "Greenleaf," respectively. Simons' personal call sign
was "Wildroot." No one would remember if it was picked at
random or for comic relief because of his thin crop of hair.

The Air Force and Army teams began jointly practicing the
assault itself in earnest on Monday, September 28. Three land-
ings or "insertions" by helicopter were rehearsed each day,
three more each night. Some were dry runs, with empty weapons; others were "live-fire," with tracer ammunition, satchel

charges, grenades, everything. By then, however, the men had walked, crawled, and run through the mock-up so many times that they knew where every round was going—every *friendly* round, that is. The location of each man at every second during the raid was precisely predetermined; a soldier who strayed by more than a yard or a second would have been turned into a 5.56 or 7.62 mm. wind tunnel by friendly M-16 automatic rifle or M-60 machine-gun fire. After some of the rehearsals, Simons personally went out and counted the holes in every target— silhouettes which had been placed around the mock-up to represent standing, crouched, or dug-in North Vietnamese. He wanted them full of holes. If they weren't, the men would go through another live-fire run. There was no room for error. The attack had to be swift, violent and lethal. Men who couldn't fire enough rounds quickly and accurately were pulled off the assault force and put in the administrative or logistics support detachment.

By now, Simons' men weren't just shooting their way through the mock-up. They were streaking into the simulated buildings, busting down doors, breaking hasps and hinges, cutting chains and shackles with blowtorches and bolt cutters—and then they took turns carrying each other out of the "village." Of Simons' 103 men, only four knew what they were really training for. To keep up the deception but prevent too much speculation, the other men were told they might have to rescue some sick diplomatic hostages at an embassy. The code name Ivory Coast suggested that the rescue would take place in the Mideast or Africa. Fearing that some of the prisoners might be insane or become irrational in the shock of the raid, Doc Cataldo had the men "resist" being carried. The soldiers learned how to cope with kicking, screaming "diplomats"—and ones too weak to lift a limb.

When the "easy" rehearsals were over, Simons began walking, then running the men through alternate plans. Plan Green would be put into operation in case his own helicopter was shot down or crashed en route. Plan Blue assumed that Meadows' compound assault team had to abort or was lost; in that case, Sydnor's team would breach the wall, clear the compound, and release the prisoners while Simons' group assumed responsibility for securing the area outside Son Tay's walls. Plan Red would be used in case Sydnor's and Cataldo's chopper failed to make it. Simons' team then would take over their functions both inside and outside the compound walls, while Donohue's gunship would be called back to spray the targets farther away with a blanket of "minigun" fire.

Again, Simons took the men through these plans in dry and live-fire exercises, in the daytime and at night, building up to the tempo and violence he expected on the raid itself. But by the end of September, Simons was worried. At night, his men still weren't getting enough rounds into the targets, and they were only two weeks away from deploying for the first possible launch window. The guard towers worried Simons most. Whichever way he juggled the ground force plan, there just weren't enough holes in the target cloth or the 2 × 4s which simulated the biggest threat. He asked Manor if the towers could be "taken out" from the air—without endangering the prisoners.

Manor suggested they try an HH-53 helicopter with 7.62 "miniguns"—small, Gatling-like six-barrel cannons—firing from each side and from the rear ramp of the helicopter. If the HH-53 flew at treetop level directly over the compound and between the two towers, it might work. The helicopters carrying the assault force would follow it into Son Tay seconds after the firing pass.

Simons was skeptical. He wanted to see it done, and he wanted to see how it was done. He didn't want the cell areas sprayed with stray lead. Marty Donohue was picked to fly the gunship helicopter. Simons decided to fly with him and fire one of the guns himself. Donohue took him up, his HH-53 loaded with enough gun barrels and ammunition to slaughter a North Vietnamese division if every bullet hit its mark. A UH-1 with a searchlight mounted on it flew overhead to illuminate the mock-up just the way Son Tay would be lit by moonlight and flares the night of the raid. When Donohue, Simons, and Donohue's three gunners made their firing pass, the belly of their HH-53 just inches above some of the cellblock roofs, Simons went deaf. He had forgotten to wear his earplugs.

He couldn't hear the next day, but his eyes were working and "God, the targets were *saturated.*" And to Simons' relief, there were no holes in the cloth panels laid out where the cells were supposed to be. Simons was "impressed." Donohue and his gunners were to get to practice that firing run on only one more flight before the raid.

Late at night on Tuesday, October 6, Manor and Simons took the entire force through a final, full-time, live-fire night rehearsal. Every twist and turn of the real route was flown, but over the southeastern United States instead of Southeast Asia. This last "profile" even included a one-hour flight to simulate the last-minute move Simons' men would make from their staging base at Takhli in central Thailand to the launch base at Udorn, just south of the Laotian border but 192 miles closer to the target. From there, it would be a long, circuitous 687-mile flight to Son Tay Prison and back.

Don Blackburn and Ed Mayer flew to Eglin to watch the dress rehearsal. Simons and his men were magnificent, Manor's crews the most unflappable, confident airmen they had ever seen. If all went well, the prisoners at Son Tay would be free men in 15 days. October 21, Manor and Simons had decided, now looked like the best launch date.

Simons was pleased with the rehearsal, but he was confronted by one final problem—and it was a big one. A helicopter could not land inside the compound, not as fast as he needed it to be done. The HH-3 was too big for the cramped area. Air Force pilots had tried every which way, but the fit was too tight. The smaller UH-1 could get in, just barely, but it held fewer troops than Dick Meadows needed. He had to have 14 men; only ten could squeeze into the Huey. Even then, it took so long to get out of the helicopter that the whole purpose of landing inside the walls would be defeated. The Huey had other drawbacks; it was not designed for aerial refueling, longer-range fuel tanks seemed impossible to come by, and it was hard pressed to fly as fast as its C-130 "mother bird" could fly slow. That meant that Meadows' small assault team would have to marry up with a Huey standing by at some CIA post on the Laotian border and

fly into North Vietnam from there. Rendezvousing with the rest
of Simons' force wouldn't be easy. It could be handled; but
Blackburn, Manor, and Simons agreed that risk of compromising the raid was too great.

Manor asked his helicopter pilots to try again with the HH-3.
By now, Herb Zehnder and his pilot, Major Herb Kalen, knew
what the real mission was and they wanted to give Meadows
and his men every split-second margin possible to get into the
POW cells before the guards did. They volunteered to crash-
land the HH-3 inside the compound. The 62-foot rotor blades
would rip into some trees on the final descent: the tree trunks
were only 65 feet and 70 feet apart, respectively, at the crucial
points. That would let Kalen slip the 73-foot-long helicopter
into an 85-foot clearing. But with luck it shouldn't hit with too
many "g's." If Meadows and his men were properly braced,
spread-eagled flat on mattresses on the helicopter floor, they
shouldn't be injured. It was the only solution, Meadows and
Kalen said. Simons and Manor finally agreed. Meadows would
set off time-delay charges just before leaving the compound to
blow up the crippled helicopter. Kalen and his two crewmen
and Meadows and his assault team would fly out of Son Tay in
one of the HH-53s that would lift out the prisoners. Kalen and
Zehnder practiced landing the HH-3 in smaller and smaller
spaces: 31 separate flights, 79½ hours. On the very last try, they
got the helicopter safely into the mock-up—with very few inches to spare.

Doc Cataldo, meanwhile, had been learning how to break
down doors with a fire ax. It was one of his "cross training" jobs
as he prepared to go on the raid. The other men kidded him
because he was "pretty wild" with the ax; he was a much better
shot with the M-16 and a .45 caliber pistol. But getting back into
top physical shape and practicing busting into a jail was the
smallest part of his workload.

Cataldo was worried, very worried, about the condition they
would find the POWs in. He had compiled detailed medical
profiles on the nine POWs who had been released by North
Vietnam, and had interviewed them to learn more about the

conditions of captivity in North Vietnam. He also reviewed carefully the pre-capture medical records of every POW suspected to be in Son Tay and weighed them against medical and psychological studies of prisoners in World War II (especially those from Japanese prison camps, "where there were severe problems") and the Korean war.

The outlook was not good.

Before his capture, the average Son Tay prisoner weighed 171 pounds, was 5 feet 10 inches tall, and thirty-three years old. Cataldo estimated that the Americans would now be down to 137 pounds, some to 108 pounds. That was his "hopeful" estimate, based on a 20 percent weight loss; in Japanese prisons in World War II, the average weight loss had been 32 percent.

Among the 61 prisoners whom the DIA had positively identified in Son Tay, Cataldo expected that 25 would have (or have had) malaria. In varying combinations, 35 would have intestinal parasites, 15 active dysentery, 12 active tuberculosis, 12 peripheral neuritis, 4 goiter—and two-thirds of them would be suffering from primary malnutrition.

Nor was his psychological "profile" of the POWs cheerful:

The POW has heard very little noise, has had very little physical exercise, and lives in dimly lit rooms. He eats two meals per day, usually consisting of cabbage soup plus bread or rice. Fish and pumpkin occasionally supplement the diet with less than two ounces of meat per week. Sometimes a banana or some other fruit is provided. Flour and sugar cookies are rarely given to the POW. Restriction of total protein intake plus physical inactivity will cause marked muscular atrophy plus a slow reaction to stimuli.

A few POWs will maintain a strong hope for liberation, and some will have given up all hope, but the majority are probably unsure and live day to day driven only by a natural desire to survive. Therefore, for most, the sudden realization that "liberation is here" will be shocking.

How would the prisoners act when liberated? Cataldo predicted that:

Army ground forces will see stunned individuals managing a weak smile. There will be no yelling on their part. The POW will be easily fatigued, having lost so much weight and muscle mass. His night vision will be poor. There will be lesions at the angles of the mouth. The skin on the arms and legs will irritate and bruises will be evident. There may be a slight swelling of the thyroid (neck) area, and the tongue will be somewhat swollen. Speech will be slow and somewhat slurred. He will complain that his feet burn. He will bruise easily, walk unsteady, and may be emotional and prone to some display of tears.

Cataldo had requisitioned some unique medical equipment; he would later teach Simons' men how to use it to care for the POWs on their ride home from Son Tay. One item was a special "M-5 medical kit" with a Duke inhaler set for use with Penthane, a noninflammable inhalation agent that acted as an anesthetic. Cataldo also made up kits for each helicopter with Ketamine HCL, a very fast-acting "knock-out" anesthetic; hemostats (scissor-like surgical clamps to stop bleeding); inflatable splints; and scissors and cannulas (hollow tubes) for cricothyroidectomies (an emergency operation like a tracheotomy, where a tube is inserted at the base of the throat to suck out fluids and force air into the lungs)—Cataldo was concerned about the borderline respiratory condition of POWs like Wes Schierman. To keep the prisoners warm, there were ponchos specially made by the Army's Natick Laboratories and vacuum-packed to conserve volume. There were also specially made sneakers, with "reinforced sponge insoles" using a Bata comfort shoe as a base. Cataldo had had them designed just for the Son Tay raid, and had lied like a bandit to explain why he needed them.

There were many other items of medical gear, including 100 sets of pajamas and bathrobes for the prisoners (and wounded raiders) to wear on their long trip back to the United States. Getting the Army's hospital at Valley Forge to give him 100 sets of pajamas and bathrobes involved a whole new line of lies and deception. Finally, Cataldo had ordered a lot of Heinz baby food—mashed rice—repackaged in plain sealed foil for security reasons.

Bullets, Blowtorches, and Bolt Cutters

On September 8, as Manor and Simons put their men through their paces at Eglin, a support detachment of 26 officers and enlisted men arrived at Auxiliary Field Number 3 to feed, house, and supply the Son Tay raiders. The detachment included a supply officer and two supply sergeants plus a three-man communications group. Equipping the Son Tay raiders with all the special gear they needed to bust into a prison quickly turned into a nightmare for them. It took a ream of top-priority but unexplained, sometimes oddball requisitions, and some devious improvisations. But the Sears Roebuck catalogue saved the day.

After the raid, Roy Manor would hint in his After Action Report that the supply section had been a little overworked. "Future operations of this nature," he said, "must include sufficient supply personnel to insure prompt reaction to sudden requirements. The original concept of one supply officer and two supply sergeants did not provide sufficient flexibility." In hindsight, Manor would suggest that the supply section should have included "an armorer, an ammunition specialist, and a light truck driver/clerk," plus "an Air Force supply liaison sergeant well versed in Air Force supply procedures and forms," and a "Class A [finance] Agent" with "a suitable amount of cash . . . for direct local procurement"; something like $4,000, he suggested, would have saved a lot of headaches. The frustrations his three supply specialists encountered made it obvious why.

Each of the raiders, it was found during training, needed a special knife to pry open doors or barricades; it had to be similar to a machete but with a heavier blade and a sharper point. The Army's Personnel Equipment Center at Natick Laboratory near Boston had developed something close to what was needed, and Fort Benning's Ranger Department had tested it with good results. But Manor's supply crew found that even by expediting the Army's purchasing system, it would take *four months* to get the few knives the raiders needed. They then turned to a special purchase section at Eglin, asking for a similar knife which they found was available locally. Again, they were told, getting the right number would be "an extremely lengthy process." But time was pressing. They asked the base machine shop to alter standard government machetes into the desired blade. After weeks of trying unsuccessfully through the high-priority special channels set up so carefully by the Pentagon for the raid, the men got the knives they needed "in a matter of days" by relying on a local grinding wheel.

Another special request came from Simons, who told the supply crew to get 250 30-round magazine clips for the raiders' M-16 rifles. Standard Army issue was a 20-round magazine, and no 30-round magazines, the supply crew was told, could be obtained through normal channels. One supply NCO tried to go directly to Colt Arms, which manufactured 30-round magazines, but then found that he still had to go back through Department of the Army headquarters before dealing with the contractor. He finally got the magazines, only to learn that the Army had no "load-bearing equipment" pouches for a soldier to carry them. The supply section quickly had a bunch of Claymore mine bags modified for that purpose.

Information about North Vietnamese prison layouts obtained from previously freed POWs made it clear that a variety of leg stocks, metal hasps, and locks might be encountered. The raiders needed two oxygen-acetylene emergency cutting outfits; they had to be lightweight, simple to operate, and have a burning time of 30 minutes. The supply section searched out a number of commercial sources without success. Then the supply department at the Naval Air Station at Pensacola, Florida, found that suitable gear was available through the federal supply system. After it got the federally supplied outfits, however, the supply section learned that the only quick way to get the oxygen and acetylene needed for them was to go back through local civilian sources.

Bolt cutters would also be needed on the raid. The supply

A low-level aerial photograph of Son Tay prison taken by a "Buffalo Hunter" reconnaissance drone in 1968, just after the first American POWs were moved to the cramped compound 23 miles west of Hanoi.

Teledyne Ryan's "Buffalo Hunter" reconnaissance drones were flown at treetop level over Son Tay prison seven times before the raid. Six of the flights malfunctioned or were shot down; the last banked too soon and returned with "perfect imagery" of the horizon beyond Son Tay.

Lockheed's SR-71 reconna
sance aircraft took most of
Son Tay target photos fr
above 80,000 feet wh
streaking over North Vietn
at more than three times
speed of sound. Cloud co
prevented an accurate "re
out" of how active the ca
really was just before the ra

An SR-71 reconnaissance
photo of the mid-1970 flood at
Son Tay caused by covert
American rainmaking operations over Laos. The river rose
to within a foot or two of the
compound's wall, and American POWs were moved from
the prison four and a half
months before the raid was
launched.

"Barbara," code name of a model of the Son Tay compound built by the
Central Intelligence Agency and used in training the Son Tay assault
force. When the prison proved to be a "dry hole," CIA officials claimed
the agency had not been included in the planning for the raid.

A specially equipped Lockheed C-130 transport, shown here in a test
flight, led the Son Tay assault force from Thailand over Laos into North
Vietnam. The C-130 had to fly a complex route in rough weather at
close to stall speed over the rugged mountains of Southeast Asia.

The men responsible for the raid on Son Tay were among the best military planners and intelligence experts in the Department of Defense.

Army Brigadier General Donald D. Blackburn, the Pentagon's "Special Assistant for Counterinsurgency and Special Activities" (SACSA).

Army Colonel E. E. Mayer, chief of the Special Operations Division of SACSA

Army Lieutenant General Donald V. Bennett *(left)*, Director of the Defense Intelligence Agency, and Air Force Major General Richard R. Stewart *(right)*, Deputy Director for Intelligence.

The air crews and assault teams that executed the raid were Special Forces volunteers, thoroughly trained in every detail of their unprecedented mission.

Lieutenant Colonel
Warner A. Britton

Lieutenant Colonel
Joseph R. Cataldo

Lieutenant Colonel
Elliott P. Sydnor

Major Frederic
M. Donohue

Captain Richard
J. Meadows

Three of the Son Tay raiders in full battle gear (left to right): Sergeant First Class Donald D. Blackard, Sergeant First Class Gregory T. McGuire, Sergeant First Class Freddie D. Doss.

Colonel Arthur D. "Bull" Simons, who led the assault on Son Tay, answers questions about the raid from the Pentagon press corps. Behind him (*left to right*): Melvin R. Laird, Secretary of Defense; Admiral Thomas H. Moorer, Chairman of the Joint Chiefs of Staff; and Air Force Brigadier General Leroy J. Manor, who commanded the overall operation.

Bull Simons being decorated by President Richard M. Nixon in a White House ceremony.

Defense Secretary Melvin R. Laird decorates the Special Forces soldiers
and airmen who assaulted the Son Tay compound deep in the heart of
North Vietnamese territory without a single serious casualty.

The "unofficial" shoulder
patch of the Son Tay raiders:
"Kept In The Dark/Fed Only
Horse Shit."

BRIDGE

SON TAY POW CAMP
(POST-ASSAULT)

SON TAY POW CAMP

N

SON TAY

U/I LIGHT INDUSTRY

SECONDARY SCHOOL

FOOT BRIDGE

An SR-71 reconnaissance photo taken immediately after the raid. The assault force discovered that the areas thought to be a "Secondary School" and an "Unidentified (U/I) Light Industry" complex were more heavily defended than the Son Tay POW camp itself.

section found what looked like just the ticket in the federal supply catalogue: 36-inch bolt cutters that should have had plenty of leverage and cutting strength. But when they arrived and Simons' men began practicing with them, they found the metal jaws so soft that they failed to cut the ¾-inch chains and padlocks which Simons' intelligence team told him to expect vithin the Son Tay cellblocks. The supply crew undertook an-
ther search and finally settled on bolt cutters of three different
zes used by local Air Force fire-fighting crews.

Simons also needed six compact, gasoline-powered chain saws, light, simple to operate, with about a 16-inch chain drive. And they had to have a waterproof ignition; it might be raining in North Vietnam. Somewhat soured by their experience with the federal supply system, the supply NCOs visited nearby hardware stores and lumber yards and bought two different models from local merchants. Both made by Skil, they weighed just over 19 pounds and cost $206.96 and $229.46, respectively, not including local sales tax.

Little things kept the supply crew busy, too. Some of the raiders would be carrying M-79 40 mm. grenade launchers and needed ammunition vests for the rounds. The vests were requisitioned through the federal supply system. But Simons' men found they would not work because the round they had been designed to carry was no longer in use. To fit the new, ogive-shaped round, the supply crew had to have Eglin's fabric shop modify the straps which secured the round in every pocket of each vest.

To document conditions under which American POWs were being held captive, Simons wanted some of his men to photograph the cells at Son Tay. Several of the Special Forces volunteers he selected, therefore, were also expert photographers. They recommended taking along six 35 mm. Pen-EE cameras. When the supply crew found that they were not available through normal supply channels, Simons' men settled on Kodak's simple S-20 Instamatic. They had "the desired ruggedness and simplicity"—but Simons would later report that the pictures they got were "worthless."

The supply section had to fill a stack of other unusual requisitions, including electrical head lamps which, Simons found, proved a nuisance when worn on the head, so he had his men hang them on their load-bearing equipment harnesses; 15 rucksacks to carry escape and evasion gear which had to be made by the fabric shop of Eglin's Special Operations Force; and three extra fire extinguishers, which would be carried in the assault helicopter that would crash-land inside the Son Tay compound. Megaphones were needed to warn the prisoners that they were being rescued and should stay calm and keep their heads down while the assault team broke into their cellblocks. Twenty raiders would be very close to exploding demolition charges and needed special ear protectors; the others needed standard earplugs so the long, noisy helicopter flight into North Vietnam would not cause them to land at Son Tay half deaf. Simons' men also needed gloves to prevent injury to their hands while locating locks to be cut. Standard summer Air Force flying gloves were decided upon; they gave a tight fit and would not have to be removed to operate weapons and other equipment.

Every man needed a set of goggles. Originally, they were to preserve night vision when the illuminating flares were set off; later, the goggles proved equally essential to protect the men from flying debris stirred up by the helicopters' rotor downwash. The goggles became a real problem. The supply team first tried standard Air Force goggles with dark amber and green lenses, but they didn't give enough protection from the brilliant flares that would light up Son Tay in the dead of night. Simons' men then tried special radiological lenses developed by the Army's Night Vision Laboratory, but they proved too hard to use. As a last resort, the supply team started combing Sears Roebuck catalogues and sporting goods stores for a solution. Finally, they improvised, coating clear-lens goggles with the red "Chart Pak" pressure-sensitive tape commonly used by commercial artists and military draftsmen to make charts and vugraphs. The Sears Roebuck catalogues later proved invaluable for obtaining ideas and rough specifications for a host of other peculiar equipment needs which Simons laid in the supply team's lap.

But it was ammunition and weapons, the basic tools of an army, which gave Simons' men their biggest headaches. Simons wanted some shotguns for area fire while clearing buildings. The Army's standard 12-gauge pump shotguns, he found, fired too small a shot pattern at 20 meters. The supply crew turned to sporting goods catalogues and came up with a five-shot, automatic gun which Simons loved: the shot pattern covered a six-foot area at 25 meters but distributed enough lead to kill anyone in it.

To help mark targets, Simons wanted some 40 mm. white phosphorous "spotting rounds" for his M-79 grenade launchers. Their incendiary filling burned brilliantly and it was lethal as well. To its disbelief, the supply team had to go through ammunition channels all the way to the Department of the Army and finally to the CIA, only to find that no such round existed. They tested what was offered and finally decided on the 40 mm. White Star Cluster. But as the pace of training quickened and the number of live-fire rehearsals increased, Simons quickly exhausted the local supply. His supply crew called Fort Bragg to order more, but was told there weren't enough in the supply system. It took a phone call to the Pentagon to get Continental Army Command Headquarters to ship 250 rounds directly from the depot.

Small arms tracer ammunition would also be used to mark targets. Simons and 50 other men would be carrying .45 caliber pistols, the standard Army sidearm dating back to World War I. But tracer ammunition for it, they found, was a "controlled item." By now, Simons' team had the highest supply priority of any Army unit anywhere in the world, but it still took special coordination with the supply manager at Joliet Arsenal in Illinois to get the tracer rounds released from Aberdeen Proving Ground in Maryland.

In 1970, the Army was spending close to $10 million a day, one-fourth of its total budget, on ammunition for Vietnam. But as Simons' share of it began arriving at Eglin, his men found that a lot of it didn't work. To set off demolition charges, 1,000 non-electric blasting caps had been requisitioned from Fort Bragg and shipped from Army stocks at Fort Benning. Simons' demolitionists reported that 22 percent of them misfired; that is, didn't fire or fired late. It took a written report to the Special Forces Center supply officer, coordination with the Fort Bragg post ammunition officer, and the resourcefulness of a Mr. Thomas at Fort Bragg's ammo dump to finally track down 100 caps that would go off as advertised—and they had to be shipped from a small, special stock held at Fort Stewart, Georgia.

Simons wanted some men to carry a few 66 mm. Light Anti-tank Weapons (LAWs) in case they had to knock out vehicles on the roads into Son Tay. Soon after the LAWs arrived, however, Fort Bragg's Thomas called with bad news: the lot shipped to Eglin had been suspended. The rounds fired reliably enough to be used for training, but not when lives depended on them. The LAW was a standard Army weapon issued in high density to infantry and tank units all over the world, but Simons' supply team had to call Joliet Arsenal in Illinois to track down 250 rounds that worked as advertised. They turned out to be located at Lone Star Ammunition Plant in Texarkana, Texas, and would have to be diverted from a shipment bound for Southeast Asia. Simons' harried supply team had to prevail upon Fort Bragg again to get the requisition filled.

Simons' growing arsenal still wasn't stocked to his satisfaction. Two kinds of satchel charges and two special demolition charges would be needed. To blast a hole in the compound wall through which the rescued prisoners could be taken to the waiting helicopters, four 30-pound satchel charges would be carried. But Simons wasn't going to rely on the standard issue; to save lives (or, as military jargon goes, "to minimize personnel exposure"), he believed that if you were going to err, err on the side of violence. Simons ordered the explosives to be "heavily overcharged." To knock out a concrete power tower just south of the target, Simons' demolitionists recommended using a five-pound satchel charge. Simons thought that was fine—and then told them to use four charges.

To blow up the helicopter that was to land Dick Meadows' assault team inside the cramped Son Tay compound, Simons' demolitionists experimented with various destruction devices;

they came up with a three-pound mixture of C-4 and Thermite
stuffed into a 30-inch length of 4-inch fire hose. It would be
placed under the helicopter's floor in a bilge sump between the
forward and aft fuel tanks. To prevent the North Vietnamese
from disabling the explosives, Simons' men decided to secure
them by a specially padlocked metal cover and set them off at
the last minute by a ten-minute time fuse. Fine, Simons told
them—but light two fuses.

To down a bridge 120 meters north of the prison, the men
recommended using two satchel charges. They could be carried
in individual rucksacks and swiftly hung over the two metal
stringers under the bridge's treadways. From standard demolition tables, the demolitionists computed the size of the charges
needed, but by now they had learned the name of the game; the
charges they ordered each weighed 30 pounds, ten times what
the formula provided. Simons agreed—but had them add two
back-up charges of equal strength.

One final, but crucial equipment need challenged Simons'
supply crew: a night sight. Twenty years after the Korean war
and at least six years into Vietnam, the Army had learned that
combat against an Asian enemy, especially, put a premium on
night combat. Since Korea, the Army had spent $18.4 billion on
research and development; since darkness covers the earth
about 50 percent of the time, a good fraction of that money
presumably was spent on equipment that would function when
the sun wasn't shining. But in 1970 the Army, Simons found,
still didn't own a rifle sight that would enable soldiers to shoot
accurately in the dark. He turned to the CIA; it didn't have one
either.

In "live-fire" rehearsals, Simons found to his dismay that at
night even his best shooters were getting only about 25 percent
of the rounds fired at 50 meters into torso-size targets which
simulated enemy soldiers standing up in a foxhole. With that
kind of accuracy, he would need to pre-position a small ammunition depot at Son Tay for the 26-minute assault. Simons was
genuinely concerned: unless night-firing accuracy could be improved dramatically, it would take far too long to neutralize the
opposition, and the lives of both the prisoners and his own men

would be jeopardized by all those stray rounds.

Early in September, however, he was relieved to learn through special supply channels of a closely guarded, secretly developed, new infra red device that might do the trick. The sight was a distinct improvement over the earlier, bulky 30-pound infra red device that the Army had used with token success late in the fifties and sixties; and the new sight weighed only six pounds. Using every priority he could muster, Simons had the Army's entire supply shipped to Eglin. But when the highly classified gear was uncrated, there were only six devices. One of Simons' supply specialists joked, "Maybe they want us to take turns using them."

Those six devices, Simons soon found out, were all the Army owned. They were hand-built items, he was told, still being tested; there was "no way" more could be provided in time for the raid.

Simons challenged the men on his supply team to come up with something that 17 years and $18 billion had been unable to produce. They were wiser now; they knew that the military supply system wasn't necessarily the answer to every soldier's prayer. Nor, they had learned, did the Army's hardware specialists always know what was available on the commercial market; they were sometimes too busy reinventing the wheel, blinded by a "not-invented-here" sort of tunnel vision. Simons' men, on the other hand, cared enough to steal the very best.

They began combing what was now a small library of sporting goods catalogues, hunting magazines, and gun advertisements. One of them—no one would remember exactly which—had a small ad from Armalite Corporation in Costa Mesa, California, for a $49.50 "Singlepoint Nite Sight." Armalite, they knew, was the firm that had privately developed Gene Stoner's design for the M-15 rifle, the one Army Ordnance had tested superficially and then rejected in favor of its own, much heavier, arsenal-designed M-14. The Army was persuaded to retest the weapon, and again the M-15 flunked, but only because the Ordnance Corps had substituted outmoded, earlier M-15 barrels for a new design that Stoner had persuaded Armalite to adopt when it bought the rights to his gun. The tests were run again, but it took almost three more years to overcome gamesmanship and oneupmanship at the highest levels of bureaucracy before the Army reluctantly admitted that the M-14 it had spent ten years and millions of dollars to develop was a lemon. In 1963, the Army finally asked for money to reequip its Vietnam forces— and eventually, all of its troops—with the Stoner-Armalite weapon. Armalite by this time had sold its rights to Colt Arms, and the redesigned weapon was finally designated the M-16.

Simons' men called Armalite on September 15, and casually asked about the availability of the $49.50 night sight and the mount that went with it. Three days later, Armalite shipped one; at Eglin's request, it was sent by air mail. As soon as the package arrived, Simons' supply section quickly read the pocket-size, 16-page operator's manual. The sight, they learned, was an old Swedish invention, patented worldwide, made in Great Britain and imported to the United States by a prominent Minnesota sporting goods firm, Normark Corporation. Every serious gun buff in America, they concluded, knew about it—except the Army.

The men hurriedly tested the sight under field conditions. The system looked promising: it weighed only 7½ ounces, was only 1 inch in diameter and 6¾ inches long, and could be dropped 8 feet onto concrete without breaking. To their chagrin, Simons' supply section noted in the operator's manual that the sight had even been designed to military specifications. There were problems with the mount; it tended to wear loose and sometimes break off—but the sight worked. Simons immediately ordered 49 more.

When they arrived and were tested further by Simons' assault force, target hits increased dramatically; shot groups from every burst were much smaller; his soldiers felt more confident of their weapons. At 25 meters, even the poorest marksman could fire all rounds into a 12-inch circle at night. At 50 meters, the same shooter could put every round into an "E-type silhouette" the size of a man's torso. In daytime tests, the sight improved speed in engaging a target and in shifting fire, although it was less accurate than the standard, open M-16 sight. At night, the situation reversed. Shooters could engage targets and shift fire just as fast, but with deadly accuracy. And the raid, of course, would be conducted in the dead of night.

The supply section was now feeling its oats and assured him the mount could be fixed, somehow. Twenty-seven more sights and mounts were ordered; by the time the last shipment arrived, at the ninth hour on October 21, Simons' three-man armament laboratory told him they had a fix for the mount— "a generous use of black electrician's tape."

All this while, Simons' support detachment had to maintain and repair a small warehouse of other equipment his troops were training with or would need on the raid, including 234 radios—just for the 56-man ground force. One reason there were so many radios was that Simons wanted two complete sets of communications gear at Eglin; one was "on loan" from higher headquarters for training, the other would be used on the mission itself. Another reason was the complexity of the operation and the need for instantaneous communications between so many elements during the short 26 minutes Simons' men would be on the ground. Simons himself would need eight separate radio nets; his troops would land with four different kinds of radios.

Two of the radio nets were for ultra-high frequency (UHF) air-to-ground transmissions. Simons would use them to call for any A-1 close support strikes his men might need, to recall helicopters to extract his force from and take the prisoners out of Son Tay, and to relay his operational reports from the objective area to Roy Manor at the Monkey Mountain command post near Danang, where he in turn would relay the raid's progress to the Pentagon. Two AN-PRC-41 radios would be taken on the raid for this purpose, one carried by Simons' radio operator, one by Sydnor's. A third net would be needed for Simons' forward air controllers to direct the close support strikes if they were called in. Ten AN-PRC-77 frequency modulated (FM) radios would be carried on backpacks for this purpose. Four more nets would be required by the ground force, one for each of the three groups in the force, and a fourth to receive orders from and relay operational reports to Simons. For this purpose, the ground force would carry 24 AN-PRC-88 "handy talkie" radios.

Finally, each of the 56 raiders would carry the compact AN-PRC-90 survival radio, not quite as long or thick as a carton of cigarettes. The men would use these in case a helicopter was shot down or had to force-land on the way to or from the objective. If something went wrong at Son Tay itself, Simons had decided, they wouldn't be needed; but he would wait until just before the mission to tell the men why not. In all, Simons and his 55 volunteers would carry 92 radios into Son Tay—almost as many as a 794-man infantry battalion takes into combat. They would be able to communicate almost 12 times better than the average front-line soldier.

Besides these 92 radios and their training counterparts, there were 50 other radios at Eglin which Simons used for spares and for administrative control during training. Keeping all 234 radios operating was a full-time chore for the supply detachment's overworked communications supervisor and his two radio operators. They speculated that ABC's Wide World of Sports used less equipment to televise the Olympics. To help them, Manor and Simons finally borrowed a complete electronics repair shop from the Air Force. But it was staffed with only one full-time noncommissioned officer; four of Simons' ground force radio operators pitched in with periodic assistance, on top of their full training schedule. Somehow, the five men kept the radios operable. During the raid, every one of them would function perfectly.

Throughout the training period at Eglin, Manor and Simons were proving an old Israeli Defense Force adage: Lean forces fight best. In 1970, the Pentagon's budget showed, there were 175,000 soldiers and civilians handling "Army logistics and materiel support." Simons' six-man supply and communications section got roughly half of the gear it needed through them—but only about half of that worked as advertised. The rest they had to improvise, buy, test, repair, and maintain on their own.

The Ivory Coast Yo-Yo

While Doc Cataldo was practicing ax marksmanship and the other Son Tay raiders were perfecting entry into and escape from a "village," Manor and Simons found their "spare time" filled with chores to "coordinate" the operation. They visited everywhere from the White House to Army and Air Force headquarters in Saigon, flying back and forth from Eglin so frequently that at times they must have felt the Pentagon had strapped them to the end of a yo-yo. Blackburn and Mayer worked hard to front for them and "run interference" as much as possible, but many of the problems required Manor and Simons' personal presence.

Soon after he was put in command of Ivory Coast, Manor flew to Scott Air Force Base near St. Louis. There, he talked personally with the commander, Military Airlift Command (MAC), and showed him the letter from the Air Force Chief of Staff ordering support of the Joint Contingency Task Group on a "no questions asked" basis. MAC would handle medical evacuation of the prisoners from Thailand back to the States. Manor had to arrange for MAC's C-141 Starlifters to be ready on a moment's notice, without anyone—including MAC's commander—knowing what for. Moreover, all of Manor's helicopter crews were from MAC's Aerospace Rescue and Recovery Service, as were the HH-53 and HH-3 aircraft he was training with at Eglin. The helicopters that would actually be used on the raid would have to be "drawn down" at the last minute from rescue assets already in place in Southeast Asia. It was becoming increasingly clear that timing of the raid would depend upon the weather —and the Air Weather Service worked for MAC.

A similar visit had to be made to Tactical Air Command headquarters near Norfolk, Virginia, since the fixed-wing C-130s and A-1s were TAC assets. Manor also hand-carried the "no questions asked" letter to the commanding general of the Air Force Systems Command (AFSC) at Andrews Air Force Base near Washington. There would be some very new and sensitive navigation and communications gear aboard many of the airplanes, some of it so new that it was still almost in the experimental stage. Special support would be needed from AFSC to install and maintain that gear; some of it had never been installed before on the kinds of planes Manor would be using. The equipment included GRC-128 very high frequency jammers for the A-1s; they would be used to disrupt voice commands from North Vietnam's ground control intercept controllers to vector any MIG fighters sent against the assault force. New forward-looking infra red navigation systems designed by Texas Instruments would be used aboard the C-130 Combat Talon mother ships. These FL-2B FLIR sets were complex to install, maintain, and operate—to the point where it would take the full-time attention of an extra navigator to identify check points en route to the target and pinpoint the objective itself. New Rockeye road denial/anti-vehicle bomblet dispensers would be needed for the A-1s; and the C-130s would have to be modified to drop illumination flares, napalm fire bombs, firefight simulators, and log flares.

Manor, Simons, and Blackburn had other worries. On Wednesday, September 2, Max Newman—"Blue Max"—discovered a "significant unauthorized disclosure of classified information" at a bar near Fort Bragg by a "former member" of SACSA's planning group. Blackburn had the man "amputated" —quietly reassigned to another post; but he was tailed everywhere he went until the raid was over.

At about the same time, the Army's chief "special operations" planner, Brigadier General Clarke T. Baldwin, asked Blackburn about the medical evacuation plan. He suggested bringing the POWs to Tripler Army General Hospital in Hawaii. Others wanted them flown directly to the Andrews Air Force Base medical center. Blackburn wrote a note to himself: "Where will all the players be when the curtain goes up?" It was a "detail" he could iron out, but Manor would have to arrange for MAC to get the C-141s to the right destination.

In some areas, Blackburn was getting "too much help." By now his boss, John Vogt, had been promoted to director of the Joint Staff. His replacement, Army Lieutenant General Melvin R. Zais, wasn't yet "wired in" on the raid. Blackburn appealed to Lieutenant General Richard T. Knowles, "the Assistant to the Chairman," to help turn down the volume and frequency of the advice and inquiries he and Mayer were getting.

In one case, for instance, a general officer who had the ear of the Army Vice Chief of Staff expressed doubt about the wisdom

of landing *inside* the Son Tay compound. Blackburn heard via
the grapevine that the officer was concerned about "losing" a
helicopter in Son Tay. When he got wind of this idle chatter,
Blackburn invited the officer down to the specially cleared
SACSA rooms and suggested they "talk things out." It was an
amicable meeting. The officer told Blackburn he had "just been
thinking out loud." Then he asked if Blackburn had thought
about the cost of the helicopter that might have to crash-land
inside the compound and be destroyed. He suggested using the
smaller Army UH-1 Huey, which cost about $350,000, instead
of the larger Air Force HH-3, which cost almost a million dollars.

Blackburn exploded: "Jesus Christ, if it's a question between
saving seconds and lives or using a God damned Huey because
it's cheaper, we're worrying about the wrong problem." He was
aghast. In six years of the Vietnam war, over 3,000 helicopters
had been shot down or destroyed; and here was an American
general officer, privy to the Son Tay rescue, worrying about
losing one more. This kind of nit-picking, distraction and doubt
came up often, but it had to be resolved. The last thing Manor
and Simons needed, Blackburn knew, was to have their attention diverted from training for the raid to sweep off "sawdust"
from termites in the Pentagon. He realized how right Vogt had
been in his decision to keep SACSA intact and let someone else
lead the raid.

There were other, more substantive problems: deception
plans to cover the task force's deployment from Eglin to Southeast Asia; special communications during the raid linking
Manor and Simons with the National Military Command Center; "little things" like picking the right code word to "execute";
whether or not a formal JCS operations order was needed to
"legalize" the raid.

The Son Tay rescue would be the first major military operation in American history conducted under direct control of the
Office, Chairman, Joint Chiefs of Staff. The key intermediate
headquarters, Commander-in-Chief, Pacific, would be "informed" and directed to "support" the operation—but not to
perturb it or redesign it. One three-star general, when finally

"read in" on the raid, questioned that it should be directed from the Pentagon. He asked Blackburn if it shouldn't be handled through Strike Command, the Army-Navy-Air Force headquarters at MacDill Air Force Base, Florida, set up early in the sixties to train and deploy joint tactical forces for overseas contingencies. The suggestion was about as useful as teats on a bull. STRICOM, as it was called, was as far removed from Southeast Asian matters as Walter Mitty was from reality. John Vogt told the officer to leave Son Tay alone and get back to work on other JCS problems.

At their end of the bureaucracy, Manor and Simons had their own troubles. A month after they were picked to lead the mission, on Wednesday, September 16, they were called before the Joint Chiefs of Staff for a status report. At three o'clock that afternoon, Manor briefed the chiefs on the "technical concept," reported the plan was feasible, and said his force would finish training and be ready to deploy by Thursday, October 8. He recommended that the rescue be made on Wednesday, October 21.

Just over a week later, on Thursday, September 24, Manor was called back to Washington to discuss the raid with Defense Secretary Laird. CIA Director Richard Helms was present at the briefing. Manor again recommended the October 20–25 launch window. Laird said he would have to "defer approval" pending "coordination with higher authority." He did not tell Manor that intensive, last-minute diplomatic efforts were under way to secure the release of the prisoners, or that if they failed, he was about to ask the President to approve the raid. But he agreed that it was finally time to brief "CINCPAC," Admiral John S. McCain, Jr., on the operation that Washington was about to execute in his back yard.

Late the next day, Friday, September 25, Blackburn and Mayer told McCain, the "Grand Old Man of the Pacific," that they were ready to launch a raid on Son Tay. They briefed him in detail—including who was known or thought to be held there. McCain knew that his son, taken prisoner three years earlier and savagely beaten by the North Vietnamese, would be one of the POWs "left behind" whether the Ivory Coast succeeded or failed. Blackburn and Mayer read in his eyes the anguish of a "concerned father" but the resolve of a very courageous man. McCain told them he appreciated the implications of their proposal. He would do everything in his power to help the operation succeed. He agreed that to preserve security, only one other person in his headquarters should be told of the mission, his Chief of Staff. McCain said that not even the commander of the Pacific Fleet need be told; SACSA could work directly with the commander of Carrier Task Force 77 in the Tonkin Gulf to coordinate the Navy diversion that would accompany the raid. Virtually the entire staff directing the war in Southeast Asia was to be kept in the dark about one of the most critical operations that had ever been launched in that area—to give 61 American POWs that much better chance of returning home alive.

At this stage in the Vietnam war, 20 months into the Nixon administration, there were 1,463 American POWs and MIAs in Southeast Asia. Their welfare had become the hottest issue in the country. The public compassion which the POW/MIA wives had aroused in less than a year of organized effort manifested itself in many ways. Millions of Americans, high-school youngsters as well as adults in a land bitter about the war, were wearing POW/MIA bracelets. The 1/4-inch-wide aluminum or copper bands carried in simple block lettering the name and date of the shootdown, capture, or disappearance of men only a few thousand of them knew; but they vowed not to take them off until "their guy" was accounted for or returned home.

Nancy Thurmond, the twenty-three-year-old wife of Senator Strom Thurmond, was leading a massive letterwriting campaign to seek more humane treatment of the POWs. Conceived by the wives in the POW/MIA League of Families, the campaign's goal was to deliver 100 tons of mail by Christmas to North Vietnam's president, Ton Duc Thang, urging better treatment and release of the prisoners. Postal service officials were hard pressed to supply the millions of 25 cent stamps Americans were suddenly buying to mail letters to Hanoi.

In August, 407 members of the House of Representatives had

signed their own appeal, protesting conditions under which the POWs were being held. Representative Roger Zion of Indiana tried to deliver it to North Vietnamese officials in Paris, without success—but its message got through to the White House. President Nixon dispatched astronaut Frank Borman on a 14-nation, 25-day global journey to tell world leaders how flagrantly North Vietnam was violating the Geneva Convention it had signed in 1957. Borman, one of the first three men to circle the moon on Christmas Eve of 1968, asked them to appeal to North Vietnam to let the International Red Cross become a go-between in obtaining better treatment for all POWs. He tried to contact the North Vietnamese, but failed. It had been easier to reach the moon than to reach Hanoi with a humane appeal.

When he returned to address an unusual joint session of Congress on Tuesday, September 22, Borman reported that not one foreign head of state had held out much hope for getting North Vietnam to budge. The POWs were too valuable as hostages for American withdrawal from Southeast Asia.

Diplomatic approaches to the North Vietnamese were faring as badly. Three days after Borman's address to Congress, Henry Kissinger flew to Paris to "confer" with Ambassador David K. E. Bruce on the eve of the 85th plenary session of the Paris peace talks. In reality, he was there to meet secretly for the second time that month with Xuan Thuy, North Vietnam's chief negotiator. His September trips followed four other secret missions to Paris earlier in the year, when he had met with Le Duc Tho, North Vietnam's foreign minister. Kissinger cabled a discouraging message. There was no progress on the POW issue.

On Sunday, September 27, President Nixon left Washington for his second trip to Europe and third trip abroad since entering the White House. The 12,000-mile journey would take him to five nations in nine days, it was announced, including visits to Yugoslavia, Italy, Spain, England, and Ireland. White House press secretary Ronald Ziegler went out of his way to announce that the President would also meet with Pope Paul VI and, on the same day, visit the Sixth Fleet during maneuvers in the Mediterranean. There was no mention that Laird and Moorer would join the presidential party, but they did.

They met with the President aboard the flagship *Springfield*.
Later that day, Laird and Moorer told Nixon of the proposal to
rescue American prisoners from Son Tay, deep inside North
Vietnam. The raid, they said, could be launched within four
weeks, but a decision would be needed soon if the force was to
deploy in time.

At that moment, Nixon was faced with the possibility of
American military involvement in the Mideast. Jordan was torn
by civil war and Syrian tanks had crossed its borders. A truce
negotiated the previous month between Israel and Egypt was
in danger of becoming unglued. Egypt's President Gamal Ab-
del Nasser had died that very day. Now Laird and Moorer were
proposing a new form of military involvement in Southeast
Asia.

Nixon reviewed the POW situation with them, and then said
that he "approved" the rescue—in principle. But he wanted
them to brief Kissinger thoroughly on it before he could make
a final decision on *when* the rescue should be made. As Laird
and Moorer departed for a three-day visit to Greece and Malta,
Nixon cabled for Bruce and his deputy, Philip Habib, to meet
him in Ireland. He wanted their unvarnished assessment of
prospects for freeing the prisoners at the conference table instead of a raid into North Vietnam, although he would not tell
them one was planned. Their report would be bleak.

On another front, however, there was more encouraging and
very important news. Communist China had just welcomed a
proposed visit by American writer Edgar Snow. On Thursday,
October 1, Snow would be invited to stand next to Chairman
Mao Tse-tung at China's "National Day" ceremonies. It signaled a clear message to Washington that Mao had given his
blessing to a move toward reconciliation with a bitter enemy of
25 years. That initiative had come to a screeching halt after the
Cambodian invasion in April and May, but now the deadlock
looked as if it had been broken.

Nixon returned to Washington on Monday, October 5, to tell
the crowd of 3,000 waiting to greet him at Andrews Air Force
Base that the United States was making progress "toward
achieving its goals in Vietnam," and then predicted with em-

phasis that "events in the future will demonstrate" this.

Soon after the President's return, Laird, Moorer, Blackburn, and Manor got word that the raid on Son Tay "might" have to be postponed from October 20–25. October 24, they knew (and would remind the White House) would be the 25th anniversary of the United Nations. They did not know that on October 25, Pakistani President Yahya Khan would meet with Nixon to discuss a mid-November visit to China, in which Khan would convey Nixon's desire for "talks in Peking at 'a high level.' " Nor did they know that in the Executive Office Building, Kissinger's staff was drafting and redrafting a toast the President would make on October 26. That night, Rumanian President Ceausescu would be honored at a White House state dinner and Nixon would hail "the uniqueness of Rumania's good relations with the United States . . . the Soviet Union . . . and the People's Republic of China." It would be the first time an American President had ever referred to Communist China as "the People's Republic of China."

If the raid was postponed, the next launch window would not occur until late November. Manor and Simons would be able to use the extra time to "fine-tune" their plan. But as the days ticked by, it seemed to some of the Son Tay planners that the raid might be canceled. To JCS Chairman Tom Moorer, "it was obvious that the President was going to approve" the raid. Yet Moorer had two concerns. There was "always a cut-off date by which you *had* to have a decision." And there was always the possibility that "they're not going to let us do this." Moorer would explain: "That was the gist of my life. In our form of government, there were always plenty of people coming forward with reasons for not doing anything. The best way of making certain you never make a mistake is never do anything." But he would also point out that Laird and President Nixon wanted to be sure "that every step had been taken" to assure success. They felt "more and more that one more month would permit 'a refinement of the training.' "

Meanwhile, "coordinating" the raid also became more refined. On Wednesday, October 7, Blackburn flew back from the full-dress night rehearsal at Eglin to brief Vice Admiral Noel

Gayler, head of NSA, on the Son Tay assault. Gayler offered
Blackburn NSA's full support. He lauded the "courageous
effort," and was "impressed as hell" that Simons would actually
land in the objective with his raiders.

The next day, Manor and Simons flew from Eglin back to
Washington. This time Blackburn took them to brief the President's Assistant for National Security Affairs, Henry Kissinger.
As they prepared to see Kissinger, Blackburn, Manor and Simons met with Don Bennett and Dick Stewart of the DIA,
NSA's Milt Zaslov, and CIA's Dick Elliott to assess the latest
intelligence. North Vietnam continually juggled its air defense
system, and one of two radars at Phuc Yen airfield, Hanoi's main
fighter base 20 miles northeast of Son Tay, had been moved.
They didn't know why and couldn't find out where. Blackburn
was worried. Had there been a leak? Had the radar been moved
to a spot where it could track the approaches to Son Tay?

The biggest threat from North Vietnamese radar would occur
about 55 minutes out of the objective area, at about the time the
assault force crossed the Laotian border. There was one radar
that could track them from the north. It was on a 5-degree
sector scan at 4½- to 5-minute intervals. The approach of the
assault aircraft would have to be precise to "thread the needle."
There was no way to mask the aircraft from the radar by terrain.
Closer to the objective, there was another radar that could pick
them up from the south. Flying low enough, however, and
along the carefully preplanned route, the C-130s, helicopters,
and A-1s could mask their approach. But if they deviated too
much in altitude or went off course, they could be picked up 8
to 15 minutes away from the objective. That was the reason the
Son Tay air crews had spent so much time practicing the approach, even though there was the hope that if the Navy diversion worked, the radar might be scanning in the wrong direction, toward Haiphong, not Laos.

Blackburn was also concerned about a Chinese signal intelligence antennae field high in the mountains of Laos, 100 miles
west of Hanoi. He asked the spooks about an air strike to knock
out the installation, but they felt it would not be needed—

provided Manor's force maintained radio silence until Simons was actually on the ground, and if radio messages to and from the staging bases in Thailand were kept at normal levels before the raid.

With the exception of the missing radar, it looked to Blackburn, Manor, and Simons as if the spooks had really come through; they had the North Vietnamese air defense order of battle down to a gnat's eyelash. But there was "something funny" going on at Son Tay—or not going on. By now, more than half of the programmed Buffalo Hunter low-level reconnaissance drones had been shot down or "crapped out." Intelligence on the camp was limited to what Building 213's photo interpreters could cull from SR-71 photos taken 80,000 feet or higher above the tiny compound.

Those photos were revealing. The camp looked empty.

On a good mission, if there weren't clouds over the target or too many shadows, the SR-71's technical objective camera could bring back stereoscopic photos sharp enough that, from 15 miles above the earth, the DIA could count the number of people inside the walls of Son Tay Prison. The last SR-71 mission, flown at three times the speed of sound on Saturday, October 3, came back with some very good photos—but no people.

As Manor was to phrase it in his After Action Report, the missions "from 6 June through 3 October" showed "an apparent decline in track activity," with "the lightest activity" evident in the latest batch of photos. But it would be "attributed to the probability that the U.S. POWs were being kept in their cells for extended periods of time." Don Blackburn would remember "sitting around [with some DIA interpreters], talking and looking at photographs, and someone said, I vaguely recall, 'It looks like they haven't been using this.'" Simons had a similar reaction. "The photographs brought to me showed a difference in vegetation," he later remarked. Weeds were growing in the compound, and "I said to myself, 'Well, it's possible that they have restricted their movements. It's possible that they have locked them up.'" But he also thought, "It's possible they have moved them."

For Bull Simons, briefing Henry Kissinger was the "hardest part of the whole operation." It was what he later called "kind of a rarefied atmosphere for a colonel in the infantry." Only four others were present: Kissinger's deputy, Major General Alexander M. Haig, Vogt, Blackburn, and Manor. They met at two-thirty in the afternoon on Thursday, October 8, in Kissinger's office in the West Wing of the White House. The meeting lasted less than 30 minutes.

Vogt introduced everyone and Blackburn outlined the overall concept for a minute or two. Then Manor launched into the detailed briefing which he and Simons had given so many times before in the past three weeks, using a portable projector and the vugraphs they had shown to the Joint Chiefs. By that time, Simons had "heard General Manor's briefing so damn many times" that it bored him. Kissinger nodded his head "sagely" as the briefing unfolded. When Manor was through, Simons covered the ground portion of the operation; it took him only "about 2½ minutes." But as he finished, he added one comment to his "canned" pitch: "I told him that we were going to use the minimum amount of fire necessary." But, Simons cautioned, the area was too confined to avoid enemy casualties. The comment caught Kissinger's attention. He asked Simons, "What in the hell are you talking about?"

Simons explained that he wasn't going on a big hunting expedition: "We're going in there to rescue prisoners, not to blow people's heads off; but we've got to move fast and we'll use whatever fire is necessary to get the job done. But not more." For one thing, he clarified, he didn't want to alert a garrison that was on the north side of the Song Con River if it could be helped. "But," Simons said, "anybody who gets in our way is going to be dead."

"You do what you need to do," Kissinger replied. "Let us take care of the international impact; we can handle that. No one in the White House is concerned about enemy casualties. Use whatever restraint is appropriate, but whatever force is essential for the most efficient operation."

Kissinger had one important question. What if the raid failed?

How sure were they that they would not just put more Americans into the prisons of North Vietnam? Blackburn told Kissinger that they could give him a "95 to 97 percent assurance of success." Manor reinforced the point; the air crews had flown 697 flight hours and 268 sorties training for this mission. It had been rehearsed something like "170 times."

Kissinger was obviously impressed. Haig had no questions or comment.

Blackburn then mentioned his concern that a "broader assessment" might be needed of the operation, a "psychological appreciation" of its impact on the Paris peace negotiations and of how North Vietnam would treat the prisoners left behind in other camps. Kissinger cut the suggestion off. "That's not your worry. Don't get mixed up in politics. That's our worry, not yours."

His reaction "sounded good" to Simons because "that's the way it ought to be." Simons found the President's Assistant for National Security Affairs "pretty swift in the head."

Manor told Kissinger that the first good weather window would occur between October 20 and 25, with October 21 the most promising date for the raid. If that launch date was acceptable to the President, his task force was ready to deploy to its staging bases in Thailand in two days, on October 10. Actually, Manor didn't use the word "President." Instead, he said the "National Command Authority." The next suitable window, he continued, would be just before Thanksgiving. But he said that he realized there might be misgivings about conducting the raid between October 20 and 25, since the President was scheduled to address the United Nations General Assembly on its 25th anniversary, October 24, while 31 heads of state were scheduled to dine at the White House that night.

Kissinger hedged. The President was out of town, he said, and final approval would have to come from him.

As the meeting broke up, Kissinger had one final question: "Who thought this up?" Vogt and Simons replied almost simultaneously: "A lot of people have been working on it. It's been a team effort." Kissinger then offered a comment which every one at the meeting would remember. "Even if it's a 'no go,' " he said, "I want to thank you, all of you, for your imagination and initiative. Thank you for coming up with something original and imaginative."

During the drive back to the Pentagon, one participant thought to himself that there had been something odd about the meeting. Henry Kissinger had not even asked how sure they were that there were any prisoners in Son Tay.

Carriers and CAS Agents

For reasons never explained to Blackburn or Manor, the White House decided soon after the Kissinger briefing to postpone the raid. As Manor would tell a group of POWs released in 1973, three years later: "The plan was enthusiastically received but it was determined that the operation should be delayed until November, our alternate date. One reason I wanted to go in October was because I was very concerned about security. However, the delay allowed us time for further training and coordination."

On Monday, October 19, JCS Chairman Tom Moorer called Blackburn to his office and said that he and Laird would make the final decision and would "go no higher."

The following Tuesday, October 27, Moorer told Blackburn he could deploy an "in-theater coordinating staff" on Sunday, November 1, and begin to deploy the task force itself two weeks later, on Tuesday, November 10. The next day, October 28, the seventh Buffalo Hunter reconnaissance drone flew over Son Tay Prison. This was the shot that banked an instant too soon and returned "perfect imagery" of the horizon beyond Son Tay. Bennett, Blackburn, and Manor decided to "terminate" the Buffalo Hunter "effort."

Later that same day, Blackburn learned that the Navy had called off *all* of its "BARCAP" flights until November 10. These were the radar-picket aircraft that kept track of all airborne North Vietnamese MIGs and vectored U.S. fighters against them. The cancellation would leave Manor's group without "eyes and ears" for 12 days. If North Vietnam were suddenly to concentrate all its fighters at the field closest to Son Tay, it might not be known until too late. The next morning, Thursday, October 29, Blackburn asked Vogt if he would get the BARCAP missions "laid back on." But there were other flights over North Vietnam he wanted "called off." They involved C-130 "psychological operations" leaflet drops "all over" North Vietnam, plus some leaflet drops from a version of Buffalo Hunter drones flying "Operation Litterbug"—better known to the men executing them as the "Bullshit bombers." Vogt agreed; it was the wrong time to "warm up" the North Vietnamese "alert system."

Blackburn had to resolve only two other "flaps" that day. One involved the Navy, the other the CIA. Months earlier, the Navy had scheduled to replace the aircraft carrier *America* with *Ranger* on station with Task Force 77 in the Tonkin Gulf. Yet *America*'s pilots were to fly some of the Son Tay diversionary raids. Because aircraft carrier "cycling" and overhauls were so complex, such transfers were scheduled months, sometimes years, in advance. But Blackburn didn't learn of the switch until October 29. In a private log labeled "Blackburn's Eyes Only," he made an entry that day: "Strange. Am presenting need to accelerate *Ranger* and *Hancock* deployments to 19 Nov., retain *Oriskany* on station until 26 Nov. Transfer pilots and aircraft from *America* to *Ranger?*" He went to see Vogt. Vogt was stunned: "Why wasn't this thought of before?" Blackburn explained that "the requirement had been laid out early in the operational planning." But as often happened in grave matters, "something fell through the cracks." The Pentagon was a 27-year-old building; it had a lot of cracks. Vogt himself was to have handled the carrier deployments, but he had been thwarted by two problems: no one would be sure when the White House would let the raid be launched; and the planners wanted everything to look as normal as possible to the North Vietnamese.

Vogt said he would get the carrier deployments fixed. It wasn't easy. When the JCS message arrived at CINCPAC headquarters, the Commander-in-Chief, Pacific Fleet, stormed in to see Admiral John McCain's Chief of Staff, Army Lieutenant General Charles A. Corcoran. "Something odd is going on," he said. "We're getting some wild orders about switching aircraft carriers all over the Pacific and they don't make sense. What the hell is going on?"

Corcoran told him, "I've never lied to you. I'm not going to now. But I'm not going to explain. I'm just asking you to ride with me on this one. Follow the orders."

That left Blackburn with only one other onion to peel on October 29. He had discovered that the CIA was "horsing around" in his back yard.

At CIA's 213-acre wooded complex in Langley, Virginia, that morning, George Carver found himself in a dilemma. Just yesterday he had assured Blackburn that none of his agents was operating in North Vietnam. Now, Blackburn was confronting him personally to challenge that assertion. In months of planning the Son Tay raid, during 16 Saturday morning coordinating sessions with Carver's hand-picked liaison man present, Blackburn had stressed time and again his concern that some CAS agent—one of the CIA's "Controlled American Sources"—might go "threshing around up north" at the wrong time or in the wrong area, get caught, and alert the North Vietnamese warning system that something big was up. Blackburn reminded Carver of his concern and told him that he had learned, through one of his own sources, that there *was* a CAS operation now under way.

Carver had to admit it. But it was "way south" of Son Tay, he insisted, down near Route 7 on the southern border with Laos. The operation couldn't possibly affect the Son Tay raid, he protested. It was a low-key insertion; that was why he hadn't thought of it when Blackburn asked about CAS teams the day before.

CIA's track record on CAS operations up north wasn't too swift, Blackburn had long felt. Almost every agent inserted there since 1964 had been "nailed"—hundreds of South Vietnamese and some North Vietnamese whom the CIA had "turned back." Soon after he took over SOG in 1965, Blackburn had learned that some CAS teams had not been resupplied for months, and he protested inserting more agents until the CIA arranged to take care of those already there. The CIA had lost some of its best agents and risked the lives of men like Dick Meadows trying to save others; but as far as Blackburn could discern, the whole CAS effort hadn't produced a thimbleful of useful intelligence.

Yet George Carver was one of Blackburn's favorite spooks. He too believed in unconventional operations, not body counts, and had supported SACSA's work steadfastly. A former Rhodes scholar and psy-ops operative, Carver was a busy, fast-talking man. He had a lot of excess energy and he loved to pick up the telephone. Asked a question in some meeting, he would often reach for a phone to find out "right now." That's what made Blackburn worry that Carver wasn't being completely candid with him; when he asked to see exactly *where* in North Vietnam that CAS agent was, Carver didn't reach for a phone to find out. He turned into a Sphinx, not denying, not confirming, suggesting by his manner that since the operation didn't affect Blackburn, he didn't need to know about it.

Blackburn controlled his temper, measuring his words. "George, you're not leveling with me. That guy went in near Site 32 way up in northern Laos, 100 miles from Son Tay. We're getting ready to launch that raid in three weeks and now I find out that one of your guys is operating in my back yard. He could screw this whole thing up. And you didn't even tell me he was there. I'm speaking for the chairman, George; we want that guy shut down, fast. The North Vietnamese can track your guys a lot easier than we can, and *we* didn't have any trouble finding him. This is one reason I included you guys on the planning team—to stop this kind of horseshit."

Carver, Blackburn would recall, responded with the "Charlie Chan" approach—sophisticated, quiet, uninformative. He said he "would see what he could do." Blackburn was "over-reacting," they were all working for the same team, et cetera, et cetera . . .

Blackburn left CIA headquarters unsatisfied, disappointed, puzzled, and concerned. *Some*thing was going on, yet the guy responsible for CIA's support of the Son Tay raid wouldn't tell him what, or why.

Five years were to pass before he finally found out all the

answers. But he learned part of the reason for Carver's discomfort a few days later, from Ed Mayer. The CIA had lost Site 32. The alternate launch base for the Son Tay raid was in communist hands, and CIA's agents were fighting like fury to get it back.

Leaks and Lost Messages

On Sunday, November 1, Blackburn, Manor, and Simons left Andrews Air Force Base for Hawaii and then South Vietnam. At the same time, a small staff from the Joint Contingency Task Group flew separately to Southeast Asia to visit every wing, squadron and base commander who would have to support the Son Tay raid. Each would be given a letter of instruction with only enough information to "perform his assigned functions." Except for the few officers whom Blackburn, Manor, and Simons would visit personally, no one else would be told the objective of the mission.

To attract as little attention as possible, the other JCTG officers flew to their destinations all over Southeast Asia on regularly scheduled flights and even on a "space available" or standby basis. In typical understatement, Manor reported later: "This proved to be very time-consuming and only numerous fortuitous connections made possible the completion of coordination on schedule. It is considered that dedicated airlift for this purpose would have obviated many of the problems encountered and allowed individuals more time to accomplish their tasks."

Blackburn, Manor, and Simons briefed Admiral McCain and his chief of staff in Hawaii at 10:45 A.M. on Monday, November 2. McCain was "visibly concerned, very fidgety in his chair." His concern was, of course, for those POWs who would be left behind—including his own son. But he supported the raid heartily. "It was a rough spot to place him in," one of those present thought. After their meeting, McCain offered Blackburn, Manor and Simons CINCPAC's "personal airplane" to fly them the 6,296 miles to Saigon. They departed Oahu at 4:45 that afternoon for the long flight across the western Pacific.

The three men were bushed. McCain's C-118 (a military version of the DC-7) was outfitted as an executive transport and airborne headquarters—"plush easy chairs, beds, great service, good food, drinks"—and it was slow, about 350 miles an hour, so they had plenty of time to catch up on their sleep. The plane touched down at Wake Island to refuel, crossed the International Date Line, and landed at 4:00 A.M. to refuel again in the Philippines. The next stop would be Saigon, where they would brief General Creighton Abrams, Westmoreland's successor as Commander, U.S. Military Assistance Command, Vietnam (MACV).

There was some work to do while they were in the air, however. Just before Blackburn left Washington, Moorer had asked him what the "impact" would be of a major bombing up north, no longer than one day in duration, just before the raid on Son Tay. It would be the first bombing of North Vietnam in over two years. The White House, Moorer said, was considering it and had proposed "tying it in" with the Son Tay rescue. Blackburn had asked Mayer to have his assessment ready by the time he returned, but on the flight to Saigon, Blackburn made his own notes:

a. Bombing would have adverse impact, nationally and internationally.
b. Might provide good excuse, if (a) is true, for NVA [North Vietnamese Army] to take reprisals against those left behind.
c. Would alert entire warning system.
d. We should "low key" our effort with view of obtaining maximum favorable impact; i.e., our mission is a humanitarian one. Bombing mission associated with this would kill this and raise a big stink.
e. Acknowledge White House view that if bombing took place before our mission, it could strengthen credibility of our Navy diversion.
f. But advantage would be far outweighed by the disadvantages, e.g., the adverse reactions.

Burly "Abe" Abrams, puffing heavily on his cigar, listened in silence as Blackburn, Manor and Simons told him for the first time of the raid on Son Tay. With him was General Lucius Clay, his air deputy and the Commanding General, 7th Air Force; and Lieutenant General Welborn Dolvin who, like Abrams, was a tanker and MACV's Chief of Staff. Abrams was a man of few words. When the briefing was over, he told Blackburn, Manor and Simons, "My God, that's a real professional job. I don't see what you've overlooked. Looks like you haven't left any stones unturned. I don't have *any* questions." Abrams then turned to Clay and asked, "Well, Lou, can you support this thing?" During the briefing, Clay's eyes had got "real big," like he was wondering, "What in tarnation, how crazy *are* you guys?" But now he told Abrams: "I'm not sure how, but we'll sure as hell manage. Sounds like we've got about ten days to get ready." Clay knew the job would not be easy, since he was in the process of removing men and equipment from every base in Southeast Asia as part of President Nixon's withdrawal program.

While Blackburn flew back to Washington to look after other SACSA business, Manor and Simons flew from Saigon by Navy plane to the Tonkin Gulf and landed aboard the aircraft carrier which Vice Admiral Frederic A. Bardshar used as "the flag" of Task Force 77. Bardshar knew "someone" was coming, but not who. He had received a high command net message* from "a friend" in CINCPAC headquarters; it told him only that two officers, an Army colonel and an Air Force brigadier general, would come aboard. Bardshar was to give them any help he could, but the visit and their mission were "very close hold." Bardshar was not to discuss them even with his own boss, the commander, Seventh Fleet or with the commander-in-chief, Pacific Fleet.

Bardshar led Manor and Simons into the flag mess. He later called in two other men, Captain Alan "Boot" Hill, his operations officer, and Commander P. D. Hoskins, his intelligence officer. Together, they were to plan the Navy diversion that

_____

*A "high command net message" was one designed to assure delivery even when radio transmitting conditions are marginal. In this case, delivery was more important than the extra measure of security that might have been gained using a "back channel" message—which general and flag officers can send to one another on an "eyes only basis" outside regular signal channels. They are not logged in or read by the action officers who read and route operational communiqués.

would mask the Son Tay raid, under a "short fuse" and circumstances that were demanding both intellectually and physically. Writing a detailed operations order for a Navy carrier air strike was like composing a symphony for an orchestra the size of the New York Philharmonic. Planning one for a major night strike to be flown simultaneously from two or three carriers was like composing a symphony for two or three orchestras that would have to perform it together without even rehearsing. And because of the "extremely limited disclosure" of the operation, Hill and Hoskins had to write a score which the musicians would see for the first time only hours before curtain time.

Blackburn was back in the Pentagon on Tuesday, November 10, to brief Moorer on the Southeast Asia trip and tell him of his concern about the proposed one-day bombing. The launch date for the raid was now about ten days away, and he tried not to think of the nightmares he had been having for weeks—"My God," he'd wake up at his home in McLean, Virginia, wondering: "What if no one's there? What if it's a 'dry hole'? What if there's been a compromise?" But there were too many other things to worry about now.

The first C-130 would leave Eglin for the objective area on Thursday, November 12. Simons and Manor had returned there to oversee the final loading of all their equipment and wish their men a safe flight. With the launch date so near, it was time to "tighten up" on security. But Blue Max came into Blackburn's office that day and told him he was concerned. There was a lot of coded traffic from CIA headquarters to its posts in Thailand and Laos; many of the messages were about the Son Tay raid.

Blackburn knew that there would have to be some last-minute traffic. CIA agents would give Simons' men their final escape and evasion briefing and there was always a chance, if the weather turned sour, that one or more of the helicopters would still have to launch from Site 32 in northern Laos. But when Blue Max showed him how much traffic was being sent, almost twice the usual average, Blackburn was alarmed. He told Moorer, who offered to call Helms and tell the CIA in no uncertain words to "tighten things up."

But the time had also arrived to let some new players in on the game. Among the first was the Pentagon's official spokesman, Daniel Z. Henkin, Laird's Assistant Secretary of Defense for Public Affairs. A long-time military journalist, and editor of the 102-year-old *Armed Forces Journal* before he joined the Pentagon public affairs staff late in 1965, Henkin was a hefty, easygoing man with greying, curly hair that looked as if he combed it only as an afterthought. He had sometimes managed to irritate the Pentagon press corps because he seemed so unperturbed by such events as the *Pueblo* capture, the Tet offensive, and the invasion of Cambodia. But a few Pentagon regulars described him as "unflappable."

When Blackburn finished briefing him on the Son Tay raid early on Thursday, November 12, Henkin thanked him almost casually and assured him that his office could "handle" the press. In Henkin's near-cavernous office in Room 2E800, halfway between the Pentagon's Mall and the River entrances, the imminent rescue of 60 to 70 American prisoners within 23 miles of Hanoi was a business-as-usual proposition. Blackburn felt almost stupid walking back to his office. Why had he been so concerned about "impact assessments" if a press expert like Henkin could take the raid in such smooth stride? Was a prisoner rescue really such small potatoes? Maybe he'd blown the raid out of all proportion in his own mind.

That same morning, Blackburn, Mayer, Manor and Simons had another meeting with Moorer. Moorer was "great," they would recall. "I've given you a job to do," he told Manor. "You're liable now to get a bunch of requests for reports or information on one thing after the other. Ignore them." The mission came first, protocol and questions second. Moorer said he'd do anything Manor and Simons needed to ease their load in the days ahead and wished them luck.

Ten minutes after Manor and Simons left the chairman's office, Blackburn received a call directly from Moorer. He wanted to know what the "impact" would be if the raid had to be delayed until December. "Just let me tell you," Moorer explained. "Something's happened. Laird is apprehensive. Something's up in Paris."

Blackburn was stunned, but he recovered enough to tell
Moorer that a delay would be "devastating." They wouldn't
have another weather window for months. The assault force
was already en route to Thailand. The men were "up" psychologically. A delay or recall now would mean serious risk of
compromise; you could keep a lid on things only so long, once
everyone was "peaked." Blackburn noted in his private log
later: "I am afraid they are looking for a rationale to fall off a
difficult, complex mission. Difficult to understand a turn-down
of this mission unless tremendous overriding factors of which
we have no knowledge. Fact that North Vietnamese may have
become more amenable to POW Christmas packages doesn't
constitute, to me, an overriding factor."

A few minutes later, Mayer received another call, this time
from Navy Captain Harry D. Train II, Moorer's executive assistant and senior aide. Moorer needed a copy of the Son Tay
briefing to take to Secretary Laird right away. Blackburn wondered what was going on. At noon, Train called him again to say
that Moorer had just met with Laird, and Laird was now on his
way to the White House. Blackburn asked, "What was Moorer's
reaction?" "Don't worry, he was smiling," Train reassured him.

At 1:45 that afternoon, Blackburn got a phone call from Vogt.
Vogt told him, "It's a 'go.' " Minutes later, Train called; Kissinger had agreed to "no bombing," and the raid was to go "on
schedule." The "no bombing" decision was to change after
North Vietnam shot down an unarmed low-level reconnaissance plane the next day, Friday the 13th, killing both crewmen. But Blackburn was relieved. All the work that he and the
other planners had done, the weeks of grueling training the
assault force had been through, would not be wasted.

Blackburn soon got more good news from another quarter.
Lieutenant General Richard Stilwell, the Army's Deputy Chief
of Staff for Operations, called to tell him that he had just ordered 30 days of "administrative leave" for Simons and his men
as soon as they returned from the operation. Blackburn had
asked Stilwell to okay it weeks ago. It was time off that wouldn't
be charged to their annual leave allowance, a way of telling
Simons' men that the Army knew they had worked long hours

under great stress, months away from their families to get ready for a job they couldn't talk about—and from which they might not even return.

Next on Blackburn's agenda was a special intelligence meeting with the DIA and NSA spooks. They reviewed the latest SR-71 photos taken on November 2 and November 6, the first of which showed a "definite increase in activity" at Son Tay. This was believed to be the result of letting the POWs spend more time outside their cells. The "Secondary School" south of the camp had also been "reactivated." The meeting adjourned with an agreement to lay on a new set of SR-71 "tracks" that would be flown on November 13, 18, and 20, just prior to the raid.

Arthur Andriatis—DIA's photo interpreter, assigned directly to Manor's Joint Contingency Task Group—had just flown to Yokota Air Base, Japan, where SR-71 photos of the Pacific area were normally processed and interpreted. There, working in the sophisticated complex that housed SAC's 67th Reconnaissance Technical Squadron, he personally would "read out" the final SR-71 photos of Son Tay Prison. SAC's regular interpreters would cover everything outside the objective area, including the approaches from Laos, in order to look for changes in surface-to-air missile (SAM) sites, antiaircraft dispositions, and the early warning/ground control intercept stations.

To save time, the DIA had arranged for several other things to be done. It was decided to concentrate on large-scale photo coverage of the area and use only one small-scale technical objective camera. SAC was also requested to limit its other reconnaissance coverage during the period ahead to make every resource available for the special missions about to be flown to "test the responsiveness of the SR-71 to special mission requirements." Procedures for processing and interpreting the new film were radically changed as well. Unloading all of the film an SR-71 normally took was a two-hour job. DIA asked SAC if the plane could be "downloaded" in 45 minutes during the tests. The missions would all be flown out of Kadena Air Base in Okinawa by the 9th Strategic Reconnaissance Wing. As soon as the film was offloaded there, a KC-135 jet tanker would rush it to Yokota. Once the film was processed and interpreted there, Andraitis would fly the interpretation results and prints to Takhli Royal Thai Air Force Base in central Thailand by special courier plane and brief Manor's air crews and the four men in Simons' assault team who knew what the objective was. Duplicate sets would be flown to Washington. Photo interpretation was a painstaking, mind-draining job. It took time; but every effort was being made to speed up the process.

The SR-71 missions of November 13 and 18 would be crucial. Besides large-scale photos of the objective itself, which would confirm "increased activity" at the prison, they would provide the first complete large-scale photography of the route from the Laotian border to Son Tay. This was needed to verify turning points, pick out emergency landing zones, and make sure that no additional SAM or AAA or early warning systems had been moved along the approach route. The last two "pre-launch" missions would be flown earlier in the day than usual on Friday, November 20, and on Saturday preliminary interpretation results would be phoned to Manor and the Pentagon Command Center. But at that late moment, there would only be time to look for some "mind-blowing change."

Blackburn was reassured by both the DIA and the NSA schedule and procedures. He was told that if there was one microsecond of North Vietnamese radio or signals traffic affecting the raid or any change in radar coverage or frequencies, the NSA would have them "locked in" and fed directly to Manor and Simons in Thailand. The Son Tay raid had been given the number-one priority of all electronic intelligence work worldwide. An "updated" electronic order of battle, air order of battle, and missile order of battle would be flown to Takhli on Thursday, November 19, just before the mission launched.

Blue Max was waiting in Blackburn's office when he returned from the special intelligence meeting, and this time the news was bad. He "thought" Blackburn "should know something." It looked as if there might be a "pigeon" in Son Tay, a prisoner who was "talking"—much too freely; had he given up, betrayed his fellow POWs, anxious to make his own miserable life more comfortable? Blue Max knew that Blackburn had planned to get a message into the camp forewarning the senior officers that rescue was imminent and how to help. Now, that plan would have to be abandoned. Blue Max wasn't sure who the pigeon was.

That hectic Thursday ended on a more positive note. About six o'clock that evening, Blackburn ran into Admiral McCain in a Pentagon corridor. McCain had just seen Secretary Laird and Admiral Moorer, and they had told him the raid on Son Tay was "a go." McCain wanted Blackburn to know that "whichever way it goes, I back what you're doing." On the drive home that night, Blackburn thought long and hard about the prisoners in Son Tay and the others who would be left behind. God, how he wished that a thirty-four-year-old naval aviator named John S. McCain III was in Son Tay Prison.

Friday, November 13, brought grim news. Six POWs were dead. Peace activist Cora Weiss had been given their names by the North Vietnamese front organization, the Committee of Solidarity with the American People. All six had been carried as POWs held in the north. Now there was an even greater urgency for the Son Tay mission.

On Saturday morning, November 14, Blackburn was at Andrews Air Force Base for an early breakfast with Manor and Simons before their long flight to Thailand. They would be leaving at 2:00 P.M. that afternoon aboard Admiral McCain's private plane; this time it was a small, but faster North American T-39, the two-engine Sabreliner executive jet. Their principal topic of conversation was the intelligence briefing Blackburn had received two days before, but their principal worry was a new threat to the security of the raid that had suddenly emerged.

Early in the planning stages, wiretaps had been placed, with the consent of all parties concerned, on the phones at Eglin Auxiliary Field Number Three and on SACSA's Pentagon phones. Tapes had been made of every conversation, and from them, Blackburn had just learned, counterintelligence teams at the Air Force Cryptologic Depot in San Antonio, Texas, had pieced together a disquieting "mosaic." They had figured out that a "big operation" was about to take place. They knew it would be in Southeast Asia. They knew that the Navy and CINCPAC were involved, that it would happen "fast" and "at night." But they had not been able to identify what the target was, the specific country in which the operation would take place, or the size of the force involved.

Had there been a leak, or was it just a clever piece of deduction? As they weighed the chances of compromise, Manor and Simons decided the odds were on their side. But just before they left Andrews for the long flight to Southeast Asia, Blackburn told them that he would make one final check and alert them after they arrived in Thailand if there was a significant danger of compromise.

The next day, Sunday, November 15, as Manor and Simons were crossing the Pacific, events in Washington began to accelerate. Messages came into the Pentagon Command Center from the CIA station chief and General Abrams in South Vietnam. The CIA wanted to borrow some of the large, armed HH-53 rescue helicopters to support an operation in southern Laos which General Vang Pao's Meo tribesmen were about to run. Abrams was opposed, but he couldn't tell his CIA counterpart in Saigon why: he wanted every HH-53 in the theater available to support Manor and Simons.

By the time Blackburn and Mayer arrived at the Pentagon early on Monday morning, the 16th, JCS action officers were having a small imbroglio over the message. Their contacts at CIA were "screaming" for the helicopters; why wouldn't MACV release them? Blackburn didn't want to do *any* explaining to anyone at this late juncture; even a hint that the aircraft were "on hold" for an operation that had anything to do with SACSA, or that Southeast Asia helicopter priorities were now being decided by the JCS, was too risky. Mayer came up with the solution. He arranged for Air Force headquarters to "ground" temporarily all HH-53s worldwide because of a "potentially catastrophic technical problem." Only "safety-related test flights" were authorized, "pending further notice."

Then Harry Train called Blackburn from Moorer's office. The President wanted a "complete briefing" on the raid, tomorrow.

He had invited Secretary of State William Rogers to sit in. Moorer would give the briefing right after lunch. Would SACSA prepare the necessary charts and briefing book?

Blackburn and Mayer spent the rest of Monday updating their briefing and having new vugraphs made. Their draftsman, a young Navy enlisted man named Larry Downing, worked late Monday evening getting all of them ready. The next morning, November 17, Blackburn and Mayer checked over his work; it was a "first-class job." They delivered everything to Train, complete with Moorer's briefing text typed out in a carefully indexed, tabbed three-ring black binder with gold-imprinted letters spelling out "Top Secret" and "Chairman's Eyes Only" on the cover.

Having just arranged for the President to "learn more about Son Tay than he ever wanted to know," Mayer discovered that the raid's commanders were apparently lost. Manor and Simons had been scheduled to land at Takhli Royal Thai Air Force Base in central Thailand at 5:30 A.M. Washington time that morning, 5:30 P.M. in the afternoon local time; Manor was supposed to send a prearranged, specially coded message to the Pentagon Command Center reporting their arrival. It was now 9:30 A.M. and the message had not yet been received. Mayer had purposely grounded about 50 Air Force planes the day before; now he was concerned that the Navy might have accidentally lost one somewhere in the western Pacific.

Mayer spent the next hour in Room 2C945, the National Military Command Center's message section, anxiously going through all the special coded cables to see if the night duty officer had misplaced Manor's message or routed it to the wrong office. There was no such message anywhere in the communications center. Blackburn told his executive officer, Air Force Colonel William P. "Pat" Ryan, to keep "bugging" the message center and track down that cable. He told Mayer they'd sweat it out until three o'clock; that was when the final contingent of Simons' raiding party was due to arrive in Thailand. Manor and Simons were to send another message then, reporting that the "Joint Contingency Task Group" had "closed in" at its staging base.

While Mayer and Ryan were trying to track down Manor and Simons, Blackburn met with NSA's Zaslov to try to track down the source of the information about the raid that had been picked up by Air Force counterintelligence at San Antonio. They reviewed the tapes of the Pentagon-Eglin phone taps at length. Zaslov concluded there was no cause for concern; neither the location or nature of the target nor the timing of the raid could be put together from the fragments of conversation on the tapes.

Blackburn didn't tell him how relieved he really was that the NSA found no cause for alarm over the phone leaks. A month before, a counterintelligence officer had come to Blackburn's office to say that some information had been compromised on a phone call from the Pentagon to Eglin. Blackburn himself had placed the call, but his impromptu "waffling" and double-talk on the phone hadn't worked: a piece of potentially serious information had been overheard, taped, and logged in by Air Force security as a fairly big disclosure—and Blackburn was the violator.

Norm Frisbie, Blackburn was told, had learned of the leak and had passed word of the goof to his superiors. The counterintelligence officer had then told Blackburn that he had to advise General Palmer, the Army Vice Chief of Staff, of the security violation. Blackburn readily agreed he should. Then he called Frisbie and asked him to get back to work on the raid. Other authorities would assess the impact of Blackburn's goof.

Despite Zaslov's reassurance, Blackburn was concerned about the leak. Later that afternoon, Mayer found him in his office "despondent as hell." They discussed Blackburn's careless slip, and Mayer told him it was a "bunch of smoke," careless but "sure as hell" nothing that would compromise the raid. Yet Blackburn was profoundly disturbed. He had gone to extraordinary measures to compartmentalize the planning and limit the "big picture" to only a few people. Not even the Commander-in-Chief of the Pacific Air Force had been "wired in." Blackburn's counterintelligence team had worked hard to have the Son Tay mock-up at Eglin torn down every time a Cosmos satellite passed overhead so that it wouldn't be detected by

Russian cameras. *He* was the one who insisted on the phone taps, even on his own. Now, he had caught the "biggest blabber of all"—himself.

Blackburn left the Pentagon early that day. At home that evening he wrote out his resignation from the United States Army. After dinner he called Mayer and asked him to come over. Blackburn showed him the resignation. Mayer read it in silence, carefully, and then tore the paper up and threw the pieces into a fire blazing in Blackburn's den. "Don't forget that we're teaching ourselves to be more careful; we haven't blown anything yet," he said. "This just means we'll have to be more careful in the future, or we're likely to blow something." Then he told Blackburn to forget the incident and get some sleep so he could get his "ass back to work." Blackburn grumbled about Mayer ripping up his resignation. "If you feel so strongly about it," Mayer said, "you can write another one in the morning."

Ed Mayer had had problems of his own that day. Train had called him at 11:15 A.M. with a "complete new set of instructions" for Moorer's White House briefing. The meeting with the President was now scheduled for 2:30 P.M., but Moorer needed "new charts, more charts and different-size charts." And he needed them by 1:30 to have some time to familiarize himself with the material.

To his horror, Mayer found that the only draftsman cleared for the Son Tay operation, Larry Downing, had gone home. He was babysitting. His wife had been taken to the hospital late the night before. There was no way, he told Mayer on the phone, that he could get a replacement babysitter in time; his regular one was in school. Mayer's own children were too old for babysitters and he had no idea where he could find one. He told Train of the problem, who commented wryly, "I don't quite believe it; the deadline is 1:30. Are you telling me this thing is going to come unglued over a babysitter?"

Mayer knew he couldn't ask Blackburn to babysit, and tracking one down was the kind of "detail" that Blackburn didn't like to be bothered with. So Mayer set to work on the charts himself. Presidential briefings, he learned belatedly, had to be made up on 20- by 30-inch flip-charts, each chart split down in the middle and then taped together on the back so it would fold just right on the Oval Office easel. Mayer called in two people from the JCS graphics section. Neither one had the proper clearance. So he called them in separately, gave one man unmarked, unclassified maps of North Vietnam and layouts of the Son Tay compound, and the other a bunch of "headlines" and labels to make up.

Mayer pasted everything together himself. Soon the unclassified maps and labels became Top Secret charts of the air approaches to Son Tay Prison, and of the prison itself. By the time he finished, his draftsmen still didn't know whether they'd been preparing flip-charts of a new atomic bomb storage site or maps for a routine SR-71 reconnaissance track over North Vietnam. Mayer told them they weren't to *speak* to each other for at least a week.

At 1:20, Mayer was ready to deliver the charts when he suddenly realized he didn't have a carrying case. Nor did the JCS graphics section. He spent the next nine minutes calling one JCS office after another and finally located a case in an office almost directly above his, the Joint Reconnaissance Center in Room 2D921. Maps and photos were its product, flip-charts its hallmark. Its director, Rear Admiral J. C. Donaldson, told Mayer he could have "any kind of carrying case SACSA ever needed."

In Room 2E873, Admiral Moorer flicked through the charts quickly without comment or question. Mayer was relieved that he had put the right labels in the right places with enough glue to keep them from falling off. But at two o'clock, the White House called: the briefing had to be postponed; Moorer was to be in the Oval Office tomorrow at eleven o'clock.

Mayer went to Blackburn's office. The Son Tay assault force was due to arrive in Thailand that afternoon at 3:00 P.M. Washington time. There should be a message confirming their arrival within minutes. Addressed to Mayer's attention, all it would read was "Electric Ray." But there was still no message from Manor and Simons. Three o'clock passed; then three-thirty. Blackburn and Mayer began to wonder not only what would happen at the White House, but where in the hell their raiders were.

Late that afternoon, Blackburn met Moorer, who was leaving the Pentagon for home at an hour much earlier than usual for him. "Can I ask how it went, Admiral, with Mr. Laird at the White House?" Blackburn said.

"Fine, Don, fine, I'd say," Moorer replied. "We'll know after I brief the President tomorrow."

Blackburn had not yet received a message from Manor or Simons, but he decided not to tell the Chairman that he'd "lost" the Son Tay raiders.

By 7:30 P.M. that evening, when Blackburn and Mayer left the Pentagon exhausted from a hectic day, the messages they had been waiting for still hadn't arrived. But Manor and Simons weren't lost; their messages were—at a relay station in Japan. Manor had sent the messages on time: one reporting his and Simons' arrival left Takhli at 5:30 A.M. Pentagon time; the second, reporting that Simons' 56-man assault force had arrived, left Takhli at 3:00 P.M. Pentagon time. But because of the special codes used, they had to be handled manually at an automatic switching station in Japan whose procedures were geared to general communications. Manor's "flash" messages didn't reach the National Military Command Center until about nine o'clock that evening. By that time, Mayer had found Simons by placing a frantic but unauthorized phone call to Thailand. "Fudging it" as best he could on the unsecure voice circuit, he verified that Simons, Manor, and their troops were indeed alive, well, and ready to raid North Vietnam.

It was just the first of a series of communication foul-ups that were to plague the Son Tay raiders.

The Oval Office

On Wednesday morning, November 18, Admiral Moorer was driven to the White House to brief President Nixon on the Son Tay raid. That day was the 80th anniversary of the launching of America's first battleship, U.S.S. *Maine*. It was also a day of decision—when, or if, to launch the raid. The admiral hoped the operation would have smoother sailing than the *Maine*.

Moorer arrived at the Oval Office at precisely 11:00 A.M.

There he found President Nixon, Henry Kissinger, Melvin Laird, CIA Director Richard M. Helms, and Secretary of State William P. Rogers. After a businesslike exchange of greetings, Moorer began to set up the elaborate 20- by 30-inch flip-charts Ed Mayer had assembled in such a panic the day before. Laird had already briefed the President on the concept, but had decided Nixon should hear the "full pitch" before making his final decision. And he knew the briefing had impressed Kissinger: it was imaginative, almost entertaining.

The way Oval Office briefings were handled in 1970, Moorer would be flipping his own charts. "You don't take a 'horseholder' to the White House," he would later joke. He hadn't had much time to look all the charts over and wondered if they were in the right order. When he was given the signal to proceed by the President, Moorer opened his carefully tabbed briefing book and began: "Mr. President, the code name for this operation is 'Kingpin.'"

Of those present in the Oval Office that morning, only Secretary of State Rogers had not been briefed about the raid before. Yet, as Moorer began to read through the briefing book, tapping the charts with a telescoping metal pointer to illustrate the text, and occasionally adding a soft-spoken comment of his own, his audience was obviously enthralled. A few minutes into the briefing, Kissinger picked up the phone to summon his deputy, Major General Alexander M. Haig. He entered the Oval Office moments later, and he, too, listened attentively.

"This is the scenario, Mr. President," Moorer said, continuing with details of the airborne approach of Simons' assault force from Thailand to Son Tay: the precise route that had to be taken to avoid detection by enemy radar, the complex procedures of aerial rendezvous and refueling, the dangers of detection and destruction on the final leg of the flight. Moorer described the Navy diversion that would be launched over Haiphong Harbor 20 minutes before the landing at Son Tay to trigger a conventional air attack response by the North Vietnamese and distract their attention from the approach of the assault force. The President was absorbed by his description of the intricate aerial ballet that would take place over an area covering 300,000 square miles of Southeast Asia.

Unveiling a large, schematic diagram of the Son Tay Prison compound, Moorer said: "Here, Mr. President, is how the assault landing and rescue will be made." Surprise, speed, and simplicity would be the keys to the success of the assault, he said, and went on to explain in detail the air and ground tactics that had been perfected through long hours of practice at Eglin Air Force Base. Moorer then added a few illustrations of how meticulously the raid had been planned. "The ground commander is positive that the operation will succeed, Mr. President. He has personally selected every man in this mission. They are all volunteers, dedicated and free from any discernible defect. The training was thorough, definitive, and intense. The air crews are among the best available. They were also individually selected and all aircraft commanders are volunteers."

Kissinger interrupted for the first time. "I talked with the two leaders, Colonel Simons and General Manor, over a month ago, Mr. President. Most impressive. Simons swears he can get into that camp and back safely with all of his men. He said the odds are 97 out of 100 in his favor. Someone told me they'd rehearsed this more than 100 times." Laird added that planning for the operation had been under way since May.

Moorer went back to his briefing to describe the tight security under which the planning and training stages of the operation had taken place. Special security measures would also be in force while the raid itself was under way. He assured the President that "if resources in support of this operation reveal that the enemy may have determined our objective, the operation will be canceled." The President protested that he didn't want that to happen.

Flipping to another chart, Moorer described the major threats, both from the air and the ground, to the assault force. It was clear from the intriguing details he provided about North Vietnamese defenses that the intelligence behind the raid was of the highest caliber. Moorer was able to tell the President, for instance, that four of the six qualified MIG-21 night intercept pilots at Phuc Yen, the airfield closest to Son Tay, had been redeployed to Vinh airfield, far to the south. Moreover, he pointed out, there was no night alert at Phuc Yen, so the remaining planes would be slow to react. There were four MIG-17 night interceptor pilots at the Haiphong-Tien airfield, Moorer added, but there was no night alert there either. And, he said, those planes, even if scrambled, would be committed against the Navy diversion. Finally, he noted that while MIG-17 all-weather fighters were also positioned at Kep airfield, there were "no known night-qualified pilots there."

Lastly, Moorer spoke of the objective of the mission—the POWs at Son Tay. "This is the only confirmed active POW camp outside Hanoi, Mr. President. The Son Tay camp has a prisoner population of 70 Americans. Of these, 61 have been tentatively identified by name and service: 43 Air Force, 14 Navy, 4 Marines." Lieutenant Commander C. D. Clower, U.S. Navy, "promoted to commander since capture," he said, had assumed the position of senior ranking officer. The North Vietnamese had moved the two previous SROs out in January and May, respectively, he explained. Again, the President seemed to be impressed by the precise detail which the Pentagon had on the target.

After cautioning that the weather would be a "critical factor" in the operation, Moorer concluded his remarks: "If you approve the operation, I plan to release General Manor to execute the raid any time he elects between the November 21 and 25 launch windows. That's all I have, Mr. President. Are there any questions I can fill you in on?"

The President looked up. "That was great, Tom, just the right amount of detail, not too much. Ah, I know you need a final decision as soon as possible and I plan to give you one soon. But what's the latest you can wait, without fouling Manor up?"

Moorer hoped his eyes wouldn't betray his concern. He knew the President made his decisions alone, and that he would want to check to see if Kissinger, Haig, or Laird had any private qualms. But the question implied another long hold, and this was no time for delay. The operation was too unprecedented and sensitive. Moorer responded carefully to the President's question: "Mr. President, if we miss this launch window, the earliest we could try again would be March. The right combina-

tion of quarter-moonlight and weather comes up only four or
five times a year in that area. We missed one window on October 21, as you know. If we're going to make this one, I should
send an 'Execute' message no later than 24 hours from now,
sooner if possible. General Manor and Colonel Simons are in
Thailand, ready to launch."

Moorer explained his problem: "There's a lot of last-minute
activity triggered by this kind of an operation—ships, airplanes,
men, special reconnaissance missions, standby search and rescue forces. It takes three days to get everything in full gear. But
we don't want to start it up if we're not going to go; too many
people would be asking too many questions. That could jeopardize our next chance. However, once approved by you, the
operation can still be aborted at any time prior to launch or
canceled and, if necessary, recalled at any time. We have prearranged code word and RED ROCKET communications to handle either a last-minute cancellation or recall."

The President replied quickly: he understood Moorer's concern. It wasn't a question of "whether" to make the rescue; that
had already been decided. The only question was "when."
Nixon assured Moorer that he would have a decision "very
soon." But he had one more question: "What if the raid failed?
Had adequate cover stories been devised?"

There were five cover stories, Moorer explained. He turned
again to his briefing book. If the raid was successful but some
aircraft and men were lost, the word would be simple—the
results justified the risk. If somehow the operation was disclosed
prior to launch, the Pentagon would say only that it involved a
highly classified mission and no details would be available. If the
mission had to be aborted or was disclosed after launch, the
aborted venture would be described as a search and rescue
effort for a downed reconnaissance airman. If the raid failed at
the target or if no POWs were rescued and word got out, the
line would be that intransigence of the North Vietnamese made
the attempt necessary, and that results would have been worth
the risk.

The President nodded. One last question. What was the earliest anyone would know if the raid had succeeded or failed?

Moorer explained briefly the complex communications hook-up between Simons' assault force, Manor's command post at Danang, the Pentagon Command Center, and the White House situation room. Washington would know within a minute or two exactly what was going on at Son Tay. The whole operation, Moorer reminded the President, was keyed to Simons being on the ground not more than 30 minutes, hopefully only 20. As soon as he called the choppers back to extract the assault force, the code word would be passed on how many prisoners had been rescued. It would take only two minutes to get the message to Washington.

"How many more POWs will we find out are dead if we wait much longer?" the President said. It was a reference to the death of six more American POWs on the list turned over by Cora Weiss on the previous Friday, November 13. The only similar list had been turned over by North Vietnam the preceding January, naming five dead U.S. airmen—all of whom, it was reported, had died before they hit the ground. But this latest list caused the Pentagon and the White House grave concern about the treatment of Americans held prisoner in the north. Two names, in particular, raised haunting questions. The first man on the list was Air Force Major Edwin L. Atterbury. The DIA had learned that he had escaped early in 1969 in "fairly robust health," but was recaptured soon after he got "over the fence." Yet, the DIA also knew, Ed Atterbury had never been seen or heard from again by a fellow POW. North Vietnam would only report that he "died in captivity" on May 18, 1969.

Another airman on the new list was Air Force Major Wilmer N. "Newk" Grubb, shot down almost five years earlier, in January of 1966. North Vietnam had released five photographs taken of him after his capture. Except for a minor knee injury, Grubb looked in good health; he appeared strong, head held high. Those pictures were published in at least ten Communist countries. Although his wife, Evelyn, never received a letter from him, the photos had sustained her for almost five years, knowing he was alive and "wonderful to see." But when the list of November 13, 1970, was "clarified" by North Vietnam's representatives in Paris, they said that Newk Grubb had died on

February 4, 1966, of "injuries sustained in his plane crash." That was only nine days after his capture, *before* any of the pictures of him had been published. One picture caption had spoken of how "humanely" Major Grubb was being treated. But, if Hanoi's latest information was correct, the photo was printed days *after* he died.

The grim significance of Grubb's death was on everyone's mind in the Oval Office as the President deliberated about the proposed Son Tay rescue. Had Hanoi propagandized to the whole world the humane treatment of a dead man? Were his captors fostering thoughts of life and hope, when there was only death? Why had Hanoi let those hopes linger for almost *five years?* If Newk Grubb died nine days after his capture, North Vietnam had perpetrated a deliberate, premeditated deception of a kind that only barbarians would consider. Were the other prisoners living, or dying, an equally uncertain and cruel fate?

The President mused silently for a few moments. Finally, he asked, "How could anyone *not* approve this?" It was a rhetorical question. The President told Moorer, "Tom, I know you guys have worked months on this. I want those POWs home too. Hell, if this works, we could even have them here for Thanksgiving dinner, right here at the White House. But I don't want to put any more into those camps, either."

And, the President added, he couldn't afford any more near-riots. The march on Washington just six months earlier, after the Cambodian invasion, still haunted him. "Christ, they surrounded the White House, remember? This time they will probably knock down the gates and I'll have a thousand incoherent hippies urinating on the Oval Office rug. That's just what they'd do."

The President also wondered if Fulbright would call the raid "an invasion" of North Vietnam. "This one could hurt, Tom," he concluded. "But I know you're up for it. I'm sure we'll go; just give me a little time to mull it over. Whatever happens, good luck." He got up and stuck out his hand to shake Moorer's; it was a warm, appreciative gesture, the kind Richard Nixon wasn't too noted for.

Haig asked Moorer quietly if he could leave an extra copy of his briefing book for the President to review in private—charts, maps, and all. Before he left the Oval Office, Moorer quickly segregated materials to be left with the President from those he would take back to the Pentagon.

In the hallway outside the Oval Office, one of the participants at the meeting stopped Moorer briefly. He spoke very softly. "Tom, you did one hellova job. The boss was visibly moved; I can tell you that. He'll approve it." Then he paused awkwardly: "One thing, Tom. If this thing fails, maybe we could find a way to let the Old Man off the hook? He's taken nothing but bum raps on every decision he's made about Vietnam. We can't let him down on this one. You know what I mean."

Moorer drove back to the Pentagon in silence. As soon as he arrived, he asked Train to pass his thanks to Blackburn and Mayer for the effective changes in the charts and a well-laid-out briefing book. But what Blackburn would really want to know, Train realized, was, "Did we get a go-ahead?" Train didn't know. He decided to pass the word that Moorer was "very pleased" and they'd have a decision "shortly."

Moorer thought he knew, but he wasn't really sure. The President had seemed very positive, almost effusive in his few compliments. He'd asked only a few questions. Yet he seemed worried, apprehensive, more thoughtful than Moorer had seen him in many of their so-called decision briefs. What really bothered Moorer, however, was that remark about "a way to let the Old Man off the hook."

The President made his decision rapidly. Late that afternoon he gave Laird the go-ahead for the raid. Moorer was gratified by the decision, and Blackburn and Mayer began immediately to set the necessary wheels in motion. But still troubled by that conversation in the hallway outside the Oval Office, Moorer told Blackburn: "Don, there's one thing we'd all ought to think about." He spoke in a confidential tone. "Ah, I don't think the President knows about this one."

Moorer would not recall the exchange and denied categorically that anyone ever suggested he might have to take the "rap" if something went wrong at Son Tay. But then it was not likely that he would feel free to admit any such suggestion had been made. Blackburn, however, would remember the encounter vividly and made a cryptic note of it in his personal daily log. "Moorer didn't need to tell me," he would recall later, "that if we screwed up, he would take the rap, no one else. And he was reminding me that the purpose of his White House visit that day was for only a few to know and that we might all end up keeping out mouths shut about Son Tay."

The Cigarettes

When word came late in the afternoon of November 18 that the President had approved the raid, the SACSA team swung into action. For months this was the moment Blackburn and Mayer had been working and planning for. But some anxious—and ludicrous—moments lay ahead. Mayer quickly encoded the "Execute" message from a prearranged code pad and took it to Vogt for approval. The message was brief, something very close to: "Mumbletypeg, Amputate Kingpin." But Vogt looked at it and said, "For Christ's sake, this doesn't make any sense." Mayer explained that it would when Manor looked up the prearranged code words. Vogt didn't believe it. There had already been one communications foul-up, and Mayer couldn't convince him there wasn't about to be another. He had to go back down to his office in the Pentagon basement, unlock a secure filing cabinet within a secure vault, take out the communications plan for Kingpin, lock up the cabinet and vault again, and hurry back to Vogt's office to show him that the message was correct. Vogt finally initialed the order; Mayer then had to take it to Moorer, who took it to Laird, who signed it. Then Moorer initialed it, and Mayer could send it, praying that it wouldn't get lost somewhere between the Pentagon and Thailand.

It left the JCS message center at 5:30 P.M. that afternoon on a RED ROCKET transmission, a special, ultra-fast, direct message procedure usually reserved for the kind of international crises suggesting that World War III might be imminent.

While Mayer was flapping to get the "Execute" message approved and sent, Blackburn got bad news about weather. Typhoon Patsy had hit Manila with winds of 105 miles an hour and gusts of 140; and it was moving west at about 80 miles an hour. Satellite photos taken of the objective area showed that it was clear, but a cold front was moving toward it from China. The typhoon and cold front might converge over North Vietnam. Blackburn recalled that meteorologists had sifted through years of Southeast Asia weather data to pick November 20 to 25 as a good window. Now that the President had given a final okay, it looked like they had picked dead wrong.

But there was still a lot of last-minute coordination to be done. Blackburn met with Jim Allen and Navy Captain Don Engen to resolve Air Force and Navy responsibilities for processing the prisoners, and for their medical care once they arrived home. The normal procedure for evacuating wounded men from Southeast Asia was to send them to whatever military hospital was closest to their homes. Where to take the rescued POWs, however, had spawned an inter-service debate that became "one of the biggest problems" Mayer had grappled with for weeks. In this case, *every* service wanted the POWs, and each had "yakked for hours and hours, day after day," to make its case. Mayer told Blackburn the debate had become "as laughable as the second 'attack' on Aparri" in northern Luzon —all because the "POWs meant publicity out the kazoo." At one point, Mayer had proposed a compromise. There were no Army POWs at Son Tay, he reminded everyone, so the freed men should be flown first from Thailand to Tripler Army General Hospital in Hawaii—it was "neutral." Once cleared for further travel, they could be flown to the hospital closest to their homes. But the Air Force insisted that *its* POWs were going to be in Air Force hospitals, not Army or Navy ones; and the Navy wanted *its* prisoners, including the Marine POWs, in Navy hospitals, no one else's. Blackburn was determined not to let the raid on Son Tay become another public relations attack. Allen and Engen agreed with him: care of the POWs came first, not the image of their services. The three decided that after a quick physical in Thailand, the prisoners would all be flown to the closest big hospital, at Clark Air Force Base in the Philippines. Then they could be evacuated, Blackburn conceded, to the respective Air Force or Navy hospitals closest to their homes.

As Blackburn left the Pentagon around six that evening, he was concerned that the large-scale redeployment of rescue units—medical evacuation C-9A jet transports from the Philippines to stand by in Thailand, as well as HH-53 rescue helicopters moving from their staging bases in central Thailand to the northern launch sites closer to North Vietnam—would "light up" the North Vietnamese warning system. When he arrived home, he was still wondering what more, if anything, could be done to prevent that system from "going hot." Then a new and bigger problem came up.

Rear Admiral James C. Donaldson was calling from the Pentagon. Donaldson was the JCS Deputy Director, J-3, for Reconnaissance. He asked Blackburn if a certain Air Force colonel, who had deployed to Thailand with Manor, was "one of your people?" Yes, Blackburn acknowledged noncommittally, the officer was; what was the problem? The officer had called Strategic Air Command headquarters in Omaha from Southeast Asia, Donaldson explained, alerting them that "the operation" might "go early" and that some refueling missions and preplanned reconnaissance tracks might have to be rescheduled. SAC's reconnaissance center didn't know what the hell the officer was talking about, but he wouldn't go into detail. SAC's reconnaissance office had called Donaldson for clarification. Donaldson wanted to know if the officer was authorized to make that kind of call on an unsecure voice circuit. He thought that any such rescheduling would come from Manor through his office.

Blackburn was livid. No, the officer wasn't authorized to tell SAC a thing, he said. So compartmentalized was the Son Tay planning that *no* one in SAC was cleared to know why it was flying all those SR-71, Buffalo Hunter, and Big Bird reconnaissance satellite missions over western Vietnam, or what the KC-135 and RC-135 missions laid on for November 20–25 were all about. SAC's officers were also savvy enough not to ask.

Blackburn asked Donaldson to stand by in the National Military Command Center, while he got back to the Pentagon as soon as he could. But before leaving home, Blackburn called Air

Force Colonel Franklin C. Rice at home and asked him to meet Donaldson and him in the command center "right away." Rice had been on the Son Tay planning group to arrange everything that would have to be handled in the command center, including communications from the Pentagon to Manor, CINCPAC headquarters in Hawaii, Task Force 77, and all of the commands that would support the operation from the SR-71 reconnaissance base in Okinawa to the medical evacuation plane standing by at Clark Air Force Base in the Philippines. Blackburn told Rice that he might need a fast telephone "patch" to their "friend" overseas.

At the Pentagon, Blackburn got on the phone with Donaldson and Rice to SAC headquarters. He asked to talk directly with the officer to whom the call from Thailand had been made. He was Colonel John Clancey, the SAC reconnaissance office duty officer. Blackburn explained that he was just going to ask questions, not answer any. Did the "character in the plot" say the operation "might" go early or "would" go early? Clancey told him, "might." Did he indicate "what operation?" "No," Clancey said, that's why he had decided to call Donaldson: they couldn't figure out what was going on, much less what it was that SAC was supposed to do.

Blackburn asked Rice to get Manor on the phone right away. There was no secure voice circuit to Takhli, Rice explained, so they would have to talk "in the clear." When Blackburn reached Manor, he told him he had been talking with some friends in the Midwest and suggested that Manor might want to strangle one of his officers with a "piano wire" because he had been playing some unauthorized "music." All the music had done, Blackburn concluded, was confuse an audience that shouldn't have been invited to the concert anyway.

It was close to midnight when Blackburn arrived back home. He still didn't have the foggiest notion why SAC had been alerted that the operation might go "early." Nor had Manor been able to clear it up in their guarded phone conversation. He had sounded as confused and irritated as Blackburn was.

Blackburn was to get only a few hours' sleep. Shortly after 4:00 A.M. he was awakened by the phone. It was Ed Mayer calling from the Pentagon Command Center. A message had just arrived from Manor, logged in at 4:11. Simons' men and Task Force 77 were ready, but "a delay due to weather was possible." Blackburn wondered what the hell was going on; was the raid going "early" or was it going to be "delayed"?

When he arrived at the Pentagon a few hours later, Thursday, November 19, his confusion mounted. He learned that if the raid didn't go on schedule, if it was delayed just one day, it might "foul up other operations." No one would tell him what those "other operations" entailed. But if the raid had to be delayed, he was told, the President would be at Camp David Saturday and wanted to be kept "in close contact" with every development.

It was only two days from the "primary launch date"; and when Blackburn saw Moorer at eight o'clock that morning, he told him of the weather problem. All they could do now, of course, was sweat it out. But weather turned out to be the least of their problems that day. Another kind of typhoon was brewing.

Blackburn spent much of the day reviewing NSA's latest electronic intercepts; an updated "air order of battle" message was sent to Takhli, giving Manor a last-minute status report on North Vietnam's air defense system. When he returned to his office about 4:30 P.M. that afternoon, he learned that DIA's General Bennett was looking for him, "excited as hell, really agitated" about something, and on his way to the chairman's office.

They caught up with each other just as Bennett was entering Moorer's suite. "Don, I've got bad news," Bennett told him. Once inside Moorer's office, he dropped his bomb: "It looks like Son Tay is empty." The prisoners had been moved.

Moorer was stunned: "Oh, my God, don't tell me that now."

The "Execute" message had gone out 24 hours before. Blackburn couldn't believe that six months of work had led to this. "Now wait a minute," he interjected, "who says so?"

Bennett said the information was straight from Hanoi.

"The word" had come from Nguyen Van Hoang. Early that week, he had met an old friend in Hanoi's Chi Lang Park, six

blocks northwest of Hoa Lo Prison and four blocks from the
Ba Dinh Sports Club, where they first became acquainted.
Hoang's friend was "Alfred"—an "elf-in-council" or "good
counselor"—the U.S. code name for a senior and long-time
staff member of the three-nation International Control Commission. Set up as a result of the 1954 Geneva accords which
partitioned North and South Vietnam, the ICC was powerless
to enforce that armistice, but its members were occasionally
very effective spies—for one side or the other, sometimes
both. Twice weekly, flights carried them from Hanoi's Gia
Lam commercial airport to Vientiane, Laos; there, connections could be made to Bangkok and then home for leave or
"diplomatic consultations."

For years, some members of the ICC staff had tried to help
American intelligence pin down the location of North Vietnam's POW camps. They worked hard at it, but with little
success. Figuring that North Vietnam wouldn't allow commercial flights to fly directly over any of the outlying POW camps
during their approaches into Gia Lam, they carefully noted
such minute details as the time and duration of every bank and
turn on the Vientiane-Hanoi flights.

In the fall of 1969, Alfred tried a more direct approach, quietly cultivating the trust of Nguyen Van Hoang. He did so at
first by accidentally dropping some information Hoang's interrogators had been trying to extract from POWs, but which
American officials were reasonably sure, from their debriefings
of the two POWs released by Hanoi in August of that year, had
not been compromised. Alfred made it sound as if some drunk,
offensive American colonel had done too much bragging on a
flight from Bangkok for three days of "R&R" in Hong Kong. It
was, of course, a carefully planted nugget, something Hoang
could report to his superiors as having pieced together from the
POW interrogations. The DIA and SACSA worked carefully to
make sure that the information was soon corroborated for
North Vietnam's defense ministry through other sources.

After a time, Alfred became an invaluable, if infrequently
seen friend of Hoang. The "research" office of North Vietnam's
Enemy Proselyting Office had been thwarted for years by its

inability to obtain much hard intelligence from POW interrogations, but it was now providing an occasional gem. Hoang's humor and eloquence improved; coincidentally, harsh treatment of the POWs eased somewhat. By late September of 1970, Alfred had reported that he believed Hoang was ready for the "hook"—an outright trade of information. The opportunity arose in early November. Alfred told Hoang he would be flying home for "consultations" in a few days; in fact, he confided, it might be about a big promotion. The only thing conceivably blocking it was his foreign ministry's frustration over Alfred's inability to evoke any new response from Hanoi on the POW issue. His foreign office, like others on the "neutral" ICC, was playing both sides against the middle, trying to please Washington as well as Hanoi. In fact, Alfred noted, he had almost been "challenged" in a recent cable to report on how many POWs were really held in the north. American diplomats weren't "buying" a list of only 339 men released by Hanoi early the previous April and were putting pressure on foreign offices all over the world to find out. Alfred mused aloud: "They must really be uptight: I bet they would give anything for a convincing answer." Hoang suggested they meet again, perhaps for a stroll in Chi Lang Park, a day or two before Alfred was to fly home.

When they met again, they enjoyed a pleasant meeting. Hoang wished Alfred success on his pending promotion and then apologized for having to break off their visit early. He had to check on some POWs who would be shown to American peace activist Peter Weiss (husband of Cora) on his visit to Hanoi later in the week. As they broke up, Hoang handed Alfred a package of Thuoc La Bien cigarettes. Alfred would remember his words vividly. "Here, you might enjoy these on your trip. They're pretty strong, so don't smoke them too fast," Hoang said. Alfred noticed that the pack was partially open. "Just wanted to make sure they were fresh," Hoang added, smiling. Waiting at Gia Lam Airport the next day for his plane, Alfred casually lit up one of the cigarettes: it was awful. Besides, he didn't smoke, and Hoang knew it. Obviously, there was some significance to this pack. On arriving in Hong Kong, Alfred immediately turned the cigarettes over to a friend for examination.

Hoang's package of cigarettes was decoded in Washington by midday the following Thursday, just a few hours before Bennett met Blackburn in Moorer's office. DIA's analysts were intrigued at how clearly Hoang had used one version of the POW's own tap code to spell out the number of men held in each camp. They hoped he had not broken the other versions. But Son Tay was not on the prison list. According to Hoang's head count, most of the POWs, about 150 of them, were in a new camp never heard of before, at a place called Dong Hoi.

When DIA's photo interpreters hauled out their most recent reconnaissance photos of the converted Army barracks at Dong Hoi, they saw that the sprawling compound had been enlarged significantly. New walls divided the complex into smaller compounds, and the guard towers were manned. At the same time, however, the photo specialists showed Bennett the latest SR-71 photos of Son Tay. Some of them were infra red imagery and revealed that the camp was active; *someone* had moved back to Son Tay.

That was Bennett's bad news, and after explaining where it had come from, he told Moorer and Blackburn that he rated this new information "B-3"—close to tops. "B" meant it was a foreign intelligence source in the field; "3" meant that the source was "usually reliable," with direct access to the information supplied.

Listening to Bennett, Blackburn was not entirely convinced that Son Tay might now be empty. He told Moorer and Bennett, "That pigeon hasn't clucked before. I don't completely buy this: I'd like to see how they arrived at that conclusion." He asked Moorer if he could report back to him at six the next morning with his own assessment. Moorer and Bennett readily agreed.

As they left Moorer's office, Bennett told Blackburn to go down to DIA's "Collection and Surveillance" center in Room 2D921 "and make my guys lay it all out for you. If you need any help, call me. But I'm afraid we're too late."

Bennett's emotion welled up as he said "too late," for there was other bad news. Whatever the situation at Son Tay, even if *all* of the prisons were about to be busted successfully, it was too late for several more American POWs. In addition to the six dead POWs whose names peace activist Cora Weiss had released on the previous Friday, the 13th, Bennett had just learned there were 11 more. Their names were on a list she had just received but was not to turn over to the government for another four days, until Monday, November 23. Nevertheless, its secret had been unlocked by DIA's and NSA's "Gamma" intercepts.

For more than a year, Cora Weiss had been a courier for the American intelligence community—but she didn't know it.

From 1969 on, every time Cora Weiss stepped off an airplane from Hanoi or from a visit to North Vietnam's peace delegation in Paris, she was placed under surveillance. The NSA also set up intercepts of her telegrams, cables, and long-distance telephone calls through the microwave stations which relayed them. She was only one of many such "targets," which also included Black Panther leader Eldridge Cleaver, actress Jane Fonda, antiwar activist Tom Hayden, and anyone else who visited North Vietnam. It was all part of the Gamma special intelligence operation run by the NSA and the DIA, and illegal as hell because it was targeted against American citizens using domestic as well as foreign intercepts. It was an elaborate, expensive procedure—and occasionally very effective. The few officers cleared to know of the intercepts had taken a "blood oath" never to utter the word Gamma.

There were about 20 different code designations for the Gamma intercepts, all four-letter suffixes like "Gamma Gilt," "Gamma Goat," or "Gamma Gyro," with the suffix designating a specific target, method, or source. One of them referred to mail openings, or the "mail cover," as the CIA preferred to call it; Cora Weiss's mail was opened regularly. Another part of this special intelligence operation was code-named "Delta," although it concerned only information picked up about Russian military operations. At the DIA, all such intercepts were handled by the "Gamma-Delta officer," and information from them was classified "Top Secret (Trine)," followed by the appropriate Gamma designation. "Trine" was the highest and most sensitive of three designations for special intelligence of this nature.

What the NSA and the DIA were looking for, in Cora Weiss's case, was advance word that she had new POW or casualty lists, who was on them, which POWs and North Vietnamese officials she had spoken with or seen, and everything she had observed —but might not report to U.S. authorities. This latest intercept confirmed the desperate plight of the American POWs. Of the 17 newly known dead on her two lists, 11 were known to have been held as POWs in the north, 5 had been listed as missing in action there, 1 as missing in Laos. There was no information on the cause of their deaths.

That news made it even more imperative to find out whether or not American POWs were still being held at Son Tay. Blackburn hurried back to his own office and told Mayer to call Spots Harris at the DIA. He wanted to meet with Harris' "entire team" and personally go over "every shred" of evidence, every "stitch" of data.

It was now close to 5:30 P.M. Mayer made the call and came back to Blackburn's office with more bad news. All of DIA's "guys" had left for the day.

Blackburn was incredulous—and mad. He picked up the phone, got Harris on the line, and told him to call everyone back. Harris suggested that DIA's team could come in "early in the morning for another look." They were probably all in traffic jams about now. Blackburn said he'd gladly wait until Harris got them into reverse gear. All Blackburn wanted was for "every swinging dick" to be back in the Pentagon as soon as Harris could round up his scattered herd; and he wanted them to bring every "thread" they had on Son Tay. He didn't care if they spent the next 12 hours there; Moorer was expecting a report at 6:00 A.M. If they were right and Son Tay was empty, Moorer would have to recall the raid. But if they didn't work fast enough, it might even be launched—while the nation's military intelligence experts were sound asleep in their suburban Virginia beds.

Harris got the men back. Late that night, Blackburn, Mayer

and Harris looked, listened, and read as DIA's experts spelled out how they had learned the prisoners were no longer in Son Tay. They also argued about what it meant.

Mayer bought their evidence. He thought Blackburn should recall the raid. To Mayer, the new camp at Dong Hoi looked like an even more promising target; it was almost as isolated as Son Tay and there were more prisoners in it. He thought everyone should "back off" and hit the new camp in a month or two.

Blackburn said he still wasn't convinced. Hoang's message, he agreed, was unambiguous; the POWs had been moved, and the DIA knew where. But the message was from a source whose reliability, in Blackburn's view, was unproven, if not suspect. DIA's photo interpreters, on the other hand, were certain that "somebody" was back in Son Tay. The camp *was* active, much more so than it had been for weeks. They just didn't know *who* was in it.

Blackburn didn't understand how anyone could form *any* conclusions from the mess in front of him. He had Harris' people go through every method of analysis, from beginning to end. He still couldn't see, he badgered them, "how in the hell" they could make "heads or tails out of the data." He was "flabbergasted" by their interpretation. One minute they were "sure" the prisoners were gone, the next they were "suspicious" that POWs had been moved back into Son Tay.

He later recalled telling them in exasperation: "Look you clowns, don't waffle it. I need an answer. I'll be back at five in the morning. At six, I'm going in with General Bennett to tell the chairman that they are there, or they are not there. All I want out of you guys is an answer—at five o'clock tomorrow morning: *Are* they there, or *aren't* they? That's all. No waffling, no explanations, no chatter, no talk. Just tell me they *are* there or they are *not* there. Because at six tomorrow morning the chairman and the President have got to decide, go or no go. Are we going to go or aren't we?"

Blackburn told them he didn't have the "foggiest notion" of what that decision would be. "But I want an *unequivocal* answer," he said. "And you're not going to dream one up in your sleep. I want it based on some decent intelligence. You guys get

your asses back to Arlington Hall or wherever, because at five
A.M., we need answers, not a bunch of bullshit."

Blackburn was sure in his own mind what the answer should
be. The raid should go. Even with doubt that the prisoners were
there, but with a 95 to 97 percent confidence factor that Simons
could get in and out safely, it was more than worth the try. If
it turned out that POWs had been moved back to Son Tay but
no attempt was made to rescue them, it would have been unfor-
givable—and, Blackburn feared, "we'd never be given another
chance."

There was nothing more he could do. He and Mayer drove
home. They had barely fallen asleep when their phones rang
shortly after 4:00 A.M. A message had been received from
Manor at 3:56 A.M.; the raid would be *advanced* 24 hours.
Manor had given a "final go" to Simons and Task Force 77, and
advised CINCPAC headquarters. In the dark of that Friday
morning, November 20, Blackburn and Mayer rushed back to
the Pentagon, bleary-eyed from a week of nightmares that
might soon come true.

"God Almighty," Blackburn thought to himself on the drive
down the George Washington Parkway, "the spooks are going
to convince Moorer to call the whole thing off." To him, a
successful raid into a "dry hole" would be better than no raid
at all.

Mayer had the opposite concern. Heading for the Pentagon,
he thought: "That crazy Blackburn is going to invade North
Vietnam so Bull Simons can land in an empty prison camp." But
he had other problems to worry about. *If* the raid was going to
go, he had only a few hours to get the Pentagon Command
Center ready. And Moorer, Laird, and all the "brass" would
have to have briefing books before them as the operation unfolded. He had left the Pentagon a few hours ago thinking that
they could be made up on Friday, for a raid that wasn't scheduled until Saturday.

As soon as he reached the Pentagon, Mayer got on the phone
to call in his command center duty officers and alert the service
DCSOPS that Kingpin would launch that day. Meanwhile,
Blackburn met again with Harris and his DIA experts. It was

five o'clock in the morning when he asked them calmly, "Yes or No?" They began to hedge: "Yes, but . . ." Blackburn cut them off. "Don't give me any buts. All I want is, 'Are they there or not?' That's what I'm telling the chairman, that's what your boss has to tell the chairman. If the chairman asks any questions, you can answer them then. But *first* you tell him 'They're there' or 'They're not.' He needs answers, not questions."

It was time for him to meet with Moorer and Bennett in the Chairman's office. Bennett was candid. He held a stack of cables, photos, and messages in one hand. "I've got this much that says 'They've been moved,' " he told Moorer. In the other hand was another thick folder: "And I've got this much that says 'They're still there.' "

Moorer asked him, "What do you recommend?"

"I recommend we go," Bennett said.

Blackburn tried not to reveal his relief.

"Bennett had the death warrant in his hand," he said later. "I thought, 'Damn, the whole thing's about to collapse.' Hell, I knew Bull would get in there and bring his guys back. I wanted to *go.*"

Moorer took Bennett "in tow" and headed for Room 3E880, Laird's office. There, over breakfast, they told the Secretary of Defense that Leroy Manor had already issued the launch order to rescue POWs from a camp which they now knew, but Manor didn't, might be empty. Bennett told Laird the prisoners were "gone," but that it was his opinion they "might have been reintroduced" into Son Tay.

Admittedly, results of the latest photo reconnaissance flights were inconclusive. The Buffalo Hunter failures and the lack of recent low-level coverage made interpretation difficult. The weather made it impossible. The November 6 mission, for instance, had produced a perfect photo—of the only cloud within a mile or so of the camp. It was directly over the compound. On November 13, there had been wisps of clouds directly over the compound, and so many shadows that the large-scale photos were of only marginal quality. The rest of the objective area appeared "normal." The last chance for photographic "prisoner verification" had been with the mission flown on Wednesday,

November 18. But that SR-71 had an airborne emergency ("equipment problems") and had to land in Thailand. Because there was no special equipment there to "download" the sensor payload, or personnel cleared even to see what the working guts of the plane looked like, the film would not arrive back at Yokota where it could be processed and "read" until Friday evening, the 20th. By then, the raid would be under way.

When Bennett got word that the November 18 "shot" had gone awry, he immediately arranged to "lay on" another mission very early on the morning of the 20th. Two passes would be made over the objective. SAC's crews and DIA's interpreters would work quickly to see what the photos looked like, and the information would be relayed from Yokota to Manor at Monkey Mountain near Danang by "Autovon" telephone "in coded form" at eight in the evening, three and a half hours before Simons' men would take off from Udorn into North Vietnam.

If the news was bad, the raid could still be recalled by RED ROCKET message, Moorer told Laird. But, he added, there was still a "50-50" chance. He wanted to try. He wanted to "go" even if there was only a "10 percent chance." News of those 17 dead POWs weighed heavily on his mind. Yet Moorer was torn. "Nothing is ever black or white," he would explain later. With cruel irony, on the same day he had learned from one source that the raid at Son Tay would be too late, he also learned from another that it was all the more urgent to launch one.

Laird agreed. He told Moorer to let the raid on Son Tay go as planned. If the camp was empty, if the raid failed for any other reason, they might find a way to conceal that the operation had ever been launched.

Long after the raid was over, Ed Mayer would remark, "It was probably the toughest decision that Laird ever had to make."

Soon after Moorer and Bennett left his office, Richard Helms, the CIA's Director, arrived. Laird went over the Gamma intercepts and conflicting intelligence reports with him, but told Helms he had decided the raid should go as planned. Laird noted, ironically, that Cora Weiss's husband would be in Hanoi as the raid was underway. When Helms left, Laird checked the

Southeast Asia weather reports once more: two of the "decision points" spelled out in the Kingpin briefing book before him were a "Final weather 'Go/No Go' " by 9:18 A.M., Washington time, and a final chance to "Abort operation prior to launch" at 10:08. Laird picked up a direct, secure phone to the White House and asked to speak with the President. He briefed Nixon on the grim news that Bennett and Moorer had presented over breakfast, that NSA's and CIA's latest Gamma intercepts revealed that Cora Weiss had a list of 11 more dead POWs, making a total of 17 so far that month. Worse yet, three of the men on the latest list had died in 1970, one of them in October and one only 15 days ago. Then Laird told the President that he now had a report that Son Tay prisoners had been moved but that SR-71 photos showed the camp had been reoccupied by "someone." He had decided, Laird said, to let the raid "go." Nixon agreed. He asked Laird to keep him posted as the operation unfolded.

FOUR

"Kingpin"

Takhli Royal Thai Air Force Base

The Son Tay raiders landed under cover of darkness at Takhli, Thailand, after a grueling 9,500-mile, 28-hour flight from Eglin Air Force Base via California, Hawaii, Guam, and the Philippines. Manor and Simons were on hand to greet them when they stepped off the plane. It was 3:00 A.M. Wednesday, November 18, in Thailand—12 hours ahead of Washington time.

Even at this late date, only four men in the ground force—Simons, Sydnor, Cataldo, and Meadows—knew what the target was or how soon the raid would be launched. But everyone sensed that the real show was imminent. Security was intense. Aboard the plane from the States, for instance, none of the men wore any insignia of rank or any U.S. Army identification on their uniforms. Even their green berets had been collected at Eglin and flown to Thailand ahead of time on a C-141 which also carried their specially rigged satchel charges and other explosives. When they stepped down the C-141's rear loading ramps at Takhli, they were quickly boarded into closed vans, not buses, for the short ride to their billets in a secure area on a remote corner of the sprawling base.

Simons' men were given only six hours to sleep and recover from the "jet lag" of the monotonous, fatiguing trip. At two that afternoon, Manor and Simons briefed them for half an hour. But still they were not told the target, or even where they were. They knew they were somewhere in Southeast Asia, but that could cover a tract of land from Taiwan to Indonesia; for all they knew, the C-141s could have been flying in wide circles for half the trip across the Pacific. Manor and Simons simply said they were now "ready," gave them a rough schedule for the next two days, told them there wouldn't be any time to waste, went through the general air and ground plans they had been rehearsing for weeks, and said they would learn the target as soon as—and "if"—final approval for the mission arrived from Washington.

After a half-hour break, while Sydnor briefed the platoon leaders, the assault teams went through their detailed plans once again. Then they began unpacking their personal gear and web equipment. Chow was served from five to six. For those who wanted to attend, a movie was shown at 8:30 P.M.; some recall that it was the Burt Lancaster prison film, *Bird Man of Alcatraz*. Whatever it was, most of the men thought it was lousy.

At 3:30 A.M. the next morning, November 19, Leroy Manor was awakened and handed a coded RED ROCKET message. It was the one Mayer had had so much trouble getting Vogt to approve. In just three words, it told Manor that the President had given his approval to execute. He had a "final go." Manor was now faced with his toughest decision of the entire operation: when to launch the raid.

It involved the weather. As the Son Tay raiders flew to Southeast Asia, Typhoon Patsy was forming east of the Philippines. By Thursday, the 19th, the typhoon had hit the Philippines and begun moving west, bringing with it some of the foulest weather Southeast Asia had seen in a decade. To make matters worse, a front was moving down from China, and the two were forecast to converge over Hanoi on Saturday, November 21, the primary launch date.

The only thing that could save the day, Manor's weather experts told him, was a high-pressure ridge that might form over Hanoi. If that happened, the clouds might move out of the Hanoi area for a few hours, giving the aircraft just enough of a weather window to get Simons into the target with the quarter-moon visibility on which the entire ground operation would depend.

Manor knew that for the raid to succeed, a rare and precise combination of weather and light conditions had to exist over a distance that spanned 500 miles. A one-quarter to three-quarter moon, 15 to 45 degrees above the eastern horizon, was required for navigation to the target, to reduce detection, and give Simons' men adequate light on the ground. The aircraft could take off from Thailand under instrument conditions, but good visibility was needed between 5,000 and 10,000 feet en route so the A-1s, C-130s, and assault helicopters could join up in close formation. Only light turbulence aloft could be tolerated or the helicopters would not be able to refuel. As the planes crossed over Laos into North Vietnam's Red River Valley, there could be no more than scattered low- and middle-altitude clouds or the assault helicopters would not be able to navigate into the target, since they needed reflections from lakes and rivers for their check points. Only scattered clouds could exist below 3,500 feet or the A-1s could not deliver the cannon fire, fire the rockets, or drop the bombs that might be needed to seal the target off from North Vietnamese reaction forces. Visibility had to be good on the ground and surface winds light for the helicopters to land. For the Navy diversion, seas in the Tonkin Gulf could be no worse than light to moderate; visibility had to be good. Over North Vietnam's coast, ceilings had to be high enough for the Navy attack aircraft to operate all the way up to 17,000 feet.

After six months of planning and three months of rehearsals, everything now hinged on the weather. Manor needed hourly, around-the-clock updates of precise weather information at specific locations all the way from Takhli in Thailand, to Son Tay and Haiphong in North Vietnam, and Yankee Station in the Gulf of Tonkin. But when he settled down in the electronic marvel that was the Takhli Royal Thai Air Force Base operations center, he discovered that he might not be able to get that information. The Air Weather Service had its own rigid set of security restrictions and release authority for access to its classified weather data. Manor, the mission commander of the most sensitive operation of the Vietnam war, found out that he did not have the right clearance.

The Commander, 1st Weather Group, flatly denied Manor access to the last-minute data essential to make the one decision that was his alone. Trying to save prisoners, Manor had become hostage to the bureaucracy. The situation was ludicrous. Manor could not tell the weatherman what the operation was all about, and *he* could not tell Manor what the weather was like. Moreover, Manor learned from his own staff weather officer, there was not time to get the needed approval and clearance from the group commander's higher headquarters, the Military Airlift Command's Air Weather Service at Scott Air Force Base in Illinois. Even if there had been time, security precluded Manor from telling both headquarters why he needed the clearance; he had no secure communications link from Takhli with either headquarters and thus could not even hint at what was going on. The 1st Weather Group commander had a secure voice link of his own, but he would not give Manor access to it. Every military asset in Southeast Asia was ready to support Manor at this juncture, but he could not get a blip of weather information.

In desperation, Manor solved the clearance problem by arranging for a personal, "back channel" message to be sent from the Director of Air Force Operations in the Pentagon directly to the Vice Commander, Seventh Air Force in Saigon. The Commander, 1st Weather Group, soon got a phone call. Although he only "supported" Seventh Air Force instead of reporting to it, he was told in no uncertain terms by a three-star Air Force general that his career would come to a halt unless he gave Manor whatever he needed, immediately, without one more question.

Manor's relief was short-lived, however. No sooner had he been cleared for the data so vital to his operation than he found that Takhli no longer had the right communications net in Thailand to handle the classified weather data. Nor was there a secure voice circuit from Takhli to Monkey Mountain, the elaborate electronics command post north of Danang where Manor would coordinate the raid's air, sea, and ground elements and monitor its progress. There would be no way that he could discuss the weather with Bull Simons and the Air Force flight leaders.

Moreover, the security people were now nervous about all the curiosity being stirred up by last-minute requests to reinstall the weather facsimile display and map plots which long ago had been stored or shipped out as air units redeployed from Thailand in the first three increments of Nixon's withdrawal from Southeast Asia. It was almost the last straw. Manor told his security people to concoct any kind of cover story they wanted to, but get the maps and weather facsimiles released, installed, and operating—fast.

That problem was solved, but the communications problem remained, and needed a quick solution. Manor's communicators at Monkey Mountain and their counterparts at Takhli got to work jury-rigging a workable setup. Without time to fine-tune a secure voice circuit, they settled for clear voice hook-ups backed up by the slower radioteletype. Through double-talk and verbal codes concocted as they conversed, the communications men would be able to convey the essentials of weather information without compromise; that is, if conditions permitted the raid to be launched at all.

The weather wasn't cooperating. When Manor was finally able to get the information he needed, he learned that Typhoon Patsy was forecast to bring high winds, low clouds, rain, and poor visibility to the northern half of South Vietnam, the panhandle of North Vietnam, and the southern Gulf of Tonkin by the evening of Saturday, the 21st. By Sunday, a cold front was expected to enter the Red River Valley; at least four days of very poor weather would follow.

There was one possibility, but a slim one—the high pressure ridge that might form over the Hanoi area. There was some evidence that the ridge was building as forecast: the weather was clearing in southeast China and was just beginning to enter North Vietnam. Manor might have a launch window after all, but it would be marginal, much shorter in duration—hours, not days—and earlier than planned.

It was clear that by Saturday, November 21, Typhoon Patsy would force the raid to be canceled. Within 48 hours, Manor knew, Task Force 77 would be hit by the typhoon itself. The seas were already getting rough. Thus, Manor had two choices: delay for at least five to seven days, hoping for improved weather but marginal light conditions at best; or launch early on the 20th under marginal conditions en route to the target. At 4:11 Thursday afternoon, November 19, he advised the JCS and CINCPAC that a delay due to weather was possible. But by the next morning, November 20, an early launch that night looked like a better bet. Manor sent a message to Admiral Bardshar at 10:10 A.M. It advised him of a "preliminary go."

Manor then ordered a special weather reconnaissance mission flown along the border of Laos and North Vietnam. The RF-4 landed at Takhli early in the afternoon and the report was good. The anticipated high-pressure ridge had moved in over Hanoi. The en route weather was forecast to be scattered to broken clouds from 5,000 to 8,000 feet, no turbulence, good visibility. In the Red River Valley, a few clouds, good visibility, light northwest winds. At 3:56, Manor sent a message to CINCPAC and the National Military Command Center at the Pentagon advising them of his "final go" decision: the raid would be launched 24 hours ahead of schedule. Thirty minutes later, Fred Bardshar got a similar message. Right after issuing the "final go" order, Manor took off for the command post at Monkey Mountain. His decision would prove to be the right one. By Saturday night, the 21st, Typhoon Patsy was less than 100 miles off North Vietnam. The Navy air diversion would have then been impossible; and the raid itself would have been halted by the high winds, extensive clouds, and poor visibility that covered the North Vietnam panhandle. Poor weather would continue into the following week. The night of November 20/21 was the only date within weeks when the Son Tay raid would have been possible. General Dwight D. Eisenhower had been

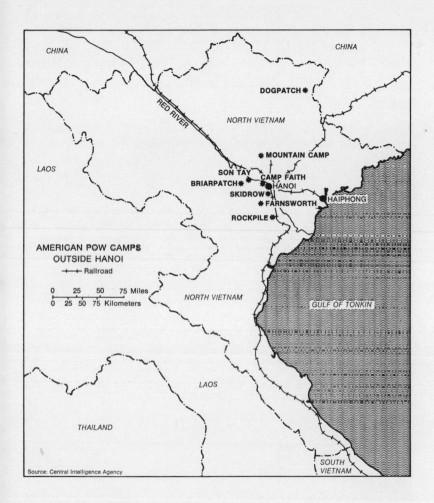

CHINA

CHINA

RED RIVER

DOGPATCH✳

NORTH VIETNAM

LAOS

✳ MOUNTAIN CAMP

SON TAY

CAMP FAITH

BRIARPATCH✳ ✳

✳HANOI

SKIDROW✳ ✳

✳ FARNSWORTH

HAIPHONG

ROCKPILE ✳

AMERICAN POW CAMPS
OUTSIDE HANOI
―✦― Railroad

0   25   50   75 Miles
0   25 50 75 Kilometers

NORTH VIETNAM

GULF OF TONKIN

LAOS

THAILAND

Source: Central Intelligence Agency

SOUTH
VIETNAM

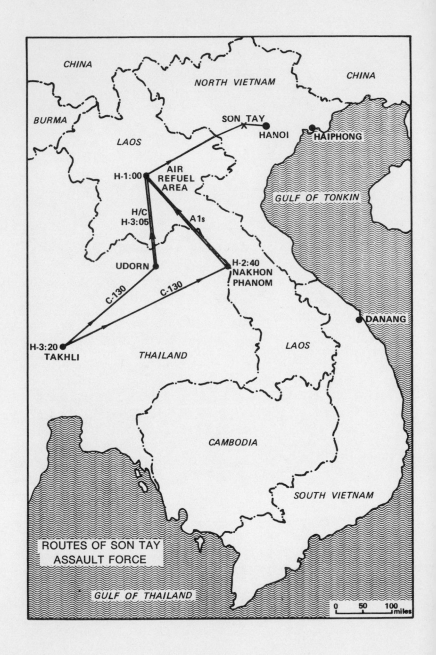

ROUTES OF SON TAY
ASSAULT FORCE

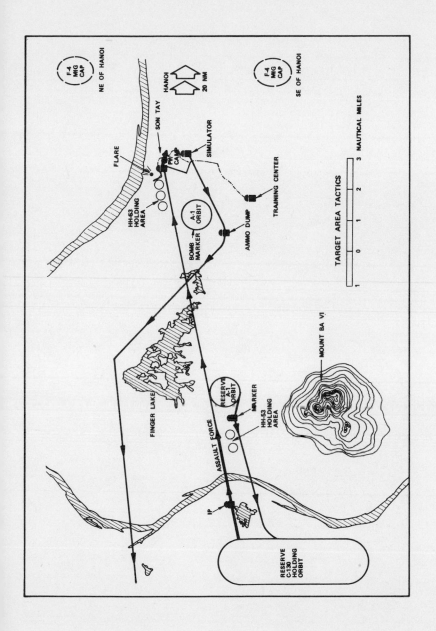

TARGET AREA TACTICS

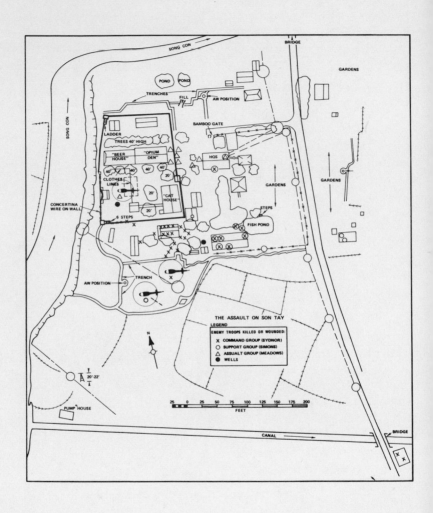

THE ASSAULT ON SON TAY
LEGEND
ENEMY TROOPS KILLED OR WOUNDED:
X COMMAND GROUP (SYDNOR)
○ SUPPORT GROUP (SIMONS)
△ ASSUALT GROUP (MEADOWS)
● WELLS

25 0 25 50 75 100 125 150 175 200
FEET

faced with a similar decision on June 5, 1944—the day before
D-Day. In 1970, Manor didn't think back to the invasion of
Normandy as he grappled with his own weather decision. But,
by slashing through bureaucratic thickets and jury-rigging communications, he too had been able to make a correct but narrow
call.

Udorn Royal Thai Air Force Base

Breakfast on the morning of Thursday, November 19, was
served to Simons' men at six. By nine, they were drawing their
ammunition and satchel charges. After an early, light lunch, the
local Air Force search and rescue commander gave a one-hour
briefing. He showed them how to operate their survival radios,
gave them call signs for the rescue aircraft, and told them,
"Here's how we run a search and rescue mission in *this* theater." He didn't have to tell them that if the SAR effort failed,
they could use their pen-sized signal flare as a pointblank pencil
—either to kill an approaching enemy, or to commit suicide.

Early that afternoon, the three assault teams each spent 45
minutes on the range under Dick Meadows' supervision, test-
firing their weapons. Again, the men and their weapons were
transported by closed van. The firing was not extensive, just
enough for each man to check his weapon and be sure that it
would function properly. Back in the billets, the men cleaned
their weapons quickly. None was disassembled; the men just
cleared the barrels with a cleaning patch and solvent. Then
they began unpacking and checking their satchel and demolition charges.

There was no movie after dinner that night. Instead, the
CIA's operations chief from Udorn, George Morton, gave a
one-hour escape and evasion briefing. A specialist in CAS operations, he talked about Laos, not North Vietnam. Most of his
briefing was on special code signals that the men could use to
alert reconnaissance aircraft when a clandestine pickup might
be made. Finally, Morton gave each man a small, plastic escape
and evasion map and his personal "blood chit." This was a small
piece of silk with a map on one side and an almost invisible,

micro-thin compass sewn into one corner; the other side had such phrases spelled out phonetically, in Lao and Vietnamese, as "Which way is north?"—"I need water"—"Can you find me a doctor?"—or "I am an American." By nine, Simons' men were bunked down, lights out.

On Friday, November 20, the pace quickened. After breakfast, night vision and infra red viewing devices were issued, fitted, checked, and stowed carefully in each man's web harness. After an early lunch, Doc Cataldo surprised everyone by issuing sleeping pills—and then checking personally to make sure that every man swallowed one, even Simons. Manor issued the "final go" order at 3:56 that afternoon, while Simons and his men were asleep. They were awakened at five for chow. Cataldo told them to eat hearty. They would take off in 5 hours; this would be their last meal in 12 hours.

Simons and Sydnor held the final briefing at six o'clock. It lasted 45 minutes. Simons spoke first, for less than three minutes. Right off, he told the men, "We are going to rescue 70 American prisoners of war, maybe more, from a camp called Son Tay. This is something American prisoners have a right to expect from their fellow soldiers. The target is 23 miles west of Hanoi."

For a second or two, there was absolute silence. "You could hear a pin drop," Simons recalled. "I want to tell you it got pretty quiet. Very quiet."

A few men let out low whistles. Then, spontaneously, they stood up and began applauding. Reports would conflict. Some would say "Cheers went up"; but Simons would remember, "No, no, there was no cheering. They just applauded." But their response told him they were ready. "They made me feel good; they wanted to do it, that was obvious—and God damn it, I thought, they ought to want to do it."

Simons had one other thing to say: "You are to let nothing, nothing interfere with the operation. Our mission is to rescue prisoners, not take prisoners. And if we walk into a trap, if it turns out that they know we're coming, don't dream about walking out of North Vietnam—unless you've got wings on your feet. We'll be 100 miles from Laos; it's the wrong part of the world for a big retrograde movement. If there's been a leak, we'll know it as soon as the second or third chopper sets down; that's when they'll cream us. If that happens, I want to keep this force together. We will back up to the Song Con River and, by Christ, let them come across that God damn open ground. We'll make them pay for every foot across the sonovabitch."

Simons turned the briefing over to Sydnor and strode down the aisle. The men stood up again and applauded. As he left the theater, he heard one man say, "Jesus, I'd hate to have this thing come off and find out tomorrow I hadn't been there." Simons told Blackburn later that for the first time in his life, tears came to his eyes.

After Simons' men had "harnessed up" in their barracks and stowed their personal effects—family photos, letters, money, anything that should be returned to their next of kin—they took another ride in the closed vans, this time to the base's biggest hangar. There, a four-engine C-130 waited to take them on board. They made a final equipment check that lasted one hour and 45 minutes. Every weapon was checked, every bandolier of ammunition opened and inspected. It was quite an arsenal for 56 men, 111 weapons in all: 2 M-16 automatic rifles (1,200 rounds of ammunition), 48 CAR-15 assault rifles (with 18,437 rounds), 51 .45 caliber pistols (1,162 rounds), 4 M-79 40 mm. grenade launchers (219 rounds), 4 M-60 machine guns (4,300 rounds), and 2 12-gauge shotguns (100 shells); in addition, they carried 15 Claymore mines, 11 special demolition charges, and 213 hand grenades. Finally, each man strapped a specially made 6-inch knife to his thigh.

Next came a careful check of the special rescue equipment: 11 axes, 12 pairs of wire cutters, 11 bolt cutters, 7 coils of rope, 2 oxyacetylene cutting torches, 2 chain saws, 5 crowbars, 17 machetes, 34 miners' lamps, 6 pairs of handcuffs, one 14-foot ladder, 2 crash hatchets, 4 fire extinguishers, one set of hammer and nails, 5 bullhorns, 6 infra red flashlights, 6 strobe lights, 6 night vision devices, 6 baton lights, 14 "beanbag" lights, and 2 cameras.

Lastly, the platoon leaders carefully went over each man's personal gear: goggles, AN/PRC-90 survival radio, pen flare, pen light, survival kit, strobe light, aviators' gloves, compass, and earplugs. By about ten o'clock, the plane was loaded. The last detail was for each man to camouflage or darken his face and pin his insignia of rank on his collar. The deception was over.

The C-130 taxied to its marshaling apron. It took off at 10:32, Southeast Asia time, 10:32 Friday morning at the White House. From Monkey Mountain, Manor signaled to the Pentagon Command Center at 10:45: Simons' men had departed the Takhli staging base for Udorn.

When they arrived at Udorn, the men transferred quickly from the C-130 to three of the five helicopters waiting at a heavily guarded parking apron. Next to them were two C-141 aeromedical evacuation planes, waiting to fly the prisoners home. In silence, Simons and his troops made a final check of the special medical supplies pre-loaded on the helicopters, 2,-690 pounds in all. They included 150 cans of water, 100 cans of survival food, the special sneakers and lined "poncho-blankets" to keep the prisoners warm—and lots of Doc Cataldo's Heinz baby food. There were also earplugs for every prisoner, to protect him from the roar of the helicopters after years of silence in a prison cell.

At 11:25 P.M., Manor sent another message from Monkey Mountain: the last HH-53 had taken off from the launch base at Udorn with the assault force at 11:18, led by the tanker C-130. But as those helicopters lifted off and began to marry up, an unidentified aircraft flew through the formation on the opposite heading, causing them to disperse. They quickly rejoined, however, and aboard his helicopter, "Apple One," Bull Simons decided to get some more sleep. In exactly three hours, he should land at Son Tay; Simons told his men to wake him up when they were 20 minutes away from the objective.

One of the planes almost didn't make it. The Combat Talon C-130 which was to guide the assault force after the tanker refueled the helicopters couldn't get its number-three, right inboard engine started. Maintenance crews were unable to find anything wrong. Manor ordered the plane to take off with three engines. But as he prepared to take off, Major Irl Franklin, the pilot, made one more try; inexplicably, the engine started, but Franklin was 23 minutes behind schedule.

At four minutes after midnight, another Combat Talon and the A-1s took off from Nakon Phanom to rendezvous with the helicopters and Franklin over Laos. The raid was underway.

Yankee Station

In the Tonkin Gulf aboard the aircraft carrier *Oriskany*, Admiral Bardshar was handed a top-priority, specially coded message at 6:25 on the morning of Thursday, November 19—about the time Simons' men were making a final check-out of their personal gear. The cryptic message was from Manor: "NCA approval received." It meant that the raid would go; the only question now was when. Bardshar set things in motion to launch the Navy diversionary strikes. The weather from Typhoon Patsy was closing in, however, and his carriers were tossing "moderately" in gale-force seas. Two of the carriers would be conducting their first night operations on the eve of their deployment. Bardshar knew he could probably *launch* the planes —his pilots would be glad to be off the heaving, rolling ships— but recovering them in this weather would be a "sporty proposition."

Bardshar had one other problem. His pilots were about to fly one of the largest and most concentrated Navy air operations ever made over North Vietnam—but there was "no authorization for the Navy forces to drop bombs." How the hell, Bardshar wondered, do you send pilots into the North Vietnamese air defense network with no bombs? What do you tell them? There wasn't much he *could* tell them.

Thus, when his carrier and air wing commanders got their preliminary planning briefing, they were read what was probably the oddest operational order ever given to a Navy strike force. They would be flying over Haiphong in the dark, both literally and figuratively. All they could tell their air crews about the purpose of their mission was this:

A special operation will be conducted by a Joint Contingency Task Group in the near future. It will be supported by elements of Task Force 77 whose function will be to create a diversion in order to assist in the successful execution of the basic mission. Security considerations prohibit full disclosure of the exact nature and timing of the operation. . . . Should any questions arise concerning the conduct of this operation, they will be directed to me [Bardshar personally signed the order] personally, by courier whenever possible.

Bardshar had not even permitted the operations order to be transmitted electrically: couriers flew it to the other two carriers, whose commanders were told that they would be waging war with blank ammunition. Bardshar's order read: "It is doubtful that political considerations will permit the expenditure of air-to-ground ordnance other than flares. Within these limits, the objective is to create as much confusion in the NVN command and control system as possible."

No Navy strikes had been flown over North Vietnam for more than two years, since October 31, 1968. Yet Navy carriers had remained on station in the Tonkin Gulf, ready to launch them any day. Finally, the air crews were to be sent back north—but in planes dropping *flares* over the heaviest air defenses in the world. Without being told why. It was bizarre, an archetypical moment of the Vietnam war.

Commander Douglas F. Mow, the skipper of Combat Air Group 19 aboard *Oriskany*, Captain J. E. McKnight, commanding Combat Air Wing 2 aboard *Ranger*, and Captain G. H. Palmer, leading Combat Air Wing 21 from *Hancock*, opened their operations orders. With them were the three carriers' commanders, Captains Frank S. Haak, J. L. Coleman, and T. C. Johnson. The detailed plan which Commander P. D. Hoskins had drawn up in less than ten days told them which planes would launch when and from what carrier, how they would rendezvous, what radio frequencies they would monitor, which call signs would be used, where the planes would orbit and refuel, what navigation tracks would be flown, and precisely when and where the pilots would "attack" Haiphong with Naval aviation "lightbulbs." One of the skippers quipped, "We've flown 300,000 sorties over the north and we're finally going to make them see the light."

Bardshar's operations order wasn't all bad news, however. "Search and Air Rescue efforts over land in NVN are authorized," it read. And if someone was shot down, four A-7 attack aircraft would be "authorized to expend" Rockeye cluster munitions and 20 mm. cannon fire "in support of SAR efforts." But Bardshar had to remind his crews again: "No air-to-ground ordnance is authorized with the exception of the flares carried by Strike aircraft and the Rockeyes and guns carried aboard the Rescue Combat Air Patrol." Bardshar would be able to ease those restrictions at the last minute, however; a few planes could carry "Shrike" radar-homing missiles to suppress North Vietnamese air defense SAMs and radar-directed antiaircraft batteries.

Bardshar's operations order closed with some "special instructions" that clamped a tight lid of security over the naval division:

(1) Once this plan is opened by the designated addressees, disclosure of such portions as necessary to accomplish your assigned mission is authorized. Such disclosure will be restricted to those with an absolute need to know and will be accomplished as late as possible in order to minimize the chances of compromise. Once this plan has been opened, no personal mail will leave your unit and personnel will be transferred only in emergency cases until the operation has been terminated or canceled.

(2) Scheduled D-Day and H-Hour are _____ at _____ [the exact times would be filled in when Bardshar got Manor's "final go"]. These will never be transmitted electrically. . . .

(5) No public statements regarding this operation are permitted even after its completion, unless specifically authorized by [the Commander of Task Force 77]. . . . Additionally, press and other visits to units involved in this operation are to be discouraged whenever possible, provided that such incidents will not lead to unnecessary speculation. Refer all decisions on these matters to [the Commander of Task Force 77]. . . .

(8) Upon termination of this operation, this [operations order] will be destroyed. Message report to originator stating that destruction has been accomplished is required.

Late the next morning, on November 20 at 11:10 A.M. Tonkin Gulf time, Bardshar received another message from Manor; it advised of a "preliminary go." At 4:56 that afternoon, a new message advised of a "final go." Boot Hill and Hoskins both flew from carrier to carrier to brief Task Force 77's air wing and squadron commanders personally. They explained that "D-Day" would be early the next day: the first planes would launch at 2:23 A.M. Tonkin Gulf time (1:23 A.M. over Son Tay). Still they could not divulge the purpose of the mission, although Hill said cryptically that when they learned the real objective, they would approve of it heartily. Hill had the commanders instruct their armament crews to break out a few Shrike missiles, some 20 mm. gun ammunition, and all the flares *Oriskany, Ranger,* and *Hancock* carried. The largest night air operation ever flown over North Vietnam would launch exactly 55 minutes before Bull Simons and his men were to land in Son Tay Prison. Their helicopters would have finished refueling over Laos four minutes after the first A-7 was catapulted off *Ranger*'s pitching flight deck.

A few minutes after 2:00 A.M. on November 21, a newly married Navy lieutenant climbed up to the 1,039-foot-long flight deck of the 78,000-ton U.S.S. *Ranger*. Making the usual walk-around inspection of his A-7 attack plane, he noticed that, just as he'd been briefed, every bomb rack was loaded with *flares.* He decided to resign his commission from Naval aviation as soon as his tour in the western Pacific was over. His father was the Commander, Naval Air Forces, Pacific. The young aviator knew that his father probably wouldn't understand. In fact, the admiral had no idea that his son—or any other Navy pilots—would be flying over Haiphong Harbor that night, armed only with flares.

As *Oriskany*'s deck crews watched the engine plumes of the A-7s and F-8s fade into the night toward Haiphong Harbor, Bardshar made his way below. His brow was furrowed. He had two concerns: would the diversionary raid create enough confusion to prevent air action against the helicopters; and would North Vietnamese MIGs come up to oppose Task Force 77's aircraft? In the carrier's sealed-off Combat Information Center, he put on a set of earphones. Through one part of a "split phone," he would be able to listen to conversations between the strike aircraft, and between them and their carriers; through the other earphone, he would listen to a translation of every intercept from North Vietnam's fighter control net. Thus, he would know on a second-by-second basis what instructions the North Vietnamese air controllers were giving their MIGs. The North Vietnamese were slow to react. For 30 to 35 minutes, that earphone was silent.

It came alive at 2:17 A.M., Son Tay time, exactly one minute before Simons' helicopters were to land at Son Tay. Bardshar heard an excited North Vietnamese MIG pilot asking the control tower at Phuc Yen airfield to "give me a vector, give me a vector." He wanted to know what compass heading to fly, "where the action was." The controller told him to wait. For a moment, Bardshar grew apprehensive. One of the runways at Phuc Yen took off right over the camp at Son Tay, only 22 miles to the southwest; there was now at least one "hot" MIG ready to launch while the raid was under way. But Phuc Yen's control tower remained silent as more pleas came from the pilot—"Give me a vector, give me a vector," he called.

Four long minutes passed. Finally, at 2:21 A.M., Son Tay time, Bardshar heard Phuc Yen's controller tell the MIG pilot, "It doesn't make any difference, they're *all over!*" When the pilot asked him to clarify those instructions, Bardshar heard the controller tell him in desperation, "I don't care what you do. Go to China if you want to."

Bardshar relaxed. The Navy diversion was working. The North Vietnamese were thoroughly confused, and he knew that Simons' force would get in and out of Son Tay without any interference from the air. But there was one thing he didn't know. Bull Simons had just added to North Vietnam's confusion by blowing up the wrong camp.

Son Tay

Nearing Son Tay, Marty Donohue banked his HH-53, "Apple Three," into a tight downward left turn to break off from the rest of the formation. His helicopter was only one of 105 planes launched from five air bases in Thailand and three aircraft carriers in the Gulf of Tonkin now converging on their targets in the most extensive night operation of the Southeast Asia conflict.

Donohue and the assault helicopters behind him descended quickly through the thin layer of scattered clouds hanging 2,000 feet over the Red River Valley. On the ground 500 feet below, his check points came up rapidly, just as advertised—the Black River ten miles west of the target, Finger Lake seven miles out, finally the Song Con River as it turned sharply north two miles south of Son Tay. Donohue slowed to 80 knots as the Combat Talon C-130 pulled up and away from the helicopters. The last two helicopters, "Apple Four" and "Apple Five," climbed to 1,500 feet to perform their role as spare flare-ships in case flares and fire-fight simulators dropped by the C-130 failed to ignite or were off mark.

The Combat Talon pilots had timed the 337.7-mile flight from Udorn perfectly. Irl Franklin had made up his 23-minute delay in departure by eliminating dog legs planned for just such a contingency. After three hours and 23 minutes of twisting, turning, terrain-hugging flight over Laos and down into the Red River Valley, they were less than one minute ahead of schedule. The timing was important. The guards at Son Tay changed on the hour or half-hour, and the raiders wanted to land as close as possible to the quarter hour. That would give the guards who had just come off duty time to fall asleep, and those who had just gone on duty time enough to "settle down."

Donohue wracked the lumbering bird into a hard right 270-degree turn and slowed his chopper to 70 knots. Two and a half months of intensive training, 40 night training flights, and 15 "live-fire" rehearsals were behind him, but only two of those flights involved what he had to do now. Ahead of him, "the lights of Hanoi were beautiful," Donohue recalled later. Suddenly, "just beyond them, the Navy planes had the sky over Haiphong Harbor lit up like the Fourth of July with flares."

Donohue was now two miles from Son Tay.

It was 2:18 Saturday morning, November 21, Hanoi time. The most important five seconds of Marty Donohue's life were coming up, after 16 years and 6,300 hours in the cockpit of a helicopter.

He would be the first man over Son Tay Prison. At treetop level, moving at only a few knots forward air speed, Apple Three would fly between the two guard towers on Son Tay's west wall. Two Gatling gun-like cannons, one mounted in each side door, would open fire and spew out a cone of converging tracer bullets at 4,000 rounds a minute to knock out the guard towers and then a guard barracks just outside the gate on the east wall. Donohue was not to fire on the guard tower at the gate. Beneath it, the DIA had warned him, was the cramped hutch where prisoners were often tortured or kept huddled in solitary. If that guard tower came crashing down, it might kill one of the POWs they were trying to rescue.

Just as the prison came into sight, the sky above Son Tay exploded in brilliant light. The C-130 flare-ship had timed its job perfectly. Donohue and his crew would have been blinded for two or three minutes if they looked directly at the bright flares. Two miles east of Son Tay city and to its south, Donohue could see the fire-fight simulators exploding, as if a ground battle was raging there.

Suddenly, the yellow warning light on his instrument panel started flashing: "Transmission," "Transmission." Donohue's copilot, Captain Tom Waldron, pointed to it excitedly, jabbing at it with his finger. Donohue pushed the intercom button and told his crew, "Hold, hold," meaning not to fire. On any other mission, the "chip light" would have been tantamount to an order for an emergency landing, even over water, and to declare that emergency to any aircraft nearby. Transmission trouble in a helicopter is not something to fool around with: too many transmissions had disintegrated catastrophically when pilots failed to land quickly enough. This time, however, Donohue quietly told his copilot, "Ignore the sonovabitch." He decided not to declare the emergency, knowing that it could cause confusion and concern.

In the last seconds of their approach to Son Tay, there was another tense moment—a "near-miss." As they set up their firing pass, amid the distractions of the ominous flashing of the transmission warning light and the exploding C-130 flares, Donohue and Waldron were unaware that wind changes and lack of reference had caused them to drift slightly to the south, less than 200 yards, of their planned approach. Donohue saw an installation very similar to the Son Tay compound still farther to the south, another 200 yards or so. He turned there momentarily, realized it wasn't the right place—there was no river outside its nearest wall—and quickly corrected course 400 yards to the north. Then he saw the towers on the west wall of Son Tay Prison—but the trees inside the compound just beyond it were higher than he had expected, much higher. Everyone had forgotten how much those 40- or 50-foot trees, photographed so carefully in June, would grow in the heavy summer rains by the time the raid was launched.

Instantly, Donohue pulled up on his collective stick to give the helicopter blades more bite, eased off on the throttle to slow down while he gained precious feet of altitude, and told his crew calmly, "Okay, ten seconds and open fire." Then he eased the helicopter over the trees in the prison courtyard, pushed the intercom button again, and ordered, "Ready—Fire!"

Donohue was too busy flying to see it, but the northwest tower came crashing to the ground within seconds, its 4 × 4-inch support posts chewed to sawdust by an almost solid hail of machine-gun bullets. The southwest tower and a guard barracks beyond the camp were chewed to shreds by subsequent bursts. Donohue's gunners, Staff Sergeants James J. Rogers and Angus Sowell, came on the intercom: "We got 'em, we got 'em. They're out." Donohue applied full throttle, turned to the north as he picked up some altitude, and searched for a small rice paddy east of Finger Lake. There, he set the helicopter down in a "holding area" about one and a half miles west of the objective. All he could do now was sit and wait until Bull Simons' men and the rescued prisoners were ready to be extracted from the target. Donohue and Waldron turned up the volume on their radio sets. For the next 27 minutes, they would monitor a bank of electronics gear as Simons and his men raided the Son Tay compound. Suddenly three hours of radio silence was finally broken. Their cockpit echoed with a cacophony of harsh, discordant FM, UHF, and VHF transmissions. Donohue tried to monitor them all.

The crash landing inside the Son Tay compound was harder, much harder, than Dick Meadows had expected, even lying flat, pressed against a mattress on the HH-3's floor to let his whole body absorb the impact. Meadows did not know it at the time, but his pilot, Herb Kalen, almost lost control of Banana One at the last second when it skimmed the trees and then hit a clothesline strung across the middle of the small compound, hardly as big as a volleyball court. One tree, Herb Zehnder, Kalen's copilot, would recall, "must have been 150 feet tall, much higher than we thought. We tore into it like a big lawn mower. There were limbs, brush, branches, and leaves everywhere. There was a tremendous vibration, the rotor system was damaged and we were down." As the helicopter's blades severed a ten-inch tree trunk, the helicopter twisted violently 30 or 40 degrees to the right, then hit the ground.

The impact was so hard that a fire extinguisher tore loose from its bracket and hit Kalen's flight engineer, Technical Sergeant Leroy Wright, with such force that it broke his ankle. First Lieutenant George L. Petrie, a blond, thirty-one-year-old Green Beret, wasn't supposed to be the first man to exit the helicopter, but he was. He wasn't braced right for the impact. "The crash landing *threw* me out," he explained later.

Dick Meadows got to his feet quickly and ran down the rear ramp clutching his bullhorn. At that moment, it was more important than any weapon he had ever carried; the CAR-15 assault rifle in his other hand and the .45 caliber pistol in his shoulder holster were almost incidental to the job ahead. Fifteen yards from the helicopter, Meadows crouched in a kneeling position, pressed the bullhorn's "trigger," and gasped for his breath to come back. He announced in a calm voice: "We're

Americans. Keep your heads down. We're Americans. This is a
rescue. We're here to get you out. Keep your heads down. Get
on the floor. We'll be in your cells in a minute."

His voice reverberated over the compound.

There were no answering cries.

The thirteen other men in Meadows' assault team streaked
for the cellblocks and front gate. As the whine of the HH-3's
engines died, Son Tay Prison came alive, crackling with automatic weapons fire. Meadows stayed crouched on one knee and
announced once more: "We're Americans. We're here to get
you out." His radio operator called Simons on the command
net, "Wildroot, this is Blueboy. We're in."

Three minutes into the raid, a blast from the south wall
knocked Meadows to the ground, but he was relieved when he
saw the gaping hole there. It meant that Bull Simons' support
group and Bud Sydnor's command team had landed safely outside the compound and the satchel charges had worked. Now
they had a way to get the prisoners out quickly. Meadows saw
a group of men rush through the breached wall and run to their
covering positions inside the compound.

But Meadows was wrong. They weren't Simons' men; they
were all Sydnor's.

Bull Simons had landed at the wrong camp. He and 21 other
men, the biggest part of the Son Tay raiding force, were 400
meters south of the target, plunked down by mistake outside
the compound that the spooks had labeled "Secondary School"
on all of their maps.

Three days before the raid, ironically, intelligence men had
warned Simons and the helicopter pilots that the "Secondary
School" might be mistaken for the real target. Its compound
was about the same size; the canal north of the school could
easily be mistaken for the Song Con River as it turned east just
to the north of Son Tay; and if there were moderate winds in
the Red River Valley, the helicopter formation could easily drift
a few hundred yards south during its final run into Son Tay.
Donohue had drifted south, and trailing Donohue in his HH-3,
Herb Kalen had also turned toward the installation to the south,

but both men caught the mistake and corrected course to the Son Tay compound. Donohue almost broke radio silence to warn the helicopters behind him of the error, but decided against it. Every second of surprise counted. Behind him, however, Warner Britton was too far atrail and too busy concentrating on his landing zone outside the south compound wall to see Kalen change course in the last few seconds.

Piloting Sydnor's chopper, John Allison was far enough above the first three helicopters to see Kalen turn away from the southern complex; he set Sydnor's command group down outside the walls of Son Tay "right on the money." But as Apple Two, Sydnor's chopper, approached its landing point a few yards south of the Son Tay compound, he realized immediately that Simons had landed at the wrong target. He wondered, "What's that crazy sonovabitch doing over there?" At H-Hour plus two minutes and 45 seconds*, Sydnor instinctively told the crew of Apple Two and his own men to put Plan Green into effect. It was the alternate plan they had rehearsed over and over again in Florida in case Simons' support group helicopter aborted or was shot down en route to Son Tay. Sydnor realized that he'd have to pull off the raid with 22 fewer men than planned because the largest part of the raiding force was visiting the wrong part of North Vietnam. The thought didn't bother him very much. He knew exactly what had to be done. Men who had served with him described his reaction to crises this way: "Bud Sydnor has ice water in his veins." As Apple Two slowed to set Sydnor and his men down, John Allison ordered his door gunners to open fire with their miniguns on the guard buildings that Simons' helicopter would have taken under fire.

At the "Secondary School" south of Son Tay, it took Simons only a second or two, after his helicopter landed, to realize that he was in trouble. The school's walls were ringed with barbed wire. Otherwise, the compound and ground outside it looked and sounded like what he expected at Son Tay. Small arms fire

*Times given in this chapter are based on actual tapes of the UHF and FM radio transmissions made during the raid by one of the EC-121 radio relay aircraft.

cracked and thumped all around him. But one thing was missing: he did not hear Meadows bellowing over that bullhorn.
That meant Simons was outside the wrong compound. But he
wasn't worried. There were two soldiers in the United States
Army, Simons knew, who would not screw up: one was Dick
Meadows, the other was Bud Sydnor. That's why he had picked
them. Simons was confident that they would pull off the raid.
His main concern now was to get back to the right landing zone
before it was all over. "I hated to be left out," he recalled later,
"and I knew it would all be over in 26 minutes."

Simons soon had a more immediate concern, however. A fire
fight was exploding all around him, and he saw a startled North
Vietnamese stand up from a foxhole near the compound's
southwest corner. He was clad only in skivvies, naked from the
waist up in the warm night air, but he was armed—and only a
few feet away.

"He was frightened, I mean really frightened, dumb-
founded," Simons would recall. "The guy was looking at me like
I was made out of green cheese. I don't blame him; we landed
out of nowhere. I remember thinking, 'This is a lousy time of
night for introductions.' I shot him through the chest."

Simons turned to his radio operator, Staff Sergeant Walter L.
Miller, who was calmly taking the brunt of everything that was
going wrong. He'd worked with Simons before in Laos and for
three years at the Special Warfare Center. "Get that fucking
chopper back in here," Simons bellowed at him. "Tell Sydnor
to go into Plan Green." Then he turned to his other signal
specialist, Staff Sergeant David S. Nickerson. "Turn that strobe
light on fast; mark the landing zone."

Overhead, Warner Britton saw the explosions and firing 400
meters north of where he'd set Simons down and realized the
mistake he made. It was, he thought, "an incredible blunder."
Before Nickerson's strobe light even began flashing, Britton
wracked Apple One into another tight turn and headed back
down to pick up Simons and his men.

Three violent ground battles were now raging within two
miles of Son Tay: the fake one to the south and east, Meadows'
and Sydnor's assault on the prison, and Bull Simons' accidental

exposure to North Vietnam's secondary education system.

While Britton maneuvered his chopper down into the thick of the fire fight, Simons' support group was turning the "Secondary School" into a blazing ruin. Simons would say that he simply launched a "preemptive strike." "There was a hell of a fire fight going on and suddenly the place lit up like a damn Christmas tree." He speculated later that "perhaps some tracer rounds ignited some gasoline barrels." His men used only small arms fire, no satchel charges, he said, but their "attack was pressed with great violence—because surprise doesn't work if you don't use violence and speed." How they "blew" the compound's south wall without using satchel charges isn't clear; but they did, and Simons' men streaked into the compound and killed a lot of soldiers rushing out from two of the "school's" four buildings. "In five minutes the place was burning like a Roman candle."

Warner Britton's "mistake" may have saved the lives of half the Son Tay raiders. The "Secondary School" was bristling with hostile troops—but only the guards were North Vietnamese. Simons' men noted as they took the others under fire that they were *much* taller—"5 feet 10 inches to 6 feet, Oriental, not wearing the normal NVA dress, but instead . . . T-shirts and fitted dark undershorts." All of them were "much better equipped" than the guards at Son Tay. "Ground forces personnel," Manor wrote later, "were unable to determine [their] nationality."

Were they Russians . . . or Chinese?

In five minutes, Simons' 22 men killed somewhere between 100 and 200 of them.

Bull Simons had eliminated "the primary external ground threat" to his 56-man force—and it was only 400 yards, not several miles, from the objective. Warner Britton's "blunder" proved to be the most fortuitous break of the Son Tay raid. Early in November, photo reconnaissance had revealed that the "Secondary School" had been "reactivated," but only later was it learned that the heavily guarded compound housed Russian or Chinese troops who were training North Vietnamese air defense technicians on "early warning/ground control interceptor equipment" that had been moved into the "light industrial complex" about 300 yards east of the "school." Manor's After Action Report, in the classic understatement of the entire operation, would recommend that the "Secondary School" be "reclassified as a 'military installation' as numerous armed personnel were encountered at this location."

As Britton landed his helicopter to extract Simons' force—it was like flying into the middle of a burning ammunition dump —and put them down outside Son Tay, Simons called for "insurance," an "air strike" on the footbridge between Son Tay Prison and the "Secondary School." His men were still under fire as they broke contact with the enemy and reboarded Britton's HH-53. The Son Tay raid was now eight minutes old.

Nine minutes into the raid, Simons radioed Meadows and Sydnor from Apple One to "revert back to the basic plan." Thirty seconds later, Britton landed Simons and his men outside the walls of Son Tay. He may have set a new record: three combat assault sorties in nine and a half minutes. He took off immediately, as planned, and flew to the holding area. Simons' demolition team raced into position to knock out the bridge north of the prison, while Sydnor's men executed the few elements of the basic plan not yet carried out: destroying the power station and power poles outside the compound, and clearing the pumphouse on the canal southwest of the camp.

Inside Son Tay, Dick Meadows and his men—unaffected by the change of plans—were still clearing and searching the prison. They were taking sporadic fire, but they had landed with devastating surprise. The heaviest fire came from an AK-47 machine gun near a well inside the compound as guards rushed through the front gate. Sydnor's team came under heavy fire from a building just south of the compound's west wall. As many as 22 North Vietnamese were killed or wounded south of the compound. By the time Simons landed, there was little resistance left, but his men stirred up a hornet's nest when they cleared the headquarters or command building outside the front gate and a large guard barracks south of it. They accounted for another ten dead North Vietnamese.

Most of the North Vietnamese guards at Son Tay Prison,

about 55 of them, were dead or wounded before their eyes could focus on the crazy Americans who were shooting up an empty prison. For by now, Meadows' men were reporting "Negative items" (no prisoners) as they broke into one cell after another. Ten minutes into the raid, Meadows radioed over the command net: "Wildroot, this is Blueboy: Negative items at this time." He ran into the cellblocks to check for himself. One minute later he radioed again: "Search complete: Negative items." Son Tay Prison was a dry hole.

Simons reacted instantly: "Prepare to withdraw to LZ [the landing zone] for extraction. Blueboy and Redwine exit on first extraction helicopter. Set up LZ security: Redwine to west, Greenleaf to east."

Simons sent one of his photographers racing through the breached wall to photograph the empty cells. Then he called for an A-1 to strafe the bridge to the north. Fourteen minutes into the raid, he ordered one of the HH-53s to take off from the holding area and land back at Son Tay. He told Nickerson to fire off a flare as a directional aid. Eighteen minutes and 50 seconds into the raid, Warner Britton's HH-53 was back at Son Tay, in the rice paddies 150 feet southeast of the compound. Simons told Meadows to get his 13 men aboard, plus the three Air Force crewmen—Kalen, Zehnder, and Wright—from Banana One. Sydnor was directed to board his men as well, with the exception of a security group, his pathfinders and his "Marshalling Area Control Officer" (MACO).

The MACO's job was to count every man boarding the departing helicopters; Simons was going to leave Son Tay with exactly as many men as had flown in there with him. The MACO reported, "Count 26: count correct." Simons signaled the helicopter to get the hell out of North Vietnam. Britton lifted Apple One off and headed west.

Twenty-two minutes into the raid, Simons called for the second HH-53 to land. There were now 33 men left at Son Tay: Simons' team, part of Sydnor's and Dick Meadows. While Simons' men "readjusted the landing zone security"—and fired M-79 grenade launchers at four small vehicles racing up from the light industrial complex 600 meters southeast of the objec-

tive and about to cross the footbridge south of the compound
—Dick Meadows reentered the prison courtyard and set the
demolition charges inside Herb Kalen's badly bent-up, million-
dollar HH-3.

By now, surface-to-air missiles were exploding all over the sky
above them. As the "flying telephone poles" streaked through
the skies of North Vietnam, someone joked that they would be
the first Americans to describe what a Russian SA-2 looked like
from the ground. Twenty-seven minutes into the raid, the last
30 raiders and Simons, Sydnor, and Meadows were aboard the
second HH-53. Simons told the pilot of Apple Two, John Allison,
"Count 33, count correct," and the plane lifted off. As it
streaked for the Laotian border, Simons learned with relief that
only one man had been wounded, a sergeant with a flesh wound
in the inner thigh.

Apple Two was six minutes out of Son Tay when there was
a huge explosion in the target area. The HH-3 demolitions had
detonated on schedule.

Simons' assault teams and Britton's pilots had performed
flawlessly. The landing had been fast and violent. Surprise was
total. The search had been swift, fire precise, reactions unflappable, the withdrawal smooth. It was "beautiful."

There was only one thing wrong. Not a single prisoner was
with them as they headed back to marry up with refueling
tankers over Laos.

The flight back to Thailand was quiet but not uneventful.
Simons' men were "very let down, very quiet." They knew they
had done their job, and done it well—but it was not the job they
had wanted to do. Forty-five minutes out of Son Tay, when he
was supposed to report on the condition of the rescued prisoners, Simons pulled out a code book and composed a message for
Manor. He looked up the word for "prisoners," put the word
"Negative" in front of it. He looked up the word "moved," put
"Previously" in front of it. Then he asked Allison to relay the
message to Monkey Mountain.

It was now 3:35 A.M. at Manor's command post near Danang,
1 hour and 17 minutes since Meadows had landed in Son Tay.
Manor received Simons' message. There were no prisoners at

Son Tay. They had been previously moved. Simons thought Manor already knew that by monitoring Meadows' transmissions while the assault force was still on the ground. But the "dry hole" was news to Manor. He read the message again: "Negative prisoners. Previously moved." He asked for the message to be repeated, but got back only a "garbled" transmission. Within seconds, he sent a flash message that would reach the Pentagon Command Center ten minutes later: "Possibly negative POWs. Leaving TACC-NS for Udorn." It meant that he was taking off from Danang to be on hand personally to clarify the situation when Simons landed at Udorn.

Because technology had failed him again, Manor had been able to pick up only a hazy picture of what had happened at Son Tay. Two EC-121 "College Eye" airborne radar platforms had taken off from Korat Royal Thai Air Force Base in Thailand as scheduled to orbit over the Tonkin Gulf and let Manor monitor, as it happened, every radio transmission of the Son Tay raid. But one of the planes had broken an oil line, lost an engine, and had to abort, landing at Danang. The back-up plane reached its orbit point over the Gulf of Tonkin, but then "experienced IFF/SIF equipment failure and was unable to receive IFF/SIF returns at extended ranges." This meant that it could no longer maintain voice contact with some of the friendly planes over Son Tay. A spare unit was installed—"with negative results." Moreover, there was so much interference on the key frequencies that Manor, sitting in front of three of the six huge display consoles in Monkey Mountain's electronic brain, had at best a confused idea of events at Son Tay. Beyond 30 or 40 miles' range, the signals weren't reliable. He said later, "There is no adequate explanation for the interference or lack of IFF/SIF returns," but then added, "It must be noted, however, that the Navy was jamming NVN radars at this time."

To add to the confusion, a "computer-buffer" operated by the Marine Corps to link the Air Force and Navy's "automated systems" had also failed. This deprived Manor of the display he was supposed to have before him of what the Navy planes were doing. A back-up, automated teletype was finally hooked up, but it gave him the information only "after the fact."

All of this, however, should not have prevented Manor from monitoring the raid's key radio traffic "in real time." Something else did. Before leaving the States, he had arranged with SAC to have an RC-135 "Combat Apple" radio relay aircraft orbit over the Tonkin Gulf. It normally operated with four UHF channels; but to monitor "all of the discrete frequencies" that would be used by the assault force, Manor asked SAC to have four additional channels installed. The necessary equipment, he was told, was already in Southeast Asia. But after he arrived there, "the in-country personnel had no knowledge of their location." As a result of these unexpected "cavities," Combat Apple could relay ground force transmissions to Manor only when simultaneous FM and UHF contact was possible. He had not heard Meadows' FM radio message to Simons, "Count complete. Negative items."

The communications plan for Kingpin was perhaps more complex and sophisticated than for any other operation in the Vietnam war. It had failed Manor at the crucial moment. The commander of the raid on Son Tay had been without his "eyes and ears." It was a situation that could have resulted in serious trouble. What if some last-minute event had necessitated canceling the raid? Could Manor have recalled the assault force after the raid had been launched, as the President had been assured? It probably would have been possible through the many permutations and combinations of radios and frequencies that were available. But Manor would have had to act swiftly, "jury-rigging" the same kind of communications patch that it had taken to get the weather information he needed. But what if something had gone wrong at Son Tay? When would Manor have learned of it? And in a crisis, when every second counted, what action could he have taken?

About an hour out of Son Tay, Simons was a very troubled man. He couldn't believe it: there were only 25 men, not 26, aboard the first helicopter. "Oh, my God," he thought, "we blew it!" They'd left someone behind. Simons requested a recount. Without the aid of cabin lights, several counts and recounts were taken. What seemed like an eternity passed before

Simons was reassured that all 59 men of his assault force were airborne on their way back to Thailand. There were only 25 men aboard the first helicopter, but there were 34, not 33, in his.

As the first extraction helicopter had been about to take off, one of Sydnor's men—who should have boarded it, and did—noticed there were "hot wires" on the ground from a power-transmission tower he had blown. He knew another chopper would land there soon and jumped back out the rear ramp to cut the wires. Then he had scampered aboard the second aircraft, before the marshalling officer could begin his count for the final extraction.

On the long ride back to Udorn, Bull Simons wondered, half chuckling to himself, what the North Vietnamese would make of it all. Someone—they could not be sure who, because there wouldn't be any bodies to examine or prisoners to interrogate—had assaulted an empty compound 23 miles from Hanoi; blown up a remote command center nearby and killed a "shit pot full" of Chinese or Russians; apparently landed a few miles to the south and east and had "one hellova fire fight, without even engaging North Vietnamese troops; and had 'raided' Haiphong, would you believe it, with a flock of *flares.*" It was "good stuff," he thought, "going in and twisting the tails of those sonsovbitches 20 miles from Hanoi."

And they were all on the way back home, so far as Simons knew, without losing one man or one plane. He was unaware that Marty Donohue was still on the ground in Apple Three—and that another plane which had taken part in the raid had been shot down.

East of Finger Lake, on the ground in the holding area a few miles west of Son Tay, Marty Donohue and Tom Waldron couldn't believe what they had been hearing on the radio. First it sounded like Simons' chopper had been shot down; why else had Sydnor called for Plan Green? Soon they saw missiles going off all around them. They counted 18 of them, four close enough to be of concern. "They lit up the sky," Donohue later said, "just like a launch at Cape Kennedy."

Then Donohue and Waldron heard Meadows report, "Negative items at this time," followed only a minute later by: "Search complete: Negative items." Their reaction was one of "complete disbelief. Everything had gone so well," Donohue later remarked. "There was less confusion than any mission I had been on. But I just couldn't believe it. It didn't really come through. We just sat there." He turned to Waldron: "Did you hear that?" "I heard it," Waldron replied, "but I don't believe it. Let's wait." They agreed: "Let's make sure. It *can't* be right."

They were on the ground in a rice paddy surrounded on three sides by a crook in the winding Song Con River where it was about 20 feet wide. A minigun on the rear ramp covered the ground behind them. They sat there waiting. In the dark of night, they could see people, 20, maybe 30 of them, in fields across the water. They were obviously looking for something— the noisy helicopters that had landed nearby. Donohue and the four other men in Apple Three couldn't tell if they were soldiers or civilians. They were less than 50 yards away.

Donohue waited there for clearance to depart. He heard Simons' code-word messages calling in Apple One and Apple Two to extract the ground force. Then he heard "more traffic" and saw Apple Four and Five lift off and head west. That left him, Apple Three. More SAMs were going off; "it was pretty busy." Still he waited.

Donohue was listening on his UHF channel for the code word telling him to "bug out" when he overheard Allison relay Simons' report on the long-range HF net to Manor: "Negative items." But there was a "lot of interference." The HF signal was "bouncing" and not that clear; nor could Donohue hear the acknowledgment from Manor. Several transmissions followed, however, reconfirming the bad news. There were no prisoners.

Soon it got very quiet. Donohue's helicopter was to be the "clean-up ship," the last one out. The "SAMs were all over [finished firing] by then," Donohue remembered. He and Waldron had been on the ground longer than they had expected, but still there was no signal releasing them. They didn't want to spend the winter in North Vietnam. "Somebody," they joked apprehensively, "may have forgotten us for a while." Had someone forgotten to send the final bug-out message to the last five men who would leave North Vietnam that night? Or was something else wrong?

Suddenly the radios came alive again. Donohue listened with mounting concern as Apple One and Two discovered their "head counts" were wrong, wondering if a man had been left behind at Son Tay. To keep North Vietnamese signal intercept centers from sending out word that an immediate, thorough search at Son Tay might produce a new prisoner for the empty cells there, the two helicopters were communicating on their FM net, whose range was limited to about 15 miles.

But this meant that as the helicopters continued their flights toward Laos, the signals Donohue was trying to monitor were getting weaker and weaker. He and Waldron strained to hear what was going on as Apple One and Two passed their count back and forth two or three times, but the outcome wasn't clear to either of them. Donohue radioed on his longer range UHF set, asking if they had "figured it out."

He was about to ask them to let him fly back to Son Tay and try to "police up the stray" when he heard another FM transmission. It sounded like Apple One was telling Apple Two, "Count Correct." The signal was much too faint for him to be sure, however. Almost in desperation, Donohue radioed one of the A-1 pilots "in the clear": "Did I 'read' that right, 'Count Correct'?" The "Sandy driver" confirmed the good news. He told Donohue he was "clear"; there was nothing left to clean up. Apple Three was finally released. Donohue should "get the hell out of there." Even at full throttle, it took him almost half an hour to catch up with the other helicopters.

Donohue would swear that, in their frustration, none of his men goosed a baby water buffalo up the rear ramp of his helicopter and flew a "prisoner" out of North Vietnam. A few days later, Henry Kissinger was convinced that *someone* had.

The National Military Command Center

In the Pentagon, Ed Mayer barely had everything ready when the Joint Chiefs of Staff began assembling just after noon on November 20, Washington time, in the National Military Command Center. By then, Simons' assault force had taken off from Udorn and was headed north over Laos. The complex routes, intricate time schedules, and target area tactics were mapped out on four huge, back-lit, Plexiglass display panels hanging overhead.

As progress reports came in from General Manor at Monkey Mountain, they were posted for all to see. The raid seemed to be unfolding on schedule:

12:04 P.M.   "HC-130s and A-1Es off on time."
12:43 P.M.   "Situation satisfactory."
 1:23 P.M.   "Navy diversion launched."
 1:27 P.M.   "Refueling complete."
 1:40 P.M.   "Task group crossed NVN border."

Tension began to build. Then Blackburn and Mayer realized that General William C. Westmoreland had shown up. He had been the Army's Chief of Staff for more than two years, but had left the operational side of the Army up to his Vice Chief, General Bruce Palmer. To the best of most people's recollection, this was Westy's first presence at a working meeting of the Joint Chiefs. He had been very busy—traveling around the nation and the world, trying to rebuild his image and bolster the Army's. And it was the first time the Joint Chiefs had ever used the command center to monitor, or "command," a real operation.

Blackburn and Mayer had drawn up a precise roster, approved by Vogt, of those who were authorized entry to the command center to watch the raid's progress. Aside from SACSA personnel, the command center duty officers on watch at the time, the Joint Chiefs and their deputies for operations, there were only 19 other names on the list. Mayer was "stunned," therefore, when Defense Secretary Laird walked into the room around 1:30 P.M., followed by an entourage of about 15 people, mostly civilians. Laird's military assistant, Air Force Brigadier General Robert Pursely, shrugged his shoulders, raised his eyebrows discreetly, and thus "told" Mayer to let everyone in.

Laird's entourage and most of the others present sat in a low balcony at the back of the command center, the Service Deputy Chiefs of Staff for Operations in the front row with elaborate communications consoles before them. Laird, Moorer, and Vogt sat with Mayer in a soundproofed, glass-enclosed room to their right—the "National Command Authority" room. The Joint Chiefs sat at a conference table below the balcony, looking up at the display consoles. With them was General Bennett of the DIA, the man who—unbeknownst to all but a few of those present—had "blown the whistle" about 20 hours earlier, signaling that Son Tay might be empty. But instead of his usual seat on the far left of the Joint Chiefs, Bennett was sitting at the end of the table, facing them and in front of a podium from which Blackburn and Spots Harris would "brief" those present on the raid's progress.

"Sitting there, doing what?" Bennett was asked later.

"Sitting there, dying!" he answered.

Suddenly the reports began to accelerate. At 2:29, Manor signaled, "MIG threat"; one minute later, "Landed in objective area safely." Blackburn checked the Kingpin timetable on the huge screen above them. The assault was 11 minutes behind schedule, but there was no explanation. He did not know that the raiders were "right on the button" but that Manor's communications system was way off its mark. Another three minutes passed, then "MIG threat all clear"; three more minutes, "Situation satisfactory."

There were no more reports for a quarter of an hour, then: "All aircraft departed objective area."

Periodically, Vogt would call the White House situation room, or Al Haig, with a crisp progress report on the raid. Everyone was waiting to hear one thing: had Simons rescued any POWs? There was no word about the prisoners at Son Tay.

Twenty-five minutes later, at 3:15 P.M., there was another signal from Manor: "Task Group crossed Laos border." Still no word on the prisoners, or about casualties among Simons' force. Forty-six minutes had passed since the planes had landed "safely."

Twelve more minutes passed before the next message: "SAR effort required. F-105 down."

Vogt almost leapt out of his chair: "F-105! What the hell's an F-105 doing up there?" He turned to Mayer. "Where did *it* come from? What's going on?"

Mayer didn't have the foggiest notion, nor did Blackburn. Nowhere in planning or training for the Son Tay mission had the use of F-105s been mentioned. Every aircraft employed in the raid was spelled out in the black, three-ring binder Kingpin briefing book, before the senior officers in the room. No one could find any F-105s listed.

Everyone had different thoughts. It was the only "glitch" so far, at least as far as anyone in the command center could tell. But it *could* be a big one. Blackburn wondered if "some crazy, frustrated bastard" had taken off from Thailand to renew the air war or challenge the North Vietnamese air force all by himself. Or was it part of that "other operation" he had heard of, but wasn't cleared to know about? If so, why was Manor sending the message?

The F-105s were Manor's idea. At the last minute, in Thailand, he had decided to have the raiding force escorted by a flight of five F-105 "Wild Weasel" aircraft from the 388th Tactical Fighter Squadron at Korat. They would work as "decoys" to jam North Vietnam's "Fan Song" radars, direct SA-2 missiles away from the assault force, knock out the "hot" SAM batteries with Shrike radar-homing missiles, and help protect the ten F-4s flying combat air patrol against MIGs.

They were, to put it bluntly, "bait."

In the crush of all the problems they had to wrestle with between November 17 and 20, Manor and his staff simply forgot to tell Washington that the F-105s had been added to the Son Tay strike force.

The two pilots in each Wild Weasel fighter knew they were bait. They were flying at only 13,000 feet, well within the SA-2s' lethal range. Only minutes after Marty Donohue flew over Son Tay Prison, the first SAM went off—but it was aimed at the F-105s, not the helicopters. In all, 16 of the 18 SAMs fired near

Son Tay were directed at the F-105s. At one time, six of them were airborne at the same time. The "bait" worked; all of the SAMs were "high flyers."

Twelve minutes into the raid, however, one of the F-105s, Firebird Three, had a close call. Two SAMs were streaking toward it; but when the "flying telephone poles" got within a mile of his plane, Major William J. Starkey rolled over and dived to 5,000 feet. As the two missiles arched down to follow his aircraft, he forced the plane into a hard pull-up. The first SAM passed over him and detonated behind the F-105. The second passed under him and exploded below and slightly behind his left wing. For 12 to 15 seconds, it looked like Starkey's wing was on fire. His "back seater," Major Everett D. Fansler, couldn't believe it when he saw the fire go out and Starkey told him calmly the plane was now flying normally.

Six minutes later, Firebird Five was hit. A SAM had detonated close enough to fill the cockpit with a "brilliant flash." The plane shuddered in a "mild shock wave." Major Donald W. Kilgus knew he had lost his "stability augmentation control system." In an F-105, that was bad news. He could not get it to reengage. Captain Clarence T. Lowry, Kilgus' back seater, knew the news was going to get worse; his fuel gauges told him the plane was leaking more fuel than its engines were burning. Kilgus headed for southern Laos and, hopefully, Thailand. Over the Plaine des Jarres in Laos, at 32,000 feet, the F-105 "flamed out." Kilgus and Lowry fought to restart the engine until 8,000 feet; then they pulled their eject handles. Their "silk afterburners" worked perfectly, but they landed in very unfriendly territory.

About this time, Marty Donohue finally took off in Apple Three from his holding position near the Son Tay compound. Apple Five, piloted by Major Kenneth Murphy, had just intercepted him, to escort Donohue home, when the radio crackled that an F-105 was down. Donohue picked up "trail" on John Allison in Apple Two, while Murphy in Apple Five and Lieutenant Colonel Royal C. Brown in Apple Four stood by in the area to refuel and rescue the downed pilots. Soon a C-130 dropped flares where the survivors were thought to be. Murphy located

both men, but started taking ground fire. Another refueling
followed, and then several A-1 strike planes arrived to protect
the helicopters. Everyone decided to wait for "first light" to
make the "pickup." Finally, Brown swooped down and rescued
Kilgus, while Murphy went in half a mile away and hoisted his
back seater, Lowry, out of the jungle.

By then, Murphy and Brown had been flying their HH-53s for
more than nine hours, almost all of it over hostile terrain and
at night. But they brought the last two Son Tay raiders home
alive.

As Simons' helicopters flew the last leg of their lonely, long
flight back to Udorn, Manor's cryptic message, "Possibly Negative PWs" arrived at the Pentagon Command Center. It was
3:35, Friday afternoon, November 21.

The message was in code, of course. When it was deciphered,
an Army brigadier general who was the senior command center
"watch officer" that afternoon grabbed it and rushed to the
Command Authority room. He was supposed to hand all incom-
ing messages to Mayer or Vogt and a copy to Blackburn. Instead, he strode through the door waving the message and
announced over and over, idiotically, "There are no prisoners
in Son Tay! There are no prisoners in Son Tay!"

That was not the news the men in the command center had
been waiting for; their reactions were a combination of disbelief, disappointment, anger.

Vogt called Haig: "Looks like a bust, Al. No prisoners. Manor
said 'Possibly,' but we'd better expect the worst." Within minutes, the President was on the phone to Laird and Moorer. He
asked them to convey his personal thanks to everyone concerned for a "courageous" effort.

Laird got up and left without much comment, not abruptly,
not in disgust or anger, but obviously disappointed. "Well," he
said, "these things happen. At least we tried." Moorer left the
room with him. With Laird gone, the room "erupted," as Mayer
would describe it, in a cross fire of recriminations. The comments, Mayer recalled, were *very* critical."

Westmoreland was livid; *"Another* intelligence failure," he said, shaking his head. Others among the Joint Chiefs made critical and sometimes bitter comments. John Vogt finally interrupted to say very quietly, "Gentlemen, before we come to any conclusions, we're going to go back and examine what *did* go wrong."

As the meeting broke up, the JCS J-3, Lieutenant General Melvin R. Zais, injected a note of humor: "Well, I guess we'll have to fire Blackburn." He was trying to make light of things, but no one thought it was very funny.

That Friday afternoon and evening, a lot of men spent some very rough hours. At Fort Belvoir, Claude Watkins was told of Manor's 3:35 message, "Possibly negative PWs" and went to the latrine and puked. After he and others from the 1127th Field Activities Group were pulled off the planning group, he never knew when, or even if, the raid would be launched. "It went so fucking long I decided they weren't going to have it. But I woke up every morning," he would recall, "wondering if it had taken place." Six and a half months after he had prepared briefing charts for an "urgent rescue," the Pentagon had drilled a dry well.

Don Bennett drove to his quarters at Fort Myer, Virginia, went to his study, and just buried his head in his hands. His wife, Bets, a sensitive, supportive woman, knew it was no time to ask why. Ed Mayer cried in front of his wife, Claire, for the first time in his Army career. Don Blackburn drove home to McLean, Virginia, and in typical humor told his wife, "Well, Ann, I really blew it." She understood. For months, she had listened to his nightmares about a "dry hole," but never told him.

It was 4:28 in the morning by the time Bull Simons and his force landed at Udorn Royal Thai Air Force Base. Manor was there, waiting. Simons strode out of the helicopter, shrugged his shoulders, and told him, "No prisoners."

Manor couldn't believe it. "For *real?*" He had received Simons' message, but the transmission had been garbled.

"Yeah, it's real; you're damned right," replied Simons, then raised his eyebrows and pursed his lips as if to add, "So what else is there to say?"

He told Manor that Meadows and his men were sure the camp had been empty for a long time; one of the cells had a bunch of cement bags in it. There weren't even leg irons or shackles left in the others.

While Simons watched his men debark from the second helicopter and assured himself that everyone was accounted for, Manor headed for the operatioñs center to call the Pentagon Command Center. When Simons entered a few minutes later, Manor and Laird were talking on the phone. It was a nonsecure voice line, so Manor's report was very brief. He would cable a coded, more complete report in a few hours. Manor asked Simons if he wanted to speak with Laird. Simons told him, "What the hell for? I don't have anything to say to him."

Simons' men and the air crews were bushed, but it would be a long time before they could get some sleep. Intelligence teams were standing by for debriefings that would last for hours. Marty Donohue was one of the luckier ones; he was debriefed by a very pretty girl.

Before they could turn in for some rest, the senior officers had to write out a detailed "Summary of Operations." It was put on the teletype at 9:15 that morning, directed to Moorer.

It got lost.

As the report was being completed, Manor and Simons got word that they were to fly back to Washington immediately. Simons asked Sydnor to assemble the men. He wanted them to know how he felt, and he felt "very strongly." He told them, "I know you are disappointed. We had the place right by the ass. But you have nothing to feel bad about, nothing to be ashamed of. You did your job and you did it as well as any combat commander could ask of you. We don't have a thing to be ashamed of. The operation, as far as what *you* did, was successful. You could not have done it better."

Simons would not recall their reactions. "Hell, I wasn't looking for any reaction. It was just something I wanted to say. I didn't give a God damn what their reaction was."

Manor and Simons climbed aboard a small courier plane, flew to Saigon, and there boarded another plane for the flight home. It was their fourth trip across the Pacific in three weeks. Admiral McCain met them in Hawaii and took them aboard one of CINCPAC's flying command posts, a modified KC-135 tanker called "Looking Glass." Simons would remember the plane vividly: "Jesus, it was unrecognizable. It was crammed solid with radios and electronic equipment, the whole damn thing. I mean from asshole to appetite. *Solid!* An electronic *jungle.*" McCain took them to the rear of the plane; he showed them a small compartment where they could sleep, "which," Simons said, "I promptly did."

They arrived at Andrews Air Force Base at about three o'-clock in the morning, Monday, November 23. Blackburn met the plane, said they were to have breakfast with Laird and Moorer, and took them to the Visiting Officers Quarters so they could freshen up and get some more sleep.

Simons told him about landing in the wrong camp. He thought that was "pretty funny. I bet we really shook those bastards up." But everything else had gone like clockwork, he said, "a real smooth operation." Blackburn remarked that the Joint Chiefs were probably more shook up than the North Vietnamese.

That bothered Simons. "What are you telling me, Don, that we got a black eye? *I'm* not mad at anybody. I thought the thing was *great.* Okay, so we didn't get 'em. Christ, the thing was worth doing *without* getting them."

Disarray

The Pentagon Press Room

Manor and Simons caught only a few hours' sleep before they were escorted to Laird's office in Room 3E880 of the Pentagon. Moorer was there and greeted them warmly. Laird apologized for having to recall them so quickly; there had been a change in plans, he said. He would explain over breakfast.

Laird led them next door into his private dining room, where Pentagon spokesman Dan Henkin joined them. The five men sat down at a conference table in the middle of a room big enough to host comfortably a cocktail party for 120 people. The room, in fact, was often used for that purpose, after a major award ceremony or whenever a new presidential appointee was sworn in to the Pentagon hierarchy. Out its windows, across the Potomac, the Jefferson Memorial, the Washington Monument, and the White House were in clear view.

Filipino stewards in short, powder blue mess jackets served orange juice and poured coffee as Laird explained what was up. The White House had called him "almost immediately" after being notified that Son Tay was empty, but that everyone had been recovered safely. Laird was ordered to bring back the two commanders "immediately"; the President wanted to decorate them personally. And Laird had been advised that two enlisted men were to be decorated as well. One of them, the White House insisted, had to be black.

Manor and Simons were asked to recommend the two enlisted men—with the proviso laid down by 1600 Pennsylvania Avenue—but their reaction was "not enthusiastic." Everyone who had crash-landed inside Son Tay Prison, they felt strongly, should be treated equally. Laird and Moorer acknowledged their feeling, but explained that it "wouldn't sell." Ed Mayer had already been given instructions to draft the appropriate citations—"fast." Manor and Simons could pick the men, of course, and "fine-tune" the proposed citations. The White House's flair for public relations won out over Manor and Simons' concept of fairness.

The awards ceremony, moreover, would be public. That meant, Laird noted, that the Pentagon would have to reveal a lot more about the Son Tay raid than had ever been intended. Until that call from the White House, the cover plans had one purpose: never to reveal that the operation was unsuccessful, if that's the way it should turn out.

Laird and Henkin wondered now whether that would have been feasible. Given the number of people involved, they asked, could the raid really be kept secret on a long-term basis, or could they keep only a "short lid" on it? Should the Pentagon "break" the story now or try to "hold it," at least until the White House awards ceremony? How much of what really happened would get out anyway? What was the *least* that could be said? What was the most that *should* be said? How should the press be told, although Laird didn't phrase the question quite this way, that the Pentagon had sent 56 men deep into North Vietnam, only to plunk them down in a "dry hole"?

It was an odd meeting, Simons would recall. At the very seat of American military power, "They were mainly concerned about a press release, and we haggled back and forth over eggs and bacon."

Laird finally asked Simons what he felt should be done. By then, Simons had decided to give Laird a recommendation "anyway," whether he asked for one or not. He told Laird to have the press conference "now." The only question, in Simons' view, was a choice of a "fist fight" over "their" story—as the press would write it, if it broke without the Pentagon's initiative —or whether, he told Laird, it would come out as "your story." "This is a perfectly legitimate operation," he said. "These are American prisoners. This is something that Americans traditionally do for Americans. For Christ's sake, what is it we're afraid of here?"

Simons would not recall if anyone else agreed with him, "but Mr. Laird did and he was the only guy I was talking to. I really didn't give a God damn whether anybody else agreed with me or not." Nor would he remember how Laird voiced his opinion, but "Five minutes later we were planning the press briefing."

The raid on Son Tay had been planned and executed in the strictest secrecy. Now, the final act was about to unfold in a glare of publicity and public relations. The five men at Laird's conference table focused all their attention on how to put the raid in the best possible light. There was almost no discussion of what had gone wrong, or right. Asked later if he told Laird that he had landed in the wrong compound, Simons replied: "No, no." It wasn't the kind of conversation, he pointed out, that got into "tactical details." Both Manor and Simons, however, assumed that Laird and Moorer knew of the fortuitous "blunder" that landed the biggest part of the raiding force in a hornet's nest at the "Secondary School." Manor had spelled it all out in the short after action summary cabled to the Pentagon Command Center just before he and Simons left Udorn. They did not know that the message had gotten lost. It wasn't to reach Washington until almost a week after the raid—and then columnist Jack Anderson would get part of it before Laird saw any of it.

As the public relations conference went into the "fine details" of how the Son Tay press release would be phrased, it became obvious that there was "no way" it could be ready in time for the usual daily press briefing. Henkin ordered the "eleven o'-clock follies" postponed until mid-afternoon. No one was to tell the 55 newsmen and radio/TV commentators accredited to the building why.

Laird strode into the Pentagon newsroom at 3:30 P.M. that afternoon, accompanied by Moorer, Manor, and Simons. As he stepped onto a low platform and adjusted the microphones, high-intensity lights came on to illuminate the four men for the TV cameras. There was an air of expectancy among the reporters; they knew a big story was about to unfold. Laird cleared his throat and told the reporters that he wanted to give them details of an "operation that took place north of the 19th parallel this past weekend."

Notebooks snapped open; pencils moved quickly. The reporters were well aware that until the preceding weekend, North Vietnam had not been bombed for more than two years. But this story would obviously be about something more than a bombing; in the glare of the Klieg lights before them was not only an Air Force general, but also a very well decorated soldier who clearly was not from some headquarters staff.

Laird spoke of North Vietnam's "adamant refusal" to exchange prisoners of war or abide by the Geneva Convention. He said that "some months ago" he had prepared a contingency plan to rescue "as many of our prisoners as possible." The pencils and pens were literally flying now across the reporters' notepads. A special Army-Air Force task force had been assembled for a rescue mission, Laird continued; its training had been "meticulous, intensive, often around the clock." A "key factor" in his final decision to launch "this search and rescue mission" was "new information that we received this month that some of our men were dying in the prisoner-of-war camps" of North Vietnam. Flash bulbs began popping.

A raid, Laird announced, had been made on a prisoner-of-war compound "approximately 20 miles west of Hanoi" at about 2:00 A.M., Hanoi time, the previous weekend. TV crews checked to see if their recorders were getting it all down; cameramen and photographers jostled each other to get closer to the podium.

Laird said that the two distinguished officers beside him—Manor and Simons—had led the operation. Brigadier General Leroy J. Manor was in overall command, and Colonel Arthur D.

Simons led the team in the search and rescue attempt. Simons and his men, Laird clarified, "landed, entered, and searched the compound." Laird spoke for over three minutes before he admitted: "Regrettably, the rescue team discovered that the camp had recently been vacated. No prisoners were found."

There was a murmur of surprise among the newsmen. Laird went on to give them some of the more general details of the raid, then opened the news conference to questions. The newsmen were ready. But they wanted more information about how the raid was executed—and why it was launched against an empty POW compound—than the Pentagon was willing to give them.

"Was this the first time that American forces had been used in North Vietnam?" Laird: "We have carried on search and rescue missions in North Vietnam quite regularly." "How many men were in the mission?" Simons: "I cannot tell you." Would Simons give them a "narrative dispatch right straight through what happened?" "No, sir, I can't do that." "Did the mission have a code name?" "I can't answer that question." "Did you fly from an aircraft carrier?" "I can't answer that." "What kind of a helicopter was it?" "I can't answer that." "How many men did you hope to free?" "I can't answer the question." "Did you have an alternate target that you might hit?" Manor: "I can't answer that." He wasn't about to reveal that they *had* hit an "alternate target"—by mistake. "Did you take any prisoners?" "I can't answer that." "Did you fire your weapons?" "Yes, we did fire our weapons." "Did you kill anybody?" Simons: "Yes, I would imagine so."

One question caused Simons to gulp noticeably: "Did you land right in the prison?" It was awfully close to, "Did you land in the right prison?" He hesitated, then answered "Yes."

Laird fielded 10 of the reporters' 35 questions himself. The smooth-talking defense chief offered a stark contrast to the gruff, matter-of-fact Simons, who at times could barely get a word in edgewise. Because of "security," Manor and Simons would reply, "I can't answer that," or "I can't comment," or "I cannot tell you," to 40 percent of the questions they "answered."

Manor and Simons were relieved by the interference that Laird was running for them. But some of Laird's answers were later to cause a credibility problem. He told the reporters that "There was no ordnance involved [in the air part of the operation]." Only four days later, President Nixon would tell White House visitors that "an air raid was carried out on a military installation next to Son Tay to keep North Vietnamese troops pinned down before the helicopters landed." Dan Henkin was forced to "clarify" the discrepancy the following day.

Laird was also asked if the raid was the first search and rescue mission that had "ever been run" of "approximately this scope," not involving SAR attempts immediately after a shootdown. Laird wasn't about to open Pandora's box, or dilute the impact of this briefing, by telling the press that there had been more than 60 POW raids in South Vietnam and Cambodia—the net result of which had been to recover exactly one American POW, who died two weeks later of wounds inflicted by his captors as the rescue was under way. So he told the press: "This is the first SAR mission conducted in North Vietnam on prisoners of war during this war."

At 4:12, Laird cut off any further questions with, "Thank you very much, gentlemen." The reporters rushed out of the pressroom to write up a story that was to dominate the news media for weeks. But what did they really know about the raid? They had been given a hard news story full of drama, yet empty of detail. They knew only that a raid had been launched into the heart of North Vietnam to rescue American prisoners of war. The raid was a success in that no American lives were lost. But the Son Tay compound was empty, and had been for "several weeks." To the newsmen the implications were clear; there had been an "intelligence failure." But when asked on whom he blamed the intelligence failure, Simons had replied: "I can't answer the question at all. I am not sure what you mean by 'intelligence failure.' "

The Pentagon had told the story its way, but to the reporters present at the briefing, it was obvious that they had not been told the whole story. The news dominated that evening's newscasts; most of the next day's front-page headlines reflected the only conclusion the reporters had been able to draw from the briefing: Son Tay was a failure. Nixon was once again blamed for undertaking a perilous new policy. The North Vietnamese canceled the upcoming session of the Paris peace talks in protest. On Capitol Hill, the reaction was far from favorable. Senator J. William Fulbright, Chairman of the Senate Foreign Relations Committee, called the raid "a major escalation of the war . . . a very provocative act to mount a physical invasion. . . ." Fulbright's committee agreed unanimously on new hearings on the political implications of the raid.

The "fist fight" that Bull Simons had predicted was going to be a tough one.

The Halls of Congress

Less than 24 hours after Laird's dramatic announcement to the Pentagon press corps, both floors of Congress locked in acrimonious debate over the raid. Senator Henry Jackson said the rescue attempt was "fully warranted." Senator Edward M. Kennedy said of the raiders, "I admire their courage. I just deplore the policy that permitted them to go." Senator Birch Bayh told newsmen he feared such raids might "result in . . . POWs being executed." He called the raid a "John Wayne approach." Senator Robert Dole introduced a resolution praising the men who had risked their lives in the abortive mission. He said the raid was successful in "demonstrating American concern. Some of these men have been languishing in prison for five years." Senator Kennedy snapped back, "And they're still there."

In the House, emotions ran equally strong and were just as divided. Congressman Charles Vanik said it was "incredible that our military intelligence should have risked the lives of brave men in raiding a prison which was unused for weeks. This vain action jeopardizes the life of prisoners of war who still survive in North Vietnam." Minority leader Gerald R. Ford said he hoped America would launch "other operations of a similar nature which will be successful." Representative Robert Leggett said the raid "must have been planned by the Saigon army or perhaps by the script-writer of a grade 'C' war movie." It was, he charged, a "first magnitude blunder" and the only thing "that kept it from being an even greater blunder was the fact that there were no POWs in the camp." The North Vietnamese, he was sure, would have shot them all. Moreover, he predicted, the operation had "radically decreased our chances of negotiating better treatment" for the POWs.

Later that same day, Defense Secretary Laird met with a hostile Senate Foreign Relations Committee. The hearing, open to the public, had been called under the guise of getting Department of Defense testimony on a $255-million supplemental foreign aid request for Cambodia. But by the time it adjourned at 6:25 that evening, not one question had been asked about the Cambodian appropriation.

Laird had notified the committee at noon that he could appear later that day. It was 4:05 P.M. when the hearing opened, a time when congressional offices were usually closing so everyone could get a head-start on Washington's rush-hour traffic. Notwithstanding the hour and last-minute scheduling, 10 of the committee's 15 members were present as Laird began his prepared statement. Its chairman, Senator Fulbright, had agreed in advance to let the Secretary of Defense speak "uninterrupted" for 15 minutes.

Laird spoke for only a third of that time. He added few new specifics to what he had already given the press about the Son Tay raid. There wasn't much he *could* add. For one thing, he still hadn't received the after-action operations summary which Manor had cabled from Thailand. "I didn't get that darned thing for *days*," he would note later, "and I was really there 'naked' for a while." But after 22 months as Secretary of Defense, Laird suspected he didn't really have the full story. "I learned one thing," he would explain: "You don't accept the first report, you don't accept the second report, you don't accept the third report; maybe by about the fourth time, you get the straight information." There were, he told the committee, reports from "unofficial sources" that "even more Americans, in addition to the six reported earlier this month, have died in captivity in North Vietnam." On a human interest level, he noted that Colonel Simons was a journalism graduate from the University of Missouri. A former Congressman himself, Laird was skillful in handling the legislative critics. One of the Senate Foreign Relations Committee's most vocal members, Senator Stuart Symington, represented that same state of Missouri.

Laird closed by telling the committee of the Son Tay raid: "I have not faced a more challenging decision since I have been Secretary of Defense." And he added, "It is my firm belief that if there had been prisoners of war at Son Tay they would be free men today." The rest of his remarks expressed his respect for and gratitude to the soldiers and airmen who had "performed heroically."

For the next two and a third hours, Fulbright and the other members of the committee questioned Laird intensively. Joint Staff Director John Vogt, not Moorer, sat beside him, but Laird handled every single question himself. He knew the hearing would be a "no win" proposition and had decided to "take the heat" himself: Vogt never got to say a word.

The issue Fulbright focused on early in the hearing was "not whether this was a brave or a valorous attack, but whether it was a wise attack." He granted that "There is certainly no question . . . about the valor and heroism of the men who conducted it. The men performed perfectly." But when he added that "whoever directed it, did not," laughter broke out. "There was something wrong with the intelligence," Fulbright said bluntly.

"It was not a failure, Mr. Chairman," Laird said.

In that case, Fulbright replied, "There was something wrong with the plan."

"These men knew full well the chance that there might not be POWs present," Laird insisted.

By "these men," Laird must have been referring to the raiders. But Manor and Simons certainly did not know. When Simons was later asked if he had been told before launching for Son Tay that the prisoners had been moved, he said vehemently, "Absolutely not." Asked if he had been told that the prisoners had been moved "but that the camp might have become active again," Simons replied, "I don't remember anybody ever saying that to me." Asked to what extent, before he launched from Udorn, it was ever suggested to him that the camp *"might* be empty," Simons said categorically, "Nobody *ever* suggested it to me." He would add, however: "I suggested it to myself. I considered that it *was* a possibility." But the first time he *ever* heard that the prisoners might have been moved in July, Simons said, was when he talked with some of the POWs he tried to rescue after they came home in 1973.

Laird continued trying to deflect Fulbright's concern about an intelligence failure. "I would like to tell you, Mr. Chairman," he said, "we have made tremendous progress as far as intelligence is concerned." The hearing again broke out in laughter. Laird's next statement was interrupted, but he made a telling point, which became probably the most widely quoted single comment on the entire raid: "We have not been able to develop a camera that sees through the roofs of buildings." Except for that, he said, "The intelligence for their mission was excellent." Laird tried to tell, and show, the hearing how much *was* known about the camp and North Vietnamese air defenses, but Fulbright cut off each of his next four sentences with another question. "I do not think this is relevant," he said finally. "There weren't any prisoners there. What difference does it make?"

The committee then began to zero in on the question that clearly troubled its members: *When* was the mission authorized, and *why* was it authorized if there were no prisoners at Son Tay? Laird was evasive.

He testified that his recommendation to President Nixon to proceed ["execute the mission," he clarified in the next sentence]"was made very early Friday morning." He did not go into detail, or reveal that the RED ROCKET message telling Manor to execute Kingpin was sent precisely at 5:30 P.M. on *Wednesday* afternoon, but that he had consulted with the President again before the actual launch on Friday.

Laird was pressed on his announcement about "even more" POW deaths than the six reported earlier in the month. "When did you receive these reports?" one Senator wanted to know. "Well," Laird hedged, not wanting to be pinned down, "those reports were received earlier this month. But since that time we have had further reports within this past week—these have been confirmed, of course—but these reports had come through channels that have contacts in Hanoi." Asked next if his recommendation to proceed with the raid had followed or preceded "these reports [of the POW deaths]," Laird was very specific: "It followed those reports."

No one asked him how he had learned on Friday, the 20th, of information Cora Weiss had not released to the State Department until Tuesday, November 23. But Laird's testimony would cause near-panic in the intelligence community; although the Gamma intercepts were one of the few sources of "hard intelligence" on the POWs, some of them were highly illegal. Moreover, peace activists like Cora Weiss weren't the only targets of those intercepts. It was a massive operation, and one of the targets was none other than Senator Fulbright himself. Laird had come close to compromising one of the nation's most carefully guarded secrets in a public hearing. Yet not one member of the committee or its staff would catch the significance of his statement, and in the weeks that followed, only one Washington journalist would pursue its implications.

Laird had problems with other questions that afternoon. Again defending the quality of the Pentagon's intelligence, he said to the committee, "Everything was exactly as [the raiders] had been told. . . . Every bit of intelligence proved to be correct." He still had not been told, of course, that the compound the intelligence experts had dubbed a "Secondary School" was, in fact, a military installation bristling with hostile troops.

Senator Frank Church, who five years later would head the Senate's special committee investigating the American intelligence community, asked Laird what could have been the most probing question of the entire hearing: "Was there any evidence that the prisoners had been evacuated just before the mission or within a day or two?"

"No, there was no evidence of that," Laird replied truthfully. There was evidence, of course, that the prisoners had been evacuated *months* before the raid. Had Church's question been rephrased only slightly—"Was there any evidence, just before the mission or within a day or two, that the prisoners had been evacuated?"—Laird would have had to answer "Yes," or to hedge, lest he reveal the Gamma intercepts. But no one asked that question.

Senator Albert Gore asked Laird an intriguing question: "Was the decision on the final execution postponed at any time before that final date?" This time Laird's reply was less than precise: "No. The decision had not been postponed. As a matter of fact, there was no postponement as far as the plan was concerned."

The committee soon turned its attention to another matter. Laird was badgered at length about the "limited duration, protective reaction strikes" flown south of the 19th parallel only hours after the Son Tay raid. Had the Department of Defense resumed large-scale bombing of the north? No, Laird said; the strikes were flown to retaliate for an unarmed RF-4 reconnaissance plane shot down ten days earlier, on November 13. Both crew members were lost. No parachutes were sighted.

The shootdown, Laird contended, violated "an understanding" made with the North Vietnamese when the bombing halt was called in 1968, that U.S. reconnaissance flights could continue to be flown over North Vietnam. A further part of the "understanding" was that the North Vietnamese would no longer shell major population centers in South Vietnam. Yet, he said, North Vietnam had shot down nine other reconnaissance planes or their escorts since the bombing halt, and had indiscriminately shelled Saigon and Hue earlier in the month. The strikes, which involved 225 strike aircraft and lasted over a period of "only seven hours," were flown in retaliation.

Laird did not mention, however, that the strikes—one of the most concentrated aerial missions of the entire war—had been planned for almost a month *before* the shootdown of the reconnaissance plane. Moorer had asked Blackburn's opinion about the possible consequences of such a strike early in November.

Again Laird, a 17-year veteran of the Congress himself before he had been appointed Secretary of Defense, had to be less than candid before the branch of government he had served so well. The committee was frankly skeptical of his explanation of the air strike, and newsmen, with only a few exceptions, gave

Laird's testimony the worst possible interpretation. The humanitarian aspects of the Son Tay raid were ignored by many editors and television commentators decrying the resumption of large-scale bombing over North Vietnam.

Blackburn's and Mayer's worst fears had come true. Asked weeks before to comment on the possible impact of such strikes, they had warned, in writing, that it would be devastating. The reasons were obvious. "Rescue" and "retaliation" were two pages apart in Webster's Dictionary and two light years apart in public opinion. But even more critical, in their opinion, was the fact that retaliatory strikes might provoke actions against the remaining prisoners that, they hoped, the raid itself would not.

Blackburn and Mayer had been told that Kissinger had agreed to "no bombing." But then came those odd, last-minute hints that a 24-hour delay in the Son Tay raid might "interfere with other operations" they were no longer privy to. The two missions had been launched almost simultaneously—105 planes supporting the rescue of prisoners of war near Hanoi meshed with 225 strikes in the south of North Vietnam retaliating for one RF-4 shot down ten days earlier. The timing of those retaliatory raids on Saturday, November 21, only hours after the abortive rescue attempt, was "to haunt us for months," Mayer would recall. Around the world, newspapers which lauded the rescue attempt in one sentence deplored resumption of the bombing in the next. The whole purpose of the Son Tay mission was getting lost in the flak.

Having been equally evasive before the Foreign Relations Committee about both the retaliatory strikes and the Son Tay rescue, Laird tripped on one crucial fact that day. Asked by Senator Stuart Symington about losses on both missions, Laird said, "We had no losses of any planes in the protective reaction attacks south of the 19th parallel this weekend and we had only two casualties in the operation to rescue the POWs." The statement was true. But it didn't sound that way a few days later when word leaked to the press that an F-105 on the Son Tay raid had been shot down and lost over Laos. Some newspaper editorials suggested that Laird was "quibbling"—and wondered what else had happened on the raid that the administration was not making public.

Members of the committee felt Laird was also quibbling on other matters. One of his biggest supporters, Senator Jacob Javits of New York, obviously didn't like the retaliatory strikes, but that, he said, was "separate" from the Son Tay raid. "War is not a pink tea business," he acknowledged in one of the hearing's most friendly remarks. But when Javits asked Laird if this was the first such POW rescue attempt, Laird told him, "It was the first time in Southeast Asia in this conflict. I apologize if I gave the impression that I was referring to the history of our country."

Javits would remember that answer when newspapers revealed, in the next three weeks, sketchy accounts of three or four other rescue attempts. They had occurred in South Vietnam and in Cambodia, and they, too, had been "dry holes." Members of Javits' staff were piqued that Laird hadn't spelled them out. When they asked the Pentagon about those other rescue attempts, they became even more miffed when they learned that the news accounts touched only the tip of an iceberg. Its full dimensions, however, would remain hidden for five years.

Son Tay was not only *not* the first rescue attempt "in Southeast Asia in this conflict": it was, in fact, the 71st "dry hole." In South Vietnam, Cambodia, and Laos, 91 such rescue operations were mounted between 1966 and 1970. At least 45 of them, probably closer to 50, were triggered by reports of U.S. POWs. Seventy-nine of the operations involved outright "raids." Of the 91 rescue operations, 20 succeeded—in rescuing 318 South Vietnamese soldiers and 60 civilians. But of 45 raids mounted to rescue American prisoners, only one succeeded. Army Specialist Fourth Class Larry D. Aiken was rescued on July 10, 1969, from a Viet Cong POW camp, but he died in an American hospital 15 days later of wounds inflicted by his captors just before his rescue. The raid, apparently, had been compromised at the last minute.

All of the rescue missions before Son Tay had been handled within the Joint Personnel Recovery Center (JPRC), a separate

staff section within MACV Headquarters in Saigon. The results
of the JPRC's efforts were no less heartbreaking than the raid
on Son Tay. In December of 1966, for instance, a confidential
informant passed word of American prisoners being held by the
Viet Cong. The JPRC found his information credible and
launched a raid. There was a heavy fire fight in which 35 Viet
Cong were killed and 34 others detained. During interrogation,
they confirmed that Americans had been held in the camp. The
prisoners had been moved just before the raid.

Some of the JPRC's raids failed because intelligence was compromised, others because the rescues weren't launched quickly
enough. This happened on one raid in 1967 when a South Vietnamese escapee from a Viet Cong POW camp reported the
location of two camps containing American prisoners. His report was challenged at first, then finally verified. A raid was
launched, and at one camp, 21 South Vietnamese prisoners
were recovered. The other camp was empty. Yet evidence
showed that American POWs had been there. The released
South Vietnamese POWs said that the Americans had been
moved about 30 days before the raid, after the escapee first
reported the presence of American prisoners there.

After Aiken's 1969 rescue, efforts to find POW camps and
free prisoners in South Vietnam and Cambodia intensified. In
1970 alone, 24 separate rescue operations were conducted in
the south. They failed to unearth even the remains of a single
U.S. prisoner. The rescue missions continued even after the
failure of the Son Tay raid. By 1973 such missions would total
119, including 98 raids. Aiken would remain the only American
ever to be recovered.

Against that backdrop, the Son Tay raid was not the spectacular failure, or at least not the unique failure, that it seemed to
be to the hostile senators who had questioned Laird. By denying
that other similar rescue missions had been attempted, Laird
missed an excellent opportunity to put the Son Tay "failure" in
better perspective. Yet he may not have known the tragic history of those earlier recue missions. Ed Mayer knew of them,
for instance, but Blackburn his immediate boss, would insist
that *he* never did. Had the Congress and the American people

been informed, they might have better understood the motives behind the Son Tay raid—and the slim chance for its success.

Laird had not sounded candid with the Congress or the American people. Perhaps it was because the Pentagon is reluctant to admit its failures; perhaps because the committee's pejorative questions and comments ridiculed a mission in which Laird believed deeply; or perhaps because Senator Fulbright was viewed as a public enemy only a shade less dangerous than North Vietnam's General Vo Nguyen Giap by an administration that felt that any information given to him was too much.

Whatever the reason, Laird's testimony shed little light on the Son Tay rescue and contributed so much misinformation that it only added to the controversy. Soon after he became Secretary of Defense, a small restaurant/bar on Connecticut Avenue nine blocks from the White House had paid Laird a special tribute by naming one of its sandwiches after him: "The Melvin R. Laird: provolone and baloney, $1.85." But Laird had offered one comment at the Fulbright hearing that would prove to be anything but baloney. Senator Javits asked him, "What signal do you want Hanoi to get on our commando raid on the POW camps?" Laird told him, "That we will take rather unusual means to see that these men are returned as free Americans." And when Senator Claiborne Pell asked him what he thought North Vietnam would do about the POWs "as a result of the raids," Laird's response was prophetic:

"I would assume that they might be guarded more closely."

Public Relations

At the White House on Wednesday, November 25, President Nixon personally decorated four of the Son Tay raiders.

Some time before the ceremony, Laird ushered Manor and Simons into the Oval Office. Nixon had asked to meet with them privately, to express his thanks—and ask what had happened. The President was "very cordial," but he didn't find out much.

Stewards from the White House mess offered drinks or coffee as the men "relaxed" with their Commander-in-Chief in deeply upholstered chairs arranged around a rug with a huge seal,

"President of the United States," woven into it. Asked later what he and the President had talked about, Bull Simons would recall, "Not much. He asked me what year I had graduated from West Point. I told him I didn't, that I was a reserve officer commissioned out of ROTC from Missouri. That seemed to faze him. He said, 'Oh!' and turned to Manor. They did the rest of the talking." The meeting was "very thoughtful of the President," Simons said, "but I wouldn't call it a thought-provoking visit. In fact, it was kind of dull and uncomfortable."

The ceremony began at 4:05 P.M. in the White House State Dining Room. Nixon delivered a short, prepared introduction before Laird read each man's citation. Simons was awarded the Distinguished Service Cross for "extraordinary heroism," the nation's second highest award for valor. Army Sergeant First Class Tyrone J. Adderly, the M-79 grenadier and ground guide in Elliott Sydnor's command group who had twice come under heavy automatic weapons fire but "eliminated the threat to the force," received the same award. Air Force Technical Sergeant Leroy M. Wright, his foot in a heavy cast from the fire extinguisher that had torn loose from the wall of Banana One when it crash-landed inside the walls of Son Tay, received its equivalent, the Air Force Cross. Leroy Manor was awarded the Distinguished Service Medal. The President pinned on each man's decoration personally.

The President's remarks and the citations were very general, adding little to what the press had been told about the raid two days earlier. Nixon expressed his pride in the "mission of mercy" to free men held captive "under the most barbaric conditions." The raid, he said, had been carried out not only with "incomparable bravery" but with "incomparable efficiency," as though Senator William Proxmire might otherwise launch an investigation into what it had cost. (The best estimate was about $7 million, but some would suggest an estimate closer to $70 million.)

Nixon then told those present, "Before I gave the final order, I asked some very searching questions." He discovered, he said, that "each man who participated in this mission was a volunteer." That was true enough. But the President's next remarks, which may have been provided by his speech writers or may have been made up on the spot, certainly came as news to the men who were being decorated. "I [also] found out," he said, "that each man who participated in this mission knew before he went that there was a 50 percent chance the mission might not succeed." Then he added, "And I found out that each man who participated in this mission knew there was a 50 percent chance that he might lose his life."

Nixon invited Laird, Moorer, Admiral McCain, several POW wives, and the gaggle of congressmen and reporters present to congratulate the four men "personally." At 4:18, the President left the room. The ceremony had lasted 13 minutes—half as long as the raid.

All three TV networks carried clips of the scene that evening. But if the White House thought the ceremony would quell the storm of controversy about the raid, it was mistaken. CBS commentator Eric Sevareid noted caustically that although "Everyone admires the brave men who tried it, a great many cannot help feeling there was something harebrained about the concept." ABC's John Scali noted that "Outdated, inadequate intelligence is being blamed for the failure of the mission. And the finger is being pointed at the Pentagon's Defense Intelligence Agency, not the government's Central Intelligence Agency which was not involved." Scali did not say who had "pointed" the finger, or on what basis he could report that the CIA had not been "involved."

It was the opening shot of another behind-the-scenes CYA— cover your ass—effort launched from CIA headquarters in Langley. Newsmen with a "good pipeline" to CIA headquarters would later report that the raid had been planned and executed without consulting the CIA. The DIA, which had provided the intelligence for the mission, was criticized for giving the Son Tay planners POW information that was "at least six months old." Vice President Spiro T. Agnew exacerbated the situation by decrying the "faulty intelligence"—although his assistant for military and foreign affairs would admit later that Agnew had never been briefed on the raid, before it *or* after.

This new controversy further obscured the humanitarian motives for the raid, and led to another bitter clash between Laird and Fulbright. Called once again to testify before the Senate Foreign Relations Committee, Laird denied Fulbright's assertion that the CIA had not been consulted about the raid. "All agencies were consulted," he said, and "information taken from all of them."

Fulbright interrupted with a statement that came close to accusing Laird of being a liar: "That is not very accurate," he said. "I personally asked the Director of the Intelligence Board if he was consulted and he said 'No.' "

"I don't think that can quite be the case," Laird said, seething; "he was consulted and advised."

Fulbright remained unconvinced. At Langley, where the words "And Ye Shall Know The Truth, And The Truth Shall Make You Free" are carved in 7-inch letters on the marble wall of the entrance lobby, a CIA spokesman declined to comment on the Laird-Fulbright exchange. The buck was skillfully being passed to the DIA for the Son Tay "snafu," further straining relations within America's already fractionalized intelligence community.

On Thanksgiving Day, Thursday, November 26, President Nixon shared his Thanksgiving dinner with 106 servicemen wounded in Vietnam and made a promise to "free the prisoners of war at any cost." Hanoi's delegation to the Paris peace talks called a press conference. North Vietnam's spokesman condemned the "protective reaction strikes" launched the previous Saturday, claiming they had killed 49 civilians and wounded 40 others. He refused to acknowledge that a raid had been made to free prisoners from a camp near Hanoi, referring only in general terms to "acts of war."

That same day in North Vietnam, which was usually quick to charge the United States with aggressive acts but obviously embarrassed that American helicopters had been able to land undetected within 23 miles of its capital, Hanoi finally informed its population of the raid on Son Tay. North Vietnam claimed that the futile, inept effort had cost frightful casualties among the American raiders and that a "number" of POWs had been "wounded" in the raid. In Moscow, *Pravda* charged that the

raid was the first step toward "spreading the land war into the
territory of North Vietnam."

North Vietnam's claim that there were casualties among the
Son Tay raiders and the POWs they were attempting to rescue
spawned a new controversy about how much—or how little—
the Pentagon had revealed about the raid. In the absence of
hard facts, "inside" reports abounded, one of them claiming
that the raiders had seized "a few" North Vietnamese prisoners
at the empty compound and taken them to an undisclosed
location in Southeast Asia for interrogation. The report was
wrong. Blackburn and Simons had flatly ruled out the advisabil-
ity of taking enemy prisoners long before the training at Eglin
began. Simons would later explain why: "I wanted *nothing* to
distract us from the real mission. Moreover, a helicopter is a
very fragile machine. In the rush of boarding to get out of there
in the dark, what do you do? Flash a guy down, turn up nothing,
and then find out he's got a grenade in his jock strap? You'd lose
the plane. So I scratched that idea off my list. We didn't do it."

But Henry Kissinger was convinced that Simons' men had
taken one prisoner—a baby water buffalo. Just where the rumor
started is uncertain, but one of Kissinger's key deputies asked
a reporter to check it out "off the record." Kissinger, he said,
was livid. If word leaked out, the operation would look even
more ludicrous, and there was already more egg on everyone's
face than the White House could stomach. Asked on what basis
Kissinger concluded that a water buffalo had been kidnapped,
the deputy explained that there had been rumors of a prisoner
being seized. The raiders denied it, but when the White House
ordered the helicopters to be searched with a fine-tooth comb,
there were unmistakable traces of water buffalo dung beneath
the floorboards. Since the White House would look kind of silly
asking too many questions about water buffalo dung, could the
reporter make a few quiet inquiries and report back? Concern
for the POWs in North Vietnam that had motivated the raid on
Son Tay had deteriorated into a White House flap over a baby
water buffalo.

When the reporter queried Blackburn about the rumor, he
laughed, incredulous. "You're out of your raving mind!" he said.

"May be," the reporter replied, "but why don't you check quietly? Maybe your Special Forces group on Okinawa is babysitting the tike until it's safe to bring him into the country." Later that afternoon, Bull Simons thought Blackburn had lost his marbles. "A *water* buffalo, for Christ's sake? No, my God, we don't have a water buffalo!" Blackburn asked him to check anyway. A few days later Kissinger learned with relief that the water buffalo either didn't exist or was hidden in impenetrable cover.

Five years later, Simons would not be amused when he was asked again about the mascot. "There is no mistake about it," he insisted. "Can you imagine running out in the dark and grabbing a water buffalo by the ass in the middle of all that? The idea is ridiculous." He denied categorically that his men had kidnapped a water buffalo. "I know God damn well it did not come back with the ground force," he said, "because I watched them load the planes." But what about the helicopters that landed near Finger Lake? "Oh," Simons replied carefully, "I don't know about that."

Marty Donohue was the pilot of one of the helicopters that landed near Finger Lake, the only one that remained on the ground long enough to wrestle a baby water buffalo aboard. Donohue swore that he didn't kidnap the beast either.

Henry Kissinger apparently got some very strange intelligence briefings.

Early in December, as he was mulling over the 30 days' leave he would soon be taking, Bull Simons got a call from the Pentagon. Defense Secretary Laird, he was told, would fly to Fort Bragg in a few days with a plane full of congressmen and other dignitaries, plus some members of the Pentagon press corps. The secretary of defense, on behalf of the President, would personally decorate each of the Son Tay raiders for heroism and meritorious service. Because so many details of the individual citations which Simons had submitted soon after the raid were "rather sensitive," the Army had decided Laird would read just one citation covering all of the raiders. The individual citations would be processed later and put into each man's personnel file. The call was to "clear" the wording of Laird's citation with

Simons. Simons asked a few questions and then slammed down the phone.

Of the 56 men he'd led into North Vietnam, he had just been told, only two others would receive the Distinguished Service Cross which President Nixon had pinned on him and Sergeant Adderly at the White House. Two of Simons' men would receive the Silver Star; 22 would get the Bronze Star with "V" device (for valor); the remaining 30, over half of his men, would get the Army Commendation Ribbon with "V" device. Soldiers called it the "Green Weenie." As a medal, it ranked one notch above the Good Conduct Ribbon, which soldiers could earn for staying in uniform three years without catching V.D.

It was clear to Simons that the Army's decorations and awards branch had decided on a "standard G.I. issue" of medals to his men. He could just picture what had happened. Some chairborne colonel looked at the stack of citations which Simons had worked hard to draft and submit for fast approval—and then shoved them aside. He flipped through Army Field Manual 101–10–1, issued in September of 1969, which cited as a "guide for commanders" the rates at which medals are "normally" awarded. Then flicking on a desk calculator, he said: "Let's see: that'll mean 2 Silver Stars or better, 22 Bronze Stars and 30 Commendation Ribbons." Having figured out the formula, he handed some major the stack of Simons' citations: "Have these rewritten accordingly, will you?"

Disgusted by his call from the Pentagon, Simons walked out of his office and said to one of his sergeants, "You lucky sonovabitch, you're going to get the 'Green Weenie.' "

"I don't understand, sir," the sergeant said.

"It's simple, you dumb shit; the Pentagon thinks you went to a North Vietnamese tea dance. Some dumb bastard in the awards section up there flunked his map reading course: he couldn't find Son Tay if it was inside the Kremlin. He thinks you went to a tea dance in an enemy brothel."

That evening, Bull Simons decided to lay it on the line. He picked up the telephone, dialed Fort Bragg's command center, and told the operator simply, "This is Colonel Simons. Priority call. Get me the Army Chief of Staff."

Within a minute, the Army operations center in the basement of the Pentagon had Simons back on the phone; General
Westmoreland was en route from Iran and would arrive at
Andrews Air Force Base about seven the next morning. General Palmer was the acting Chief. "Did Colonel Simons want to
talk with General Palmer or wait for General Westmoreland?"

Simons refrained from swearing and asked for Palmer.

In seconds, the Army Vice Chief of Staff was on the line:
"Bull, this is Bruce Palmer. What's up?"

"General," Simons told him very calmly, "some dumb
sonovabitch is sending the secretary of defense here in a day or
two with a box full of Green Weenies. It might be best if he
didn't come; I'd hate to see some of the men turn those decorations down in front of a flock of reporters."

"Turn them down? What do you mean, Bull?"

Simons told him, "General, I don't want to embarrass the
Army, but one of my men is just likely to shove an Army Commendation Ribbon straight up Mr. Laird's ass. These men risked
their lives outside Hanoi; they weren't on a Boy Scout patrol in
the suburbs of Saigon. Your awards section is handling these
decorations as though it were business-as-usual and we were
holding up their Friday afternoon golf outing. This wasn't business as usual. These guys laid it all out; every one of them
earned at least a Silver Star. For what they did, Green Weenies
are an insult, not a decoration."

"I understand how you feel, Bull," Palmer said. "I'll look into
it."

On Wednesday, December 9, 1970, Defense Secretary Melvin Laird arrived at Fort Bragg aboard Air Force Two. He
awarded 54 medals to the Army Son Tay raiders. Four of them
were Distinguished Service Crosses; 50 were Silver Stars. There
were no Green Weenies in Laird's box of medals.

Forty-three of the raid's Air Force participants were deco-
rated in the same ceremony. John Allison, Warner Britton,
Marty Donohue, and Herb Kalen were awarded the Air Force
Cross, their service's counterpart of the Distinguished Service
Cross. Laird pinned the DSC on the blouses of Elliott Sydnor
and Dick Meadows.

Doc Cataldo got a Silver Star. Only a few days after the raid, he had gone to see Ed Mayer. He volunteered to go back to North Vietnam—as a prisoner.

Cataldo knew the POWs needed a doctor. Why not "send" them one? He told Mayer he was willing to have any kind of device implanted anywhere in his body to keep track of him— and to help him, in turn, report back on the prisoners or perhaps call in another raid. Mayer could arrange to have him shot down, if that's what was needed to make his capture plausible. Cataldo didn't know how to fly, but he was willing to take off in the back seat of an RF-4, have the pilot put the plane on autopilot, and eject over friendly territory while Cataldo "flew" into Hanoi. Once he saw or heard the North Vietnamese air defense batteries open fire, he would set off a time-delay destruct mechanism to shoot *himself* down—and bail out just before it was due to go off.

The Silver Star Laird pinned on him cost the American taxpayer $1.70.

Until that ceremony, Cataldo's family was skeptical that he had really been on the raid. Before the operation was launched, Simons, Manor, and Mayer had polled their men to ask who wanted his participation to be made public or was willing to be interviewed, within *very* tight restraints about any operational details. Most of the men asked for their names not even to be made public. That fell through, however, when Nixon and Laird decided to decorate the men in a public ceremony. It was an attempt to quell the controversy that surrounded their mission. But the detailed citations that Simons had drawn up for his men would *not* be made public. There were still a lot of questions about the raid that the administration didn't want to answer.

One award for the Son Tay raid was never made. It was an Army Commendation Medal for a sergeant first class from Company A, 7th Special Forces Group. Until a few days before the raid, he was on Simons' assault force. But "Blue Max" got wind that the man was having some serious family problems and, although a "fantastic, damned brave soldier," had developed serious doubts about the war in Vietnam. Simons "amputated" him and put the soldier in the 36-man Support Group. He was gravely disappointed. He wanted more than anything to be on the raid. After the assault force had left for Thailand, Blue Max learned that the sergeant was thinking about defecting. But he worked hard and when Simons returned, he wrote him up for an Army Commendation Medal. A few days later, the soldier deserted. He fled to Denmark, then Sweden, and became a war protester. Ed Mayer "yanked" his medal. To his great credit, however, the sergeant turned himself in to the U.S. military attaché in Sweden within weeks, and asked to return to the United States to "face the music" for deserting. To the Army's credit, it did not press court-martial charges against him, but gave him a general discharge.

Another of the most important Son Tay "awards" had already been made—in an unofficial ceremony at a cocktail party in the Virginia suburbs.

A few hours after the raiders returned to Udorn, one of Simons' noncommissioned officers snuck off base and entered a small tailor shop frequented by American GIs just outside the main gate. He asked the proprietor if he could make up about 100 embroidered shoulder patches in the next three hours. He showed the merchant a sketch. The patch was about 3 inches round. In its center against a black background was a steaming white mushroom with two beady eyes peering out from under it. On a small tab just below were the initials KITD/FOHS in black letters against a white background.

It was mid-afternoon on November 21. The sergeant's eyes were bloodshot, his face was tired; he'd been back from the Son Tay raid less than eight hours and he had not slept in two days. He was also risking a court-martial. In a flagrant breach of security, he'd left the intelligence debriefing compound to sneak off base and get these patches made up. Time was a problem. Instead of resting at Udorn for a few days, the raiders had learned, they would load aboard one of the medical evacuation C-141s which had been standing by for the rescued POWs; right after dinner, they would be flown out of Thailand directly back to Fort Bragg and Eglin. The sergeant was determined not to leave without those patches.

The tailor checked with one of the seamstresses in the crowded back room of his shop and returned to the front counter. The patches could be made, he said, but they would cost $2, American, apiece. "Can you have them ready by five o'clock?" the sergeant asked.

When the Son Tay raiders returned home and could finally tell their families what they had been up to over the months past, a few of them held cocktail parties. After the JCS After Action Report had been submitted, thank-you letters written, and recommendations for awards and decorations made, the men on the planning and support staffs could also relax; and early in December, Air Force Lieutenant Colonel Benjamin N. Kraljev, Jr., invited Blackburn to a party at his home in suburban Virginia. Kraljev had been one of Manor's key operational planners. Midway in the party, he called for silence and turned to Blackburn. "General, the men have made up their own patch. We'd like you to wear one. You earned it too." He gave Blackburn the round, black patch. Blackburn looked at the quizzical eyes peering out from beneath the mushroom, smiled, and asked, "What does this stand for: KITD/FOHS?"

Kraljev answered quietly, "Sir, that's us: Kept In Total Darkness/Fed Only Horse Shit."

Post Mortem

Whatever its public stance, the Pentagon was badly shaken by the reaction to the Son Tay raid. Shortly before Laird had flown to Fort Bragg to decorate the raiders, Manor's after action summary finally arrived from Thailand—almost a week after the assault. Part of the report—fortunately, its most innocuous pages—immediately fell into the hands of columnist Jack Anderson. Already unhappy that communications had failed at every key juncture of the raid, Laird viewed the delayed post-operations report and the Anderson leak with even greater annoyance. He and Moorer decided it was time for a shake-up of the military communications network worldwide.

Another shake-up was in the wind. Most of the criticism about the raid was directed at the various intelligence agencies that had supported it. Despite Laird's protests that the raiders had been given "excellent" intelligence, despite attempts by members of the intelligence community to pass the buck or simply retreat behind a wall of official silence, the impression left on the press and public was clear: a well-intentioned military operation had been doomed from the start by faulty intelligence. The message was not lost on the Pentagon and the White House. As a senior member of the National Security Council would later remark: "Son Tay was the last straw." At the time, the NSC viewed the raid as just one more of the snafus that prompted a major reorganization of the intelligence community put into effect one year later.

But in the meantime, the Pentagon undertook another line of investigation to determine if the cause for the raid's failure was faulty intelligence or faulty security. That investigation would turn up some significant facts about the enemy's reaction to Son Tay.

Two months after the raid, Sully Fontaine was on his honeymoon when a "counselor" from the American Embassy tracked him down and told him to be on the next flight for Hong Kong. Someone would meet him there with further instructions. Fontaine had planned to spend almost a week with his bride in Bangkok, one of his favorite cities. But after 28 years in the intelligence business, he was used to getting unexpected orders in strange places at inconvenient times.

Forty-four years old, Belgian-born of French parents, fluent in four languages, Fontaine was a professional spook, an experienced Army clandestine operator. He had joined the British Army in 1943, went through Commando training and airborne school, and parachuted into Europe to work with the American OSS, and the Dutch, Belgian, and French undergrounds. He earned the Croix de Guerre with Palm from both Belgium and France. After the war, he studied philosophy at the Belgian Military School, was posted to the United Nations for three years, and then coaxed into the United States Army for officer training while the Korean war was winding down. There, he commanded the United Nations Honor Guard, a crack, 99-man American unit augmented by special platoons of elite troops from seven other countries. Fontaine had his own private international peacekeeping force. But he was soon back in the "underground" commanding one of the Army's first Special Forces' training teams in Korea.

For the next three years, Fontaine's assignments fluctuated between military intelligence and more Special Forces work. Sent to the 10th Special Forces Group in Germany in 1959, he organized "special missions" in Africa and the Middle East instead. In 1963, he was sent to Vietnam to organize a Special Forces camp where the Mekong River crosses into Cambodia, and to help train South Vietnamese and Cambodian units. He did his job well and ended up in Don Blackburn's Special Operations Group. Blackburn put him in charge organizing agent networks, recruiting Montagnards and supervising special operations in Cambodia and Laos.

After three tours in Vietnam, Fontaine was put into criminal intelligence work in Europe. One of his duties was to serve as the U.S. military liaison officer to Interpol. Two years later he was back in Southeast Asia, investigating international crime organizations throughout the Far East. At the time his honeymoon was so abruptly interrupted, Fontaine was on leave from a tour as deputy commander of all Army criminal investigatory work in the western United States. He had been looking forward to introducing his bride to life in San Francisco when their honeymoon was over.

Fontaine and his bride flew immediately to Hong Kong. There, another embassy "counselor" met his plane and handed him an envelope. His leave was canceled; he was directed to fly to Washington.

In Washington, Fontaine was escorted to the Pentagon and ended up, he would recall, "in a cellar someplace." There, in a cramped office with a "Special Access Only" sign on the door, he was told: "We have just received an order to investigate a leak on the Son Tay raid. You're in charge." It was not a routine investigation. His orders were signed personally by the acting Army Chief of Staff, General Bruce Palmer, "by direction of the Secretary of the Army."

Fontaine knew only what he had read about the raid. For two days, he examined the Son Tay files: draft after-action reports, counterintelligence assessments, security files, "everything involved." He concluded that investigating a possible leak was ludicrous. With professionals like Simons and Blackburn behind the raid, there couldn't have been any. Moreover, he knew that if there had been a leak, Simons and his men would have been creamed seconds after landing in North Vietnam. Simons had brought all his men back virtually untouched. Fontaine had served with Simons—"the greatest soldier I ever met."

But Fontaine's Pentagon contact was adamant: "No, we had a leak. As you know, there was nobody there when they arrived. Somewhere along the line before the raid, somebody knew that raid was going to be made. We feel that foreign intelligence knew about the raid, told the North [Vietnamese] and that is why they cleared out."

To Fontaine the whole investigation sounded like a "political imbroglio" between different intelligence outfits trying to lay the blame on someone else. But he hand-picked a team of investigators, sent one of them to Fort Bragg and another to Eglin Air Force Base, while he flew back to Southeast Asia— without his bride.

In Pnom Penh, Cambodia, Fontaine contacted his "French connections." Given his experience with Britain's Special Operations Executive, the European underground, and American Army special missions in Europe and North Africa, he had some very close French friends. Fontaine had two requests to make of one in particular. First, he wanted to find out what the Chinese knew about the Son Tay raid. That would be "no problem," his friend told him. Second, Fontaine wanted to have dinner with a certain Russian intelligence operative. But it had to be set up through an impeccable, neutral intermediary both could trust. The Frenchman was glad to oblige; he knew Fontaine was in the American Army but suspected he was really working for the French.

That night, Fontaine received a call from a Polish intelligence officer who told him: "I have a Russian I'd like you to meet. You two have many common interests; why don't you have dinner with us?" The Pole and Fontaine, it turned out, had trained together in SOE. Fontaine was elated. "The Poles," he would explain years later, "have the best intelligence in that side of the world. The professional Polish intelligence can run circles around any NKVD, KGB, MI-6, or other agent you want."

At the Café de la Paix the next night, Fontaine knew the Russian was "no flunky" before they'd finished their first drink. The two had known of each other, but only by reputation, word-of-mouth, and dossiers. The Russian, Fontaine found, was slightly mystified; this odd meeting had been set up through a Pole by a Frenchman who swore that Fontaine was part of *his* team. He asked Fontaine bluntly if he was a double agent. Fontaine disappointed him. No, he just needed some information. What could the Russian tell him about Son Tay?

The question startled the Russian; he told Fontaine that the raid had been a total surprise. But his next remark gave away the Russian reaction to the raid. If the Americans could hit Son Tay, he said, they could " 'hit' anything in North Vietnam," couldn't they?

The next day, Fontaine's French contact met him at the same restaurant. Now, he explained, the Russian had a favor to ask. He wanted to know what the next target was. Was it the Lang Chi Dam near Son Tay?

Fontaine didn't have to lie. He said he didn't know. The Russian, Fontaine's French friend exhorted, wanted to know what Fontaine *thought,* not just what he knew. "You can go back and say, 'I don't know nothing about it,' " Fontaine said, "not a thing!"

The question about the Lang Chi Dam left Fontaine "flabbergasted." It was such an obvious target. The Russians had to be intensely worried about it to have probed him, through a cutout, on *future* operations. "One thing came out loud and clear" from his visit to Pnom Penh; the Russians were worried about the dam near Son Tay.

The Chinese reaction, Fontaine found, was different. The raid had caught them by surprise too, but it made them mad. "Something was wrong someplace," Fontaine was told, if North Vietnam couldn't handle a small military force operating close to its own capital. The Chinese didn't ask about the dam. What they wanted to know was, did Fontaine have any ideas for infiltrating the North Vietnamese—so China could find out how badly screwed up things really were in Hanoi? The Chinese, he would report to Washington, "were really shook" by the raid. "They thought the whole goddamn country [North Vietnam] was about to be overrun by a platoon of American hippies."

From other sources, Fontaine became convinced that there had been no leak about the raid through friendly intelligence channels. His British contacts were one such tip-off. "If you want to know what's going to happen next week in Washington," Fontaine had always thought, "don't go to Washington, go to London." And one British contact, the head of British military intelligence in North America at the time, told him admiringly, "We were shocked. For once, none of you big mouths even talked."

As good as he was, there *was* a security leak about the raid that Fontaine was not to uncover. It happened in Hawaii, where only three officers knew of the operation beforehand. One was Admiral John S. McCain, Jr., Commander-in-Chief, Pacific. The second was Army Lieutenant General Charles A. Corcoran, his Chief of Staff. And the third was an Air Force officer seven ranks junior to them, Andrew Porth. Porth, however, wasn't "cleared" to know of the raid. In the parlance of military intelligence, he simply "G-2'd it," or figured it out on his own.

Porth was a young intelligence captain in the Escape and Evasion Branch of Headquarters, Pacific Air Force (PACAF), at Hickam Air Force Base. The 5-foot 11-inch, blond, wavy-haired officer was responsible for all POW information and planning for "Egress Recap," the processing of returned POWs. He made sure that every fighter group in PACAF had its own display board of North Vietnam showing photos of the known POW camps. All of the "traffic" on prisoners of war—messages, reconnaissance photos, and intelligence analyses—crossed his desk. He worked closely with the 548th Reconnaissance Technical Group, which compiled the so-called PACAF Index. This was almost a bible for those concerned with POW intelligence; it contained every POW's and MIA's picture, and statements from key witnesses about the circumstances of his shootdown or disappearance. The book was widely used in interrogating defectors or captured Viet Cong or North Vietnamese. Porth's office was literally a vault which he shared with reconnaissance specialists who controlled the "air assets" for certain intelligence missions.

In September and October of 1970, Porth began to notice that routine traffic once classified only "Confidential" was being upgraded to "Secret." And that what used to be "Secret," in turn, soon became "Top Secret." This was particularly true of reconnaissance missions flown over North Vietnam. Photos he used to see regularly no longer crossed his desk; he had no "need-to-know." He sensed that "something was up." Yet, due to a quirk in counterintelligence planning as the Son Tay operation was being "tightened up," he still saw regular data on the "tracks" of proposed reconnaissance missions.

There were other indications that something was brewing. Porth received calls from offices that were now "cut out of the loop," asking him what was going on. All over the Pacific, "assets" were being shifted about—airplanes, missions, people, special communications equipment. As weeks went by, it was becoming harder and harder for PACAF officers to do their jobs. They couldn't manage their part of the war very well when the tools they were supposed to control were taken away without explanation for missions they knew nothing about.

On Wednesday, November 11, nine days before the Son Tay raid, a medical service major in PACAF's Surgeon General's Office called Porth, perplexed. He wanted to know if Porth could tell him anything about a medical-evacuation C-141 that had been pulled off regular Vietnam flights and put on alert at Clark Air Force Base in the Philippines. It was specially configured to handle 55 ambulatory or litter patients. It was now standing by on "moment's notice," the officer told Porth, to "launch." The major couldn't figure out what for, and he felt the plane might be needed for regular medical-evacuation missions. (There was still a very real war under way in South Vietnam—312 Americans were killed and 1,940 wounded in October of 1970.)

Porth told the major he had no idea. Then, the number 55 hit him—an airplane specially configured for 55 patients? That was the number of prisoners, according to the latest DIA estimate Porth had seen, of POWs still held in Son Tay. He rechecked the map coordinates of reconnaissance tracks whose photographs he was no longer cleared to see. They were over Son Tay. Porth was suddenly very sure that someone was going to raid Son Tay.

He also knew it was an operation he wasn't cleared for, something he shouldn't discuss with anyone. Still, the idea haunted him. The following Monday, November 16, he put together an intelligence briefing board—a chart on which photographs and maps could be stuck as the briefing progressed, yet quickly removed, put into an envelope, and secured in a vault or locked file drawer. His briefing board spelled out the "indicators" that told him a raid on Son Tay was imminent. Porth put it away, but that Wednesday he told the watch officer on duty in PACAF's intelligence warning center to call him immediately if he came across *any* new mention of POWs—whether on radio news bulletins, the wire services, foreign newspapers, or wherever.

Two days later, on the night of November 20, Porth received a sudden summons to report to PACAF's headquarters building. There he found a "big gaggle" of people. "Something" was going on in North Vietnam. They were "really agitated," stirred up—the air defense system was "hot," missiles were going off like a string of Chinese firecrackers, radio traffic was at a level PACAF hadn't seen in years—and no one knew why.

Porth watched his boss, Colonel Pat E. Goforth, PACAF's Deputy Director of Intelligence, survey all this confusion. PACAF's Vice Commander, Lieutenant General John P. Lavelle, joined the group. Everyone stood around, explaining to Lavelle what the North Vietnamese were doing—but no one could explain *why* they were doing it. Porth went to his office, took his briefing board out of the vault, pasted it all together, shrouded it with a cloth, and carried it back to the headquarters building. He approached the watch director, a full colonel named Walter Stevens. "I think I know what's going on, sir," he reported.

By now, it was close to 9:30 P.M. Still no one had been able to tell the vice commander, Pacific Air Forces, what in hell was stirring up so much action in North Vietnam. Finally, Lavelle was told that a Captain Porth might have something worth hearing. Porth unveiled his briefing board and said: "I believe it's a raid on Son Tay. Here's why I think it adds up."

Lavelle listened to the short briefing, looked Porth in the eye, and told him bluntly, "You're out of your God damn mind, Captain."

Porth quickly retired from the scene. He would recall just one reaction to the encounter: "It was odd. General Lavelle usually doesn't cuss."

Lavelle went to his office, he would relate later, picked up a red phone, his "hot line" direct to CINCPAC headquarters, and asked the officer who answered to speak with Admiral McCain. McCain was in his operations center and could not be disturbed, Lavelle was told. Then he asked to speak with General Corcoran; but Corcoran was with McCain and he could not be interrupted either. Lavelle told the aide to carry a note into them. It explained his concern that something "big" was up in North Vietnam. Within seconds, a rear admiral was on the line: "They know all about it," he said—whatever "it" was—and the situation was under control. Lavelle was asked to have his "guys 'cool it,' lay off, don't speculate."

Three days later, November 23, Lavelle was listening to Secretary of Defense Laird brief the Pentagon press corps about a raid on a POW compound at a place called Son Tay. One of the little-known wonders of military communications is that the Pentagon's daily press briefing can be heard as it is under way in every major headquarters around the world. Few members of the Pentagon press corps were ever aware that their impertinent questions about the Vietnam war were sometimes listened to "live" everywhere from Teheran to Saigon.

At work in his vault that same day, Porth got a call to report to the "vice commander's office, fast." When he entered, Lavelle was still listening to the Laird briefing. "Sit down, Captain," Lavelle said. "I thought you'd enjoy listening to this with me." It was one of the most effective, unspoken tributes of the entire Son Tay episode. When the press conference ended, Lavelle asked Porth, "Are you *sure* you weren't told beforehand that this was going to come off?" Porth told him, "No, sir, I just guessed."

Blackburn and Mayer would not hear of the Porth incident for five years. "This could not have happened," one of them would protest; it meant something had slipped through the elaborate security precautions taken to mask the raid. Nor could they believe that if it had happened, it would not have surfaced sooner; that meant something was wrong with the post-raid assessment. But Mayer would also doubt five years later that Fontaine's investigation of Son Tay security had even taken place; he had not heard of it before and would question, if it had, why no one on the team had grilled him.

From his viewpoint, Fontaine would be equally piqued, five years later, to learn from a journalist that Bull Simons had landed at the wrong camp.

There was another, even more disturbing aspect of the raid that remains a mystery even today. Who were those "100 to 200" men killed in Bull Simons' "pre-emptive strike" at the "Secondary School" south of Son Tay Prison? CIA's George Carver would insist that he had never been told and, when he checked his agency's records, "could not find out." He deferred the question to the DIA, calling it a "military matter." When the DIA checked its records, no entry could be found even indicating that the question had ever been listed as a collection requirement. It might seem, in the aftermath of the Son Tay failure, that the nation's security apparatus went out of its way to avoid learning any more bad news about the operation.

Were those troops at the "Secondary School" Chinese? If so, Bull Simons and his men had slaughtered an entire company of elite Chinese troops and left their billets in North Vietnam "burning like a Roman candle" at the very time when Henry Kissinger and Richard Nixon were massaging every diplomatic channel they could think of to open a dialogue with Peking. Or were they Russians? If they were, they had been killed by American troops almost one year to the day after Moscow and Washington opened their first round of Strategic Arms Limitation Talks. Is it possible that the CIA didn't *want* to know who those troops were—and that the DIA didn't want to report that the Pentagon might have just "blown" Kissinger's secret "game plan" in world power politics?

Soon after the raid, it became clear, from sources independent of Fontaine's inquiries, that both Moscow and Peking were shook up by the peculiar events at Son Tay, perhaps because they thought the real purpose of the raid was to give some sort of devious signal that the war was going to get very rough—and on someone else's territory. The Russians reacted almost at once. Soviet armed forces became much more intent about rear area security; units were reorganized and forces shifted to establish special reaction forces at critical targets all over the world. One of them was the Lang Chi hydroelectric plant, the dam 65 miles northwest of Hanoi whose turbogenerators would soon become operational and more than replenish the North Vietnamese power sources taken out by the American bombing effort that had also put so many prisoners into the cells of North Vietnam. Not long after the raid on Son Tay, a ground security element of about a battalion in size was deployed there. Despite the failure to rescue any POWs at Son Tay, the appearance of that force proved that the enemy feared Blackburn and Manor's unconventional brand of warfare more than they did an "invasion" of Cambodia, or some other orthodox military operation, where their units could choose to "stand and fight" or fade into the jungle and avoid battle.

Ironically, the failure of the Son Tay raid discouraged the Pentagon and the White House from launching similar "pinprick" operations. Blackburn and Mayer had been planning a raid against the Lang Chi Dam for almost a year before Son Tay. Son Tay had been designed in part to give Blackburn the license to unleash it. But in the glare of publicity that surrounded the Pentagon's failure to rescue any POWs, the military hierarchy forgot that Simons had executed the rest of the mission almost to perfection. And when the new security forces were discovered, the Joint Chiefs would not even formally consider the proposal to knock out the dam. The operation was scrubbed from SACSA's list of "new initiatives."

The dam *was* finally taken out, not in a raid but in a bombing attack. On June 10, 1972, eight Air Force F-4s hit the complex with 15 laser-guided 2,000-pound bombs, one of the first uses of "smart bombs." The strike worked. Generators in the concrete portion of the dam were severely damaged, while the earthen portion was not damaged at all, thus avoiding a flood down the Red River Valley that undoubtedly would have caused a furor of protest around the world. Power available to North Vietnam's national transmission network was once again in such short supply that in Hanoi itself, electricity was rationed.

The Chinese proved equally concerned about rear area security in North Vietnam. All over the country and in northern Laos, where Chinese "engineers" were not only improving railroads and building roads and bridges but also actually manning air defense batteries, a lot of "construction crews" were soon guarding instead of building. And a week and a half after the raid, it was learned, a Chinese senior delegation traveled from Peking to Hanoi and met with leaders of the Lao Dung Party in a hastily scheduled "review" of the situation in Southeast Asia. Precisely what went on is probably not known, but years later White House sources would admit having learned that Hanoi's leaders were subjected to a "brutal" interrogation. Phrases like, "Have you lost not only the candle, but the hour?" were used. And there were hints, it was reported, that China had reconsidered its generous flow of aid to support North Vietnam's struggle in the south. Perhaps to reinforce that point, a large shipment of Soviet materiel moving to Hanoi by rail through China was inexplicably held up at the Chinese border. The Chinese would only explain that there were "technical problems" with the Russian shipping documents.

It was, at least in part, the growing enmity between China and Russia that finally enabled the Nixon administration to extricate itself from Vietnam. At last, the three great powers—America, Russia, and China—had had enough of the Vietnamese morass; and the North Vietnamese, fearing Russian and Chinese influence no less than American intervention, were equally eager to be rid of them. Doors that had been locked and bolted for years began to open slowly, and each nation involved in the struggle attempted to extricate itself with some shred of political or military advantage. It was a time-consuming process as North Vietnam, with a skill far beyond its experience in international power politics, played one great nation off against the other to achieve its ultimate goals.

For the Americans, it was an agonizing process. The North Vietnamese still refused to play their trump card: the American POWs. The year 1971 saw American combat deaths in Vietnam fall to 1,380, one-seventh of what they were during Nixon's first year in office; and 177,000 American soldiers returned home safely. But no POWs. At the end of the year, there were 478 known POWs and 1,013 Americans missing in action.

The Joint Staff spent a lot of time that year working on a plan it had sketched out soon after the Son Tay raid. Desperate to get the POWs home, the Pentagon was ready to recommend a replay of the raid on Son Tay, but on a scale of vastly different proportions and with far graver implications. Early in 1972, a "close hold" meeting of the Joint Chiefs of Staff reviewed the plan. Moorer thought well enough of it that he invited Laird to sit in the second time it was presented, early in May.

By then, there were only 62,600 Americans left in Vietnam, but more than 525 POWs and 1,150 MIAs somewhere in Southeast Asia. The President had visited China, but North Vietnam had just unleashed a savage attack in the south. America responded by mining Haiphong Harbor. Bombing of the north was resumed. Yet North Vietnam still refused to budge on the POW issue. America was desperate—and the Joint Chiefs were ready to consider anything to get those men home.

The proposal which JCS planners presented in "the Tank" would show how hopeless the POW situation had become, and how much America cared about those men. It proposed a "raid" by three and a half *divisions* into North Vietnam, an invasion involving 57,500 men to rescue some 500 Americans. The raid would be a simultaneous airborne, amphibious, and airmobile

assault to envelope Hanoi and ring it with American troops,
cutting every avenue of escape. Small Special Forces teams
would seize Hoa Lo Prison, the Plantation, and outlying camps
like the Zoo where prisoners were known to be held. To
"cover" deployment of airborne forces to within striking distance of Hanoi, a ruse was devised that joint maneuvers were
to be conducted in the western Pacific, in which the entire 82nd
Airborne Division would participate for the first time. After
"marshaling" on an island en route to those maneuvers, the
82nd would parachute instead on "choke points" outside Hanoi
—while Special Forces teams parachuted into the prisons inside
the city. The planning was so meticulous—many of the Son Tay
planners were involved once again—that detailed maps of the
sewer systems from Hoa Lo had been obtained from some of the
very French designers and engineers who had laid them out
years before.

Such a raid would be an incredible gamble. More raiders
would die than POWs could be rescued, its planners knew; and
they couldn't be sure of locating every outlying prisoner-of-war
camp—the DIA, it would turn out, had confirmed the location
of nine of the 13 POW camps North Vietnam had used or was
using by then—or of freeing all those in the ones that had been
identified. But another element of the plan made them confident Hanoi would release any POWs the raiders would be unable to free.

Some of the Special Forces teams would have a much freer
license than Bull Simons' men had been given. Their job was
not only to recover as many POWs as possible, but to pick up
any hapless, high-ranking North Vietnamese officials they could
lay their hands on—the higher the rank, the better—and "extract" them as well. North Vietnam could then be invited to
exchange the POWs who hadn't been freed for those members
of its high command on whom the tables had been turned.

Although planning reached the point where a Marine division was ready to embark and other forces were "ready to go,"
the alert order for the raid was never issued. One of the planners would state later that, in his opinion, the raid would have
"ended the war." "The God damn country was really that des-

perate. This is what we were almost forced to do." Had the operation been launched, he felt, the war would have been "all over in two weeks."

The war did not end for another 11 months. Years later, the CIA would profess to know nothing of any proposal to ring Hanoi with three and a half divisions. CIA's memory would prove to be equally bad about a raid that had actually taken place—Son Tay. Its records were "incomplete." "Not that much about Son Tay was ever put in writing," a deputy director would explain. A few "sensitive" records at the Pentagon would turn out to be missing; the files were "cleaned up" in 1973. Memories of some of the men who planned the raid would be more convenient, or protective, than others. A lot more is known today about the raid on Son Tay than was ever made public in 1970. Yet many questions remain.

Contrary to impressions at the time, the intelligence supporting the raid was remarkable. But did it, like the planning and execution of the raid, border on "overkill"? Had the raid been launched soon after the Pentagon learned of the POWs at Son Tay, would they have been rescued? Had the Pentagon forgotten one of General George Patton's favorite dictums: "A good plan violently executed now is better than a perfect plan next week"? Or was the Pentagon right, knowing that the plan had to be not only good but almost perfect if Bull Simons and his men were to get in and out of North Vietnam alive, let alone rescue the POWs at Son Tay?

Yet if the intelligence for the raid was so good, why was it discovered only at the last minute that the prisoners had been moved four and a half months before because of a flood? Or was it known earlier, but never told to those so intimately involved in planning the raid—and those ready to risk their lives executing it?

One senior member of the intelligence community would confirm that the information *was* known well before the raid, but known only to a very few. He would say bluntly, in an interview that he knew was being tape-recorded: "In July of 1970 they had a tremendously harsh typhoon season in North

Vietnam. The river outside Son Tay flooded. It stopped flooding when it was two feet from the outer wall. The North Vietnamese were concerned, so they moved out of Son Tay."

Asked if he found out "later" or before the raid that the prisoners had been moved, he replied: "In July. And then *some*body moved back in September. Now, I changed the word right there: *Some*body. We weren't sure who. This is the key part of it right here. . . . I am not sure how well known it was, but they moved out because of the rain, the flooding in July."

Were the July floods caused by Operation Popeye? Those cloud-seeding operations, conducted over North Vietnam in 1967 and 1968 and shifted to Laos from 1969 to 1972, entailed some of the most carefully guarded secrets of the Vietnam war. Testimony at a Top Secret briefing of the Senate Foreign Relations Committee in March 1974 would reveal that information about the program was so sensitive that it was denied to the President's closest advisers. So high was Popeye's classification, an Air Force witness explained, that information about the program was even withheld from a National Security Council interagency panel formed in 1972, while the war was still underway, formed specifically to look into "weather modification and geophysical activities as weapons of war." Another witness, the Deputy Assistant Secretary of Defense for East Asia and Pacific Matters—and the man to whom the Pentagon's Vietnam Task Force reported—would admit that "The first *I* heard of it was as a result of a Jack Anderson column." But he wasn't the only senior defense civilian kept in the dark. The Secretary of Defense himself, Melvin Laird, had told that same committee in 1972 that "We have never engaged in that type of activity over North Vietnam." Two years later, in 1974, he had to write Senator Fulbright that he had "just been informed that such activities were conducted." Without explaining further why the Pentagon's number one civilian had not been clued in, Laird expressed his "regret that this information was not available to me [earlier]."

Was it possible that, because of the tightly compartmentalized secrecy surrounding Operation Popeye, the Son Tay planners were not told when, or why, the POWs were moved? CIA's

George Carver failed to see any connection at all between the flood or their move and Operation Popeye. Recalling, incorrectly, that few Popeye missions were flown over the area west of Son Tay that summer, he would remark: "I think you're all wet about that one." But Carver would admit in 1976 that he hadn't even thought about connecting the "coincidences" before. Another senior intelligence official would confirm, however, that his agency did know in July or early August that the prisoners had been moved. Asked if the planners would have been told, he would reply: "Yes, yes, yes." Would they have been told *before* the raid? "Yes, at the Manor level, that level." Would the Joint Chiefs of Staff have been told? "That's kind of a tough one. They might not have."

The fact is that not one of the Son Tay planners was told. "I'll castrate anyone who knew that the prisoners had been moved, or thought it, and didn't tell me," Blackburn would remark. Even though the DIA had dramatic photos of the flood as it occurred, Mayer would insist that no one knew until November that the prisoners had been moved: "I would unequivocally, face to face, call whoever says otherwise a liar." Moorer would also deny that he was given any such information. It was not until the eve of the raid that the Son Tay planners learned, through Nguyen Van Hoang's pack of cigarettes, that the prisoners had left. And even then it was believed that "someone" had moved back to Son Tay.

The quantity—and quality—of the intelligence made available to the Son Tay planners was indeed remarkable. Otherwise Bull Simons and his men would not have gotten in and out of Son Tay alive, with or without any POWs. But in retrospect, the planning, execution, and aftermath of the raid must be viewed in light of the information that they did *not* have. Not until the last minute did they discover that the POWs they hoped to rescue had been moved. Not until the last minute did Blackburn discover that the CIA had inserted a CAS agent in the vicinity of Son Tay, an agent whose activities might have compromised the security of the raid. Moorer knew, DIA's Don Bennett knew. But Blackburn found out about it only by accident. Not until *after* the raid did the planners realize that the

Pentagon and the White House intended to launch massive "protective reaction strikes" over North Vietnam almost simultaneously with the Son Tay rescue.

Yet Blackburn and the other Son Tay planners still knew a lot more than Manor, the man who commanded the raid, and Simons, the man who led it. Should not Manor and Simons have been warned that the camp would probably be empty? In an operation where minutes—seconds—counted, should not Simons have been prepared to touch down, look around, and get the hell out if the prisoners weren't there? It is possible that the planners thought the prospect of attacking a "dry hole" would have an adverse effect upon the morale of the raiders. It is also possible that they were hoping for some last-minute confirmation that "someone" was still at Son Tay. Whatever the reason, the raiders were not told, and with intelligence which indicated that the POWs had, in fact, been moved but that "someone" was still at Son Tay, the raid was launched anyway.

Why? Why was a raid once thought to have a 95 percent chance of success launched at all when the odds looked more like 10 or 20, or at best 50, percent? The Army's Vice Chief of Staff, Bruce Palmer, would insist that "the Joint Chiefs were never made aware, before the raid, that it had only a 50-50 chance." CIA's George Carver, whose boss would claim soon after the raid that the CIA had not been consulted, would say that the last-minute "traffic" was "fragmentary." It indicated a "possibility" of a "dry hole." "*One* interpretation was that the guys were gone," he said. "There was a conscious last-minute debate," and Carver himself would admit that he had been "back and forth" on the phone with Laird about whether or not to "go."

But Mayer would recall that "the evidence was overwhelming," so much so in his view that "The operation would never have gone had it not been for Don Blackburn." In his own defense, Blackburn would claim that the evidence was not that conclusive. "Had I known, I'd have had to call it off." But he would admit candidly, "I didn't *want* to know. I wanted to *go*. I was looking for any straw I could find to keep that mission alive. I wanted to demonstrate that we could get in there and pull their chain. Sure, I wanted to find POWs; but I didn't *want* to know the truth, I just wanted a shred of evidence to let us hang in there. It was bigger than getting the POWs out. There were too many people who didn't have the perception to understand what this was really about, or could accomplish."

What *did* the raid on Son Tay accomplish? Some of Blackburn's cohorts, years later, would claim the only thing it proved was how hard it is to call off an operation once military planners set their minds on it, and once the Joint Chiefs and the Pentagon put momentum behind it. The weight of the military bureaucracy. Blackburn's enthusiasm, the possibility that "someone" was still at Son Tay, the desperate plight of the POWs in North Vietnam—all undoubtedly influenced Laird's final decision to "go." Like his advisers, like the President himself, he was willing to risk failure.

Ironically, the Pentagon had avoided one failure when it learned early in the planning that Ap Lo was empty. But the news that Son Tay was empty arrived at the eleventh hour, on the heels of two reports in ten days that 5 percent of the known POWs had died in North Vietnam's prisons. The decision makers had only hours to grapple with a new conflict, to avoid another failure—or take an even bigger risk.

Was it a risk worth taking? The Son Tay raiders failed to rescue a single POW, and while the Russians, the Chinese, and the North Vietnamese were shaken up by the raid, their subsequent actions made similar rescue attempts, as well as other operations in Blackburn's catalogue of clandestine warfare, even more risky. The failure of the raid laid the Pentagon and the White House open to a new barrage of criticism about the conduct of the Vietnam war. But it did demonstrate to the world America's outrage at the treatment of the POWs by North Vietnam, and the determination of the administration to do everything in its power to bring those men home. The North Vietnamese got the message. The raid triggered subtle, but important, changes in their treatment of American POWs. In the final assessment, the raid may not have been a "failure" after all.

Hoa Lo Prison

From their cells in Camp Faith, Mo Baker and the other prisoners who had been moved there four and a half months earlier from Son Tay saw the raid unfold. There was a large surface-to-air-missile site next to the Camp Faith compound. But they hadn't known it until the battery suddenly opened fire, in salvo, one missile after another, at about 2:30 A.M. that morning of November 21. One "hellova noise" woke them up. It was like sitting on the end of a runway behind a flight of F-105s when they lit their afterburners to take off.

The prisoners leaped off their bunks and pressed their faces to the bars to see what was happening. They could see very little; the walls outside were too high. All they knew was that a "flock" of SAMs had gone out almost underneath their windows. Suddenly from the back side of their cellblock, some prisoners called, "Hey, come look at this." Looking to the west now, they saw flares being dropped, SAMs going off, flashes and explosions, "a lot of action." Immediately they knew: "Damn, they're raiding Son Tay!"

They began cheering and hollering. Some thought other prisoners must have been moved into the camp after they had moved out on July 14. Mo Baker would recall thinking, "Holy cow, there goes my ride home." Elation was mixed with disappointment.

The guards at Camp Faith were upset, frightened, acting as if "they had a riot on hand," one POW would remember. Guards bolted into the cellblocks brandishing rifles and AK-47s. They told the prisoners, "Get away from the windows. Lay down. Back to your bunks."

Within hours, at "very early daylight," the prisoners found out what a "panic move was like." Guards told them to "roll up" —dishes, drinking cups, everything. That afternoon, trucks (not buses this time) drove into the prison. Blindfolded, slapped into manacles, the prisoners were jammed into the trucks and, late that evening, driven to downtown Hanoi. It was dark when they arrived, but they recognized the Hanoi Hilton. This time, however, they were marched in through the back gates. Mo Baker's entire compound from Camp Faith was jammed into one huge room. It was in an old part of the prison Americans had never been held in before. Close to 50 men shared a common "bed" that night, a 15-foot-wide slab of concrete that ran 40 feet down the middle of the room.

The prisoners immediately began to pump several English-speaking guards as well as the officer in charge: "Why were we moved?" No one would tell them. "You will know in the future," was all anyone would say. But the prisoners could figure it out. The North Vietnamese were scared. Even as intelligence officials were debriefing the Son Tay raiders in Thailand, North Vietnam started to round up the POWs from scattered camps all over the north and hustle them into downtown Hanoi. The prediction that Melvin Laird was to make five days after the raid was already being fulfilled.

The roundup continued for weeks. From North Vietnam's view, Hanoi was much better defended. The prisoners wouldn't be vulnerable to another Son Tay. Not even a battalion of mad men could bust open Hoa Lo Prison. From the prisoners' view, the roundup was the best thing that ever happened to them.

Two days after Son Tay, Navy Lieutenant (j.g.) Charles Plumb was suddenly moved to his fifth prison in three years. He had been shot down just south of Hanoi on Ho Chi Minh's birthday, May 19, 1967, on a mission against a military complex called Little Detroit. He was captured in the deadliest month of the air war, only five days before he was due to come home. After weeks of learning how effective North Vietnamese torture was in New Guy Village in the Plantation, Plumb was moved to the Hanoi Hilton with just one cellmate. Four and a half months later he was taken back to the Plantation; this time, he had two cellmates. In July of 1969, he was moved to the Zoo, with three cellmates. In September 1970, he too was moved to Camp Faith, this time with seven cellmates. Two months later, on November 24, 1970, just three days after the raid on Son Tay, he was thrown back into the Hanoi Hilton for what the guards would describe only as "security reasons." There were 57 men in his cell.

It was a dramatic change from the virtual isolation he'd known for almost three and a half years. "Alone," he would recall, "we had no counsel, no power. Alone we despaired." But with 57 cellmates, it was "like walking into the Smithsonian for the first time . . . a brand-new source of information and entertainment." Plumb and his fellow prisoners were crammed into a 25 × 35-foot room with only 14 inches of bed space apiece, but they were "overjoyed to be among comrades."

Other POWs soon joined them at the Hanoi Hilton, and after his release, Plumb would write of the changed circumstances of his captivity:

Approximately 260 POWs became organized into the Fourth Allied POW Wing. We were divided in squadrons, flights and sections. Each subdivision with its own commander attained the same pride we had once known in our flying units. Now we could act as one body—mates in one cell wouldn't be on a hunger strike while fellows in the next cells ate cookies. We had bargaining power . . . SROs now had a unified force to confront the enemy. They also had authority to control behavior of the prisoners. . . . The increasing strength from unity made impact and our demands were met.*

*I'm No Hero—A P.O.W. Story as Told to Gwen de Werff by Charles Plumb. Independence, Mo.: Independence Press, 1973.

The POWs were finally allowed to bathe daily. That November of 1970, Plumb would write, "We were happy to be able to discuss, joke, and laugh together in our larger cells, but it was especially rewarding to join for prayer in prison." They decided to rename the Hanoi Hilton "Camp Unity."

Ralph Gaither was also at Camp Faith, only 15 miles away, the night of the raid on Son Tay, his former prison. "The whole sky," he would remember, "lit up" that night. The POWs at Camp Faith heard "tremendous bombing." Some thought that air attacks against the north, at a lull since 1968, had started again; others heard the helicopters and wondered if a raid might be under way.

They were washing dishes when the North Vietnamese suddenly told them to load everything—buckets, clotheslines, mops, everything—aboard some trucks. Within two or three hours they, too, were on their way to the Hanoi Hilton where they were crowded 40 to 60 men in each room, some of them only 22 by 45 or 60 feet long. "With so many men, we really got organized," Gaither would recall. "Each room became a squadron. The senior man in the room became its squadron commander, the next man down was executive officer. Other assignments were made: an education officer to correlate subject areas and persons for individual and group study; a recreation officer to correlate games, exercise and other activities; a chaplain . . . a health, welfare and sanitation officer. . . ." Within days, the POWs had made contact with most of the senior officers held elsewhere in the prison. "The new organization, the return to a high level of military efficiency, was very good for our morale." Gaither spent the next year and a half under those dramatically changed conditions. It was "a creative period" for him. He loved to write poetry and his work blossomed.

One of the Hanoi Hilton's last new guests as the Son Tay roundup continued was Navy Commander Edward H. Martin. Shot down on July 9, 1967, while leading a strike against Ninh Binh, he spent the first year of his incarceration in solitary. After months of that he was near death. He lived on one thought: "Six months from now, I'm going home." Every six months, he'd convince himself anew. It was his way of holding onto sanity while they worked him over in the Zoo, finally throwing him into a cell 78 inches long and 60 inches wide with four other men, sleeping on concrete, two of his cellmates in irons, unable to urinate, never getting a shower, not knowing how long they'd be there.

About 2:30 A.M. on November 21, Ed Martin, from his cell in the Zoo, saw the flares over, explosions around, and surface-to-air missiles flying above Son Tay. Instinctively, he knew what was up.

As SAMs arched into the sky almost due west of his prison cell, Martin watched them explode harmlessly only 19 miles away; they were detonating everywhere from 2,000 to 18,000 feet above the terrain. He had seen lots of SAMs—at much closer range. One had finally nailed his F-4 on July 9, 1967. On the morning of November 21, however, Martin realized that not one SAM had hit its target; he knew all too well what the explosion looked like when an SA-2 slammed into a plane in mid-air. He broke into tears. He knew that Son Tay was empty; but that didn't really matter, he told himself. America cared. He had his best night's sleep in three years.

Thirty-six days later, Martin found himself in relative paradise; he was moved into the Hanoi Hilton the day after Christmas, 1970. In a large room with him were 19 other POWs. Some were old Navy friends, some men he had heard being tortured in the Zoo but had never been able to talk to.

One of them was Air Force Lieutenant Colonel James H. Kastler, a hero well before he was shot down on August 8, 1966. He broke both legs on bailout and came to be held in virtual awe by his fellow prisoners. Taken to the Zoo, with Martin in a cell only 25 feet away, Kastler was put "on the ropes" one night and worked over unmercifully by a sadistic expert known only as "the Cuban." He was handcuffed, blindfolded, and beaten 700 times with a fan belt—100 strokes a day for seven days. Blindfolded, he couldn't anticipate the blows. There was no way of knowing when to tense up, when to relax; all he could do was wait. Each time he fell mercifully unconscious, the Cuban waited until Kastler came to and then started over.

Finally, Kastler said, "I surrender, I submit." Guards brought pencil and paper so he could sign his "confession." But when they told him to write, Kastler replied calmly, "I've changed my mind." His torture started all over again.

Ed Martin listened to it all. He would say of the Cuban, seven years later, "I'd pay $5,000 right now to find out who that bastard is."

Jim Kastler's fate in North Vietnamese hands wasn't made any easier by a *Time* magazine story about him that hit the newsstands just before his capture. It told of an F-105 pilot who'd become a legend among disgruntled airmen fighting an air war under "rules of engagement" imposed by Washington that made it almost impossible to hit a meaningful target, and which had turned the skies over North Vietnam into a duck-shooting gallery. But, *Time* noted, Major James Kastler somehow always got his target. No one knew how he did it. A week later he was shot down on a strike south of Hanoi. It wasn't long before Hanoi got its copy of *Time* and the North Vietnamese knew they'd nailed a big one. They kept him in solitary for years, determined to break him. Thanks to Son Tay, Jim Kastler finally got a roommate in the Hanoi Hilton.

Another of Martin's cellmates in the Hanoi Hilton was Captain Bill Lawrence, the *Constellation* attack wing commander and former aide whom Tom Moorer had heard shot down on June 28, 1967, a few weeks before he became Chief of Naval Operations. Martin *saw* Bill Lawrence go down; he was leading a strike right behind him. Two weeks later, Martin himself got smoked. Wounded when his plane was hit and beaten to a pulp later, Martin soon became very, very ill. He thought he was going to die. He used the tap code to seek help. Lawrence was the man he contacted. Lawrence told him not to give up. When he didn't hear from Martin, Lawrence tapped out a message asking for *Martin*'s help. It forced Martin to "get it together" and not give up. Thanks to Son Tay, Martin and Lawrence finished their "program" in North Vietnam together.

The most senior American POW was Colonel John P. "Jack" Flynn, shot down on October 27, 1967, on his 36th mission over the north, almost all of them on "Route Package Six" near Hanoi, the most heavily defended part of North Vietnam. Held in isolation from the other prisoners at the Hanoi Hilton with a few ranking officers, Flynn was nevertheless able to command the Fourth Allied POW Wing in every sense of the word. As North Vietnam moved more and more prisoners back into the Hanoi Hilton, his secret orders were quietly but quickly passed from cell to cell. Whether the other prisoners understood the reasons for them or not, Flynn's instructions were followed almost to the letter. One of his former officers would say of him, "He led his men through the Hanoi torture chambers when all he had left to lead them with was integrity."

Now a major general, Flynn would call Son Tay "the most magnificent operation of the war." After they consolidated the prisoners in the Hanoi Hilton, Flynn remembered, "we heard about Son Tay" from POWs who had been in the outlying camps. Some had seen the firing; some had heard it. Some thought it was a commando raid; others felt sure it was to take the POWs out of Son Tay.

"There was a wave of exuberance. Our morale soared," Flynn said. "For a while, of course, we didn't have absolute confirmation that there had been a rescue attempt, but we were pretty darned sure. What gave it away, finally, was North Vietnam's own propaganda. We heard them vilifying Vice President Agnew over the squawk box one day. They were complaining about his 'provocative' boast that the U.S. would 'go anywhere, even to the center of Hanoi,' to rescue its prisoners."

For some of the prisoners, however, word of the Son Tay raid was an omen of bad days ahead. Flynn was one of the officers who reacted this way at first. "Among the senior officers," he admitted five years after the raid, "we talked a lot about Son Tay. We reasoned, first, that it was a surprise raid of a type that could not be duplicated again. For one thing, we were all in the Hilton now; it wasn't the kind of place you could bust open very easily. Second, we asked ourselves, why would the U.S. resort to such an extreme? We concluded that the U.S. had lost its leverage at the bargaining table in Paris. Son Tay, we speculated, was a 'court of last resort'—a last chance to get us out, or to get enough of us out to regain some bargaining power, by focusing attention on the prisoner situation and showing the world how badly we were being treated.

"The conclusions discouraged us. Our original estimate had been that the war would last eight years. We said to ourselves, 'Maybe we'd better think of 15 years if we've lost that much bargaining power.' We never transmitted that to our constituents, of course. But for those of us who would have to remain (we weren't sure that there hadn't been some new prisoners in Son Tay by the time they raided it), it signaled that we'd be in North Vietnam a long, long time."

Not all of the prisoners who were moved to the Hanoi Hilton after Son Tay had been shot down over the north. Air Force Colonel Theodore W. "Ted" Guy was shot down over Laos on March 28, 1968. He had been kept in solitary for almost 1,000 days without ever having a roommate. At the Hanoi Hilton, put into an isolated cellblock with the other senior officers near Flynn's, he saw his first American in almost three years. He was still locked up alone, but finally he could "talk" with somebody besides a captor.

Another POW glad to have company was Ernie Brace, one of the earliest shootdowns, a CIA Air America pilot who managed to pass himself off as an Air Force major. He showed up at the Plantation late in 1968, having spent two and a half years held captive in a *cave* near Dien Bien Phu, five miles from the Laotian border. That entire time, over 900 days, he was kept in irons, alone. It was damp, dark, vermin-infested. Finally moved to the Plantation, he was slammed into a closet-like "room." It had a door and a barred window. He had to stand on his "honey bucket" to see out, but the North Vietnamese bolted shutters on the window when they caught him peeking out. When the other prisoners finally established communications with him, they asked how he liked his room. "Gee, this is all right," he told them. "It's a vast improvement over my cave."

Air Force Colonel Norman C. Gaddis, shot down on May 12, 1967, was another man whom the Son Tay raid brought out of hiding. Like Ted Guy, he too had spent over 1,000 days in solitary, most of them in Heartbreak Hotel, the most secure, isolated, and painful part of Hoa Lo Prison. None of the other prisoners had even seen him, but his name was in the "memory bank"; someone had spotted a picture of Gaddis' identification card in a North Vietnamese pictorial magazine. After the Son Tay raid, he was given his first roommate in four and a half years, Air Force Colonel James E. Bean, who also had been in solitary since his capture on January 3, 1968. Both had spent most of their confinement in Heartbreak Hotel, but were finally moved into another remote part of Hoa Lo, "The Mint," the senior officer cellblock where Jack Flynn and Air Force Colonel David W. Winn, another 1968 shootdown, were held separately in nearby cells. Other senior officers were there as well—such as Navy Captains James B. Stockdale and Jeremiah Denton, Jr., both 1965 shootdowns, and Air Force Colonel Robbie Risner. All had been moved in and out of Heartbreak Hotel to other remote sections, like pawns on a chessboard, making it virtually impossible, the North Vietnamese thought, for them to communicate with the other prisoners.

For Bean and Flynn, the reunion was both joyful and painful. They learned that at least three of their fellow airmen had gone insane while held captive in the north. The three were among a group of 11 POWs called "the Lonely Hearts," men whom the other POWs had identified one way or another as being "in the system" but who were kept isolated even after the Son Tay roundup. The other eight had been shot down over Laos. The POWs feared that they would be returned to the Pathet Lao and used as separate bargaining chips. When Mo Baker recalled those three men who had gone insane—and never came home —he would note quietly, "The Son Tay raid may have saved the sanity of some others."

One of the POWs everyone was happiest to see was John S. McCain III. Most of them knew how much he had suffered. His spirit amazed them—Jack McCain was the one who cheered *them* up, who had a sense of humor, who uplifted them. He showed them that human decency was not dead: Americans took that spirit to Hanoi, held onto it, and sustained each other with it.

At the Hanoi Hilton, one of McCain's cellmates was Nguyen Guoc Dat, a South Vietnamese pilot nicknamed "Max." Born in Hanoi, he fled to South Vietnam in 1954. In 1966, he was shot down over North Vietnam on an air strike led by Marshal Nguyen Kao Ky. One day Max overheard some guards talking about the raid on Son Tay, the first "positive evidence" the prisoners had of it. Word quickly passed from cell to cell; throughout the Hanoi Hilton, McCain would recall later, there was an atmosphere of "elation."

Dave Sooter, a twenty-two-year-old Army warrant officer, was flying H-23 helicopters for the 1st Cavalry Division when he was shot down over South Vietnam. It was February 17, 1967, less than seven months after he'd finished flying school, when his helicopter was suddenly hit. It exploded 50 feet above the trees. Sooter remembers breathing fire. He passed out before his burning helicopter hit the trees.

When he came to four or five hours later, Sooter was already a prisoner. His captors gave him three days to recover some strength, then marched him to a camp hidden in the jungle about ten miles inside the border of northern Cambodia. He was held there for three years. On November 2, 1967, Sooter tried to escape. He was caught within hours, and his legs and arms were put in stocks while he suffered helplessly as ants and mosquitoes feasted on his festering new wounds. Within a week, he was near death. One night he "saw Jesus' face" and began praying. The next day his captors took off his stocks. That night they put them back on. When morning came, the stocks came off again. Dave Sooter turned into a devout Christian.

As well as he can fix the date, Sooter's long march to North Vietnam began on November 8, 1969. He walked for 43 days. He guesses he walked 600 miles—over jungle-covered mountains, exhausted from the tropical heat, miserable from the frequent rains, weak from malnutrition. When he reached the Demilitarized Zone between North and South Vietnam, he was put on a truck; it drove right up the Ho Chi Minh Trail, at night, and landed him a week or two later in a prison camp near Hanoi. Sooter thinks the miserable, cramped new prison may have been at Ap Lo, near Son Tay. Wherever it was, discipline at the camp was lax; the beatings were sporadic, not regular. He could not recall where he was moved next, but less than a year later, he and his fellow prisoners heard the raid on Son Tay—

aircraft overhead, small arms firing, explosions, SAMs screaming through the air. Four days later, with no explanation, the
North Vietnamese moved them all into the Plantation in the
northern part of downtown Hanoi. Almost every prisoner who
had been moved north from South Vietnam, Cambodia, and
Laos was soon put into the same camp.

A few days after Sooter arrived at the Plantation, an English-
speaking North Vietnamese officer told them about the Son Tay
raid. He claimed that North Vietnam had known about it two
weeks ahead of time. But when no one paraded newly captured
prisoners or American bodies, Sooter knew he was lying. And
the camp guards, Sooter noticed with relief and amusement,
were too busy digging trenches and foxholes or practicing air
raid drills to hassle the prisoners much.

Even before the raid on Son Tay, North Vietnamese treatment of the POWs had begun to ease—"ease" being a relative
word. The POWs sensed the change after Ho Chi Minh's death
early in September of 1969. Some attributed it to that; others
to the massive letterwriting campaigns launched in America
urging more humane treatment of the prisoners. Many believe
it resulted from the fact that propaganda statements, so often
extracted from the prisoners under brutal torture, had
backfired. In 1966, for instance, Captain Jeremiah Denton, Jr.,
had been paraded before a foreign television crew. When U.S.
intelligence analysts examined the film clips, they noted that his
gaunt eyes were blinking oddly. In Morse code, he had
managed to spell out one word: "Torture." American diplomats
explained the film quietly to foreign officials around the world.

North Vietnam's campaign to extract military information by
torture had also failed miserably. The interrogators spoke little
English, the translators were not "hep" on military matters or
America's life style, and information extracted in one session or
camp was seldom correlated with what had been learned in
another. The men held out as long as they could, and when they
finally "talked," they came up with some of the most incredible
lies fighter pilots have ever concocted. At one time, Mo Baker's
compound was put on the racks, one by one; the North Vietnamese wanted to learn the names of every man in their squa-

drons. Through the tap code, the POWs passed the word on what the new round of torture was designed to wring out of them. The information their captors wanted was ludicrously outdated, but they agreed that each man should hold out for ten days. At that rate, it would take the North Vietnamese a year and a half to extract the dope. By the time the interrogation sessions ended, North Vietnam had pieced together an odd American "air order of battle." Dizzy Dean was Mo Baker's squadron commander, Stan Musial the operations officer, and the rest of the St. Louis Cardinals were his flying mates. Other POWs "broke" as well and named their flying mates: Clark Kent, Bruce Wayne, and Captain Marvel.

Brutal as the sessions were, some questions put to the POWs left them in stitches. One interrogator pressed hard for a working diagram of an aircraft carrier. He became outraged when the POWs wouldn't tell him where its pens for pigs and chickens were located. Word of the interrogation passed quickly among the cells. Morale soared among the battered men. Time was such a horrible waste, but not without humor.

By the time of the Son Tay raid, most of the torture sessions were to extract propaganda statements, but even these had abated dramatically. More and more men were allowed to write, and receive, letters. In the first eight months of 1970, 265 men got to write home, compared with 208 in all of 1969 and only 94 in 1968. POW families received 2,148 letters in those first eight months of 1970; only 699 had come through the year before, only 256 in 1968. Yet a lot of prisoners still went without mail, as did their families. The North Vietnamese were consistent only in their inconsistency—and brutality.

And some men still suffered horribly after Son Tay. Mo Baker was caught building a radio; it was almost complete. He told his interrogators it was to get better reception of the propaganda newscasts which blared over loudspeakers throughout Hoa Lo Prison. He finally told them how it was supposed to work. When the North Vietnamese hooked it up, the loudspeakers went dead: Baker's radio had shorted them out. The North Vietnamese found a special dungeon for him. It was very deep. They kept him there for 90 days. Communicating was hard at first. One day, he finally heard "Tap-tap . . ."—"Shave and a haircut, two bits." "Mo, you really pulled their chain," the message told him. Deep down in that solitary dungeon, he felt good that he had given his fellow prisoners something to chuckle about.

By the time Baker got out of solitary, the prisoners were "incredibly well organized." There were regular, communal church services (the starving POWs had forced the issue with a prolonged hunger strike); "movies" (each man reenacted his favorite), plays, and classes. Mo Baker taught college-level math, algebra, trigonometry, differential calculus—15 college credit hours of it. He had never had time to study foreign languages. In the months ahead, he learned to speak Spanish, French, *and* German. Time stopped being such a horrible waste.

The men were also able to give one another medical care. Some had abscessed teeth. Mo Baker was one of them; he said later that of all he suffered, the fractured thigh hurt, the torture hurt, but his abscessed tooth hurt worst. Finally, he lanced it himself. They made him the room dentist.

Spirits lifted and humor improved among all the POWs after the raid on Son Tay. Still, their release was more than two years away. The Paris peace talks dragged on; the real negotiating was done behind the scenes. By October of 1972, there were over 530 known prisoners in Southeast Asia. One of them, Army Special Forces Major Floyd S. Thompson, taken prisoner on March 26, 1964, had spent almost ten years in captivity. Some of the POWs, however, felt almost like "outcasts." They were the "new guys" shot down over the north after the October 31, 1968, bombing halt. Heartbreak Hotel had even been renamed "New Guy Village." The first "new guy" was Air Force Captain Mark J. Ruhling, whose RF-4 reconnaissance plane was bagged on November 23, 1968. In October of 1972, three years and 11 months after being taken prisoner, he tapped out a message from Room 2 of Hoa Lo Prison: "Today I've been a prisoner longer than any American held in World War II. Don't call me a 'new guy' anymore."

Later that same month, on October 26, 1972, Henry Kissinger appeared before the White House press corps and announced that "Peace is at hand." Cynics would later comment that Nixon's landslide victory in his campaign for reelection, on November 7, owed a lot to that announcement. It proved to be premature. The North Vietnamese were not yet ready to sign. When Kissinger returned to Washington after another frustrating round of negotiations, he asked JCS Chairman Admiral Thomas Moorer how many B-52s were operational throughout the world. On Sunday, December 17, they were unleashed over Hanoi.

It was December 18, about ten o'clock in the evening, Hanoi time, when the first sticks of 500-pound bombs fell. As Ed Martin would describe that night in Hoa Lo Prison, "The whole world lit up. . . . The North Vietnamese were absolutely frantic, terrified. We cheered; we cried; we hugged each other. We knew the end was close."

For the next 12 days, B-52s, F-111s, and fighter-bombers from Okinawa, Thailand, and the Tonkin Gulf pummeled North Vietnam in an around-the-clock blitz—1,353 B-52 sorties and 3,-034 fighter-bombers dropped 36,452 tons of munitions, 11 times as much destruction in 12 days as had fallen on all of North Vietnam in the three *years* of 1969, 1970, and 1971. By December 30, 27 American planes and one rescue helicopter had been shot down; 93 airmen would be reported missing; 31 had been taken prisoner.

Negotiations in Paris resumed. At 12:30 P.M. on Tuesday, January 23, 1973, Henry Kissinger and North Vietnam's chief negotiator, Le Duc Tho, initialed the "Agreement on Ending the War and Restoring Peace in Vietnam." On Saturday the 27th, the North Vietnamese and the Viet Cong released a list of 617 American POWs, 55 of whom they said had died in captivity. The list proved to be ludicrously, and in some cases tragically, inaccurate. In the weeks ahead, 566, not 562, American POWs would return home alive.

The first 116 of those men, released in Hanoi, stepped down the ramp of an Air Force medical-evacuation plane at Clark Air Force Base in the Philippines on Monday, February 12, 1973. Millions of Americans, an audience even bigger than had seen

Neil Armstrong and Buz Aldrin land on the moon in July of 1969, watched on TV, choked with emotion, grateful that their ordeal was over, hopeful that the abscess created in the hearts and minds of America by the war in Vietnam would soon heal.

The first man off that plane was Navy Captain Jeremiah A. Denton. He saluted the American flag, hesitated, stepped to a microphone, and told the world: "We are honored to have [had] the opportunity to serve our country under difficult circumstances . . . God bless America." In just 34 words, he summed up eloquently what he had lived for in seven years and seven months of captivity.

In all, 629 Americans survived captivity in Southeast Asia: the 566 men released in 1973, including 2 from China; 12 released earlier by the north; 23 released before 1973 by the Viet Cong; 2 who escaped from the Pathet Lao; 24 who escaped from the Viet Cong (13 of them in the 1968 Tet fighting, the last three in 1969); and 2 who were recovered from the Viet Cong before the war was a war, in 1962. At least 72 Americans died at the hands of their captors. And early in 1976, 763 Americans were still listed as missing in action in a part of the world their fellow countrymen were trying hard to forget.

A year after their release, the prisoners of war were asked to complete a classified "survey of returned prisoners of war." It was a comprehensive 74-page questionnaire, drawn up by Air Force Intelligence and the Monroe Corporation, a small think tank specializing in POW affairs. About 320 of the returnees completed it, including 80 Navy and 20 Marine Corps former POWs.

In one part of the survey, the prisoners were asked how seven events affected their morale while in prison: "Successful resistance (winning); Son Tay raid; Ho Chi Minh's death; attempted escapes; Tet offensive in 1968; December 1972 bombing raids on Hanoi; and Bombing Halts." Their answers to each could range from "Major negative effect" over six options to "Major positive effect" and "Essential to well-being."

Two events aided morale most—by wide margins. They were the 1972 bombing of Hanoi and the Son Tay POW raid. Seventy percent of the POWs said Son Tay had a "Major positive effect" on their morale or was "Essential to well-being." About 60 percent reported the same impact from the 1972 "Linebacker II" bombing resumption. Only 30 percent of the POWs, by comparison, felt that Ho Chi Minh's death had a "Major positive effect," even though many attributed a major relaxation of prison rules and treatment to it. Twice as many POWs called Son Tay "essential" to their well-being as felt that way about the Linebacker II bombing campaign. The difference was striking, given that so many people have attributed North Vietnam's decision to sign the Paris peace accords and finally release the prisoners to the 1972 bombing.

Dr. Roger Shields was the man coordinating all POW/MIA activities after 1971 and in charge of "Operation Homecoming" when the prisoners were finally released in 1973. He came to his job as Deputy Assistant Secretary of Defense for International Security Affairs a few months after the Son Tay raid, but from hundreds of POW debriefs after 1973 and his own extensive visits with many of the prisoners, Shields would sum up its impact this way:

"A lot of people said it was just a foolish thing to have done, that we really didn't have enough information to succeed, and therefore concluded that it was crazy.

"It *did* succeed. It was a very, very helpful operation. There is just no question whatsoever about it. After the Son Tay raid, they were all brought back to Hanoi. There, they were able to get together and organize, to mount some kind of common defense against their captors. That organization was brought about by the Son Tay raid. The North Vietnamese did feel vulnerable, they became very much concerned about this. As a result, they brought them together. They put them in a situation where the men could communicate, organize and support each other and care for the sick and wounded. Not only that, the morale boost that these men received was great. Some of them had been held incommunicado for years and didn't know what was going on. They were tremendously boosted to know that their country cared for them."

Shields would add: "Something else should come out of this. The *Mayaguez* raid worked and those men came home. But there was no guarantee before *it* went off that it would work. Just as there was no guarantee that the Son Tay raid would work.

"Son Tay was a very bold and very imaginative operation. Secretary Laird made the statement that had he the decision to make over again, he would do the same thing and I concur with that most heartily. When you think of the difficulties, no matter how much you rehearse, no matter what kind of maps you have, the first time you run through the real thing, there are going to be surprises.

"I would hate to see the day when Americans feel that we have to have a one hundred percent guarantee of success before we try something like this. That would mean if we didn't have the guarantee, we just wouldn't try, we wouldn't do anything. There is a chance of failure in everything we do."

Political cartoonist R. B. Crockett of the Washington *Star* probably said it best, and first, the day after the news of the Son Tay raid broke. At the top of the *Star*'s editorial page was a drawing of a bearded, gaunt but stooped POW. His ankle was chained to a post outside his hutch. His misty eyes were watching a small flight of American helicopters fade into the distance. He said it all in three words:

"Thanks for trying."

'THANKS FOR TRYING!'

Epilogue

When Hanoi launched its final offensive in South Vietnam during the spring of 1975, South Vietnam's defenses in the Central Highlands collapsed so quickly that nine more Americans became prisoners of war. They included five missionaries, the six-year-old daughter of a missionary couple, a U.S. consular official, and the chief provincial adviser for the Agency for International Development. For five months, the nine were shifted from one detention camp to another, held captive in leaky huts crawling with scorpions and occasionally snakes. Six of them contracted malaria. There was sufficient rice to nourish them, but little else. They lost an average of 20 pounds each. Finally, they were driven by truck to North Vietnam—and imprisoned at a little compound near Hanoi. It was Son Tay.

On the last day of October 1975, almost five years after the raid on Son Tay, they were finally released.

A few weeks before the fifth anniversary of the Son Tay raid, I got a call from Melvin Laird. "Ben, now listen," he said, "about your book. There's one thing you've got to get across: that raid was a *disgrace*. It was a *disgrace*, do you hear me?"

Why? "Because they didn't promote that colonel!" Laird said. He told me that he had tried personally to get the Army's promotion board to pick Bull Simons for brigadier general. When he failed to show up on the list of 80 colonels selected for promotion in the spring of 1971, Laird said he appealed to Westmoreland to add Simons' name to the list. Westmoreland explained to him at great length that it was "impossible"—the Army had a rigid selection system, it worked, the Chief of Staff shouldn't overrule his own promotion boards, not everyone could make general, Simons was a fine colonel but he hadn't even been to one of the war colleges, just because he was an exceptional combat leader didn't mean he'd make a good general, et cetera, et cetera.

Simons retired from the United States Army on July 7, 1971, less than a year after Blackburn asked if he would volunteer for a mission he couldn't describe.

He now raises pigs for a living. He bought a small farm in the swamps near Defuniak Springs, Florida, 70 miles west of where he trained the Son Tay raiders. The pigs, he says, "are the sweetest God damn things you ever saw."

When I asked how he felt about Son Tay, he said, "When the raid was over, I forgot it and I haven't thought about it since then." But he was concerned that the Army was decimating its Special Forces capability. "They can produce results that far outweigh their numbers," he said. "You can demand anything of them, any God damn thing you can name, and you can demand it with impunity, without any hesitation. But it takes good leaders, good training, people who know their business. And these guys will do it."

Not once since his retirement has Simons been asked to lecture at an Army service school, West Point, the Infantry School, the Special Warfare Center, the Command and General Staff College, or the Army War College. He has been invited to lecture at two of the other service schools: the United States Air Force Academy and the Armed Forces Staff College in Norfolk, Virginia. Its commandant at the time was Rear Admiral Jeremiah A. Denton, Jr., one of the Navy's first shootdowns. Denton, a prisoner for seven and a half years, believes that the Son Tay raid was the greatest thing that happened in Vietnam.

When I asked Simons if the raid was the most beautiful operation of his Army career, he said, "Son Tay was about the best." But there was one thing about the raid that I had been warned he would flatly refuse to discuss: landing at the wrong compound. He was adamant about it, until I showed him General Orders Number 32, Headquarters, Department of the Army. Dated July 13, 1971, the document was 23 pages long in single-space type. In it were all of the individual citations for the awards made to the Army Son Tay raiders. It was an unclassified document; six months earlier, I had requested the citations from the Army through normal public information channels. When I read it, I realized that the citations gave a picture of the Son Tay raid that in many respects just didn't "square" with public accounts of it.

> Captain Udo H. Walther (Silver Star): "Upon reaching his first objective, Captain Walther realized his force had been landed in an area other than, but resembling the target area. . . ."
> Captain Daniel D. Turner (Silver Star): ". . . leader of the command group . . . he noted that one of the assault helicopters had not landed as planned. Realizing that immediate action was required to institute an alternate plan. . . ."
> Staff Sergeant Walter L. Miller (Silver Star): "Realizing that the group had landed in an area approximately 400 meters south of the objective. . . ."

Simons read the citations, turning page after page in silence. He was surprised that mention of landing in the wrong place appeared in an unclassified document. Finally, I asked him again to tell me what had really happened at Son Tay. "Let me put it to you this way," he said. "I am not prepared to repudiate what that citation says." We talked about the raid for the next nine hours.

Simons, ironically, was the one who had caused the orders to come out. A week or so before he was to retire, he realized that not one of his men had received the individual citation backing up his award for valor. Simons knew how important the citations were to the men; future promotions could hinge on just such a piece of paper. Simons wanted them in every man's personnel file, before he retired. He called the Pentagon and

told some colonel that if those citations weren't on his desk
before the end of the week, he was going to call the Chief of
Staff personally and have the colonel castrated for taking seven
months to process a few pieces of paper. The colonel probably
turned to a major and said something like, "Here, get these out
fast, will you?" and forgot to remind him that the citations still
had to be cleared by "security review."

The Air Force participants were equally reluctant to discuss
details of the raid on Son Tay, particularly landing at the wrong
camp. Over a period of almost a year, I requested the United
States Air Force—verbally and in writing, several times—for
copies of the Air Force citations equivalent to Army General
Orders Number 32, which were also unclassified. I got the silent
treatment. Finally, I was advised that the *only* way they might
be released was if I wrote a formal petition for them under the
new Freedom of Information Act. I decided not to bother; by
that time I no longer needed them. But I wondered why the Air
Force public information system was so gun-shy about a 400-
yard navigation error in the dead of night deep in hostile territory, when that error may have saved half the raiders from
being slaughtered, and when men like Warner Britton reacted
so swiftly and courageously to pull Bull Simons' chestnuts out
of the fire.

Colonel Warner Britton is now retired, living in Mobile, Alabama. Colonel John Allison is Director of Safety for the Aerospace Rescue and Recovery Service. Colonel Frederic M. Donohue is working in the "Special Operations" Division, Office,
Joint Chiefs of Staff, the group that replaced SACSA. Colonel
Herb Zehnder is now retired, living at Fort Walton Beach,
Florida, near Eglin Air Force Base. Norv Clinebell is retired. So
are Colonels George J. Iles and Rudolph C. Koller. Claude Watkins is still working on escape and evasion and POW affairs at
Fort Belvoir.

Leroy J. Manor is a major general, commanding the 13th Air
Force in the Philippines. Since Son Tay, he has been involved
in several other rescues: the *Mayaguez*—swiftly executed, it
was a success but cost more lives than were saved; and the
evacuation of Hue, Danang, and Saigon, when that tragic dec-

ade and war called Vietnam finally collapsed in mid-1975.

One month after the Son Tay raid, Donald D. Blackburn learned in an almost haphazard way that he would be reassigned from the Office, Joint Chiefs of Staff, to a research and development post on the Army general staff. On his departure from the JCS, he was awarded the Distinguished Service Medal. He retired after 33 years of military service eight months after the Son Tay raid. Brigadier General Leroy J. Manor succeeded him as SACSA

Blackburn now lives in McLean, Virginia, a few miles from CIA headquarters. He is a vice president of the BDM Corporation, a civilian think tank largely involved in studies for the Department of Defense and one of the few so-called Beltway Bandits with a reputation for innovative, creative research. In the den of the white brick house which he designed and built on a heavily wooded six-acre lot, Blackburn has hung the usual memorabilia of a long and colorful military career—citations for a host of medals and decorations, his original commission, crests and badges, plaques from the units he led. Some things in the den, however, go far beyond the realm of usual military nostalgia.

One is a leather sheath housing a 6-inch knife-bayonet. It was carried into the middle of the Son Tay Prison compound by Captain Richard J. Meadows when his HH-3 helicopter crash-landed there on November 21, 1970. A leather thong, used to strap the knife to Meadows thigh, is wound around the bayonet's sheath. Stuck in it is a 3-inch piece of rice straw. Meadows found the straw on his combat jacket when he returned from the Son Tay raid. He gave it to Blackburn the day Blackburn retired. That piece of straw, Meadows told Blackburn, was "the only thing living in Son Tay Prison worth bringing home from North Vietnam." Next to the sheathed bayonet, Blackburn has framed the Son Tay patch. It sums up his last year in uniform: "Kept In Total Darkness / Fed Only Horse Shit."

Donald V. Bennett retired from the Army in mid-1974 as a four-star general, after serving as Commander-in-Chief of United Nations Forces in Korea, Commanding General of Eighth Army and, finally, Commander-in-Chief, United States

Army, Pacific. His last act in uniform was to recommend that his entire headquarters, USARPAC in Hawaii, be "dis-established" to save men and money, and eliminate an unnecessary "switchboard" in the Pentagon's worldwide chain of command. The headquarters no longer exists. He lives today on Hilton Head Island, South Carolina. He travels occasionally to consult with the government on intelligence matters.

James R. Allen is a lieutenant general, Superintendent of the United States Air Force Academy. Lieutenant Colonel John E. Kennedy, the NSA expert who found the "eye of the needle" into North Vietnam, is dead. Major General Richard R. Stewart is retired from the Air Force, consulting on intelligence matters with another of the better Washington area think tanks, Decisions & Designs, Inc. George Carver is now Deputy to the Director, CIA, for National Intelligence Officers. Harry D. Train II is now a vice admiral; after moving up to become Director of the JCS Joint Staff, he has been named to command the Sixth Fleet.

Dr. Joseph R. Cataldo retired from the Army in 1974 and now has a successful private practice in Alexandria, Virginia. There are no memorabilia from the Son Tay raid hung on his office walls, and his patients today will probably be as surprised to learn that he was on the raid as his family was in 1970.

Major Richard J. Meadows is an instructor at the Army Ranger camp at Eglin Air Force Base. A few months short of the fifth anniversary of his crash landing inside Son Tay Prison, he was passed over by an Army board for promotion from captain to major. Its members apparently felt he lacked the well-rounded career that would qualify him for duty as a senior staff officer. But in Meadows' case, unlike Simons', his combat arms branch chief—Elliott Sydnor—found that part of his record wasn't up to date, gave a stand-by promotion board an updated file, and Meadows was promoted on his record.

Five years after the Son Tay raid, 79 percent of the prisoners of war who finally came home are still in service.

Mo Baker is a colonel at Andrews Air Force Base. When he stepped off the plane at Clark Air Force Base in the Philippines on March 14, 1973, he was told that his wife had divorced him.

In mid-1974, he married the widow of Captain Vincent J. Connolly, missing-in-action for seven and a half years, an RF-101 pilot shot down by a SAM over Hanoi in November of 1966. Those who were with him felt it impossible that he could have survived the hit. Mo and Honey Baker each had two children and they get along "famously." It is one of the most beautiful, sensitive, close-knit families in America. They give can-openers to their friends as house-warming presents.

Haydn Lockhart, the Air Force's first shootdown and longest captive, is flying F-4 fighter-bombers out of Holloman Air Force Base. Brigadier General Robbie Risner is Deputy Commanding General of the Tactical Fighter Weapons School at Nellis Air Force Base. Major General John P. Flynn, who led the Fourth Allied POW Wing in North Vietnam, is Commander of the Air Force Military Training Center at Lackland Air Force Base near San Antonio. Jon Reynolds got his master's degree in history at Duke University and is now teaching at the Air Force Academy. John Dramesi, who escaped North Vietnamese prisons twice but was recaptured, once with Ed Atterbury, commands an F-111 squadron at Mountain Home Air Force Base; he was named for promotion to colonel late in 1975. Wes Schierman came home on February 12, 1973. He is back in perfect health, flying for Northwest Orient Airlines out of Spokane, Washington. Navy Captain Ed Martin has command of his own ship, the U.S.S. *Canisteo.* Bill Lawrence and James Stockdale are rear admirals. In the last such White House ceremony for the Vietnam war, Stockdale was awarded the Congressional Medal of Honor early in 1976 for his heroism as a prisoner of war, as was Air Force Colonel George E. Day. John McCain III is flying again, in command of a wing near Jacksonville, Florida, which trains Navy attack pilots. Rodney Knudson is flying again at Pensacola, Florida. He is not bitter toward the captors who tortured him so brutally. He wishes he could host them for visits at Disney World, the Houston Astrodome, and the John F. Kennedy Center for the Performing Arts. Then he would tell them, "Okay, go home now, if you want to—and enjoy that mind-blowing form of 'civilization' you tried to cram down my throat."

Charlie Plumb runs a public relations firm in Kansas City built around his experiences in North Vietnam. Whereas other men have tried to put those years behind them, Plumb has turned "professional POW," as he puts it, and earns a "very good living" lecturing around the country on the values that sustained him in Son Tay Prison and through five years and nine months of captivity. Fifty thousand copies of his book, *I'm No Hero,* have sold since 1973.

Army Chief Warrant Officer David Sooter is back on flying duty, a helicopter flight instructor at the Army Aviation Center, Fort Rucker, Alabama.

I have spoken with many of the men who were imprisoned at Son Tay. Some are bitter about the planning behind the raid. "Why," one of them asked, "did it take six or seven months?" To them, "weather" was a very unsatisfactory explanation. But they have nothing but admiration and gratitude for the men who actually landed at Son Tay. One of them put it this way: "If I ever run into the guys who made that raid, they'll never be able to buy their own drinks."

Author's Notes

There is something about a raid that is very primitive. From the days of the cave man, the Viking, and the American Indian, the most dramatic form of military action has been the calculated gamble of small, sharply honed forces on high risk ventures deep in enemy territory. Many such raids have changed the course of larger battles; some have changed the course of history. Yet the second paragraph of the JCS Son Tay After-Action report almost apologized for the raid when it said: "In retrospect, it might appear that excessive forces and resources were committed to the operation." But the 59 men who landed at Son Tay prison and the $7 million or $70 million which the raid cost are a striking contrast to the 3,091 lives and $21.7 *billion* that Americans spent in 1971, 1972, and 1973 to achieve the same goal—bring our prisoners of war home.

Military men hate criticism as much as anybody else (including authors). But in writing the story of the Son Tay raid it was not my intention to criticize it. No one needs to apologize for the "failure" at Son Tay. On the contrary, when seen in its full perspective, the raid might serve our national planners as a reminder of how much a small, elite, well-trained unorthodox force can accomplish. Nor was it my intention to add fuel to the controversy about the quality of the intelligence behind the raid. The revelation that Son Tay was a dry hole made the phrase "military intelligence" sound like the biggest contradiction in the English language for months afterward. Yet Simons and his men were given the benefit of the best intelligence available, often gathered against great odds; and it would have been impossible to plan—or execute—the raid without it. The story of the raid may also serve to remind critics of military intelligence what might have happened at Son Tay without it.

Little of what really happened at Son Tay has ever been made public. The Pentagon doesn't like to talk about its "failures": "Other than the absence of prisoners at the objective, there were no major surprises in the operation," its commander wrote in the second paragraph of his official, Top Secret After-Action Report to the Joint Chiefs of Staff. There were other surprises, of course—lots of them. They began to turn up as I quietly started researching the story behind the raid within days of when it happened, not in the "official" accounts, but from interviews with the men who took part in the operation. For 18 months, between August of 1974 and February of 1976, I had 173 such interviews with the men who planned the raid, collected intelligence for it, or executed it—and with many of the prisoners of war they had tried to free. It would be impossible to acknowledge all of them by name. For one thing, there are too many people to thank. For another, some of those interviews were granted with the understanding that they were not for attribution and would have to remain "deniable."

Most of the interviews were tape-recorded: transcripts of just the key ones fill six 3-inch-thick loose-leaf binders. One interview lasted close to nine non-stop hours. Another spanned a period of four days, including an intensive background discussion taped during a four-hour drive from Washington to a hideaway in the mountains of North Carolina where the principal and I could visit undisturbed. Notes from interviews which were not recorded grew to fill 34 "Reporter's Notebooks," and almost four file drawers of maps, photographs, official documents, news clippings and correspondence were annotated and cross-referenced to the interviews. Whenever possible, quotations in the book have been taken *verbatim* from interviews, or from notes made by the participants at the time of the raid. But others had to be reconstructed from their recall of a meeting or conversations that took place five or more years ago. I tried to interview most of the participants in such meetings, but it was not always possible. President Richard M. Nixon, for instance, has not chosen as yet to discuss the final anxious moments in which he agreed to let the raid proceed, in the face of mounting evidence that it would be futile.

It was also impossible to obtain another very important perspective on the raid. I requested, but never received, permission from the North Vietnamese to visit Son Tay prison and interview military officials in Hanoi for their impressions of and reactions to this operation.

During my interviews, many of those who planned the raid —and even more of those who participated in it—expressed surprise about things they *still* hadn't been told of an operation to which they dedicated months of their lives or risked their lives to execute. Bull Simons told me in one interview, for instance, "You know, I'm beginning to think you know more about this God damn operation than I do." Some of the officials I interviewed were aghast that I had learned the largest part of the raiding force had landed in the wrong camp. Others were concerned that I had found out that they knew, before the raid, that Son Tay had been empty of prisoners for four and a half months, and that they had corroboration of that information 24 hours before the raid was launched.

Some "facts" about the raid, of course, are still in dispute. Inevitably, I had to sort out differing recollections, some of them dimmed by time, to determine what really happened. Where such disputes were material to the story, I tried to present both sides. A case in point is the controversy over Operation Popeye and the extent to which it triggered the flood that caused the North Vietnamese to move the prisoners from Son Tay in mid-July of 1970, four and a half months before the raid. In other cases, I found that documentary evidence needed to verify points in dispute no longer existed; some of it, I discovered, was destroyed at the very time I began questioning conflicting versions of the raid. There is some uncertainty, for in-

stance, over just how much detail Air Force intelligence had, at
the time SACSA was first briefed on May 25, 1970, on the
request by six prisoners in Son Tay to be rescued. In searching
for the records of that briefing, I was told in the fall of 1975 that
they had been destroyed during an earlier, "routine" purging
of sensitive JCS files—even though they had been carefully
marked never to be destroyed.

My research was also complicated by the fact that the intelligence behind and planning for the raid was so "compartmentalized" that very few individuals were privy to "the big picture."
I am grateful for the candid and lengthy interviews I have
enjoyed with those few people who did have that visibility, and
were willing to talk about it. One Pentagon official told me
jokingly one day, "Maybe you should subtitle the book, 'More
About the Son Tay Raid Than We Ever Intended to Make
Known.'" The book has not been "censored" by the Pentagon,
however, or any other agency or individual. But I am very
grateful to several men who gave privately of their time to
review parts of the draft manuscript, pointed out errors, incon-
sistencies or conflicts, and provided leads that made it possible
to resolve most of them.

In lieu of thanking by name each individual who contributed
to my research, I simply would like to thank all of them—for
letting me tell their story. They are a unique group, dedicated
military guys who made no big deal about volunteering and
risking their lives to rescue their fellow soldiers—men who
were strangers to them.

I also want to thank several people without whose help my
manuscript might never have gone to press:
• At the Pentagon, William Beecher, then the Acting Assistant Secretary of Defense for Public Affairs and now with the
Boston Globe. When "the system" wanted to answer most Son
Tay queries with the comment, "It's all still classified," Bill
Beecher was the man who quietly challenged the wisdom of
that policy, triggered access to the JCS After Action Reports
and ultimately made possible a much more open dialogue on
one of the most secret operations of the Vietnam war. After his

departure from the Pentagon, the staff of the Defense Information Directorate patiently accepted, researched and promptly answered close to 35 more written, detailed queries and a host of informal ones over a period of 21 months; worked long hours to search out and make available previously classified records and photos; and never asked "why" but sought only for the truth to be told, without ever suggesting what "version" of it ought to prevail. In particular, my special thanks go to Colonels Robert L. Burke and Thomas D. Byrne; Lieutenant Colonels Jack T. Munsey, Nancy K. Johnson, and George W. Ogles; and Captain Hallie E. "Ed" Robertson. More special thanks go to Orval G. "Hap" Willoughby, Donald E. Baruch, John C. Becher, Francis J. Falatko, James B. Freeman, Norman J. Hatch, Bettie E. Sprigg, and Charles W. Hinkle, the Director for Freedom of Information. At the Air Force Still Photo Depository, my thanks to researcher Walter R. Cate, Jr., who tracked down the photo used on the dust jacket.

• At Wagner & Baroody, Heather David, who produced a book about the Son Tay raid and the POW situation in a near-record 17 days after it happened, who has since worked diligently on behalf of the POW/MIA families, and who graciously offered her extensive photographic files for possible use in this book.

• At *Armed Forces Journal,* F. Clifton Berry, Jr., who took over the editor's reins in 1975 and gave unselfishly of his time to free mine to finish a book he knew I wanted very much to do "right"; Nan R. Burnett and Pamela D. Cox, who transcribed an avalanche of taped interviews and patiently typed, re-typed and proofread a blizzard of drafts and re-drafts; Louise Richards, the former assistant editor, who stepped in at a crucial juncture and worked around the clock to type, proofread and help edit the final working draft; and Barbara Ann Lindland, whose husband early in 1976 is still carried as a prisoner of war, and who at the eleventh hour helped pull it all together.

• At Harper & Row, an especially warm note of thanks goes to Harriet Stanton, who typed the final manuscript faultlessly. I am also grateful to Burton Beals who, as *The Raid* took final form, became much more of a collaborator than an editor; he also became a valued personal friend whom I hold in high professional regard. To Lynne McNabb, Sally Williams, Bill Janson, and Florence Goldstein, thanks for their friendship, help and professionalism. To M. S. Wyeth, Jr., Harper & Row Vice President and Editor-in-Chief, go my sincere thanks for his enthusiasm and personal interest in my book.

• At home, I want to thank my son, Clinton Howard Schemmer, who spurred me on to write this book the way he knew his mother wanted it to be done. When I began to bog down or when answers to certain questions seemed so bizarre at times that I thought I was writing fiction, his excitement over what really happened at Son Tay, his remarks about the interviews we enjoyed being in on together, and his frequent, enthusiastic question from the University of Montana, "How's the book going, Dad?" inspired me to finish it.

The book began in earnest two months after his mother died. Sitting together at home one evening, we found a note my wife had written almost two years earlier but somehow knew I would find at that turning point in my life. It was a very beautiful note, and it reads in part, "To my beloved—because he knows the other half that hasn't been printed. Please write it now."

BENJAMIN F. SCHEMMER

Washington, D.C.
May 1976

The Son Tay Prisoners

(All of the POWs held at Son Tay were known to have been captured, as opposed to being carried on "missing-in-hostile-action" lists.)

United States Air Force

(Of the 333 USAF pilots who were captured and later returned to U.S. control by the North Vietnamese, 45, or just over 13½ percent, were imprisoned at Son Tay.)

Rank	Name	Date Shot Down or Reported Missing	Date Returned to U.S. Control
Lt. Col.	Elmo C. Baker	23 Aug 67	14 Mar 73
Maj.	Charles G. Boyd	22 Apr 66	12 Feb 73
Capt.	Richard C. Brenneman	8 Nov 67	14 Mar 73
Capt.	Edward A. Brudno	18 Oct 65	12 Feb 73
Lt. Col.	Alan L. Brunstrom	22 Apr 66	12 Feb 73
Capt.	Hubert E. Buchanan	16 Sep 66	4 Mar 73
Col.	William D. Burroughs	31 Jul 66	4 Mar 73
Capt.	William W. Butler	20 Nov 67	14 Mar 73
Capt.	Larry E. Carrigan	23 Aug 67	14 Mar 73
Capt.	Larry J. Chesley	16 Apr 66	12 Feb 73
Capt.	John W. Clark	12 Mar 67	18 Feb 73
Maj.	Thomas E. Collins, III	18 Oct 65	12 Feb 73
Lt. Col.	Thomas J. Curtis	20 Sep 65	12 Feb 73
Capt.	Myron L. Donald	23 Feb 68	14 Mar 73
Capt.	Jerry D. Driscoll	24 Apr 66	12 Feb 73
Col.	Richard A. Dutton	5 Nov 67	14 Mar 73
Capt.	Leroy F. Ellis, Jr.	17 Dec 67	14 Mar 73

Rank	Name	Date Shot Down or Reported Missing	Date Returned to U.S. Control
Maj.	Kenneth Fisher	7 Nov 67	14 Mar 73
Capt.	Frederic R. Flom	8 Aug 66	4 Mar 73
Lt. Col.	Willis E. Forby	20 Sep 65	12 Feb 73
Capt.	David E. Ford	19 Nov 67	14 Mar 73
Capt.	Henry P. Fowler, Jr.	26 Mar 67	18 Mar 73
Capt.	David F. Gray, Jr.	23 Jan 67	4 Mar 73
Maj.	Charles E. Greene, Jr.	11 Mar 67	4 Mar 73
Lt. Col.	David B. Hatcher	30 May 66	12 Feb 73
Lt. Col.	Julius S. Jayroe	19 Jan 67	4 Mar 73
Maj.	Robert D. Jeffrey	20 Dec 65	12 Feb 73
Lt. Col.	Thomas M. Madison	19 Apr 67	4 Mar 73
Lt. Col.	Louis F. Makowski	6 Oct 66	4 Mar 73
Capt.	Ronald L. Mastin	16 Jan 67	4 Mar 73
Capt.	Thomas N. Moe	16 Jan 68	14 Mar 73
Maj.	Robert D. Peel	31 May 65	12 Feb 73
Lt. Col.	Ben M. Pollard	15 May 67	4 Mar 73
Capt.	James E. Ray	8 May 66	12 Feb 73
Maj.	Jon A. Reynolds	28 Nov 65	12 Feb 73
Lt. Col.	Wesley D. Schierman	28 Aug 65	12 Feb 73
Lt. Col.	Bruce G. Seeber	5 Oct 65	12 Feb 73
Maj.	Richard E. Smith, Jr.	25 Oct 67	14 Mar 73
Lt. Col.	Robert L. Stirm	27 Oct 67	14 Mar 73
Maj.	Thomas G. Storey	16 Jan 67	4 Mar 73
Capt.	Leroy W. Stutz	2 Dec 66	4 Mar 73
Maj.	Russell E. Temperley	27 Oct 67	14 Mar 73
Lt. Col.	Irby D. Terrell, Jr.	14 Jan 68	14 Mar 73
Capt.	Gerald S. Venanzi	17 Sep 67	14 Mar 73
Capt.	Lawrence D. Writer	15 Feb 68	14 Mar 73

United States Navy

(Of the 145 Navy pilots who were captured and later returned to U.S. control by the Vietnamese, 16, or just over 11 percent, were imprisoned at Son Tay.)

Rank	Name	Date Shot Down or Reported Missing	Date Returned to U.S. Control
Lt. Cdr.	Wendell R. Alcorn	22 Dec 65	12 Feb 73
Cdr.	Claude D. Clower	19 Nov 67	14 Mar 73

Rank	Name	Date Shot Down or Reported Missing	Date Returned to U.S. Control
Cdr.	Render Crayton	7 Feb 66	12 Feb 73
Lt. Cdr.	Michael P. Cronin	13 Jan 67	4 Mar 73
Lt. Cdr.	Robert H. Doremus	24 Aug 65	12 Feb 73
Lt. Cdr.	Ralph E. Gaither, Jr.	17 Oct 65	12 Feb 73
Lt. Cdr.	Paul E. Galanti	17 Jun 66	12 Feb 73
Lt. Cdr.	Danny E. Glenn	21 Dec 66	4 Mar 73
Lt.	Wayne K. Goodermote	13 Aug 67	14 Mar 73
Lt. Cdr.	John Heilig	5 May 66	12 Feb 73
Lt. Cdr.	Wilson D. Key	17 Nov 67	14 Mar 73
Lt. Cdr.	Dennis A. Moore	27 Oct 65	12 Feb 73
Lt. Cdr.	Robert J. Naughton	18 May 67	4 Mar 73
Lt.	Theodore G. Stier	19 Nov 67	14 Mar 73
Lt.	Gary L. Thornton	20 Feb 67	4 Mar 73
Lt. Cdr.	William M. Tschudy	18 July 65	12 Feb 73

United States Marine Corps

(Of 37 Marine Corps officers who were captured by the North Vietnamese, 4, or just under 11 percent, were imprisoned at Son Tay.)

Rank	Name	Date Shot Down or Reported Missing	Date Returned to U.S. Control
Lt. Col.	John H. Dunn	7 Dec 66	12 Feb 73
CWO-4	J. W. Frederick	5 Dec 65	Died in captivity
Maj.	Orson G. Swindle, III	11 Nov 66	4 Mar 73
Capt.	James H. Warner	13 Oct 67	14 Mar 73

The Son Tay Raiders

United States Army

Support Group

Rank	Name	Parent Organization
Col.	Arthur D. Simons	Hq, XVIII Abn Corps
Capt.	Eric J. Nelson	Co B, 7th SFG
Capt.	Glenn R. Rouse	HHC, 2d Bn USAIMA
Capt.	Udo H. Walther	Co D, 6th SFG
SFC	Earl Bleacher	2d Bn, USAIMA
SFC	Leroy N. Carlson	Co C, 7th SFG
SFC	John Jakovenko	Co C, 6th SFG
SFC	Jack G. Joplin	HHC, 6th SFG
SFC	Daniel Jurich	Co B, 7th SFG
SFC	David A. Lawhon, Jr.	Co C, 7th SFG
SFC	Salvador M. Suarez	Co B, 6th SFG
SFC	Donald E. Taapken	Co C, 6th SFG
SFC	Richard W. Valentine	Co B, 7th SFG
SSgt.	Walter L. Miller	Sig Co, 6th SFG
SSgt.	Robert L. Nelson	Co B, 6th SFG
SSgt.	David S. Nickerson	Sig Co, 6th SFG
SSgt.	Thomas E. Powell	Co D, 7th SFG
SSgt.	John E. Rodriquez	Co C, 6th SFG
Sgt.	Gary D. Keel	Co C, 6th SFG
Sgt.	Keith R. Medenski	Co B, 6th SFG
Sgt.	Franklin D. Roe	Co B, 6th SFG
Sgt.	Marshall A. Thomas	Co D, 6th SFG

Assault Group

Rank	Name	Parent Organization
Capt.	Richard J. Meadows	Det 1, USAIS
Capt.	Thomas W. Jaeger	Co A, 7th SFG

Rank	Name	Parent Organization
Capt.	Dan H. McKinney	Co D, 7th SFG
1st Lt.	George W. Petrie	Co D, 6th SFG
MSgt.	Thomas J. Kemmer	Co B, 6th SFG
MSgt.	Billy K. Moore	Co C, 6th SFG
MSgt.	Galen C. Kittleson	Co B, 6th SFG
SFC	Anthony Dodge	2d Bn, USAIMA
SFC	Lorenzo O. Robbins	Co B, 6th SFG
SFC	William L. Tapley	Co C, 6th SFG
SFC	Donald R. Wingrove	Co D, 6th SFG
SSgt.	Charles G. Erickson	Co B, 7th SFG
SSgt.	Kenneth E. McMullin	HHC, 6th SFG
Sgt.	Patrick St. Clair	Co C, 6th SFG

Command Group—Security

Rank	Name	Parent Organization
Lt. Col.	Elliott P. Snydor	Det 1, USAIS
Lt. Col.	Joseph R. Cataldo	Surgeon General, Hq DA
Capt.	James W. McClam	Co A, 6th SFG
Capt.	Daniel D. Turner	Co A, 6th SFG
MSgt.	Joseph W. Lupyak	Co D, 7th SFG
MSgt.	Herman Spencer	Co C, 7th SFG
SFC	Tyrone J. Adderly	Co A, 6th SFG
SFC	Donald D. Blackard	Co B, 7th SFG
SFC	Freddie D. Doss	HHC, 6th SFG
SFC	Jerry W. Hill	2d Bn, USAIMA
SFC	Marion S. Howell	Co A, 6th SFG
SFC	Billy R. Martin	Co A, 6th SFG
SFC	Gregory T. McGuire	Co A, 6th SFG
SFC	Charles A. Masten, Jr.	Co D, 6th SFG
SFC	Joseph M. Murray	Co A, 6th SFG
SFC	Noe Quezada	Co D, 7th SFG
SFC	Ronnie Strahan	Co B, 6th SFG
SSgt.	Paul F. Poole	Co B, 6th SFG
SSgt.	Lawrence Young	2d Bn, USAIMA
Sgt.	Terry L. Buckler	Co D, 7th SFG

Support Personnel

Rank	Name	Parent Organization
Lt. Col.	Bill L. Robinson	Co D, 6th SFG
Lt. Col.	Gerald Kilburn	HHC, JFKCMA
Capt.	Randle L. Smith	HHC, JFKCMA
Sgt. Maj.	Minor B. Pylant	Co A, 6th SFG

Rank	Name	Parent Organization
MSgt.	Jesse A. Black	Co A, 7th SFG
MSgt.	Edgar C. Britt	Co A, 6th SFG
MSgt.	Bernard L. Rauscher	Co D, 6th SFG
SFC	Franklin B. Abramski	Co B, 7th SFG
SFC	James A. Bass	HHC, 6th SFG
SFC	Archie Batrez, Jr.	Co D, 6th SFG
SFC	Robert L. Dodd	Co A, 7th SFG
SFC	Charles M. Erwin	Co D, 6th SFG
SFC	James A. Green	Co A, 6th SFG
SFC	Bobby R. Hansley	Co B, 7th SFG
SFC	Roswell D. Henderson	Co D, 7th SFG
SFC	Frederick L. Hubel	Co B, 7th SFG
SFC	Bruce M. Hughes	Co D, 7th SFG
SFC	John R. Jourdan	Co B, 7th SFG
SFC	Ernest R. Pounder	Co A, 7th SFG
SFC	Aaron L. Tolson, Jr.	Co D, 6th SFG
SFC	Burley W. Turner	Co D, 7th SFG
SFC	Grady C. Vines	Co C, 7th SFG
SSgt.	Elmer D. Adams	Co D, 6th SFG
SSgt.	Rodger D. Gross	HHC, 7th SFG
SSgt.	Larry G. Stroklund	Co A, 6th SFG
SSgt.	David L. Wilson	Co C, 6th SFG
Sgt.	Brian J. Budy	Co B, 6th SFG
Sgt.	Michael G. Green	Co C, 6th SFG
Sgt.	Robert R. Hobdy	Sig Co, 6th SFG
Sgt.	John J. Lippert	Co D, 7th SFG
Sgt.	Arlin L. Olson	Co D, 6th SFG
Spec. 5	Willard F. Dezurik	Co D, 6th SFG
Spec. 5	Lawrence C. Elliott	HHC, 6th SFG
Spec. 5	Gary R. Griffin	Co D, 6th SFG
Spec. 4	Christopher Casey	Co B, 6th SFG
Spec. 4	Frank J. Closen	Co B, 6th SFG

UH-1 Aircraft Crew Members

Rank	Name	Parent Organization
1st Lt.	George W. Williams	6th SFG
CWO-2	Ronald J. Exley	6th SFG
CWO-2	Jackie H. Keele	6th SFG
CWO-2	John J. Ward	6th SFG
Spec. 6	Larry C. Boots	6th SFG
Spec. 4	Alan H. Wood	82nd Abn Div

United States Air Force

Assault Force

Aircraft	Code Name	Rank	Name	Parent Organization
HH-3	Banana 1	Lt. Col.	Herbert E. Zehnder	ARRTC
		Maj.	Herbert D. Kalen	ARRTC
		TSgt.	Leroy M. Wright	ARRTC
HH-53	Apple 1	Lt. Col.	Warner A. Britton	ARRTC
		Maj.	Alfred C. Montrem	ARRTC
		MSgt.	Harold W. Harvey	ARRTC
		MSgt.	Maurice F. Tasker	ARRTC
		SSgt.	Jon K. Hoberg	40th ARRS
HH-53	Apple 2	Lt. Col.	John V. Allison	ARRTC
		Maj.	Jay M. Strayer	40th ARRS
		TSgt.	William E. Lester	ARRTC
		TSgt.	Charlie J. Montgomery	ARRTC
		SSgt.	Randy S. McComb	40th ARRS
HH-53	Apple 3	Maj.	Frederic M. Donohue	ARRTC
		Capt.	Thomas R. Waldron	ARRTC
		SSgt.	Aron P. Hodges	ARRTC
		SSgt.	James J. Rogers	ARRTC
		SSgt.	Angus W. Sowell, III	ARRTC
HH-53	Apple 4	Lt. Col.	Royal C. Brown	37th ARRS
		Maj.	Roy R. Dreibelis	37th ARRS
		TSgt.	Lawrence Wellington	ARRTC
		SSgt.	Wayne L. Fisk	40th ARRS
		SSgt.	Donald Labarre	ARRTC
HH-53	Apple 5	Maj.	Kenneth D. Murphy	703d SO Sqdn
		Capt.	William M. McGeorge	40th ARRS
		TSgt.	David F. McLeod	ARRTC
		SSgt.	John J. Eldridge	40th ARRS
		SSgt.	Daniel E. Galde	ARRTC
HC-130P	Lime 01	Maj.	William J. Kornitzer, Jr.	ARRTC
C-130	Cherry 1	Maj.	Irl L. Franklin	7th SO Sqdn
		Maj.	Thomas L. Mosley	7th SO Sqdn
		Capt.	Randal D. Custard	7th SO Sqdn
		Capt.	Thomas K. Eckhart	7th SO Sqdn
		Capt.	William A. Guenon, Jr.	7th SO Sqdn
		Capt.	James F. McKenzie, Jr.	7th SO Sqdn
		Capt.	Thomas L. Stiles	7th SO Sqdn
		MSgt.	Leslie G. Tolman	7th SO Sqdn
		TSgt.	William A. Kennedy	7th SO Sqdn

308   A P P E N D I X   I I

Aircraft	Code Name	Rank	Name	Parent Organization
		TSgt.	Kenneth C. Lightle	7th SO Sqdn
		TSgt.	James M. Shepard	7th SO Sqdn
		SSgt.	Earl D. Parks	7th SO Sqdn
C-130	Cherry 2	Lt. Col.	Albert P. Blosch	Det 2, 1st SOW
		Maj.	John Gargus	Det 2, 1st SOW
		Maj.	Harry L. Pannill	Det 2, 1st SOW
		Capt.	John M. Connaughton	Det 2, 1st SOW
		Capt.	David M. Kender	Det 2, 1st SOW
		Capt.	Norman C. Mazurek	Det 2, 1st SOW
		Capt.	William D. Stripling	Det 2, 1st SOW
		TSgt.	Dallas T. Criner	Det 2, 1st SOW
		TSgt.	Billy J. Elliston	Det 2, 1st SOW
		TSgt.	Jimmie O. Riggs	Det 2, 1st SOW
		TSgt.	Paul E. Stierwalt	Det 2, 1st SOW
		SSgt.	Melvin B. D. Gibson	Det 2, 1st SOW

Assault Force Alternates Who Did Not Fly

Aircraft	Code Name	Rank	Name	Parent Organization
HH-3	Banana 1	Maj.	David E. Vaughn	37th ARRS
C-130	Cherry 1	SSgt.	Robert L. Renner	7th SO Sqdn
C-130	Cherry 2	Lt. Col.	Cecil M. Clark	Det 2, 1st SOW
		Capt.	Ronald L. Jones	Det 2, 1st SOW
C-130	Cherry 2	TSgt.	Failus Potts	Det 2, 1st SOW
		SSgt.	William J. Brown	Det 2, 1st SOW

Attack Group

Aircraft	Code Name	Rank	Name	Parent Organization
A-1	Peach 1	Maj.	Edwin J. Rhein, Jr.	1st SOW
		Maj.	John C. Waresh	56th SOW
A-1	Peach 2	Maj.	James R. Gochnauer	1st SOW
		Capt.	Robert M. Senko	56th SOW
A-1	Peach 3	Maj.	Richard S. Skeels	1st SOW
		Lt.	James C. Paine	56th SOW
A-1	Peach 4	Maj.	Eustace M. Bunn	1st SOW
		Capt.	Robert H. Skelton	56th SOW
A-1	Peach 5	Maj.	John C. Squires	1st SOW
		Capt.	William R. Sutton	56th SOW

MIG Combat Air Patrol Group

Aircraft	Code Name	Rank	Name	Parent Organization
F-4	Falcon 1	Maj.	Kenneth L. Gardner	13th TFS
		Capt.	Larry L. Henry	13th TFS
F-4	Falcon 2	Capt.	John D. Landin, Jr.	13th TFS
		Capt.	George E. McKibben	13th TFS
F-4	Falcon 3	Maj.	George E. Coats	555th TFS
		Capt.	Stuart B. McCurdy	555th TFS
F-4	Falcon 4	Maj.	Hubbard W. Lee	555th TFS
		Capt.	Michael T. Golas	555th TFS
F-4	Falcon 5	Maj.	James C. Malaney	13th TFS
		Capt.	Russell G. Wright	13th TFS
F-4	Falcon 11	Maj.	Orville B. Baird	555th TFS
		Capt.	Carl Paladino	555th TFS
F-4	Falcon 12	Capt.	Douglas P. Brown	555th TFS
		Capt.	Charles E. Smith	555th TFS
F-4	Falcon 13	Capt.	John L. Cantwell	13th TFS
		Capt.	Larry L. Henry	13th TFS
F-4	Falcon 14	Capt.	Ronald M. Hintze	13th TFS
		Capt.	Joseph R. Preston	13th TFS
F-4	Falcon 15	Maj.	Jimmy C. Pettyjohn	555th TFS
		1st Lt.	Thomas A. Wagner	555th TFS

Wild Weasel Decoy Group

Aircraft	Code Name	Rank	Name	Parent Organization
F-105	Firebird 1	Lt. Col.	Robert J. Kronebusch	388th TFW
		Maj.	John Forrester	388th TFW
F-105	Firebird 2	Maj.	Raymond C. McAdoo	388th TFW
		Maj.	Robert J. Reisenwitz	388th TFW
F-105	Firebird 3	Maj.	Everett D. Fansler	388th TFW
		Maj.	William J. Starkey	388th TFW
F-105	Firebird 4	Maj.	Murray B. Denton	388th TFW
		Capt.	Russell T. Ober	388th TFW
F-105	Firebird 5	Maj.	Donald W. Kilgus	388th TFW
		Capt.	Clarence T. Lowry	388th TFW

Maintenance Support Group

Rank	Name	Parent Organization
Capt.	Gerard M. Carroll	Det 2, 1st SOW
Capt.	Lionel E. Faggard	AFLC

Rank	Name	Parent Organization
MSgt.	Thomas E. Hogan	1198 OE&T Sq
TSgt.	David L. Brookover	1198 OE&T Sq
TSgt.	Ronald H. Casey	1198 OE&T Sq
TSgt.	Gerald Crisp	Det 2, 1st SOW
TSgt.	Charles W. Duff	1198 OE&T Sq
TSgt.	Billy R. Frederick	Det 2, 1st SOW
TSgt.	Tommy C. Moseley	1198 OE&T Sq
TSgt.	Bradley A. Whittier	1198 OE&T Sq
TSgt.	Richard W. Yates	1198 OE&T Sq
SSgt.	George T. Butler	1198 OE&T Sq
SSgt.	Raymond L. Chalkley	1198 OE&T Sq
SSgt.	George R. Kendall	1198 OE&T Sq
SSgt.	Donald R. Skidmore	1198 OE&T Sq
Sgt.	Robert W. Cleeland	Det 2, 1st SOW
Sgt.	Dale E. Dalton	Det 2, 1st SOW
Sgt.	David N. Dierking	Det 2, 1st SOW
Sgt.	Elliot L. Rothman	Det 2, 1st SOW
Sgt.	Kenneth A. Ruud	Det 2, 1st SOW
Sgt.	Robert D. Werner	Det 2, 1st SOW
A1C	Richard A. Bacon	Det 2, 1st SOW
A1C	Stephen P. Goodson	Det 2, 1st SOW
A1C	James R. Holder	Det 2, 1st SOW
A1C	Jerry D. Melcher	1198 OE&T Sq
CIV	Walter R. Fuller	Texas Instruments
CIV	Garry L. Hesse	Hallicrafters
GS-13	Hubert J. Hildreth	Air Force Logistics Command
CIV	Gene L. Pyle	Texas Instruments

Security Police Support Group

Rank	Name	Parent Organization
SSgt.	Wilbert Bell	464 SP Sq
AIC	Steven L. Berg	464 SP Sq
AMN	Stanley W. Crouch	464 SP Sq
AMN	Joseph T. Jernigan, Jr.	464 SP Sq
Sgt.	Clarence A. Ratcliff	464 SP Sq

Munitions Group

Rank	Name	Parent Organization
TSgt.	Teddie R. Goss	1st SOW
TSgt.	Giles C. Rose	1st SOW
Sgt.	William H. Mowder	1st SOW

APPENDIX III

Son Tay Awards for Valor

(*Decorated by President Richard M. Nixon at the White House on November 25, 1970. All others were decorated by Secretary of Defense Melvin R. Laird at Fort Bragg, North Carolina, on December 9, 1970.)

United States Army

Distinguished Service Cross

Col. Arthur D. Simons*
Lt. Col. Elliott P. Sydnor
Capt. Richard J. Meadows
MSgt. Thomas J. Kemmer
SFC Tyrone J. Adderly*
SSgt. Thomas E. Powell

Silver Star

Lt. Col. Joseph R. Cataldo
Capt. Thomas W. Jaegar
Capt. James W. McClam
Capt. Dan. H. McKinney
Capt. Eric J. Nelson
Capt. Glenn R. Rouse
Capt. Daniel Turner
Capt. Udo H. Walther
1st Lt. George W. Petrie, Jr.
MSgt. Calen C. Kittleson
MSgt. Joseph W. Lupyak
MSgt. Billy K. Moore
MSgt. Herman Spencer
SFC Donald D. Blackard
SFC Earl Bleacher, Jr.
SFC Leroy N. Carlson
SFC Anthony Dodge
SFC Freddie D. Doss
SFC Jerry W. Hill
SFC Marion S. Howell
SFC John Jakovenko
SFC Jack G. Joplin
SFC Daniel Jurich
SFC David A. Lawhon, Jr.
SFC Gregory T. McGuire
SFC Billy R. Martin
SFC Charles Masten
SFC Donald R. Mingrove
SFC Joseph M. Murray
SFC Noe Quezada
SFC Lorenzo Robbins
SFC Ronnie Strahan
SFC Salvador M. Suarez
SFC Donald E. Taapken
SFC William L. Tapley
SFC Richard W. Valentine
SSgt. Charles G. Erickson
SSgt. Kenneth E. McMullin
SSgt. Walter L. Miller
SSgt. Robert F. Nelson

Silver Star

SSgt. David Nickerson
SSgt. Paul F. Poole
SSgt. John E. Rodriquez
SSgt. Lawrence Young
Sgt. Terry L. Buckler

Sgt. Gary D. Keel
Sgt. Keith R. Medenski
Sgt. Franklin D. Roe
Sgt. Patrick St. Clair
Sgt. Marshal A. Thomas

Distinguished Flying Cross

1st Lt. George W. Williams
CWO Ronald J. Exley

CWO Jackie H. Keele
CWO John J. Ward

United States Air Force

Distinguished Service Medal

Brig. Gen. Leroy J. Manor*

Air Force Cross

Lt. Col. John V. Allison
Lt. Col. Warner A. Britton
Maj. Frederic M. Donohue

Maj. Herbert D. Kalen
TSgt. Leroy M. Wright*

Silver Star

Lt. Col. Albert P. Blosch
Lt. Col. Royal A. Brown, Jr.
Lt. Col. Herbert R. Zehnder
Maj. Eustace M. Bunn
Maj. Irl L. Franklin
Maj. John Gargus
Maj. James R. Grochnauer
Maj. Alfred C. Montrem
Maj. Kenneth D. Murphy
Maj. Harry L. Pannill
Maj. Edwin J. Rhein
Maj. Richard S. Skeels
Maj. John C. Squires
Capt. John M. Connaughton
Capt. David M. Kender
Capt. Norman C. Mazurek
Capt. Thomas L. Stiles
Capt. William D. Stripling

Capt. Thomas R. Waldron
MSgt. Harold W. Harvey
MSgt. David V. McLeod, Jr.
MSgt. Maurice F. Tasker
Sgt. Dallas R. Criner
TSgt. Billy J. Elliston
TSgt. William E. Lester
TSgt. Charles J. Montgomery, Jr.
TSgt. Jimmy O. Riggs
TSgt. Paul W. Stierwalt
TSgt. Lawrence Wellington
SSgt. Daniel E. Galde
SSgt. Melvin B. D. Gibson
SSgt. Aron P. Hodges
SSgt. Donald LaBarre
SSgt. James J. Rogers
SSgt. Angus W. Sowell, III

The Son Tay Planners

Feasibility Study Group (convened by SACSA, June 10, 1970)

Rank	Name	Service	Parent Organization
Col.	Norman H. Frisbie	USAF	Hq USAF
Col.	William C. Norman	USA	SACSA
Lt. Col.	Warner A. Britton	USAF	ARRTC
Lt. Col.	Keith R. Grimes	USAF	Air Univ
Lt. Col.	Thomas F. Minor	USA	DCSOPS
Lt. Col.	Lawrence Ropka, Jr.	USAF	Hq USAF
Maj.	Arthur A. Andraitis	USAF	Hq USAF
Maj.	Boyd F. Morris	USA	USAJFKCEN, Ft. Bragg
Capt.	James A. Jacobs	USAF	DIA
Capt.	John H. Knops	USAF	Hq USAF
Lt.	Theodore A. Grabowsky	USN	CNO
1st Lt.	James A. Brinson	USMC	DIA
SGM	Donald M. Davis	USA	6th SFGA, Ft. Bragg
GS-8	Frances L. Earley	DA	SACSA
GS-6	Barbara L. Strosnider	DAF	Hq USAF

Planning Group (convened by SACSA, August 10–14, 1970)

Rank	Name	Service	Parent Organization
Brig. Gen.	Leroy J. Manor	USAF	USAFSOF
Col.	Arthur D. Simons	USA	Hq XVIII Abn Corps
Col.	Norman H. Frisbie	USAF	Hq USAF
Capt.	William M. Campbell	USN	CNO
Lt. Cdr.	Clair R. Hershey	USN	CNO

Rank	Name	Service	Parent Organization
Lt. Col.	James V. Bailey	USA	Hq DA AC/S COMELEC
Lt. Col.	Joseph R. Cataldo	USA	Hq DA SG
Lt. Col.	Keith R. Grimes	USAF	Air Univ
Lt. Col.	Benjamin N. Kraljev, Jr.	USAF	Hq USAF
Lt. Col.	Richard A. Peshkin	USAF	Hq USAF
Lt. Col.	Lawrence Ropka, Jr.	USAF	Hq USAF
Lt. Col.	Homer Willett	USAF	Hq USAF
Maj.	Arthur A. Andraitis	USAF	Hq USAF
Maj.	Richard S. Beyea, Jr.	USAF	Hq USAF
Maj.	Thomas E. Macomber	USAF	Hq USAF
Maj.	Boyd F. Morris	USA	USAJFKCEN, Ft. Bragg
Maj.	James H. Morris	USA	7th SFGA, Ft. Bragg
Maj.	Max E. Newman	USA	USAFNTC-USAFAC
Capt.	James A. Jacobs	USAF	DIA
Capt.	John H. Knops	USAF	Hq USAF
Capt.	Richard J. Meadows	USA	Det 1, USAIS
1st Lt.	James A. Brinson	USMC	DIA
SGM	Donald M. Davis	USA	6th SFGA, Ft. Bragg
MSgt.	William S. Gann	USA	6th SFGA, Ft. Bragg
SFC	Jesse E. Sherrod	USA	6th SFGA, Ft. Bragg
GS-8	Frances L. Earley	DA	SACSA
GS-6	Barbara L. Strosnider	DAF	Hq USAF

SACSA's Administrative Support/Augmentation Group

Rank	Name	Service	Parent Organization
Capt.	John S. Harris	USN	DIA
Col.	Franklin C. Rice	USAF	NMCC
Lt. Col.	John E. Kennedy	USAF	PDAF
Maj.	Harvey D. Hallman	USAF	USAFSOF
Maj.	Frank C. Vogel	USAF	Hq USAF
1st Lt.	Michael L. Batsell	USAF	USAFSOF
MSgt.	Billy B. Baber	USAF	USAFSOF
DM 1	Larry Downing	USN	OJCS
SSgt.	Stanley G. Graves	USA	DIA
SSgt.	John J. Martin	USAF	USAFSOF
GS-8	Elneita S. Russell	USAF	USAFSOF

Bibliography

BOOKS

American Enterprise Institute for Public Policy Research. *Vietnam Settlement: Why 1973, Not 1969?* Washington, D.C.: 1973.

Buttiner, Joseph. *Vietnam: A Dragon Embattled.* Vol. II. New York: Praeger, 1967.

David, Heather. *Operation Rescue.* New York: Pinnacle Books, 1971.

Department of the Army. *Vietnam Studies: U.S. Army Special Forces, 1961–1971.* Washington, D.C.: Government Printing Office, 1973.

Dramesi, John A. *Code of Honor.* New York: Norton, 1975.

Effros, William G., ed. *Quotations, Vietnam: 1945–1970.* New York: Random House, 1970.

Gaither, Ralph. *With God in a POW Camp.* As told to Steve Henry. Nashville, Tenn.: Broadman Press, 1973.

Gallucci, Robert L. *Neither Peace Nor Honor, The Politics of American Policy in Vietnam.* Baltimore, Md.: The Johns Hopkins University Press, 1975.

Harkins, Philip. *Blackburn's Headhunters.* New York: Norton, 1956.

Kalb, Bernard, and Marvin Kalb. *Kissinger.* Boston: Little, Brown, 1974.

Littauer, Ralph, and Norman Uphoff, eds. *The Air War in Indochina.* Revised ed. Boston: Beacon Press, 1972.

McGrath, John M. *Prisoner of War: Six Years in Hanoi.* Annapolis, Md.: Naval Institute Press, 1975.

New York Times. *The Pentagon Papers.* New York: Bantam Books, 1971.

Plumb, Charles. *I'm No Hero—A P.O.W. Story as Told to Gwen de Werff.* Independence, Mo.: Independence Press, 1973.

Risner, Robinson. *The Passing of the Night: My Seven Years as a Prisoner of the North Vietnamese.* New York: Ballantine Books, 1973.

Rowan, Roy. *The Four Days of the Mayaguez.* New York: Norton, 1975.

Rowe, James N. *Five Years to Freedom.* Boston: Little, Brown, 1971.

Schemmer, Benjamin F., and the Editors of *Armed Forces Journal. Almanac of Liberty.* New York: Macmillan, 1974.

Van Dyke, Jon M. *North Vietnam's Strategy for Survival.* Palo Alto, Calif.: Pacific Books, 1972.

Westmoreland, William C. *A Soldier Reports.* Garden City, N.Y.: Doubleday, 1976.

HEARINGS

"Bombing Operations and the Prisoner-of-War Rescue Mission in North Vietnam," *Hearings before the Committee on Foreign Relations, United States Senate, Ninety-First Congress, Second Session,* Washington, D.C.: Government Printing Office, 1971.

"American Prisoners of War in Southeast Asia, 1971," *Hearings Before the Subcommittee on National Security Policy and Scientific Developments, Committee on Foreign Relations, Ninety-Second Congress, First Session,* Parts 1 and 2, Washington, D.C.: Government Printing Office, 1971 and 1972.

"Weather Modifications," *Hearings Before the Subcommittee on Oceans and International Environment of The Committee on Foreign Relations, Ninety-Third Congress, Second Session,* Washington, D.C.: Government Printing Office, 1974.

"Americans Missing in Southeast Asia," *Hearings Before the House Select Committee on Missing Persons in Southeast Asia, Ninety-Fourth Congress, First Session,* Parts 1 and 2, Washington, D.C.: Government Printing Office, 1975 and 1976.

PERIODICALS

Armed Forces Journal, "Better Deal for Service Spooks?", December 1971.

———, "Dissent," July 1974.

————, "Last Medals of Honor of the Vietnam War," March 1976.

————, "Our Outgunned Spies," December 1971.

————, "POW Profile: The Upward Trend in Letter-Writing," October 5, 1970.

————, "There's Always a Chance," March 1973.

Ruhl, Robert K. *Airman*, "Raid at Son Tay," August 1975.

Schwanhausser, Robert R. in *Armed Forces Journal*, "RPV's: Angel in the Battle, Victim in the Budget," November 1974.

Steinhauser, Thomas C. in *Armed Forces Journal*, "How to Make Flag Rank," July 1972.

Weaver, Robert A. in *Armed Forces Journal*, "A New Expanded 1975 Version of the Army Writer's Dictionary (6th Edition)," May 1975.

Weiss, George in *Armed Forces Journal*, "Battle for Control of the Ho Chi Minh Trail," February 15, 1971.

TRANSCRIPTS OF BRIEFINGS

Transcript of Secretary of Defense's Press Conference on the Son Tay Prisoner of War Raid, Office, Assistant Secretary of Defense (Public Affairs), November 23, 1970.

Operation Kingpin, Briefing Book for the Joint Chiefs of Staff and National Command Authorities, Office, Joint Chiefs of Staff, November 1970.

Briefing on the Son Tay Raid, Brigadier General Leroy J. Manor, USAF, 1971: untitled, undated.

REPORTS

Report on the War in Vietnam, Admiral U. S. G. Sharp and General W. C. Westmoreland. Washington, D.C.: Government Printing Office, 1968.

General Orders No. 32, Headquarters, Department of the Army, Washington, D.C., July 13, 1971.

"Report on the Son Tay Prisoner of War Rescue Operation," Parts I and II, Brigadier General Leroy J. Manor, USAF, Commander, JCS Joint Contingency Task Group, Office, Joint Chiefs of Staff, Washington, D.C., 1971.

"Chronology of the Vietnam War," Office of the Joint Chiefs of Staff, Historical Office, 1955–1972.

"Southeast Asia Statistical Digest," Table 6, Office, Assistant Secretary of Defense (Comptroller), Washington, D.C., 1966 through 1973.

"Written Report of Lieutenant General Vernon A. Walters, USA, Deputy Director, Central Intelligence Agency," submitted for the record to the Select Committee on Missing Persons in Southeast Asia of the U.S. House of Representatives, March 17, 1976.

"Foreign and Military Intelligence," Book 1, *Final Report of the Select Committee to Study Governmental Operations with Respect to Intelligence Activities, United States Senate, Ninety-Fourth Congress, Second Session,* Washington, D.C.: Government Printing Office, 1976.

"Intelligence Activities and the Rights of Americans," Book 2, *Final Report of the Select Committee to Study Governmental Operations with Respect to Intelligence Activities, United States Senate, Ninety-Fourth Congress, Second Session,* Washington, D.C.: Government Printing Office, 1976.

Index

319